THE INCIDENT AT
SEETHING SPRING

It was a remarkably barbaric murder.

To be sure, England was at war; passions were high, and Questing *had* been under suspicion in connection with the mysterious lights that appeared on Rangi's Peak whenever an Allied ship was sunk.

But still, Alleyn wondered: did that justify boiling the man alive?

COLOUR SCHEME

NGAIO MARSH

A JOVE BOOK

To the Family at Tauranga

This Jove book contains the complete
text of the original hardcover edition.
It has been completely reset in a typeface
designed for easy reading, and was printed
from new film.

COLOUR SCHEME

A Jove Book / published by arrangement with
Little, Brown and Company

PRINTING HISTORY
Little, Brown and Company edition published 1943
Berkley edition / May 1978
Jove edition / January 1982
Second printing / December 1982

ISBN: 0-515-06014-3

Jove books are published by Jove Publications, Inc.,
200 Madison Avenue, New York, N. Y. 10016. The words
"A JOVE BOOK" and the "J" with sunburst are trademarks
belonging to Jove Publications, Inc.

PRINTED IN THE UNITED STATES OF AMERICA

CONTENTS

CAST OF CHARACTERS

DR. JAMES ACKRINGTON M.D., F.R.C.S., F.R.C.P.

BARBARA CLAIRE, his niece

MRS. CLAIRE, his sister

COLONEL EDWARD CLAIRE, his brother-in-law

SIMON CLAIRE, his nephew

HUIA, maid at Wai-ata-tapu

GEOFFREY GAUNT, a visiting celebrity

DIKON BELL, his secretary

ALFRED COLLY, his servant

MAURICE QUESTING, man of business

RUA TE KAHU, a chief of the Te Rarawas

HERBERT SMITH, roustabout at Wai-ata-tapu

ERU SAUL, a half-caste

SEPTIMUS FALLS

THE PRINCESS TE PAPA (MRS. TE PAPA), of the Te Rarawas

DETECTIVE-SERGEANT WEBLEY, of the Harpoon Constabulary

A Superintendent of Police

MAORI WORDS USED IN THE TEXT

Aue! Aue! Aue! Te mamae i au, Alas! Alas! Alas!
  my grief

Haere mai, Welcome

Hapu, Clan

Kainga, Unfortified place of residence

Marae, Enclosed space in front of house

Matagouri (incorrect dog-Maori), *Discaria tou-
  mautu* (Prickly shrub)

Makutu, Bewitch

Na waitana?, From whom are we?

Pa, Fortified place. Used loosely for native village

Pakeha, Foreigner. Chiefly used for white man

Toki, Adze

Toki-poutangata, Greenstone-adze

Whare, House

CHAPTER I

THE CLAIRES AND
DR. ACKRINGTON

When Dr. James Ackrington limped into the Harpoon Club on the afternoon of Monday, January the thirteenth, he was in a poisonous temper. A sequence of events had combined to irritate and then to inflame him. He had slept badly. He had embarked, he scarcely knew why, on a row with his sister, a row based obscurely on the therapeutic value of mud pools and the technique of frying eggs. He had asked for the daily paper of the previous Thursday only to discover that it had been used to wrap up Mr. Maurice Questing's picnic lunch. His niece Barbara, charged with this offence, burst out into one of her fits of nervous laughter and recovered the paper, stained with ham fat and reeking with onions. Dr. Ackrington, in shaking it angrily before her, had tapped his sciatic nerve smartly against the table. Blind with pain and white with rage he stumbled to his room, undressed, took a shower, wrapped himself in his dressing gown and made his way to the hottest of the thermal baths, only to find Mr. Maurice Questing sitting in it, his unattractive outline rimmed with effervescence. Mr. Questing had laughed offensively and announced his intention of remaining in the pool for twenty minutes. He had pointed out the less hot but unoccupied baths. Dr. Ackrington, standing on the hardened bluish mud banks that surrounded the pool, embarked on as violent a quarrel as he could bring about with a naked smiling antagonist who returned no answer to the grossest insults. He then went back to his room, dressed and, finding nobody upon whom to pour out his wrath, drove his car ruthlessly up the sharp track from Wai-ata-tapu Hot Springs to the main road for Harpoon. He left behind him an atmosphere well suited to his mood, since the air, as always, reeked of sulphurous vapours.

Arrived at the club, he collected his letters and turned into the writing-room. The windows looked across the Harpoon Inlet whose waters on this midsummer morning were quite unscored by ripples and held immaculate the images of sky and white sand, and of the crimson flowering trees that bloom at this time of year in the Northland of New Zealand. A shimmer of heat rose from the pavement outside the club and under its influence the forms of trees, hills, and bays seemed to shake a little as if indeed the strangely primitive landscape were still taking shape and were rather a half-realized idea than a concrete accomplishment of nature.

It was a beautiful prospect but Dr. Ackrington was not really moved by it. He reflected that the day would be snortingly hot and opened his letters. Only one of them seemed to arrest his attention.

He spread it out before him on the writing table and glared at it, whistling slightly between his teeth.

This is what he read:—

Harley Chambers,
Auckland, C.I.

My dear Dr. Ackrington,

I am venturing to ask for your advice in a rather tricky business involving a patient of mine, none other than our visiting celebrity the famous Geoffrey Gaunt. As you probably know, he arrived in Australia with his Shake-spearean company just before war broke out and remained there, continuing to present his repertoire of plays but handing over a very generous dollop of all takings to the patriotic funds. On the final disbandment of his company he came to New Zealand, where, as you may not know (I remember your loathing of radio), he has done some excellent propaganda stuff on the air. About four weeks ago he consulted me. He complained of insomnia, acute pains in the joints, loss of appetite and intense depression. He asked me if I thought he had a chance of being accepted for active service. He wants to get back to England but only if he can be of use. I diagnosed fibrositis and nervous debility, put him on a very simple diet, and told him I certainly did not consider him fit for any sort of war service. It seems he has an idea of writing his autobiography. They all do it. I suggested that he might combine this with a course of hydrotherapy and complete rest. I suggested Rotorua, but he won't hear of it. Says he'd be plagued with lion hunters and what-not and that he can't stand the tourist atmosphere.

You'll have guessed what I'm coming to.

I know you are living at Wai-ata-tapu, and understand that the Spa is under your sister's or her husband's management. I have heard that you are engaged on a *magnum opus* so therefore suppose that the place is conducive to quiet work. Would you be very kind and tell me if you think it would suit my patient, and if Colonel and Mrs. Claire would care to have him as a resident for some six weeks or more? I know that you don't practise nowadays, and it is with the greatest diffidence that I make my final suggestion. Would you care to keep a professional eye on Mr. Gaunt? He is an interesting figure, and I venture to hope that you may feel inclined to take him as a sort of patient extraordinary. I must add that, frankly, I should be very proud to hand him on to so distinguished a consultant.

Gaunt has a secretary and a man-servant, and I understand he would want accommodation for both of them.

Please forgive me for writing what I fear may turn out to be a tiresome and exacting letter.

> Yours very sincerely,
> IAN FORSTER

Dr. Ackrington read this letter through twice, folded it, placed it in his pocket-book, and, still whistling between his teeth, filled his pipe and lit it. After some five minutes' cogitation he drew a sheet of paper towards him and began to cover it with his thin irritable script.

Dear Forster (he wrote),

Many thanks for your letter. It requires a frank answer and I give it for what it is worth. Wai-ata-tapu is, as you suggest, the property of my sister and her husband, who run it as a thermal spa. In many ways they are perfect fools, but they are honest fools and that is more than one can say of most people engaged in similar pursuits. The whole place is grossly mismanaged in my opinion, but I don't know that you would find anyone else who would agree with me. Claire

is an army man and it's a pity he has failed so signally to
absorb in the smallest degree the principles of system and
orderly control that must at some time or another have been
suggested to him. My sister is a bookish woman. However
incompetent, she seems to command the affection of her
martyred clients, and I am her only critic. Perhaps it is
unnecessary to add that they make no money and work like
bewildered horses at an occupation that requires merely the
application of common sense to make it easy and profitable.
On the alleged therapeutic properties of the baths you have
evidently formed your own opinion. They consist, as you are
aware, of thermal springs whose waters contain alkalis, free
sulphuric acid, and free carbonic-acid gas. There are also
siliceous mud baths in connection with which my brother-in-
law talks loosely and freely of radio-activity. This latter
statement I regard as so much pious mumbo-jumbo, but
again I am alone in my opinion. The mud may be miraculous.
My leg is no worse since I took to using it.

As for your spectacular patient, I don't know to what
degree of comfort he is used, but can promise him he won't
get it, though enormous and misguided efforts will be made
to accommodate him. Actually there is no reason why he
shouldn't be comfortable. Possibly his secretary and man
might succeed where my unfortunate relatives may safely be
relied upon to fail. I doubt if he will be more wretched than he
would be anywhere else in this extraordinary country. The
charges will certainly be less than elsewhere. Six guineas a
week for resident patients. Possibly Gaunt would like a
private sitting-room for which I imagine there would be an
extra charge. Tonks of Harpoon is the visiting medical man. I
need say no more. Possibly it is an oblique recommendation
of the waters that all Tonks's patients who have taken them
have at least survived. There is no reason why I should not
keep an eye on your man and I shall do so if you and he wish
it. What you say of him modifies my previous impression that
he was one of the emasculate popinjays who appear to form
the nucleus of the intelligentsia at Home in these degenerate
days. Bloomsbury.

My *magnum opus,* as you no doubt ironically call it,
crawls on in spite of the concerted efforts of my immediate
associates to withhold the merest necessities for undisturbed

employment. I confess that the autobiographical outpourings of persons connected with the theatre seem to me to bear little relation to serious work, and where I fail, Mr. Geoffrey Gaunt may well succeed.

Again, many thanks for your letter,

Yours,

JAMES ACKRINGTON

P.S. I should be doing you and your patient a disservice if I failed to tell you that the place is infested by as offensive a fellow as I have ever come across. I have the gravest suspicions regarding this person.

J.A.

As Dr. Ackrington sealed and directed this letter a trace of complacency lightened the habitual austerity of his face. He rang the bell, ordered a small whisky-and-soda and with an air of relishing his employment began a second letter.

Roderick Alleyn, Esq., Chief-Inspector, C.I.D.,
c/o Central Police Station,
Auckland,
Sir,

The newspapers, with gross indiscretion, report you as having come to this country in connection with scandalous leakages of information to the enemy, notably those which led to the sinking of S.S. *Hippolyte* last November.

I consider it my duty to inform you of the activities of a person at present living at Wai-ata-tapu Hot Springs, Harpoon Inlet. This person, calling himself Maurice Questing and staying at the local Spa, has formed the habit of leaving the house after dark. To my positive knowledge, he ascends the mountain known as Rangi's Peak, which is part of the native reserve and the western face of which looks out to sea. I have myself witnessed on several occasions a light flashing on the slopes of this face. You will note that *Hippolyte* was torpedoed at a spot some two miles out from Harpoon Inlet.

I have also to report that on being questioned as to his movements, Mr. Questing has returned evasive and even lying answers.

I conceived it my duty to report this matter to the local
police authorities, who displayed a somnolence so profound
as to be pathological.

I have the honour to be,
                     Yours faithfully,
James Ackrington M.D., F.R.C.S., F.R.C.P.

The servant brought the drink. Dr. Ackrington accused
him of having substituted an inferior brand of whisky for the
one ordered, but he did this with an air of routine rather than
of rage. He accepted the servant's resigned assurances with
surprising mildness, merely remarking that the whisky had
probably been adulterated by the makers. He then finished
his drink, clapped his hat on the side of his head and went out
to post his letters. The hall porter pulled open the door.

"War news a bit brighter this morning, sir," said the porter
tentatively.

"The sooner we're all dead, the better," Dr. Ackrington
replied cheerfully. He gave a falsetto barking noise, and
limped quickly down the steps.

"Was that a joke?" said the hall porter to the servant. The
servant turned up his eyes.

ii

Colonel and Mrs. Claire had lived for twelve years at Wai-
ata-tapu Springs. They had come to New Zealand from India
when their daughter Barbara, born ten years after their
marriage, was thirteen, and their son Simon, nine years old.
They had told their friends in gentle voices that they wanted
to get away from the conventions of retired army life in
England. They had spoken blithely, for they took an
uncritical delight in such phrases, of wide-open spaces and of
a small inheritance that had come to the Colonel. With most
of this inheritance they had built the boarding-house they

now lived in. The remaining sums had been quietly lost in a series of timid speculations. They had worked like slaves, receiving good advice with well-bred resentment and bad advice with touching gratitude. Beside these failings, they had a positive genius for collecting impossible people, and at the time when this tale opens were at the mercy of a certain incubus called Herbert Smith.

On the retirement of her distinguished and irascible brother from practice in London, Mrs. Claire had invited him to join them. He had consented to do so only as a paying guest, as he wished to enjoy complete freedom for making criticisms and complaints, an exercise he indulged with particular energy, especially in regard to his nephew Simon. His niece Barbara Claire had from the first done the work of two servants and, because she went out so little, retained the sort of English vicarage-garden atmosphere that emanated from her mother. Simon, on the contrary, had attended the Harpoon State schools, and, influenced on the one hand by the persistent family attitude of poor but proud gentility, and on the other by his schoolfellows' suspicion of "pommy" settlers, had become truculently colonial, somewhat introverted and defiantly uncouth. A year before the outbreak of war he left school, and was now taking the preliminary Air Force training at home.

On the morning of Dr. Ackrington's visit to Harpoon, the Claires pursued their normal occupations. At midday Colonel Claire took his lumbago to the radio-activity of the mud pool, Mrs. Claire steeped her sciatica in a hot spring, Simon went into his cabin to practise Morse code, and Barbara cooked the midday meal in a hot and primitive kitchen with Huia, the Maori help, in attendance.

"You can dish up, Huia," said Barbara. She brushed the locks of damp hair from her eyes with the back of her forearm. "I'm afraid I seem to have used a lot of dishes. There'll be six in the dining-room. Mr. Questing's out for lunch."

"Good job," said Huia skittishly. Barbara pretended not to hear. Huia, moving with the half-languid, half-vigorous grace of the young Maori, smiled brilliantly, and began to pile stacks of plates on a tray. "He's no good," she said softly.

Barbara glanced at her. Huia laughed richly, lifting her

short upper lip. "I shall never understand them," Barbara thought. Aloud she said: "Mightn't it be better if you just pretended not to hear when Mr. Questing starts those—starts being—starts teasing you?"

"He makes me very angry," said Huia, and suddenly she became childishly angry, flashing her eyes and stamping her foot. "Silly ass," she said.

"But you're not really angry."

Huia looked out of the corners of her eyes at Barbara, pulled an equivocal grimace, and tittered.

"Don't forget your cap and apron," said Barbara, and left the sweltering kitchen for the dining-room.

Wai-ata-tapu Hostel was a one-storied wooden building shaped like an E with the middle stroke missing. The dining-room occupied the centre of the long section separating the kitchen and serveries from the boarders' bedrooms, which extended into the east wing. The west wing, private to the Claires, was a series of cramped cabins and a tiny sitting-room. The house had been designed by Colonel Claire on army-hut lines with an additional flavour of sanatorium. There were no passages, and all the rooms opened on a partially covered-in verandah. The inside walls were of yellowish-red oiled wood. The house smelt faintly of linseed oil and positively of sulphur. An observant visitor might have traced in it the history of the Claires' venture. The framed London Board-of-Trade posters, the chairs and tables painted, not very capably, in primary colours, the notices in careful script, the archly reproachful rhyme-sheets in bathrooms and lavatories, all spoke of high beginnings. Broken *passe-partout,* chipped paint, and fly-blown papers hanging by single drawing-pins traced unmistakably a gradual but inexorable decline. The house was clean but unexpectedly so, tidy but not orderly, and only vaguely uncomfortable. The front wall of the dining-room was built up of glass panels designed to slide in grooves, but devilishly inclined to jam. These looked across the verandah to the hot springs themselves.

Barbara stood for a moment at one of the open windows and stared absently at a freakish landscape. Hills smudged with scrub were ranked against a heavy sky. Beyond them, across the hidden inlet, but tall enough to dominate the scene, rose the truncated cone of Rangi's Peak, an extinct volcano so characteristically shaped that it might have been placed in the landscape by a modern artist with a passion for simplified form. Though some eight miles away, it was actually clearer than the near-by hills, for their margins, dark and firm, were broken at intervals by plumes of steam that rose perpendicularly from the eight thermal pools. These lay close at hand, just beyond the earth-and-pumice sweep in front of the house. Five of them were hot springs hidden from the windows by fences of manuka scrub. The sixth was enclosed by a rough bath shed. The seventh was almost a lake over whose dark waters wraiths of steam vaguely drifted. The eighth was a mud pool, not hot enough to give off steam, and dark in colour with a kind of iridescence across its surface. This pool was only half-screened and from its open end protruded a naked pink head on top of a long neck. Barbara went out to the verandah, seized a brass schoolroom bell, and rang it vigorously. The pink head travelled slowly through the mud like some fantastic periscope until it disappeared behind the screen.

"Lunch, Father," screamed Barbara unnecessarily. She walked across the sweep and entered the enclosure. On a brush fence that screened the first path hung a weather-worn placard: "The Elfin Pool. Engaged." The Claires had given each of the pools some amazingly insipid title, and Barbara had neatly executed the placards in poker-work.

"Are you there, Mummy?" asked Barbara.

"Come in, my dear."

She walked round the screen and found her mother at her feet, submerged up to the shoulders in bright blue steaming water that quite hid her plump body. Over her fuzz of hair Mrs. Claire wore a rubber bag with a frilled edge and she had spectacles on her nose. With her right hand she held above the water a shilling edition of *Cranford*.

"So *charming*," she said. "They are all such dears. I never tire of them."

"Lunch is nearly in."

"I must pop out. The Elf is really wonderful, Ba. My

tiresome arm is quite cleared up."

"I'm so glad, Mummy," said Barbara in a loud voice. "I want to ask you something."

"What is it?" said Mrs. Claire, turning a page with her thumb.

"Do you like Mr. Questing?"

Mrs. Claire looked up over the top of her book. Barbara was standing at a curious angle, balanced on her right leg. Her left foot was hooked round her right ankle.

"Dear," said Mrs. Claire, "*don't* stand like that. It pushes all the wrong things out and tucks the right ones in."

"But do you?" Barbara persisted, changing her posture with a jerk.

"Well, he's not out of the top drawer of course, poor thing."

"I don't mind about that. And anyway what *is* the top drawer? It's a maddening sort of way to classify people. Such cheek! I'm sorry, Mummy, I didn't mean to be rude. But honestly, for *us* to talk about class!" Barbara gave a loud hoot of laughter. "Look at us!" she said.

Mrs. Claire edged modestly towards the side of the pool and thrust her book at her daughter. Stronger waves of sulphurous smells rose from the disturbed waters. A cascade of drops fell from the elderly rounded arm.

"Take *Cranford*," she said. Barbara took it. Mrs. Claire pulled her rubber bag a little closer about her ears. "My dear," she said, pitching her voice on a note that she usually reserved for death, "aren't you mixing up money and breeding? It doesn't matter what one *does* surely..." She paused. "There is an innate something..." she began. "One can always tell," she added.

"Can one? Look at Simon."

"Dear old Simon," said her mother reproachfully.

"Yes, I know. I'm very fond of him. I couldn't have a kinder brother, but there isn't much innate something about Simon, is there?"

"It's only that awful accent. If we could have afforded..."

"There you are, you see," cried Barbara, and she went on in a great hurry, shooting out her words as if she fired them from a gun that was too big for her. "Class consciousness is all my eye. Fundamentally it's based on money."

On the verandah the bell was rung again with some abandon.

"I must pop out," said Mrs. Claire. "That's Huia ringing."

"It's not because he talks a different language or any of those things," said Barbara hurriedly, "that I don't like Mr. Questing. I don't like *him*. And I don't like the way he behaves with Huia. Or," she added under her breath, "with me."

"I expect," said Mrs. Claire, "that's only because he used to be a commercial traveller. It's just his way."

"Mummy, *why* do you find excuses for him? Why does Daddy, who would ordinarily loathe Mr. Questing, put up with him? He even laughs at his awful jokes. It isn't because we want his board money. Look how Daddy and Uncle James practically froze out those rich Americans who were very nice, I thought." Barbara drove her long fingers through her mouse-coloured hair, and avoiding her mother's gaze stared at the top of Rangi's Peak. "You'd think Mr. Questing had a sort of *hold* on us," she said, and then burst into one of her fits of nervous laughter.

"Barbie darling," said her mother, on a note that contrived to suggest the menace of some frightful indelicacy, "I think we won't talk about it any more."

"Uncle James hates him, anyway."

"Barbara!"

"Lunch, Agnes," said a quiet voice on the other side of the fence. "You're late again."

"Coming, dear. Please go on ahead with Daddy, Barbara," said Mrs. Claire.

iii

Dr. Ackrington bucketed his car down the drive and pulled up at the verandah with a savage jolt just as Barbara reached it. She waited for him and took his arm.

"Stop it," he said. "You'll give me hell if you hurry me."
But when she made to draw away he held her arm in a wiry
grasp.

"Is the leg bad, Uncle James?"

"It's always bad. Steady now."

"Did you have your morning soak in the Porridge Pot?"

"I did not. And do you know why? That damned
poisonous little bounder was wallowing in it."

"Mr. Questing?"

"He never washes," Dr. Ackrington shouted. "I'll swear
he never washes. Why the devil you can't insist on people
taking the shower before they use the pools is a mystery. He
soaks his sweat off in my mud."

"Are you sure...?"

"Certain. Certain. Certain. I've watched him. He never
goes near the shower. How in the name of common decency
your parents can stomach him..."

"That's just what I've been asking Mummy."

Dr. Ackrington halted and stared at his niece. An
observer might have been struck by their resemblance to each
other. Barbara was much more like her uncle than her
mother, yet while he, in a red-headed edgy sort of way, was
remarkably handsome, she contrived to present as good a
profile without its accompaniment of distinction. Nobody
noticed Barbara's physical assets; her defects were inescapable. Her hair, her clothes, her incoherent gestures, her
strangely untutored mannerisms, all combined against her
looks and discounted them. She and her uncle stared at each
other in silence for some seconds.

"Oh," said Dr. Ackrington at last. "And what did your
mother say?"

Barbara pulled a clown's grimace. "She *reproved* me," she
said in a sepulchral serio-comedy voice.

"Well, don't make faces at me," snapped her uncle.

A window in the Claires' wing was thrown open, and
between the curtains there appeared a vague pink face
garnished with a faded moustache, and topped by a thatch of
white hair.

"Hullo, James," said the face crossly. "Lunch. What's
your mother doing, Ba? Where's Simon?"

"She's coming, Daddy. We're all coming. *Simon!*" screamed Barbara.

Mrs. Claire, enveloped in a dark red flannel dressing gown, came panting up from the pools, and hurried into the house.

"Aren't we going to *have* any lunch?" Colonel Claire asked bitterly.

"Of course we are," said Barbara. "Why don't you begin, Daddy, if you're in such a hurry? Come on, Uncle James."

As they went indoors, a young man came round the house and slouched in behind them. He was tall, big-boned, and sandy-haired, with a jutting underlip.

"Hullo, Sim," said Barbara. "Lunch."

"Righto."

"How's the Morse code this morning?"

"Going good," said Simon.

Dr. Ackrington instantly turned on him. "Is there any creditable reason why you should not say 'going well'?" he demanded.

"Huh!" said Simon.

He trailed behind them into the dining-room and they took their places at a long table where Colonel Claire was already seated.

"We won't wait for your mother," said Colonel Claire, folding his hands over his abdomen. "For what we are about to receive may the Lord make us truly thankful. Huia!"

Huia came in wearing cap, crackling apron, and stiff curls. She looked like a Polynesian goddess who had assumed, on a whim, some barbaric disguise.

"Would you like cold ham, cold mutton, or grilled steak?" she asked, and her voice was as cool and deep as her native forests. As an afterthought she handed Barbara a menu.

"If I ask for steak," said Dr. Ackrington, "will it be cooked..."

"You don't want to eat raw steak, Uncle, do you?" said Barbara.

"Let me finish. If I order steak, will it be cooked or tanned? Will it resemble steak or *biltong?*"

"Steak," said Huia, musically.

"Is it cooked?"

"Yes."

"Thank you. I shall have ham."

"What the devil are you driving at, James?" asked Colonel Claire, irritably. "You talk in riddles. What *do* you want?"

"I want grilled steak. If it is already cooked it will not be grilled steak. It will be boot leather. You can't get a bit of grilled steak in the length and breadth of this country."

Huia looked politely and inquiringly at Barbara.

"Grill Dr. Ackrington a fresh piece of steak, please, Huia."

Dr. Ackrington shook his finger at Huia. "Five minutes," he shouted. "Five minutes! A second longer and it's uneatable. Mind that!" Huia smiled. "And while she's cooking it I have a letter to read to you," he added importantly.

Mrs. Claire came in. She looked as if she had just returned from a round of charitable visits in an English village. The Claires ordered their lunches and Dr. Ackrington took out the letter from Dr. Forster.

"This concerns all of you," he announced.

"Where's Smith?" demanded Colonel Claire suddenly, opening his eyes very wide. His wife and children looked vaguely round the room. "Did anyone call him?" asked Mrs. Claire.

"Don't mind Smith, now," said Dr. Ackrington. "He's not here and he won't be here. I passed him in Harpoon. He was turning in at a pub and by the look of him it was not the first by two or three. Don't mind him. He's better away."

"He got a cheque from Home yesterday," said Simon, in his strong New Zealand dialect. "Boy, oh boy!"

"Don't speak like that, dear," said his mother. "Poor Mr. Smith, it's such a shame. He's a dear fellow at bottom."

"Will you allow me to read this letter, or will you not?"

"Do read it, dear. Is it from Home?"

Dr. Ackrington struck the table angrily with the flat of his hand. His sister leant back in her chair, Colonel Claire stared out through the windows, and Simon and Barbara, after the first two sentences, listened eagerly. When he had finished the letter, which he read in a rapid uninflected patter, Dr. Ackrington dropped it on the table and looked about him with an air of complacency.

Barbara whistled. "I *say*," she said—"Geoffrey Gaunt! I *say*."

"And a servant. And a secretary. I don't quite know what to say, James," Mrs. Claire mumured. "I'm quite bewildered. I really don't think . . ."

"We can't take on a chap like that," said Simon loudly.

"And why not, pray?" his uncle demanded.

"He'd be no good to us and we'd be no good to him. He'll be used to posh hotels and slinging his weight about with a lot of English servants. What'd we do with a secretary and a man-servant? What's he do with them anyway?" Simon went on with an extraordinary air of hostility. "Is he feeble-minded or what?"

"Feeble-minded!" cried Barbara. "He's probably the greatest living actor."

"Well, he can have it for mine," said Simon.

"For the love of heaven, Agnes, can't you teach your son an intelligible form of speech?"

"If the way I talk isn't good enough for you, Uncle James . . ."

"For pity's sake let's stick to the point," Barbara cried. "I'm for having Mr. Gaunt and his staff, Sim's against it, Mother's hovering. You're for it, Uncle, I suppose."

"I fondly imagined that three resident patients might be of some assistance to the exchequer. What does your father say?" He turned to Colonel Claire. "What do you say, Edward?"

"Eh?" Colonel Claire opened his eyes and mouth and raised his eyebrows in a startled manner. "Is it about that paper you've got in your hand? I wasn't listening. Read it again."

"Great God Almighty!"

"Your steak," said Huia, and placed before Dr. Ackrington a strip of ghastly pale and bloated meat from which blood coursed freely over the plate.

During the lively scene which followed, Barbara hooted with frightened laughter, Mrs. Claire mumured conciliatory phrases, Simon shuffled his feet, and Huia in turn shook her head angrily, giggled, and uttered soft apologies. Finally she burst into tears and ran back with the steak to the kitchen, where a crash of breaking crockery suggested that she had

hurled the dish to the floor. Colonel Claire, after staring in
surprise at his brother-in-law for a few seconds, quietly took
up Dr. Forster's letter and began to read it. This he continued
to do until Dr. Ackrington had been mollified with a helping
of cold meat.

"Who is this Geoffrey Gaunt?" asked Colonel Claire after
a long silence.

"*Daddy!* You *must* know. You saw him in *Jane Eyre* last
time we went to the pictures in Harpoon. He's wildly
famous." Barbara paused with her left cheek bulging. "He
was *exactly* my idea of Mr. Rochester," she said ardently.

"Theatrical!" said her father distastefully. "We don't want
that sort."

"Just what I say," Simon agreed.

"I'm afraid," said Mrs. Claire, "that Mr. Gaunt would
find us very humdrum sort of folk. Don't you think we'd
better just keep to our own quiet ways, dear?"

"*Mummy,* you *are...*" Barbara began. Her uncle,
speaking with a calm that was really terrifying, interrupted
her.

"I haven't the smallest doubt, my dear Agnes," he said,
"that Gaunt, who is possibly a man of some enterprise and
intelligence, would find your quiet ways more than
humdrum, as you complacently choose to describe them. I
ventured to suggest in my reply to Forster that Gaunt would
find few of the amenities and a good deal of comparative
discomfort at Wai-ata-tapu. I added something to the effect
that I hoped lack of luxury would be compensated for by
kindness and by consideration for a man who is unwell.
Apparently I was mistaken. I also fancied that, having gone
to considerable expense in building a Spa, your object was to
acquire a clientele. Again, I was mistaken. You prefer to rest
on your laurels with an alcoholic who doesn't pay his way,
and a bounder whom I, for one, regard as a person better
suited to confinement in an internment camp."

Colonel Claire said: "Are you talking about Questing,
James?"

"I am."

"Well, I wish you wouldn't."

"May I ask why?"

Colonel Claire laid his knife and fork together, turned

scarlet in the face, and looked fixedly at the opposite wall.

"Because," he said, "I am under an obligation to him."

There was a long silence.

"I see," said Dr. Ackrington at last.

"I haven't said anything about it to Agnes and the children. I suppose I'm old-fashioned. In my view a man doesn't speak of such matters to his family. But you, James, and you two children, have shown so pointedly your dislike of Mr. Questing that I am forced to tell you that I—I cannot afford—I must ask you for my sake to show him more consideration."

"You can't afford...?" Dr. Ackrington repeated. "Good God, my dear fellow, what have you been up to?"

"Please, James. I hope I need say no more."

With an air of martyrdom Colonel Claire rose and moved over to the windows. Mrs. Claire made a movement to follow him, but he said, "No, Agnes," and she stopped at once. "On second thoughts," added Colonel Claire, "I believe we should reconsider our decision about taking these people as guests. I—I'll speak to Questing about it. Please let the subject drop for the moment." He walked out on to the verandah and past the windows, holding himself very straight, and, still extremely red in the face, disappeared.

"Of all the damned astounding how-d'ye-do's..." Dr. Ackrington began.

"Oh, James, *don't*," cried Mrs. Claire, and burst into tears.

iv

Huia slapped the last plate in the rack, swilled out the sink, and turned her back on a moderately tidy kitchen. She lived with her family at a native settlement on the other side of the hill and, as it was her afternoon off, proposed to return there in order to change into her best dress. She walked round the house, crossed the pumice sweep, and set off along a path that skirted the warm lake, rounded the foot of Waiata-tapu Hill, and crossed a native thermal reserve that lay on the far side. The sky was overcast and the air oppressively warm and still. Huia moved with a leisurely stride. She seemed to be part of the landscape compounded of the same dark medium, quiescent as the earth under the dominion of the sky. White men move across the surface of New Zealand, but the Maori people are of its essence, tranquil or disturbed as the trees and lakes must be, and as much a member of the earth as they.

Huia's path took her through a patch of tall manuka scrub and here she came upon a young man, Eru Saul, a half-caste. He stepped out of the bushes and waited for her, the stump of a cigarette hanging from his lips.

"Hu!" said Huia. "You. What do *you* want?"

"It's your day off, isn't it? Come for a walk."

"Too busy," said Huia briefly. She moved forward. He checked her, holding her by the arms.

"No," he said.

"Shut up."

"I want to talk to you."

"What about? Same old thing all the time. Talk, talk, talk. You make me tired."

"You know what. Give us a kiss."

Huia laughed and rolled her eyes. "You're mad. Behave yourself. Mrs. Claire will go crook if you hang about. I'm going home."

"Come on," he muttered, and flung his arm around her. She fought him off, laughing angrily, and he began to upbraid her. "I'm not posh enough. Going with a *pakeha* now, aren't you? That's right, isn't it?"

"Don't talk to me like that. You're no good. You're a no-good boy."

"I haven't got a car and I'm not a thief. Questing's a ruddy thief."

"That's a big lie," said Huia blandly. "He's all right."

"What's he doing at night on the Peak? He's got no business on the Peak."

"Talk, talk, talk. All the time."

"You tell him if he doesn't look out he'll be in for it. How'll you like it if he gets packed up?"

"I don't care."

"Don't you? *Don't you?*"

"*Oh,* you are silly," cried Huia, stamping her foot. "Silly fool! Now get out of my way and let me go home. I'll tell my great-grandfather about you and he'll *makutu* you."

"Kid-stakes! Nobody's going to put a jinx on me."

"My great-grandfather can do it," said Huia and her eyes flashed.

"Listen, Huia," said Eru. "You think you can get away with dynamite. O.K. But don't come at it with me. And another thing. Next time this joker Questing wants to have you on to go driving, you can tell him from me to lay off. See? Tell him from me, no kidding, that if he tries any more funny stuff, it'll be the stone end of his trips up the Peak."

"Tell him yourself," said Huia. She added, in dog Maori, an extremely pointed insult, and taking him off his guard slipped past him and ran round the hill.

Eru stood looking at the ground. His cigarette burnt his lip and he spat it out. After a moment he turned and slowly followed her.

CHAPTER II

MR. QUESTING GOES DOWN
FOR THE FIRST TIME

"We've heard from Dr. Forster, sir," said Dikon Bell. He glanced anxiously at his employer. When Gaunt stood with his hands rammed down in the pockets of his dressing gown and his shoulders hunched up to his ears one watched one's step. Gaunt turned away from the window, and Dikon noticed apprehensively that his leg was very stiff this morning.

"Ha!" said Gaunt.

"He makes a suggestion."

"I won't go to that sulphurous resort."

"Rotorua, sir?"

"Is that what it's called?"

"He realizes you want somewhere quiet, sir. He's made inquiries about another place. It's in the Northland. On the west coast. Subtropical climate."

"Sulphurous pneumonia?"

"Well, sir, we do want to clear up that leg, don't we?"

"We do." With one of those swift changes of demeanor by which he so easily commanded devotion, Gaunt turned to his secretary and clapped him on the shoulder. "I think you're as homesick as I am, Dikon. Isn't that true? You're a New Zealander, of course, but wouldn't you ten thousand times rather be there? In London? Isn't it exactly as if someone you loved was ill and you couldn't get to them?"

"A little like that, certainly," said Dikon dryly.

"I shouldn't keep you here. Go back, my dear chap. I'll find somebody in New Zealand," said Gaunt with a certain melancholy relish.

"Are you giving me the sack, sir?"

"If only they can patch me up..."

21

"But they will, sir. Dr. Forster said the leg ought to respond very quickly to hydrotherapy," said Dikon with a prime imitation of the doctor's manner. "They simply hated the sight of me in the Australian recruiting offices. And I fancy I should have little more than refuse-value at Home. I'm as blind as a bat, you know. Of course, there's office work."

"You must do what you think best," said Gaunt gloomily. "Leave me to stagnate. I'm no good to my country. Ha!"

"If you call raising twelve thousand for colonial patriotic funds no good..."

"I'm a useless hulk," said Gaunt, and even Dikon was reminded of the penultimate scene in *Jane Eyre*.

"What are you grinning at, blast you?" Gaunt demanded.

"You don't look precisely like a useless hulk. I'll stay a little longer if you'll have me."

"Well, let's hear about this new place. You're looking wonderfully self-conscious. What hideous surprise have you got up your sleeve?"

Dikon put his attache case on the writing table and opened it.

"There's a princely fan mail to-day," he said, and laid a stack of typed sheets and photographs on one side.

"Good! I adore being adored. How many have written a little something themselves and wonder if I can advise them how to have their plays produced?"

"Four. One lady has sent a copy of her piece. She has dedicated it to you. It's a fantasy."

"God!"

"Here is Dr. Forster's letter, and one enclosed from a Dr. James Ackrington who appears to be a celebrity from Harley Street. Perhaps you'd like to read them."

"I should hate to read them."

"I think you'd better, sir."

Gaunt grimaced, took the letters and lowered himself into a chair by the writing desk. Dikon watched him rather nervously.

Geoffrey Gaunt had spent twenty-seven of his forty-five years on the stage, and the last sixteen had seen him firmly established in the first rank. He was what used to be called a romantic actor, but he was also an intelligent one. His greatest distinction lay in his genius for making an audience hear the sense as well as the music of Shakespearean verse. So accurate and clear was his tracing out of the speeches' content that his art had about it something of mathematical precision and was saved from coldness only by the apparent profundity of his emotional understanding. How far this understanding was instinctive and how far intellectual, not even his secretary, who had been with him for six years, could decide. He was middle-sized, dark, and not particularly striking, but as an actor he possessed the two great assets: his skull was well shaped, and his hands were beautiful. As for his disposition, Dikon Bell, writing six years before from London to a friend in New Zealand, had said, after a week in Gaunt's employment: "He's tricky, affected, clever as a bagful of monkeys, a bit of a bounder with the temper of a fury, and no end of an egotist, but I think I'm going to like him." He had never found reason to revise this first impression.

Gaunt read Dr. Forster's note and then Dr. Ackrington's letter. "For heaven's sake," he cried, "what sort of an antic is this old person? Have you noted the acid treatment of his relations? Does he call this letter a recommendation? Discomfort leavened with inefficient kindness is the bait he offers. Moreover, there's a dirty little knock at me in the last paragraph. If Forster wants me to endure the place, one would have thought his policy would have been to suppress the letter. He's a poor psychologist."

"The psychology," said Dikon modestly, "is mine. Forster wanted to suppress the letter. I took it upon myself to show it to you. I thought that if you jibbed at the Claires, sir, you wouldn't be able to resist Dr. Ackrington."

Gaunt shot a suspicious glance at his secretary. "You're too clever by half, my friend," he said.

"And he *does* say," Dikon added persuasively, "he *does* say 'the mud may be miraculous.'"

Gaunt laughed, made an abrupt movement, and drew in his breath sharply.

"Isn't it worth enduring the place if it puts your leg right, sir? And at least we could get on with the book."

"Certain it is I can't write in this bloody hotel. *How* I hate hotels. Dikon," cried Gaunt with an assumption of boyish enthusiasm, "shall we fly to America? Shall we do *Henry Vth* in New York? They'd take it, you know, just now. *'And Crispin, Crispian shall ne'er go by...'* God, I think I must play *Henry* in New York."

"Wouldn't you rather play him in London, sir, on a fit-up stage with the blitz for battle noises off?"

"Of course I would, damn you."

"Why not try this place? At least it may turn out to be copy for the Life. Thermal *divertissements*. And then, when you're fit and ready to hit 'em ... London."

"You talk like a Nanny in her dotage," said Gaunt fretfully. "I suppose you and Colly have plotted this frightfulness between you. Where is Colly?"

"Ironing your trousers, sir."

"Tell him to come here."

Dikon spoke on the telephone and in a moment the door opened to admit a wisp of a man with a face that resembled a wrinkled kid glove. This was Gaunt's dresser and personal servant, Alfred Colly. Colly had been the dresser provided by the management when Gaunt, a promising young leading man with no social background, had made his first great success. After a phenomenal run, Colly accepted Gaunt's offer of permanent employment, but had never adopted the technique of a man-servant. His attitude towards his employer held the balance between extreme familiarity and a cheerful recognition of Gaunt's prestige. He laid the trousers that he carried over the back of a chair, folded his hands and blinked.

"You've heard all about this damned hot spot, no doubt?" said Gaunt.

"That's right, sir," said Colly. "Going to turn mudlarks, aren't we?"

"I haven't said so."

"It's about time we did something about ourself though, isn't it, sir? We're not sleeping as pretty as we'd like, are we? And how about our leg?"

"Oh, you go to hell," said Gaunt.

"There's a gentleman downstairs, sir, wants to see you. Come in over an hour ago. They told him in the office you were seeing nobody and he says that's all right and give in his card. They says it's no use, you only see visitors by

appointment, and he comes back with that's just too bad and
sits in the lounge with a Scotch-and-soda, reading the paper
and watching the door."

"That won't do him much good," said Dikon. "Mr.
Gaunt's not going out. The masseur will be here in half an
hour. What's this man look like? Pressman?"

"Noue!" said Colly, with the cockney's singular emphasis.
"More like business. Hard. Smooth worsted suiting. Go-
getter type. I was thinking you might like to see him, Mr.
Bell."

"Why?"

"I was thinking you might. Satisfy him."

Dikon looked fixedly at Colly and saw the faintest
vibration of his left eyelid.

"Perhaps I'd better get rid of him," he said. "Did they give
you his card?"

Colly dipped his finger and thumb in a pocket of his black
alpaca coat. "Persistent sort of bloke, sir," he said, and fished
out a card.

"Oh, get rid of him, Dikon, for God's sake," said Gaunt.
"You know all the answers. I won't leer out of advertise-
ments, I won't open fetes, I won't attend amateur productions, I'm accepting no invitations. I think New Zealand's
marvellous. I wish I was in London. If it's anything to do with
the war effort, reserve your answer. If they want me to do
something for the troops, I will if I can."

Dikon went down to the lounge. In the lift he looked at the
visitor's card.

MR. MAURICE QUESTING
Wai-ata-tapu Thermal Springs

Scribbled across the bottom he read: "May I have five
minutes? Matter of interest to yourself. M.Q."

ii

Mr. Maurice Questing was about fifty years old and so much a type that a casual observer would have found it difficult to describe him. He might have been any one of a group of heavy men playing cards on a rug in the first-class carriage of a train. He appeared in triplicate at private bars, hotel lounges, business meetings and race-courses. His features were blurred and thick, his eyes sharp. His clothes always looked expensive and new. His speech, both in accent and in choice of words, was an affair of mass production rather than selection. It suggested that wherever he went he would instinctively adopt the cheapest, the slickest, and the most popular commercial phrases of the community in which he found himself. Yet though he was as voluble as a radio advertiser, shooting out his machine-turned phrases in a loud voice, and with a great air of assurance, every word he uttered seemed synthetic and quite unrelated to his thoughts. His conversation was full of the near-Americanisms that are part of the New Zealand dialect, but they, too, sounded dubious, and it was impossible to guess at his place of origin though he sometimes spoke of himself vaguely as a native of New South Wales. He was a successful man of business.

When Dikon Bell walked into the hotel lounge, Mr. Questing at once flung down his paper and rose to his feet.

"Pardon me if I speak in error," he said, "but is this Mr. Bell?"

"Er, yes," said Dikon, who still held the card in his fingers.

"Mr. Gaunt's private secretary?"

"Yes."

"That's great," said Mr. Questing, shaking hands ruthlessly, and breaking into laughter. "I'm very pleased to meet you, Mr. Bell. I know you're a busy man, but I'd be very happy if you could spare me five minutes."

"Well, I..."

"That's fine," said Mr. Questing, jamming a flat pale thumb against a bell-push. "Great work! Sit down."

Dikon sat sedately on a small chair, crossing his legs, joined his hands, and looked attentively over his glasses at Mr. Questing.

"How's the Big Man?" Mr. Questing asked.

"Mr. Gaunt? Not very well, I'm afraid."

"So I understand. Well now, Mr. Bell, I had hoped for a word with him, but I've got an idea that a little chat with you will be very very satisfactory. What'll you have?"

Dikon refused a drink. Mr. Questing ordered whisky-and-soda.

"Yes," said Mr. Questing with a heartiness that suggested a complete understanding between them. "Yes. That's fine. Well now, Mr. Bell, I'm going to tell you, flat out, that I think I'm in a position to help you. Now!"

"I see," said Dikon, "that you come from Wai-ata-tapu Springs."

"That is the case. Yes. Yes, I'm going to be quite frank with you, Mr. Bell. I'm going to tell you that not only do I come from the Springs, but I've got a very considerable interest in the Springs."

"Do you mean that you own the place? I thought a Colonel and Mrs. Claire . . ."

"Well, now, Mr. Bell, shall we just take things as they come? I'm going to bring you right into my confidence about the Springs. The Springs mean a lot to me."

"Financially?" asked Dikon mildly. "Therapeutically? Or sentimentally?"

Mr. Questing, who had looked restlessly at Dikon's tie, shoes and hands, now took a furtive glance at his face.

"Don't make it too hot," he said merrily.

With a rapid movement suggestive of sleight-of-hand he produced from an inner pocket a sheaf of pamphlets which he laid before Dikon. "Read these at your leisure. May I suggest that you bring them to Mr. Gaunt's notice?"

"Look here, Mr. Questing," said Dikon briskly, "would you mind, awfully, if we came to the point? You've evidently discovered that we've heard about this place. You've come to recommend it. That's very kind of you, but I gather your motive isn't purely altruistic. You've spoken of frankness so perhaps you won't object to my asking again if you've a financial interest in Wai-ata-tapu."

Mr. Questing laughed uproariously and said that he saw they understood each other. His conversation became thick with hints and evasions. After a minute or two Dikon saw that he himself was being offered some sort of inducement. Mr. Questing told him repeatedly that he would be looked after, that he would have every cause for personal gratification if Geoffrey Gaunt decided to take the cure. It was not by any means the first scene of its kind. Dikon was mildly entertained, and, while he listened to Mr. Questing, turned over the pamphlets. The medical recommendations seemed very good. A set of rooms—Mr. Questing called it a suite—would be theirs. Mr. Questing would see to it that the rooms were refurnished. Dikon's eyebrows went up, and Mr. Questing, becoming very confidential, said that he believed in doing things in a big way. He was not, he said, going to pretend that he didn't recognize the value of such a guest to the Springs. Dikon distrusted him more with every phrase he uttered, but he began to think that if such enormous efforts were to be made, Gaunt should be tolerably comfortable at Wai-ata-tapu. He put out a feeler.

"I understand," he said, "that there is a resident doctor."

He was surprised to see Mr. Questing change colour. "Dr. Tonks," Questing said, "doesn't actually reside at the Springs, Mr. Bell. He's at Harpoon. Only a few minutes by road. A very very fine doctor."

"I meant Dr. James Ackrington."

Mr. Questing did not answer immediately. He offered Dikon a cigarette, lit one himself, and rang the bell again.

"Dr. Ackrington," Dikon repeated.

"Oh, yes. Ye-e-s. The old doctor. Quite a character."

"Doesn't he live at the hostel?"

"That is correct. Yes. That is the case. The old doctor's retired now, I understand."

"He's something of an authority on muscular and nervous complaints, isn't he?"

"Is that so?" said Mr. Questing. "Well, well, well. The old doctor, eh? Quite a character. Well, now, Mr. Bell, I've a little suggestion to make. I've been wondering if you'd be interested in a wee trip to the Springs. I'm driving back there to-morrow. It's a six hours' run and I'd be very very delighted to take you with me. Of course the suite won't be poshed up by then. You'll see us in the raw, sir, but any suggestions you cared to make..."

"Do you live there, Mr. Questing?"

"You can't keep me away from the Springs for long," cried Mr. Questing evasively. "Now about this suggestion of mine . . ."

"It's very kind of you," said Dikon thoughtfully. He rose to his feet and held out his hand. "I'll tell Mr. Gaunt about it. Thank you so much."

Mr. Questing wrung his hand excruciatingly.

"Good-bye," said Dikon politely.

"I'm staying here to-night, Mr. Bell, and I'll be right on the spot if . . ."

"Oh yes. Perfectly splendid. Good-bye."

He returned to his employer.

iii

Late on the afternoon of Saturday the eighteenth, old Rua Te Kahu sat on the crest of a hill that rose in an unbroken curve above his native village. The hill formed a natural barrier between the Maori reserve lands and the thermal resort of Wai-ata-tapu Springs where the Claires lived. From where he sat Rua looked down to his right upon the sulphur-corroded roof of the Claires' house, and to his left upon the smaller hip-roofs of his own people's dwelling houses and shacks. From each side of the hill rose plumes of steam, for the native *pa* was built near its own thermal pools. Rua, therefore, sat in a place that became him well. Behind his head, and softened by wreaths of steam, was the shape of Rangi's Peak. At his feet, in the warm friable soil, grew manuka scrub.

He was an extremely old man, exactly how old he did not choose to say; but his father, a chief of the Te Rarawa tribe, had set his mark to the Treaty of Waitangi, not many years before Rua, his youngest child, was born. Rua's grandfather, Rewi, a chieftain and a cannibal, was a neolithic man. To find his European counterpart, one would look back beyond the dawn of civilization. Rua himself had witnessed the full impact of the white man's ways upon a people living in a stone age. He had in turn been warrior, editor of a native newspaper, and member of Parliament. In his extreme age he had sloughed his European habits and returned to his own sub-tribe and to a way of life that was an echo in a minor key of his earliest youth.

"My great-great-grandfather is a hundred," bragged little Hoani Smith at the Harpoon primary school. "He is the oldest man in New Zealand. He is nearly as old as God. *Hu!*"

Rua was dressed in a shabby suit. About his shoulders he wore a blanket, for nowadays he felt the cold. Sartorially he was rather disreputable, but for all that he had about him an air of greatness. His head was magnificent, long and shapely. His nose was a formidable beak, his lips thin and uncompromising. His eyes still held their brilliance. He was a patrician, and looked down the long lines of his ancestry until they met in one of the canoes of the first Polynesian searovers. One would have said that his descent must have been free from the coarsening of Melanesian blood. But for his colour, a light brown, he looked for all the world like a Jacobite patriot's notion of a Highland chieftain.

Every evening he climbed to the top of the hill and smoked a pipe, beginning his slow ascent an hour before sunset. Sometimes one of his grandchildren, or an old crony of his own clan, would go up with him, but more often he sat there alone, lost, as it seemed, in a long perspective of recollections. The Claires, down at the Springs, would glance up and see him appearing larger than human against the sky and very still. Or Huia, sitting on the bank behind the house when she should have been scrubbing potatoes, would wave to him and send him a long-drawn-out cry of greeting in his own tongue. She was one of his many great-grandchildren.

This evening he found much to interest him down at the Springs. A covered van had turned in from the main road and had lurched and skidded down the track which the Claires called their drive, until it pulled up at their front door. Excited noises came from inside the house. Old Rua heard his great-granddaughter's voice and Miss Barbara Claire's unmelodious laughter. There were bumping sounds. A large car came down the track and pulled up at the edge of the sweep. Mr. Maurice Questing got out of it followed by a younger man. Rua leant forward a little, grasped the head of his stick firmly and rested his chin on his knotted hands. He seemed rooted in the hilltop, and part of its texture. After a long pause he heard a sound for which his ears had inherited an acute awareness. Someone was coming up the track behind him. The dry scrub brushed against approaching legs. In a moment or two a man stood beside him on the hill-top.

"Good evening, Mr. Smith," said old Rua without turning his head.

"G'day, Rua."

The man lurched forward and squatted beside Te Kahu. He was a European, but his easy adoption of this native posture suggested a familiarity with the ways of the Maori people. He was thin, and baldish. His long jaw was ill-shaved. His skin hung loosely from the bones of his face, and was unwholesome in colour. There was an air of raffishness about him. His clothes were seedy. Over them he wore a raincoat that was dragged out of shape by a bottle in an inner pocket. He began to make a cigarette, and his fingers, deeply stained with nicotine, were unsteady. He smelt very strongly of stale spirits.

"Great doings down at the Springs," he said.

"They seem to be busy," said Rua tranquilly.

"Haven't you heard? They've got a big pot coming to stay. That's his secretary, that young chap that's just come. You'd think it was royalty. They've been making it pretty solid for everybody down there. Hauling everything out and shifting us all round. I got sick of it and sloped off."

"A distinguished guest should be given a fitting welcome."

"He's only an actor."

"Mr. Geoffrey Gaunt. He is a man of great distinction."

"Then you know all about it, do you?"

"I think so," said old Rua.

Smith licked his cigarette and hung it from the corner of his mouth.

"Questing's at the back of it," he said. Rua stirred slightly. "He's kidded this Gaunt the mud'll fix his leg for him. He's falling over himself polishing the old dump up. You ought to see the furniture. Questing!" Smith added viciously. "By cripes, I'd like to see that joker get what's coming to him."

Unexpectedly Rua gave a subterranean chuckle.

"Look!" Smith said. "He's got something coming to him all right, that joker. The old doctor's got it in for him, and so's everybody else but Claire. I reckon Claire's not so keen, either, but Questing's put him where he just *can't* squeal. That's what I reckon."

He lit his cigarette and looked out of the corners of his eyes at Rua. "You don't say much," he said. His hand moved shakily over the bulge in his mackintosh. "Like a spot?" he asked.

"No, thank you. What should I say? It is no business of mine."

"Look, Rua," said Smith energetically. "I like your people. I get on with them. Aways have. That's a fact, isn't it?"

"You are intimate with some of my people."

"Yes. Well, I came up here to tell you something. Something about Questing." Smith paused. The quiet of evening had impregnated the countryside. The air was clear and the smallest noises from below reached the hill-top with uncanny sharpness. Down in the native reserve a collection of small brown boys milled about, squabbling. Several elderly women with handkerchiefs tied over their heads sat round one of the cooking pools. The smell of steaming sweet potatoes was mingled with the fumes of sulphur. On the other side, the van crawled up to the main road sounding its horn. From inside the Claires' house hollow bumping noises still continued. The sun was now behind Rangi's Peak.

"Questing's got a great little game on," said Smith. "He's going round your younger lot talking about teams of *poi* girls and kids diving for pennies, and all the rest of it. He's offering big money. He says he doesn't see why the Arawas down at Rotorua should be the only tribe to profit by the tourist racket."

Rua got slowly to his feet. He turned away from the Springs side of the hill to the east and looked down into his own hamlet, now deep in shadow.

"My people are well contented," he said. "We are not Arawas. We go our own way."

"And another thing. He's been talking about having

curios for sale. He's been nosing round. Asking about old times. Over at the Peak." Smith's voice slid into an uncertain key. He went on with an air of nervousness. "Someone's told him about Rewi's axe," he said.

Rua turned, and for the first time looked fully at his companion.

"That's not so good, is it?" said Smith.

"My grandfather Rewi," Rua said, "was a man of prestige. His axe was dedicated to the god Tane and was named after him, Toki-poutangata-o-Tane. It was sacred. Its burial place, also, is sacred and secret."

"Questing reckons it's somewhere on the Peak. He reckons there's a lot of stuff over on the Peak that might be exploited. He's talking about half-day trips to see the places of interest, with one of your people to act as guide and tell the tale."

"The Peak is a native reserve."

"He reckons he could square that up all right."

"I am an old man," said Rua affably, "but I am not yet dead. He will not find any guides among my people."

"Won't he! You ask Eru Saul. He knows what Questing's after."

"Eru is not a satisfactory youth. He is a bad *pakeha* Maori."

"Eru doesn't like the way Questing plays up to young Huia. He reckons Questing is kidding her to find guides for him."

"He will not find guides," Rua repeated.

"Money talks, you know."

"So will the tapu of my grandfather's *tokipoutangata*."

Smith looked curiously at the old man. "You really believe that, don't you?" he said.

"I am a *rangitira*. My father attended an ancient school of learning. He was a tohunga. I don't believe, Mr. Smith," said Rua with a chuckle. "I know."

"You'll never get a white man to credit supernatural stories, Rua. Even your own younger lot don't think much..."

Rua interrupted him. The full magnificence of his voice sounded richly on the evening air. "Our people," Rua said, "stand between two worlds. In a century we have had to swallow the progress of nineteen hundred years. Do you wonder that we suffer a little from evolutionary dyspepsia? We are loyal members of the great commonwealth: your enemies are our enemies. You speak of the young people. They are like voyagers whose canoes are in a great ocean between two countries. Sometimes they behave objectionably and are naughty children. Sometimes they are taught very bad tricks by their *pakeha* friends." Rua looked full at Smith, who fidgeted. "There are *pakeha* laws to prevent my young men from making fools of themselves with whisky and too much beer," said Rua tranquilly, "but there are also *pakehas* who help them to break these laws. The *pakehas* teach our young maidens that they should be quiet girls and not have babies before they are married, but in my own *hapu* there is a small boy whom we call Hoani Smith, though in law he has no right to that name."

"Hell, Rua, that's an old story," Smith muttered.

"Let me tell you another old story. Many years ago, when I was a youth, a maiden of our *hapu* lost her way in the mists on Rangi's Peak. In ignorance, intending no sacrilege, she came upon the place where my grandfather rests with his weapons, and, being hungry, ate a small piece of cooked food that she carried with her. In that place it was an act of horrible sacrilege. When the mists cleared, she discovered her crime and returned in terror to her people. She told her story, and was sent out to his hill while her case was discussed. At night she thought she would creep back, but she missed her way. She fell into Taupo-tapu, the boiling mud pool. Everybody in the village heard her scream. Next morning her dress was thrown up, rejected by the spirit of the pool. When your friend Mr. Questing speaks of my grandfather's *toki*, relate this story to him. Tell him the girl's scream can still be heard sometimes at night. I am going home now," Rua added, and drew his blanket about him with precisely the same gesture that his grandfather had used to adjust his feather cloak. "Is it true, Mr. Smith, that Mr. Questing has said a great many times that when he takes over the Springs, you will lose your job?"

"He can have it for mine," said Smith angrily. "That'll do me all right. He doesn't have to talk about the sack. When Questing's the boss down there, I'm turning the job up." He dragged the whisky bottle from his pocket and fumbled with the cork.

"And yet," Rua said, "it's a very soft job. You are going to drink? I shall go home. Good evening."

iv

Dikon Bell, marooned in the Claires' private sittingroom, stared at faded photographs of regimental Anglo-Indians, at the backs of blameless novels, and at a framed poster of the Cotswolds in spring. The poster was the work of a celebrated painter, and was at once gay, ordered, and delicate—a touching sequence of greens and blues. It made Dikon, the New Zealander, ache for England. By shifting his gaze slightly, he saw, framed in the sitting-room window, a landscape aloof from man. Its beauty was perfectly articulate yet utterly remote. Against his will he was moved by it as an unmusical listener may be profoundly disturbed by sound forms that he is unable to comprehend. He had travelled a great deal in his eight years' absence from New Zealand and had seen places famous for their antiquities, but it seemed to him that the landscape he now watched through the Claires' window was of an age far more remote than any of these. It did not carry the scars of lost civilization. Rather, it seemed to make nothing of time, for it was still primeval and its only stigmata were those of a neolithic age. Dikon, who longed to be in London, recognized in himself an affinity with this indifferent and profound country, and resented its attraction.

He wondered what Gaunt would say to it. He was to return to his employer next day by bus and train, a long and fatiguing business. Gaunt had bought a car, and on the following day he, Dikon and Colly would set out for Wai-ata-tapu. They had made many such journeys in many countries. Always at the end there had been expensive hotels or flats and lavish attention—amenities that Gaunt accepted as necessities of existence. Dikon was gripped by a sensation of panic. He had been mad to urge this place with its air of amateurish incompetence, its appalling Mr. Questing, its incredible Claires, whose air of breeding would seem merely to underline their complacency. A bush pub might have amused Gaunt; the Springs would bore him to exasperation.

A figure passed the window and stood in the doorway. It was Miss Claire. Dikon, whose job obliged him to observe such things, noticed that her cotton dress had been most misguidedly garnished with a neck bow of shiny ribbon, that her hair was precisely the wrong length, and that she used no make-up.

"Mr. Bell," said Barbara, "we were wondering if you'd advise us about Mr. Gaunt's *rooms.* Where to *put* things. I'm afraid you'll find us very *primitive.*" She laid tremendous stress on odd syllables and words, and as she did so turned up her eyes in a deprecating manner and pulled down the corners of her mouth like a lugubrious clown.

"Comedy stuff," thought Dikon. "Alas, alas, she means to be funny." He said that he would be delighted to see the rooms, and, nervously fingering his tie, followed her along the verandah.

The wing at the east end of the house, corresponding with the Claires' private rooms at the west end, had been turned into a sort of flat for Gaunt, Dikon and Colly. It consisted of four rooms: two small bedrooms, one tiny bedroom, and a slightly larger bedroom which had been converted into Mr. Questing's idea of a celebrity's study. In this apartment were assembled two chromium-steel chairs, one large armchair, and a streamlined desk, all of rather bad design, and with the dealer's tabs still attached to them. The floor was newly carpeted, and the windows in process of being freshly curtained by Mrs. Claire. Mr. Questing, wearing a cigar as if it were a sort of badge of office, lolled carelessly in the armchair. On Dikon's entrance he sprang to his feet.

"Well, well, well," cried Mr. Questing gaily, "how's the young gentleman?"

"Quite well, thank you," said Dikon, who had spent the greater part of the day motoring with Mr. Questing, and had become reconciled to these constant inquiries.

"Is this service," Mr. Questing went on, waving his cigar at
the room, "or is it? Forty-eight hours ago I hadn't the
pleasure of your acquaintance, Mr. Bell. After our little chat
yesterday. I felt so optimistic I just had to get out and get
going. I went to the finest furnishing firm in Auckland, and I
told the manager, I told him: 'Look,' I told him, 'you've got
the right stuff! It's modern and it's quality. Listen!' I told him.
'I'll take this stuff, if you can get it to Wai-ata-tapu, Harpoon,
by to-morrow afternoon. And if not, not.' That's the way I
like to do things, Mr. Bell."

"I hope you have explained that even now Gaunt may not
decide to come," said Dikon. "You have all taken a great deal
of trouble, Mrs. Claire."

Mrs. Claire looked doubtfully from Questing to Dikon.
"I'm afraid," she said plaintively, "that I don't really quite
appreciate very up-to-date furniture. I always think a
homelike atmosphere, no matter how shabby... However."

Questing cut in, and Dikon only half-listened to another
dissertation on the necessity of moving with the times. He
was jerked into full awareness when Questing, with an air of
familiarity, addressed himself to Barbara. "And what's Babs
got to say about it?" he asked, lowering his voice to a rich and
offensive purr. Dikon saw her step backwards. It was an
instinctive movement, he thought, uncontrollable as a reflex
jerk, but less ungainly than her usual habit. Its effect on
Dikon was as simple and as automatic as itself; he felt a stab
of sympathy and a protective impulse. She was no longer
regrettable; she was, for a moment, rather touching.
Surprised, and a little disturbed, he looked away from
Barbara to Mrs. Claire, and saw that her plump hands were
clenched among sharp folds of the shining chintz. He felt that
a little scene of climax had been enacted. It was disturbed by
the appearance of another figure. Limping steps sounded on
the verandah, and the doorway was darkened. A stocky man,
elderly but still red-headed and extremely handsome in an
angry sort of way, stood glaring at Questing.

"Oh, James," Mrs. Claire mumured, "there you are, old
man. You haven't met Mr. Bell. My brother, Dr. Ackrington."

As they shook hands, Dikon saw that Barbara had moved
close to her uncle.

"Have a good run up?" asked Dr. Ackrington, throwing a

needle-sharp glance at Dikon. "Ever see anything more disgraceful than the roads? I've been fishing."

Startled by this *non sequitur,* Dikon murmured politely: "Indeed?"

"If you can call it fishing. Hope you and Gaunt aren't counting on catching any trout. What with native reserves and the damned infamous behaviour of white poaching cads, there's not a fish to be had in twenty miles."

"Now, now, now, Doctor," said Questing in a great hurry. "We can't let you get away with that. Why, the greatest little trout streams in New Zealand . . ."

"D'you enjoy being called 'Mister'?" Dr. Ackrington demanded, so loudly that Dikon gave a nervous jump. Questing said uneasily: "Not much."

"Then don't call me 'Doctor,'" commanded Dr. Ackrington. Questing laughed uproariously. "That's just too bad," he said.

Dr. Ackrington looked round the room. "Good God," he said, "What are you doing with the place?"

"Mr. Questing," began Mrs. Claire, "has very kindly . . ."

"I might have recognized the authentic touch," said her brother, turning his back on the room. "Staying here tonight are you, Bell? I'd like a word with you. Come along to my room when you've a moment."

"Thank you, sir," said Dikon.

Dr. Ackrington looked through the doorway. "The star boarder," he said, "is returning in his usual condition. Mr. Bell is to be treated to a comprehensive view of our amenities."

They all looked through the doorway. Dikon saw a shambling figure cross the pumice sweep and approach the verandah.

"Oh dear!" said Mrs. Claire. "I'm afraid . . . James, dear, could you. . . ?"

Dr. Ackrington limped out to the verandah. The newcomer saw, stumbled to a halt, and dragged a bottle from the pocket of his raincoat.

To Dikon, watching through the window, the intrusion of a drunken white figure into the native landscape was at once preposterous and rather pathetic. A clear light, reflected from the pumice track, rimmed the folds of his shabby

garments. He stood there, drooping and lonely, and turned
the whisky bottle in his hand, staring at it as if it were the
focal point for some fuddled meditation. Presently he raised
his head and looked at Dr. Ackrington.

"Well, Smith," said Dr. Ackrington.

"You're a sport, Doc," said Smith. "There's a couple of
snifters left. Come on and have one."

"You'll do better to keep it," said Dr. Ackrington quite
mildly.

Smith peered beyond him into the room. His eyes
narrowed. He lurched forward to the verandah. "I'll deal
with this," said Questing importantly, and strode out to meet
him. They confronted each other. Questing, planted squarely
on the verandah edge, made much of his cigar; Smith clung to
the post and stared up at him.

"You clear out of this, Smith," said Questing.

"You get to hell yourself," said Smith distinctly. He
looked past Questing to the group in the doorway, and very
solemnly took off his hat. "Present company excepted," he
added.

"Did you hear what I said?"

"Is that the visitor?" Smith asked loudly, and pointed at
Dikon. "Is that the reason why we're all sweating our guts up?
That? Let's have a better look at it. Gawd, what a sissy."

Dikon wondered confusedly which of the party felt most
embarrassed. Dr. Ackrington made a loud barking noise,
Barbara broke into agonized laughter, Mrs. Claire rushed
into a spate of apologies, Dikon himself attempted to suggest
by gay inquiring glances that he had not understood the tenor
of Smith's remarks. He might have spared himself the
trouble. Smith made a plunge at the verandah step shouting:
"Look at the little bastard." Questing attempted to stop him,
and the scene mounted in a rapid crescendo. Dikon, Mrs.
Claire, and Barbara remained in the room. Dr. Ackrington
on the verandah appeared to hold a watching brief, while
Questing and Smith yelled industriously in each other's faces.
The climax came when Questing again attempted to shove
Smith away from the verandah. Smith drove his fist in
Questing's face and lost his balance. They fell simultaneous-
ly.

The noise stopped as suddenly as it had begun. An

inexplicable and ridiculous affair changed abruptly into a piece of convincing melodrama. Dikon had seen many such a set-up at the cinema studios. Smith, shaky and bloated, crouched where he had fallen and mouthed at Questing. Questing got to his feet and dabbed at the corner of his mouth with his handkerchief. His cigar lay smoking on the ground between them. It was a shot in technicolour, for Rangi's Peak was now tinctured with such a violence of purple as is seldom seen outside the theatre, and in the middle distance rose the steam of the hot pools.

Dikon waited for a bit of tough dialogue to develop and was not disappointed.

"By God," Questing said, exploring his jaw, "you'll get yours for this. You're sacked."

"You're not my bloody boss."

"I'll bloody well get you the sack, don't you worry. When I'm in charge here..."

"That will do," said Dr. Ackrington crisply.

"What *is* all this?" a peevish voice demanded. Colonel Claire, followed by Simon, appeared round the wing of the house. Smith got to his feet.

"You'll have to get rid of this man, Colonel," said Questing.

"What's he done?" Simon demanded.

"I socked him." Smith took Simon by the lapels of his coat. "You look out for yourselves," he said. "It's not only me he's after. Your dad won't sack me, will he, Sim?"

"We'll see about that," Questing said.

"But *why*..." Colonel Claire began, and was cut short by his brother-in-law.

"If I may interrupt for a moment," said Dr. Ackrington acidly. "I suggest that I take Mr. Bell to my room. Unless, of course, he prefers a ring-side seat. Will you come and have a drink, Bell?"

Dikon thankfully accepted, leaving the room in a gale of apologies from Mrs. Claire and Barbara. Questing, who seemed to have recovered his temper, followed them up with a speech in which anxiety, propitiation, and a kind of fawning urgency were most disagreeably mingled. He was cut short by Dr. Ackrington.

"Possibly," Dr. Ackrington said, "Mr. Bell may prefer to

form his own opinion of this episode. No doubt he has seen a chronic alcoholic before now, and will not attach much significance to anything this particular specimen may choose to say."

"Yes, yes. Of course," Dikon murmured unhappily.

"As for the behaviour of Other Persons," Dr. Ackrington continued, "there again, he may, as I do, form his own opinion. Come along, Bell."

Dikon followed him along the verandah to his own room, a grimly neat apartment with a hideous desk.

"Sit down," said Dr. Ackrington. He wrenched open the door of a home-made cupboard, and took out a bottle and two tumblers. "I can only offer you whisky," he said. "With Smith's horrible example before you, you may not like the idea. Afraid I don't go in for modern rot-gut."

"Thank you," said Dikon, "I should like whisky. May I ask who he is?"

"Smith? He's a misfit, a hopeless fellow. No good in him at all. Drifted out here as a boy. Agnes, my sister, who is something of a snob, talks loosely about him being a public-school man. Her geese are invariably swans, but I suppose this suggestion is within the bounds of possibility. Smith may have originated in some ill-conducted establishment of dubious gentility. Sometimes their early habits of speech go down the wind with their self-respect. Sometimes they keep it up even in the gutter. They used to be called remittance men, and in this extraordinary country received a good deal of entirely misguided sympathy from native-born fools. That suit you?"

"Thank you, sir," said Dikon, taking his drink.

"My sister chooses to regard him as a sort of invalid. Some instinct must have led him ten years ago to the Springs. It has proved to be an ideal battening ground. They give him his keep and a wage, in exchange for idling about the place with an axe in his hand and a bottle in his pocket. When his cheque comes from Home he drinks himself silly, and my sister Agnes gives him beef-tea and prays for him. He's a complete waster but he won't trouble you, I fancy. I confess that this evening I was almost in sympathy with him. He did what I have longed to do for the past three months." Dikon glanced up quickly. "He drove his fist into Questing's face,"

Dr. Ackrington explained. "Here's luck to you," he added. They drank to each other.

"Well," said Dr. Ackrington after a pause, "you will doubtless lose no time in returning to Auckland and telling your principal to avoid this place like the devil."

As this pretty well described Dikon's intention he could think of nothing to say, and made a polite murmuring.

"If it is of any interest, you may as well know you have seen it at its worst. Smith is not always drunk and Questing is not always with us."

"Not? But I thought..."

"He absents himself. I rejoice in the event and deplore the motive. However."

Dr. Ackrington glared portentously into his glass and cleared his throat. Dikon waited for a moment, but his companion showed no sign of developing his theme. Dikon was to learn that Dr. Ackrington could exploit with equal mastery the embarrassing phrase and the disconcerting silence.

"Since we have mentioned him," Dikon began nervously, "I confess I'm in a state of some confusion about Mr. Questing. May I ask if he is actually the—if Wai-ata-tapu Springs is his property?"

"No," said Dr. Ackrington.

"I only ask," Dikon continued in a hurry, "because you see I was approached in the first instance by Mr. Questing. Although I've warned him that Gaunt may decide against the Springs, he has been at extraordinary pains and really very considerable expense to—to alter existing arrangements and so on. And I mean—well, Dr. Forster's note suggested that it was to Colonel and Mrs. Claire that we should apply."

"So it is."

"I see. But—Questing?"

"If you decide against the Springs," said Dr. Ackrington, "you should convey your decision to my sister."

"But," Dikon repeated obstinately, "Questing?"

"Ignore him."

"Oh."

Steps sounded outside the window, and voices: Smith's voice slurred but vicious; Colonel Claire's high-pitched, perhaps a little hysterical; and Questing's the voice of a bully.

As they came nearer, odd sentences separated out from the general rumpus.

"... if the Colonel's satisfied—it's not a fair pop."

"... never mind that. You've been asking for it and you'll get it."

"... sack me and see what you get, you—"

"... most disgraceful scene—force my hand ..."

"... kick you out to-morrow."

"This is too much," Colonel Claire cried out. "I've stood a great deal, Questing, but I must remind you that I still have some authority here."

"Is that so? Where do you get it from? You'd better watch your step, Claire."

"By God," Smith roared out suddenly, "you'd better watch yours."

Dr. Ackrington opened the door and stood on the threshold. Complete silence followed this move. Through the open door came a particularly strong wave of sulphurous air.

"I suggest, Edward," Dr. Ackrington said, "that you continue your conversation in the laundry. Mr. Bell has no doubt formed the opinion that we do not possess one."

He shut the door. "Let me give you another drink," he said courteously.

CHAPTER III

GAUNT AT THE SPRINGS

"Five days ago," said Gaunt, "you dangled this place before me like some atrocious bait. Now you do nothing but bemoan its miseries. You are strangely inconsistent."

"In the interval," said Dikon, wrenching the car out of a pothole, and changing down, "I have seen the place. I implore you to remember, sir, that you have been warned."

"You overdid it. You painted it in macabre colours. My curiosity was stimulated. For pity's sake, my dear Dikon, drive a little further away from the edge of the abyss. Can this mountain goat-track possibly be a main road?"

"It's the only road from Harpoon to Wai-ata-tapu, sir. You wanted somewhere quiet, you know. And these are not mountains. There are no mountains in the Northland. The big stuff is in the South."

"I'm afraid you're a scenic snob. To me this is a mountain. When I fall over the edge of this precipice, I shall not be found with a sneer on my lips because the drop was merely five hundred feet instead of a thousand. There's a most unpleasant smell about this place."

"It's the thermal smell. People are said to get to like it."

"Nonsense. How are you travelling, Colly?"

Fenced in by luggage in the back seat, Colly replied that he kept his eyes closed at the curves. "I didn't seem to notice it so much this morning in them forests," he added. "It's dynamite in the open."

The road corkscrewed its way in and out of a gully and along a barren stretch of downland. On its left the coast ran freely northwards in a chain of scrolls, last interruptions in its firm line before it tightened into the Ninety Mile Beach. The thunder of the Tasman Sea hung like a vast rumour on the freshening air, and above the margin of the downs Rangi's Peak was slowly erected.

"That's an ominous-looking affair," said Gaunt. "What is it about these hills that gives them an air of the fabulous? They are not so very odd in shape, not incredible like the Dolomites or imposing like the Rockies—not, as you point out in your superior way, Dikon, really mountains at all. Yet they seem to be pregnant with some tiresome secret. What is it?"

"Perhaps it's something to do with the volcanic silhouette. If there's a secret the answer's in the Maori language. I'm afraid you'll get very tired of that cone, sir. It looks over the hills round the Springs." Dikon waited for a moment. Gaunt had a trick of showing a fugitive interest in places, of asking for expositions, and of growing restless when they were given to him.

"Why is the answer in Maori?" he said.

"It was a native burial-ground in the old days. They tipped the bodies into the crater. It's extinct you know. Supposed to be full of them."

"Good Lord!" said Gaunt softly.

The car climbed higher, and the base of Rangi's Peak, a series of broad platforms and slopes, came into sight. "You can see quite clearly," Dikon said, "the route they must have followed. Miss Claire tells me the tribes used to camp at the foot for three days holding a *tangi,* the Maori equivalent of a wake. Then the body was carried up the Peak by relays of bearers. They said that if it was a chief who had died, and if the air was still, you could hear the singing as far away as Wai-ata-tapu."

"Gawd!" said Colly.

"Can you look into the crater and see. . . ?"

"I don't know. It's a native reserve, the Claires told me. Very tapu of course."

"What's that?"

"Tapu? Taboo. Sacred. Forbidden. Untouchable. I don't suppose the Maori people ever climb up the Peak nowadays. No admittance to the *pakeha,* of course; it would be much too tempting a hunting-ground. They used to busy the chiefs' weapons with them. There is a certain adze inherited by the chief Rewi who died about a hundred years ago and was buried on the Peak. This adze, his favourite weapon, was hidden up there. It had featured prominently and bloodily in the Maori wars, and had been spoken of in their oral schools of learning for generations before that. Rewi's *toki-poutangata*. It has a secret mark on it, and was said to be invested with supernatural power by the god Tane. There it is, they say, a collector's plum if ever there was one, somewhere on the Peak. The whole place belongs to the Maori people. It's forbidden territory to the white hunter."

"How far away is it?"

"About eight miles."

"It looks less than three in this uncanny atmosphere."

"Kind of black, sir, isn't it?" said Colly.

"Black and clear," said Gaunt. "A marvellous back drop."

They drove on in silence for some time. The flowing hills moved slowly about as if in a contrapuntal measure determined by the progress of the car. Dikon began to recognize landmarks. He felt extremely apprehensive.

"Hullo," said Gaunt. "What's that affair down on the right? A sort of doss-house, one would think."

Dikon said nothing, but turned in at a ramshackle gate.

"You don't dare to tell me that we have arrived," Gaunt demanded in a loud voice.

"Yes, sir."

"My God, Dikon, you'll writhe for this. Look at it. Smell it. Colly, we are betrayed."

"Mr. Bell warned you, sir," Colly said. "I daresay it's very comfortable."

"If anything," said Dikon, "it's less comfortable than it looks. Those are the Springs."

"Those reeking puddles?"

"Yes. And there, on the verandah, I see the Claires assembled. You are expected, sir," said Dikon. Out of the tail of his eyes he saw Gaunt's gloved fingers go first to his tie and then to his hat. He thought suddenly: "He looks terribly like a famous actor."

The car rocked down the last stretch of the drive and shot across the pumice sweep. Dikon pulled up at the verandah steps. He got out, and taking off his hat approached the expectant Claires. He felt nervous and absurd. The Claires were grouped after the manner of an Edwardian family portrait that had taken an eccentric turn. Mrs. Claire and the Colonel were in deckchairs, Barbara sat on the steps grasping a reluctant dog. Dikon guessed that they wore their best clothes. Simon, obviously under duress, stood behind his mother's chair looking murderous. All that was lacking, one felt, was the native equivalent of a gillie holding a couple of staghounds in leash. As Dikon approached, Dr. Ackrington came out of his room.

"Here we are, you see," Dikon called out with an effort at gaiety. The Claires had risen. Impelled by confusion, doubt, and apology, Dikon shook hands blindly all round. Barbara looked nervously over his shoulder and he saw with a dismay which he afterwards recognized as prophetic that she had gone white to her unpainted lips.

He felt Gaunt's hand on his arm and hurriedly introduced him.

Mrs. Claire brought poise to the situation, Dikon realized, but it was the kind of poise with which Gaunt was quite unfamiliar. She might have been welcoming a bishop-suffragan to a slum parish, a bishop-suffragan in poor health.

"Such a long journey," she said anxiously. "You must be so tired."

"Not a bit of it," said Gaunt, who had arrived at an age when actors affect a certain air of youthful hardihood.

"But it's such a dreadful road. And you *look* very tired," she persisted gently. Dikon saw Gaunt's smile grow formal. He turned to Barbara. For some reason which he had not attempted to analyze, Dikon wanted Gaunt to like Barbara. It was with apprehension that he watched her give a galvanic jerk, open her eyes very wide, and put her head on one side like a chidden puppy. "Oh hell," he thought, "she's going to be funny."

"Welcome," Barbara said in her sepulchral voice, "to the *humble abode*." Gaunt dropped her hand rather quickly.

"Find us very quiet, I'm afraid," Colonel Claire said, looking quickly at Gaunt and away again. "Not much in your line, this country, what?"

"But we've just been remarking," Gaunt said lightly, "that your landscape reeks of theatre." He waved his stick at Rangi's Peak. "One expects to hear the orchestra." Colonel Claire looked baffled and slightly offended.

"My brother," Mrs. Claire mumured. Dr. Ackrington limped forward. Dikon's attention was distracted from this

last encounter by the behaviour of Simon Claire, who
suddenly lurched out of cover, strode down the steps and
seized the astounded Colly by the hand. Colly, who was
about to unload the car, edged behind it.

"How are you?" Simon said loudly. "Give you a hand with
that stuff."

"That's all right, thank you, sir."

"Come on," Simon insisted and laid violent hands on a
pigskin dressing-case which he lugged from the car and
dumped none too gently on the pumice. Colly gave a little cry
of dismay.

"Here, here, here!" a loud voice expostulated. Mr.
Questing thundered out of the house and down the steps.
"Cut that out, young fellow," he ordered and shouldered
Simon away from the car.

"Why?" Simon demanded.

"That's no way to treat high-class stuff," bustled Mr.
Questing with an air of intolerable patronage. "You'll have to
learn better than that. Handle it carefully." He advanced
upon Dikon. "We're willing," he laughed, "but we've a lot to
learn. Well, well, well, how's the young gentleman?"

He removed his hat and placed himself before Gaunt. His
change of manner was amazingly abrupt. He might have
been a lightning impersonator or a marionette controlled by
some pundit of second-rate etiquette. Suddenly, he oozed
deference. "I don't think," he said, "that I have had the
honour—"

"Mr. Questing," said Dikon.

"This is a great day for the Springs, sir," said Mr.
Questing. "A great day."

"Thank you," said Gaunt, glancing at him. "If I may I
should like to see my rooms."

He turned to Mrs. Claire. "Dikon tells me you have taken
an enormous amount of trouble on my behalf. It's very kind
indeed. Thank you so much." And Dikon saw that with this
one speech, delivered with Gaunt's famous air of gay
sincerity, he had captivated Mrs. Claire. She beamed at him.
"I shall try not to be troublesome," Gaunt added. And to Mr.
Questing: "Right."

They went in procession along the verandah. Mr.
Questing, still uncovered, led the way.

ii

Barbara sat on the edge of her stretcher-bed in her small hot room and looked at two dresses. Which should she wear for dinner on the first night? Neither of them was new. The red lace had been sent out two years ago by her youngest aunt who had worn it a good deal in India. Barbara had altered it to fit herself and something had gone wrong with the shoulder, so that it bulged where it should lie flat. To cover this defect she had attached a black flower to the neck. It was a long dress and she did not as a rule change for dinner. Simon might make some frightful comment if she wore the red lace. The alternative was a short floral affair, thick blue in colour with a messy yellow design. She had furbished it up with a devilish shell ornament and a satin belt and even poor Barbara wondered if it was a success. Knowing that she should be in the kitchen with Huia, she pulled off her print, dragged the red lace over her head and looked at herself in the inadequate glass. No, it would never become her dress, it would always hark back to unknown Aunty Wynne who two years ago had written: "Am sending a box of odds and ends for Ba. Hope she can wear red." But could she? Could she plunge about in the full light of day in this ownerless waif of a garment with everybody knowing she had dressed herself up? She peered at her face, which was slightly distorted by the glass. Suddenly she hauled the dress over her head, fighting with the stuffy-smelling lace. "Barbara," her mother called. "Where are you? Ba!" "Coming!" Well, it would have to be the floral.

But when, hot and desperate, she had finally dressed, and covered the floral with a clean overall, she pressed her hands together. "O God," she thought, "make him like it here! Please, dear God, make him like it."

iii

"Can you possibly endure it?" Dikon asked.

Gaunt was lying full length on the modern sofa. He raised
his arms above his head. "All," he whispered, "I can endure
all but Questing. Questing must be kept from me."

"But I told you—"

"You amaze me with your shameless parrot cry of 'I told
you so,'" said Gaunt mildly. "Let us have no more of it." He
looked out of the corner of his eye at Dikon. "And don't look
so tragic, my good ass," he added. "I've been a small-part
touring actor in my day. This place is strangely reminiscent of
a one-night fit-up. No doubt I can endure it. I *should* be
dossing down in an Anderson shelter, by God. I do well to
complain. Only spare me Questing, and I shall endure the
rest."

"At least we shall be spared his conversation this evening.
He has a previous engagement. Lest he offer to put it off, I
told him you would be desolated but had already arranged to
dine in your rooms and go to bed at nine. So away he went."

"Good. In that case I shall dine *en famille* and go to bed
when it amuses me. I have yet to meet Mr. Smith, remember.
Is it too much to hope that he will stage another fight?"

"It seems he only gets drunk when his remittance comes
in." Dikon hesitated and then asked: "What did you think of
the Claires, sir?"

"Marvellous character parts. Overstated, of course. Not
quite West End. A number-one production on tour, shall we
say? The Colonel's moustache is a little too thick in both
senses."

Dikon felt vaguely resentful. "You captivated Mrs.
Claire," he said.

Gaunt ignored this. "If one could take them as they are,"
he said. "If one could persuade them to appear in those
clothes and speak those lines! My dear, they'd be a riot. Miss
Claire! Dikon, I didn't believe she existed."

"Actually," said Dikon stiffly, "she's rather attractive. If
you look beyond her clothes."

"You're a remarkably swift worker if you've been able to
do that."

"They're extraordinarily kind and, I think, very nice."

"Until we arrived you never ceased to exclaim against them. Why have you bounced round to their side all of a sudden?"

"I only said, sir, that I thought you would be bored by them."

"On the contrary I'm agreeably entertained. I think they're all darlings and marvellous comedy. What *is* your trouble?"

"Nothing. I'm sorry. I've just discovered that I like them. I thought," said Dikon, smiling a little in spite of himself, "that the tableau on the verandah was terribly sad. I wonder how long they'd been grouped-up like that."

"For ages, I should think. The dog was plainly exasperated and young Claire looked lethal."

"It is rather touching," said Dikon and turned away.

Mrs. Claire and Barbara, wearing their garden hats and carrying trowels, went past the window on tiptoe, their faces solemn and absorbed. When they had gone a little way Dikon heard them whispering together.

"In heaven's name," cried Gaunt, "why do y stalk about their own premises like that? What are th otting?"

"It's because I explained that you liked to reiax before dinner. They don't want to disturb you. I fancy their vegetable garden is round the corner."

After a pause Gaunt said: "It will end in my feeling insecure and ashamed. Nothing arouses one's self-abasement more than the earnest amateur. How long have they had this place?"

"About twelve years, I think. Perhaps longer."

"Twelve years and they are still amateurs!"

"They try so terribly hard," Dikon said. He wandered out onto the verandah. Someone was walking slowly round the warm lake towards the springs.

"Hullo," Dikon said. "We've a caller."

"What do you mean? Be very careful, now. I'll see no one, remember."

"I don't think it's for us, sir," Dikon said. "It's a Maori."

It was Rua. He wore the suit he bought in 1936 to welcome the Duke of Gloucester. He walked slowly across the pumice to the house, tapped twice with his stick on the central verandah post and waited tranquilly for someone to take notice of him. Presently Huia came out and gave a suppressed giggle on seeing her great-grandfather. He addressed her in Maori with an air of austerity and she went back into the house. Rua sat on the edge of the verandah and rested his chin on his stick.

"Do you know sir," said Dikon, "I believe it might be for us, after all. I've recognized the old gentleman."

"I won't see anybody," said Gaunt. "Who is he?"

"He's a Maori version of the Last of the Barons. Rua Te Kahu, sometime journalist and M.P. for the district. I'll swear he's called to pay his respects."

"You must see him for me. We did bring some pictures, I suppose?"

"I don't think," Dikon said, "that the Last of the Barons will be waiting for signed photographs."

"You're determined to snub me," said Gaunt amiably. "If it's an interview, you'll talk to him, won't you?"

Colonel Claire came out of the house, shook hands with Rua and led him off in the direction of their own quarters.

"It's not for us, after all, sir."

"Thank heaven for that," Gaunt said but he looked a little huffy nevertheless.

In Colonel Claire's study, a room about the size of a small pantry and rather less comfortable, Rua unfolded the purpose of his call. Dim photographs of polo teams glared down menacingly from the walls. Rua's dark eyes rested for a moment on a group of turbaned Sikhs before he turned to address himself gravely to the Colonel.

"I have brought," he said, "a greeting from my *hapu* to your distinguished guest, Mr. Geoffrey Gaunt. The Maori people of Wai-ata-tapu are glad that he has come here and would like me to greet him with a cordial *Haere mai.*"

"Oh, thanks very much, Rua," said the Colonel. "I'll tell him."

"We have heard that he wishes to be quiet. If however he would care to hear a little singing, we hope that he will do us the honour to come to a concert on Saturday week in the evening. I bring this invitation from my *hapu* to your guests and your family, Colonel."

Colonel Claire raised his eyebrows, opened his eyes and

mouth, and glared at his visitor. He was not particularly surprised, but merely wore his habitual expression for absorbing new ideas.

"Eh?" he said at last. "Did you say a concert? Extraordinarily nice of you, Rua, I must say. A concert."

"If Mr. Gaunt would care to come."

Colonel Claire gave a galvanic start. "Care to?" he repeated. "I don't know, I'm sure. We should have to ask him, what? Sound the secretary."

Rua gave a little bow. "Certainly," he said.

Colonel Claire rose abruptly and thrust his head out of the window. "*James!*" he yelled. "Here!"

"What for?" said Dr. Ackrington's voice at some distance.

"I want you. It's my brother-in-law," he explained more quietly to Rua. "We'll see what he thinks, um?" He went out to the verandah and shouted, *"Agnes!"*

"Hoo-oo?" replied Mrs. Claire from inside the house.

"Here."

"In a minute, dear."

"Barbara."

"Wait a bit, Daddy. I can't."

"Here."

Having summoned his family, Colonel Claire sank into an armchair, and glancing at Rua gave a rather aimless laugh. His eyes happened to fall upon a Wild West novel that he had been reading. He was a greedy consumer of thrillers, and the sight of this one lying open and close at hand affected him as an open box of chocolate affects a child. He smiled at Rua and offered him a cigarette. Rua thanked him and took one, holding it cautiously between the tips of his fingers and thumb. Colonel Claire looked out of the corners of his eyes at his thriller. He was long-sighted.

"There was another matter about which I hoped to speak," Rua said.

"Oh yes?" said Colonel Claire. "D'you read much?"

"My eyesight is not as good as it once was, but I can still manage clear print."

"Awful rot, some of these yarns," Colonel Claire continued, casually picking up his novel. "This thing I've been dipping into, now. Blood-and-thunder stuff. Ridiculous."

"I am a little troubled in my mind. Disturbing rumours
have reached me..."

"Oh?" Colonel Claire, still with an air of absentminded-
ness, flipped over a page.

"...about proposals that have been made in regard to
native reserves. You have been a good friend to our people,
Colonel..."

"Not at all," Colonel Claire murmured abstractedly, and
felt for his reading glasses. "Always very pleased..." He
found his spectacles, put them on and, still casually, laid the
book on his knee.

"Since you have been at Wai-ata-tapu, there have been
friendly relations between your family and my *hapu*. We
should not care to see anyone else here."

"Very nice of you." Colonel Claire was now frankly
reading, but he continued to wear a social smile. He
contrived to suggest that he merely looked at the book
because after all one must look at something. Old Rua's
magnificent voice rolled on. The Maori people are never in a
hurry, and in his almost forgotten generation a gentleman led
up to the true matter of an official call through a series of
polite approaches. Rua's approval of his host was based on
an event twelve years old. The Claires arrived at Wai-ata-
tapu during a particularly virulent epidemic of influenza.
Over at Rua's village there were many deaths. The Harpoon
health authorities, led by the irate and overworked Dr.
Tonks, had fallen foul of the Maori people in matters of
hygiene, and a dangerous deadlock had been reached. Rua,
who normally exercised an iron authority, was himself too ill
to control his *hapu*. Funeral ceremonies lasting for days,
punctuated with long-drawn-out wails of greeting and
lamentation, songs of death, and interminable after-burial
feasts maintained native conditions in a community lashed
by a European scourge. Rua's people became frightened,
truculent, and obstructive, and the health authorities could
do nothing. Upon this scene came the Claires. Mrs. Claire
instantly translated the whole affair into terms of an English
village, offered their newly built house as an emergency
hospital and herself undertook the nursing, with Rua as her
first patient. Colonel Claire, whose absence-of-mind had
inoculated him against the arrogance of Anglo-Indianism,

and who by his very simplicity had fluked his way into a sort of understanding of native peoples, paid a visit to the settlement, arranged matters with Rua, and was accepted by the Maori people as a *rangitira,* a person of breeding. He and his wife professed neither extreme liking nor antipathy for the Maori people, who nevertheless found something recognizable and admirable in both of them. The war had brought them closer together. The Colonel commanded the local Home Guard and had brought many of Rua's older men into his division. Rua considered that he owed his life to his *pakeha* friends and, though he thought them funny, loved them. It did not offend him, therefore, when Colonel Claire furtively read a novel under his very nose. He rumbled on magnificently with his story, in amiable competition with Texas Rangers and six-shooter blondes.

". . . there has been enough trouble in the past. The Peak is a native reserve and we do not care for trespassers. He has been seen by a certain rascal coming down the western flank with a sack on his shoulders. At first he was friendly with this no-good young fellow, Eru Saul, who is a bad *pakeha* and a bad Maori. Now they have quarreled and their quarrel concerns my great-granddaughter Huia, who is a foolish girl but much too good for either of them. And Eru tells my grandson Rangi, and my grandson tells me, that Mr. Questing is behaving dishonestly on the Peak. Because he is your guest we have said nothing, but now I find him talking to some silly young fellows amongst our people and putting a lot of bad ideas into their heads. Now that makes me very angry," said old Rua, and his eyes flashed. "I do not like my young people to be taught to cheapen the culture of their race. It has been bad enough with Mr. Herbert Smith, who buys whisky for them and teaches them to make pigs of themselves. He is no good. But even *he* comes to me to warn me of this Questing."

The Colonel's novel dropped with a loud slap. His eyebrows climbed his forehead, his eyes and mouth opened. He turned pale.

"Hey?" he said. "Questing? What about Questing?"

"You have not been listening, Colonel," said Rua, rather crossly.

"Yes, I have, only I didn't catch everything. I'm getting deaf."

"I am sorry. I have been telling you that Mr. Questing has been looking for curios on the Peak and boasting that in a little while Wai-ata-tapu will be his property. I have come to ask you in confidence if this is true."

"What's all this about Questing?" demanded Dr. Ackrington, appearing at the doorway in his dressing gown. "'Evening, Rua. How are you?"

"It began by being about Gaunt and a concert party," said the Colonel unhappily. "It's only just turned into something in confidence about Questing."

"Well, if it's in confidence, why the devil did you call me? There seems to be a conspiracy in this house to deny my sciatica thermal treatment."

"I wanted to ask you if you thought Gaunt would like to go to a concert. Rua's people have very kindly offered..."

"How the devil do I know? Ask young Bell. Very nice of you, Rua, I must say."

"And then Rua began to talk about Questing and the Peak."

"Why don't you call him Quisling and be done with it?" Dr. Ackrington demanded loudly. "It's what he is, by God."

"James! I really must insist—You have no shred of evidence."

"Haven't I? Haven't I? Very well. Wait and see."

Rua stood up. "If it is not troubling you too much," he said, "perhaps you would ask Mr. Gaunt's secretary...?"

"Yes, yes," the Colonel agreed hurriedly. "Of course. Wait a minute, will you?"

He stumbled out of the room, and they heard him thump along the verandah towards Geoffrey Gaunt's quarters.

Rua's old eyes were very bright and cunning as he looked at Dr. Ackrington, but he did not speak.

"So he's been trespassing, has he?" asked Dr. Ackrington venomously. "I could have told you that when the *Hippolyte* was torpedoed."

Rua made a brusque movement with his wrinkled hands but still did not speak.

"He does it by night sometimes, doesn't he?" Dr. Ackrington went on. "Doesn't he go up by night, with a flash-lamp? Good God, my dear fellow, I've seen it myself. Curios be damned."

"Somehow," Rua said mildly, "I have never been able to enjoy spy stories. They always seem to me to be incredible."

"Indeed!" Dr. Ackrington rejoined acidly. "So this country, alone in the English-speaking world, stands immune from the activities of enemy agents. And why, pray? Do you think the enemy is frightened of us? Amazing complacency!"

"But he has been seen digging."

"Do you imagine he would be seen semaphoring? Of course he digs. No doubt he robs your ancestors' graves. No doubt he will have some infamous booty to exhibit when he is brought to book."

Rua pinched his lower lip and became very solemn. "I have felt many regrets," he said, "for old age which compelled me to watch my grandsons and great-grandsons set out to war without me. But if you are right, there is still work in Ao-tea-roa for an old warrior." He chuckled, and Dr. Ackrington looked apprehensively at him.

"I have been indiscreet," he said. "Keep this under your hat, Rua. A word too soon and we shan't get him. I may tell you I have taken steps. But see here. There's a certain amount of cover on the Peak. If your young people haven't altogether lost the art of their forbears—"

"We must arrange something," said Rua composedly. "Yes. No doubt something can be arranged."

"What is it, dear?" said Mrs. Claire, appearing abruptly in the doorway. "Oh! Oh, I thought Edward called me, James. Good evening, Rua."

"I *did* call you about half an hour ago," said her husband crossly from behind her back, "but it's all over, now. Old Rua was here with some—oh, you're still there, Rua. Mr. Gaunt's secretary says they'll be delighted."

Barbara came running distractedly from the kitchen. She and her parents formed up in a sort of queue outside the door.

"What is it, Daddy?" she asked. "What do you want?"

"Nobody wants anything," shouted her father angrily. "Everybody's delighted. Why do you all come running at me?"

"My people will be very pleased," said Rua. "I shall go now and tell them. I wish you all good evening."

As he walked along the verandah his great-granddaughter, Huia, flew out and excitedly rang the dinner-bell in his face. He gave her a good-natured buffet and struck out for home. Dikon, looking startled, came out on the verandah followed by Gaunt. Huia, over-stimulated by her first view of the celebrity, flashed her eyes, laughed excitedly and continued to peal her bell until Barbara took it away from her.

"I think that must be dinner," said Mrs. Claire with a bright assumption of surprise, while their ears still rang with the din. She turned with poise towards Gaunt. "Shall we go in?" she asked gently, and they formed up into a kind of procession, trailing after each other towards the dining-room door. At the last moment Simon appeared, as usual from the direction of the cabins, where he had a sort of workshop.

But the first night's dinner was not to go forward without the intrusion of that particular form of grotesque irrelevance which Dikon was learning to associate with the Claires, for as Gaunt and Mrs. Claire approached the front door, a terrific rumpus broke out in the kitchen.

"Where's the Colonel?" an agitated voice demanded. "I've got to see the Colonel."

Smith, dishevelled and with threads of blood crossing his face, blundered through the dining-room from the kitchen, thrust Gaunt and Mrs. Claire aside, and seized the Colonel by his coat lapels. "Here," he said, "you've got to do something You've got to look after me. He tried to kill me."

CHAPTER IV

RED FOR DANGER

Dikon, mindful of his only other encounter with him and influenced by an exceedingly significant smell, came to the conclusion that Mr. Smith was mad drunk. Perhaps a minute went by before he realized that he was merely terrified. It was obvious that the entire Claire family made the same mistake for, they all, together and severally and entirely without success, tried to shut Smith up and hustle him away into the background. Finally it was Dr. Ackrington who, after a sharp look at Smith, said to his brother-in-law: "Wait a minute now, Edward, you're making a mistake. Come along with me, Smith, and tell me what it's all about."

"I won't come along with anyone. I've just been along with someone and it's practically killed me. You listen to what I'm telling you! He's a bloody murderer."

"Who is?" asked Simon from somewhere in the rear.

"Questing."

"Smith, for God's sake!" said the Colonel, and tried to lead him away by the elbow.

"Leave me alone. I know what I'm talking about. I'm telling you."

"Oh, Daddy, *not* here!" Barbara cried out, and Mrs. Claire said: "No, Edward, *please.* Your study, dear." And as if Smith were some recalcitrant schoolboy, she repeated in a hushed voice: "Yes, yes, much better in your study."

"But you're not listening to me," said Smith. And to the acute embarrassment of everybody except Gaunt, he began to blubber. "Straight out of the jaws of death," he cried piteously, "and you ask a chap to go to the study."

Dikon heard Gaunt give a little cough of laughter before he turned to Mrs. Claire and said: "We'll remove ourselves."

"Yes, of course," said Dikon.

The doorway, however, was blocked by Simon and Mrs. Claire, and before they could get out of the way Smith roared out: "I don't want anybody to go. I want witnesses. You stay where you are."

Gaunt looked good-humouredly from one horrified face to another, and said: "Suppose we all sit down."

Barbara took her uncle fiercely by the arm. "Uncle James," she whispered, "stop him. He mustn't. *Uncle James, please.*"

"By all means let us sit down," said Dr. Ackrington.

They filed solemnly and ridiculously into the dining-room and, as if they were about to witness a cabaret turn, sat themselves down at the small tables. This manoeuvre appeared to quieten Smith. He took up a strategic position between the tables. With the touch of complacency which must have appeared in the Ancient Mariner when he cornered the wedding guest, he embarked upon his story.

"It was over at the level crossing," he began. "I'd been up the Peak with Eru Saul and I don't mind telling you why. Questing's been nosing around the Peak and the Maoris don't like it. We'd seen him drive along the Peak road earlier in the evening. Eru and I reckoned we'd cut along by the bush track to a hideout in the scrub. We didn't see anything. He must have gone up the other face of the hill if he was there at all. We waited for about an hour and then I got fed up and came down by myself. I hit the railroad about a couple of chains above the level crossing."

"By the railroad bridge?" said Simon.

"You're telling me it was by the bridge," said Smith with extraordinary violence. "I'll say it was by the bridge. And get this. The 5:15 from Harpoon was just about due. You know what it's like. The railroad twists in and out of the scrub and round the shoulder of the hill and then comes through a wee tunnel. You can't see or hear a thing. Before you know what's happening, she's on top of you."

"She is, too," agreed Simon, with an air of supporting Smith against unfair opposition.

"The bridge is the worst bit. You can't see the signals but you can see a bend in the Peak road above the level crossing. To get over the gully you can hop across the bridge on the sleepers, or you can wade the creek. I stood there wondering

if I'd risk the bridge. I don't like trains. There was a Maori
boy killed on that bridge."

"There was, too."

"Yes; well while I was kind of hesitating I saw Questing's
car come over the crest of the road and stop. He leant out of
the driving window and saw me. Now listen. You've got to
remember he could see the signal and I couldn't. It's the red
and green light affair they put in after the accident. I saw him
turn his head to look that way."

Smith wiped his mouth with the back of his hand. He
spoke quietly now, was no longer ridiculous, and held the
attention of his audience. He sat down at an empty table and
looked about him with an air of astonishment.

"He waved me on," he said. "He could see the signal and
he gave me the all-clear. Like this. I didn't move at first and
he did it again. See? A bit impatient, too, as much as to say:
'What's eating you? Hop to it.' Yes, well I hopped. I've never
liked the bridge. It's a short stride between sleepers and you
can see the creek through the gaps. Look. I'd got half-way
when I heard her behind me, blowing her whistle in the
tunnel. It's funny how quick you can think. Whether to jump
for it or swing from the end of a sleeper, or stand waving my
arms and, if she didn't pull up in time, dive for the engine. I
thought about Questing, too, and how, if she got me,
nobody'd know he gave me the office. And all the time I was
hopping the sleepers like a bloody ballet dancer, with the
creek below clicking through the gaps. Like one of those
dreams. Look, she was on the bridge when I jumped. I was
above the bank by then. I suppose it wasn't more than ten
feet. I landed in a *matagouri* bush. Scratched all over, and
look at my pants. I didn't even try to get out of it. She
rumbled over my head, and muck off the sleepers fell in my
eyes. I felt funny. I mean my body felt funny, as if it didn't
belong to me. I was kind of surprised to find myself climbing
the bank and it seemed to be someone else that was winded
when I got to the top. And yet all the time I was hell-set on
getting at Questing. And had he waited for me? He had not.
'Struth, I stood there shaking like a bloody jelly and I heard
him tooting his horn away along the Peak road. I don't know
how I'd have got home if it hadn't been for Eru Saul. Eru'd
come down the hill and he saw what Questing swung across

me. He's a witness to it. He gave me a hand to come home.
Look, Eru's out there in the kitchen. You ask him. He
knows." He turned to Mrs. Claire. "Can I get Eru to come in,
Mrs. Claire?"

"I'll get him," said Simon, and went out to the kitchen. He
returned, followed by Eru, who stood oafishly in the
doorway. Dikon saw, for the first time, a fleshy youth dressed
in a stained blue suit. His coat was open, displaying a brilliant
tie, and an expanse of puce-coloured shirt stretched tight
across the diaphragm. He showed little of his Maori blood,
but Dikon thought he might have served as an illustration of
the least admirable aspect of colonization in a native country.

"Here, listen, Eru," said Smith. "You saw Questing swing
it across me, didn't you?"

"Too right," Eru muttered.

"Go on. Tell them."

It was the same story. Eru had come down the hillside
behind Smith. He could see the bridge and Questing's car.
"Questing leant out of the window and beckoned Bert to
come on. I couldn't see the signal, but I reckoned he was
crazy, seeing what time it was. I yelled out to Bert to turn it
up and come back, but he never heard me. Then she blew her
whistle." Eru's olive face turned white. "Gee, I thought he
was under the engine all right. I couldn't see him, like, from
where I was. The train was between us. Gee, I certainly
expected the jolt. I never picked he'd jump for it. Crikey, was
I relieved when I seen old Bert sitting in the prickles!"

"The engine driver pulled her up and they come back to
inquire, didn't they, Eru?"

"Too right. They looked terrible. You know, white as a
sheet. They'd got the shock of their lives, those jokers. We
had to put it down in writing he'd blown his whistle. They had
to protect themselves, see?"

"Yeh. Well, that's the whole works," said Smith. "Thanks,
Eru."

He rubbed his hands over his face and looked at them. "I
could do with a drink," he said. "You may think I've had
some by the way I smell. I swear to God I haven't. It broke
when I went over."

"That's right," said Eru. He looked round awkwardly.
"I'll say good-day," he added.

He returned to the kitchen. Mrs. Claire glanced after him dubiously, and presently got up and followed him.

Smith sagged forward, resting his cheek on his hand as though he sat meditating alone in the room. Dr. Ackrington limped across and put his hand on Smith's shoulder.

"I'll fix you up," he said. "Come along."

Smith looked up at him, got to his feet, and shambled to the door.

"I could have him up, couldn't I, Doc?" he said. "It's attempted murder, isn't it?"

"I hope so," said Dr. Ackrington.

ii

Mrs. Claire stood in the centre of her own kitchen looking up at Eru Saul. The top of her head reached no farther than his chin, but she was a plumply authoritative figure and he shuffled his feet and would not look at her. Huia, with an air of conscious virtue, was dishing up the dinner.

"You are going home now, Eru, I suppose," said Mrs. Claire.

"That's right, Mrs. Claire," said Eru, looking at Huia.

"Huia is very busy, you know."

"Yeh, that's right."

"And we don't like you waiting about. You know that."

"I'm not doing anything, Mrs. Claire."

"The Colonel doesn't wish you to come. You understand?"

"I was only asking Huia what say we went to the pictures."

"I'm not going to the pictures. I told you already," said Huia loudly.

"There, Eru," said Mrs. Claire.

"Got another date, haven't you?"

Huia tossed her head.

"That will do, Eru," said Mrs. Claire.

"Too bad," said Eru, looking at Huia.

"You'll go now, if you please," Mrs. Claire insisted.

"O.K., Mrs. Claire. But listen, Mrs. Claire. You wouldn't pick Huia wasn't on the level, would you? I didn't pick it right away, but it's a fact. Ask Mr. Questing, Mrs. Claire. She's been over at the Bay with him this afternoon. I'll be seeing you, Huia."

When he had gone Mrs. Claire's round face was rosy-red. She said: "If Eru comes here again you must tell me at once, Huia, and the Colonel will speak to him."

"Yes, Mrs. Claire."

"We are ready for dinner." She walked to the door and hesitated. Huia gave her a brilliant smile.

"You know we trust you, Huia, don't you?"

"Yes, Mrs. Claire."

Mrs. Claire went into the dining-room.

They dined in an atmosphere of repressed curiosity. Dr. Ackrington returned alone, saying that he had sent Smith to bed, and that in any case he was better out of the way. Throughout dinner, Gaunt and Dikon, who had a small table to themselves, made elaborate conversation about nothing. Dikon was in a state of confusion so acute that it surprised himself. From where he sat he could see Barbara—her lamentable clothes, her white face, and her nervous hands clattering her knife and fork on the plate and pushing about the food she could not eat. Because he tried not to look, he looked the more and was annoyed with himself for doing so. Gaunt sat with his back to the Claires' table, and Dikon saw that Barbara could not prevent herself from watching him.

During the years of their association, Dikon's duties had included the fending away of Gaunt's adorers. He thought that he could interpret Barbara's glances. He thought that she was sick with disappointment, and told himself that only too easily could he translate her mortification and misery. He was angry and disgusted—angry with Gaunt, and so he said to himself, disgusted with Barbara—and this reaction was so foreign to his habit that he ended by falling quite out of humour with himself. Presently he became aware that Gaunt was watching him sharply and he realized that he had been speaking at random. He began to stammer and was actually relieved when, upon the disappearance of Huia, Colonel and

Mrs. Claire embarked in antiphony upon an apologetic chant of which the theme was Smith's unseemly behaviour. This rapidly developed into a solo performance by Mrs. Claire in the course of which she attempted the impossible feat of distributing whitewash equally between Questing and Smith. Her recital became rich in *cliches:* "More sinned against than sinning . . . A dear fellow at bottom . . . Means well but not quite . . . So sorry it should have happened . . ." She was encouraged by punctual ejaculations of "Quite" from her distracted husband.

Gaunt was beginning to get out of an impossible situation as gracefully as might be when Dr. Ackrington spared him any further recital.

"My dear Agnes," said Dr. Ackrington, "and my dear Edward. I expect we are all agreed that attempted murder is not in the best possible taste and a vague distribution of brummagem haloes will not persuade us to alter our opinion. Suppose we leave it at that. I have one suggestion—let us call it a request—to make, and I should like to make it at once. That fellow may return at any moment."

The Claires fidgeted. Simon, who seemed to be unable to speak in any mode but a truculent roar, said that he reckoned he was going to ask Questing what the hell he thought he was up to. "It's crook, that's what it is," Simon shouted angrily. "By cripey, I reckon it's crook. I'm going to ask him flat out—"

"You will ask him nothing, if you'll be so good," his uncle said briskly, "and I shall be obliged if you will suffer me to finish."

"Yes, but—"

"Simon, *please,*" his mother implored.

"I was about to ask," Dr. Ackrington went on, "that you allow *me* to speak to Mr. Questing when he arrives. I have a specific reason for making this suggestion."

"I thought perhaps," said Mrs. Claire unhappily, "Edward might take him to his study."

"Is Edward's study the Ark of the Tabernacle of the Lord," cried Dr. Ackrington in a fury, "that Questing should be subdued in it? Why this perpetual itch to herd people together in Edward's study, which, when all's said and done, is no bigger than a lavatory and rather less comfortable? Will you listen to me? Will you indulge me so far as to keep quiet while I speak to Questing, here, openly, in the presence of you all?"

Dikon's attention was momentarily diverted by Gaunt, who said in a fierce whisper: "If you forget a syllable of that speech I shall sack you."

The Claires were all speaking together again but their expostulations died out when Dr. Ackrington cast himself back in his chair, turned up his eyes and began to whistle through his teeth. After an uncomfortable silence Mrs. Claire said timidly: "I'm sure there's been some mistake."

"Indeed?" said her brother. "Do you mean that Questing miscalculated and that Smith has no right to be alive?"

"No, dear."

"What was Smith saying about lights?" asked Colonel Claire suddenly. "I didn't catch all that about lights."

"Will someone explain to Edward about railway signals?" Dr. Ackrington asked dangerously, but Colonel Claire went on in a high complaining voice. "I mean, suppose Questing didn't happen to notice the signals."

"You, Edward," his brother-in-law interrupted, "are the only person of my acquaintance from whom I can conceive such a display of negligence, but even you could scarcely fail to glance at a signal some twenty-two yards in front of your nose before inviting a man to risk his life on a single-track railway bridge. I find it impossible to believe that Questing didn't act deliberately and I have good reason to believe that he did."

There was another silence broken unexpectedly by Geoffrey Gaunt. "In fact, Dr. Ackrington," said Gaunt, "you think we have a potential murderer among us?"

"I do."

"Strange. I've never thought of a murderer being an insufferable bore."

Barbara gave a yelp of unhappy laughter.

"Wait on!" said Simon. "Listen!"

They all heard Questing's car come down the drive. He drove past the windows and round the house to the garages.

"He'll come in here!" Barbara whispered.

"I implore you to leave him to me, Edward."

Colonel Claire threw up his hands. "Shall Barbie and I—?" Mrs. Claire began, but her brother silenced her with an

angry flap on his hand. After that nobody spoke and
Questing's footfall sounded loud as he came round the house
and along the verandah.

Perhaps Dikon had anticipated, subconsciously, a sinister
change in Questing. Undoubtedly he experienced a shock of
anticlimax when he heard the familiar and detestable
inquiry.

"Well, well, well," said Mr. Questing, beaming in the
doorway, "how's tricks? Any dinner left for a little feller? Am
I hungry or am I hungry! Good evening, Mr. Gaunt. And
how's the young gentleman?"

He sat down at his own table, rubbed his hands together,
and shouted: "Where's the Glamour Girl? Come on,
Beautiful. Let's have a slant at the me-and-you."

It was at this moment that Dikon, to his unspeakable
horror, discovered in himself a liking for Mr. Questing.

iii

To Dikon's surprise, Dr. Ackrington did not go at once
into the attack. Huia brought Mr. Questing's first course and
received an offensive leer with a toss of her head. Mrs. Claire
murmured something to Barbara and they went out together.
With an air of secret exultation, Gaunt began to make
theatrical conversation with Dikon. The other three men did
not utter a word. To Dikon, the tension in the room seemed
almost ponderable, but Questing did not appear to notice it.
He ate a colossal dinner, became increasingly playful with
Huia, and, on her final withdrawal, leant back in his chair,
sucked his teeth, produced a cigar case and was about to offer
it to Gaunt when at last Dr. Ackrington spoke.

"You did not bring Smith back with you, Mr. Questing?"

Questing turned indolently and looked at him. "Smith?"
he said. "By gum, I meant to ask you about Smith. Hasn't he
come in?"

"He's in bed. He's knocked about and is suffering from shock."

"Is that so?" said Questing very earnestly. "By gum, now, I'm sorry to hear that. Suffering from shock, eh? So he would be. So he would be."

Dr. Ackrington drew in his breath with a sharp whistle and by this manoeuvre seemed to gain control of himself.

"I bet that chap's annoyed with me," Questing added cheerfully, "and I don't blame him. So would I be in his place. It's the kind of thing that would annoy you, you know. Isn't it?"

"Smith appears to find attempted murder distinctly irritating," agreed Dr. Ackrington.

"Attempted murder?" said Questing, opening his eyes very wide. "That's not a very nice way to put it, Doctor. We all of us make mistakes."

Dr. Ackrington uttered a loud oath.

"Now, now, now," Questing chided, "what's biting you? You come out on the verandah, Doc, and we'll have a little chat."

Dr. Ackrington beat his fist on the table and began to stutter. Dikon thought they were in for a tirade, but with a really terrifying effort at self-control Dr. Ackrington pulled himself up, gripped the edge of the table and at last addressed Questing coherently and with a kind of calmness. He outlined the story of Smith's escape, adding several details that he had evidently gleaned after leaving the dining-room. At first Questing listened with the air of a connoisseur, but as Dr. Ackrington went on he began to get restless. He attempted several interjections but was ruthlessly talked down. Finally, however, when his inquisitor enlarged upon his abominable behaviour in deserting a man who might have been fatally injured, Questing raised a cry of protest. "Fatally injured, my foot! He came charging up the bank like a horse, don't you worry. It was me that looked like getting a fatal injury."

"So you turned tail and bolted?"

"Don't be ridiculous. I didn't want a lot of unpleasantness, that's all. I wasn't deserting the chap. There was another chap there to look after him. He came bowling down the hill after it happened. A chap in a blue shirt. And the train

stopped. I didn't want a lot of humbug with the engine driver.
Smith was all right. I could see he wasn't hurt."

"Mr. Questing, did you or did you not look at the signal
before you beckoned Smith to cross the bridge?"

For the first time, Questing looked acutely uncomfortable. He turned very red in the face and said: "Look, Doctor,
we've got a very, very distinguished guest. We don't need to
trouble Mr. Gaunt—"

"Not at all," said Gaunt. "I'm enormously interested."

"Will you answer me?" Dr. Ackrington shouted.
"Knowing that the evening train was due, and seeing the
fellow hesitated to cross the railway bridge, did you or did
you not look at the signal before waving him on?"

"Of course I looked at it." Questing examined the end of
his cigar, glanced up from under his eyebrows and added in a
curiously flat voice: "It wasn't working."

Dikon experienced that wave of personal shame with
which an amateur reciter at close quarters can embarrass his
audience. It was such a bad lie. It was so clearly false.
Questing so obviously knew that he was not believed. Even
Dr. Ackrington seemed deflated and found nothing to say.
After a moment Questing mumbled: "Well, *I* didn't see it,
anyway. They ought to have a wig-wag there."

"A red light some ten inches in diameter and you didn't see
it."

"I said it wasn't working."

"We can check up on that," said Simon.

Questing turned on him. "You mind your own business,"
he said, but his voice missed the note of anger, and it seemed
to Dikon that there was something he could not bring himself
to say.

"Do you mind telling us where you had been?" Dr.
Ackrington continued.

"Pohutukawa Bay."

"But you were on the Peak road."

"I know I was. I thought I'd just take a run along the Peak
road before I came home."

"You'd been to Pohutukawa Bay?"

"I'm telling you I went there."

"To see the trees in flower?"

"My God, why shouldn't I go to see the pootacows! It's a

great sight isn't it? Hundreds of people go, don't they? If you must know I thought it would be a nice little run for Mr. Gaunt. I thought I'd take a look-see if they were in full bloom before suggesting he went over there."

"But you must have heard that there is no bloom this year on the *pohutukawas*. Everybody's talking about it."

For some inexplicable reason Questing looked pleased. "I hadn't heard," he said quickly. "I was astonished when I got there. It's very, very disappointing. Just too bad."

Dr. Ackrington, also, looked pleased. He got up and stood with his back to Questing, his eyes fixed triumphantly on his brother-in-law.

"Yes, but I don't know what the devil you're getting at both of you," Colonel Claire complained. "I've been—"

"Do me the extraordinary kindness to hold your tongue, Edward."

"Look here, James!"

"Cut it out, Dad," said Simon. He looked at his uncle. "I reckon I'm satisfied," he said roughly.

"I am obliged to you. Thank you, Mr. Questing. I fancy we need detain you no longer.

Questing drew at his cigar, exhaled a long dribble of smoke and remained where he was. "*Wait* a bit, *wait* a bit," he said, speaking in the best tradition of the cinema boss. "You're satisfied, huh? O.K. That's fine. That's swell. What about me? Just because I've got an instinct about the right way to behave when we've distinguished guests among us, you think you can get away with dynamite. I've tried to save Mr. Gaunt the embarrassment of this scene. I apologize to Mr. Gaunt. I'd like him to know that when I've taken over this joint the resemblance to a giggle-house will fade out automatically." He walked to the door. "But we *must* have an exit line," Gaunt muttered. Questing turned. "And just in case you didn't hear me, Claire," he said magnificently, "I said *when* and not *if*. Good evening."

He did his best to slam the door but true to the tradition of the house it jammed half-way and he wisely made no second attempt. He walked slowly past the windows with his thumbs in the armholes of his waistcoat, making much of his cigar.

As soon as he had passed out of earshot, Colonel Claire raised a piteous cry of protest. He hadn't understood. He would never understand. What was all this about Pohutuka-wa Bay? Nobody had told him anything about it. On the contrary—

With extraordinary complacency, Dr. Ackrington cut in: "Nobody told you it was a bad year for *pohutukawas*, my good Edward, for the conclusive reason that it is a phenomenally good year. The Bay is ablaze with blossom. I laid for your friend Questing, Edward, and, as Simon's intolerable jargon would have it—did he fall!"

iv

After the party in the dining-room had broken up, Gaunt suggested that he and Dikon should go for a stroll before night set in. Dikon proposed the path leading past the Springs and round the shoulder of the hill that separated them from the native settlement. Their departure was hindered by Mrs. Claire, who hurried from the house, full of warnings about boiling mud. "But you can't miss your way, really," she added. "There are little flags, white for safe and red for boiling mud. But you will take care of him, Mr. Bell, won't you? Come back before dark. One would never forgive oneself if after all this . . ." The sentence died away as a doubt arose in Mrs. Claire's mind about the propriety of saying that death by boiling mud would be a poor sequel to an evening of social solecisms. She looked very earnestly at Gaunt and repeated: "So you *will* take care, won't you? Such a horrid place, really. When one thinks of our dear old English lanes . . ."

They reassured her and set off. Soon after their arrival Gaunt had taken his first step in the Elfin Pool. Whether through the agency of free sulphuric acid, or through the stimulus provided by the scene they had just witnessed, his leg was less painful than it had been for some time, and he was in good spirits. "I've always adored scenes," he said, "and this was a princely one. They can't keep it up, of course, but really, Dikon, if this is anything like a fair sample, I shall do very nicely at Wai-ata-tapu. How right you were to urge me to come."

"I'm glad you've been entertained," Dikon rejoined, "but honestly, sir, I regard the whole affair as an exceedingly sinister set-up. I mean, *why* did Questing lie like a flat-fish?"

"Several most satisfactory theories present themselves. I am inclined to think that Miss Claire is the key figure."

Dikon, who was leading the way, stopped so suddenly that Gaunt walked into him. "What can you mean, sir!" Dikon cried. "How can Questing's relations with Smith have any possible connection with Barbara Claire?"

"I may be wrong of course, but there is no doubt that he has his eye on her. Didn't you notice that? All that frightful line of stuff with the Maori waitress was undoubtedly directed at Barbara Claire. A display of really most unpalatable oomph. I must say she didn't seem to care for it. Always the young gentlewoman, of course." They walked on in silence for a minute, and then Gaunt said lightly: "Surely you can't have fallen for her?"

Without turning his head Dikon said crossly: "What in the name of high fantasy could have put that antic notion into your head?"

"The back of your neck has bristled like a hedgehog ever since I mentioned her. And it's not such an antic notion. There are possibilities. She's got eyes and a profile and a figure. Submerged it is true in dressy floral *ninon,* but there nevertheless." And with a touch of the malice with which Dikon was only too familiar, Gaunt added: "Barbara Claire. It's a charming name, isn't it? You must teach her not to hoot."

Dikon had never liked his employer less than he did at that moment. When Gaunt prodded him in the back with his stick, Dikon pretended not to notice, but cursed softly to himself.

"I apologize," said Gaunt, "in fourteen different positions."

"Not at all, sir."

"Then don't prance along at such a rate. Stop a moment. I'm exhausted. What's that noise?"

They had rounded the flank of the hill and now came in sight of the native settlement. The swift northern dusk had fallen upon the countryside with no suggestion of density. The darkening of the air seemed merely to be a change in translucence. It was very still, and as they stood listening Dikon became aware of a curious sound. It was as if a giant somewhere close at hand were blowing thick bubbles very slowly and complacently; or as if, over the brink of the hill, a vast porridge pot had just come to boiling point. The sounds were irregular, each one mounting to its point of explosion. Plop. Plop-plop . . . Plop.

They moved forward and reached a point where the scrub and grass came to an end and the path descended a steep bank to traverse a region of solidified blue mud, sinter mounds, hot pools and geysers. The sulphurous smell was very strong. The track, defined at intervals by stakes to which pieces of white rag had been tied, went forward over naked hillocks towards the hip-roofs of the native settlement.

"Shall we go further?" asked Dikon.

"It's a detestable place, but I think we must see this infernal brew."

"We must keep to the track, then. Shall I go first?"

They walked on and presently, though the soles of their feet received a strange experience. The ground beneath them was unsteady, quivering a little, telling them that, after all, there was no stability in the earth by which we symbolize stability. They moved across a skin and the organism beneath it was restless.

"This is abominable," said Gaunt. "The whole place works secretly. It's alive."

"Look to your right," said Dikon. They had come to a hillock; the path divided, and, where it turned to the right, was marked by red flags.

"They told me you used to be able to walk along there," Dikon explained, "but it's not safe now. Taupo-tapu is encroaching."

They followed the white flags, climbed steeply, and at last, from the top of the hillock, looked down on Taupo-tapu.

It was perhaps fifteen feet across, dun-coloured and glistening, a working ulcer in the body of the earth. Great bubbles of mud formed themselves deliberately, swelled, and broke with the sounds which they had noticed a few minutes before and which were now loud and insistent. With each eruption unctuous rings momentarily creased the surface of the brew. It was impossible to escape the notion that Taupo-tapu had some idiotic purpose of its own.

For perhaps two minutes Gaunt looked at it in silence. "Quite obscene, isn't it?" he said at last. "If you know anything about it, don't tell me."

"The only story I've heard," Dikon said, "is not a pretty one. I won't."

Gaunt's reply was unexpected. "I should prefer to hear it from a Maori," he said.

"You can see where the thing has eaten into the old path," Dikon pointed out. "The red flags begin again on the other side and rejoin our track just below us. Just as well. It would be an unpleasant error to mistake the paths, wouldn't it?"

"Don't, for God's sake," said Gaunt. "It's getting dark. Let's go home."

When they turned back, Dikon found that he had to make a deliberate effort to prevent himself from hurrying, and he thought he sensed Gaunt's impatience too. The firm dry earth felt wholesome under their feet as once more they circled the hill. Behind them, in the native village, a drift of song rose on the cool air, intolerably plaintive and lonely.

"What's that?"

"One of their songs," said Dikon. "Perhaps they're rehearsing for your concert. It's the genuine thing. You get the authentic music up here."

The shoulder of the hill came between them and the song. It was almost dark as they walked along the brushwood fence towards Wai-ata-tapu. Steam from the hot pools drifted in wraiths across the still night air. It was only when she moved forward that Barbara's dress and the blurred patches of white that were her arms and face told them that she had been waiting for them. Perhaps the darkness gave her courage and balance. Perhaps any voice would have been welcome just then, but it seemed to Dikon that Barbara's had a directness and repose that he had not heard in it before.

"I hope I didn't startle you," she said. "I heard you coming down the path and thought I should like to speak to you."

Gaunt said: "What is it, Miss Claire? More excursions and alarms?"

"No, no. We seem to have settled down again. It's only that I wanted to tell you how very sorry we all are about that frightful scene. We shan't go on apologizing, but I did just want to say this: Please don't think you are under an obligation to stay. Of course you know you are not, but perhaps you feel it's rather difficult to tell us you are going. Don't hesitate. We shall quite understand."

She turned her head and they saw her in profile against a shifting background of steam. The dusk, simplifying her ugly dress, revealed the beauty of her silhouette. The profile lines of her head and throat were well-drawn, delicate, and harmonious. It was an astonishing change. Perhaps if Gaunt had not seen her so translated, his voice would have held less warmth and friendliness when he answered her.

"But there is no question of our going," he said. "We have not thought of it. As for the scene, Dikon will tell you that I have a lust for scenes. We are very sorry if you're in difficulties, but we don't in the least want to go."

Dikon saw him take her arm and turn her towards the house. It was a gesture he often used on the stage, adroit and impersonal. Dikon followed behind as they walked across the pumice.

"It's awfully nice of you," Barbara was saying. "I—we have felt so frightful about it. I was horrified when I heard what Mr. Questing had done, badgering you to come. We didn't know what he was up to. Uncle James and I were horrified."

"He didn't badger *me,*" said Gaunt. "Dikon attended to Questing. That's why I keep him."

"Oh." Barbara half-turned her head and laughed, not with her usual boisterousness, but shyly. "I wondered what he was for," she said.

"He has his uses. When I start work again he'll be kept very spry."

"You're going to write, aren't you? Uncle James told me.

Is it an autobiography? I do hope it is."

Gaunt moved his hand above her elbow. "And why do you hope that?"

"Because I want to read it. You see, I've seen your Rochester, and once somebody who was staying here had an American magazine, I think it was called the *Theatre Arts,* and there was an article in it with photographs of you as different people. I liked the Hamlet one the best because—"

"Well?" asked Gaunt when she paused.

Barbara stumbled over her next speech. "Because—well, I suppose because I know it best. No, that's not really why. I didn't know it at all well until then, but I read it again, lots of times, and tried to imagine how you sounded when you said the speech in the photograph. Of course after hearing Mr. Rochester it was easier."

"Which photograph was that, Dikon?" asked Gaunt over his shoulder.

"It was with Rosencrantz..." Barbara began eagerly.

"Ah, I remember."

Gaunt stood still and put her from him, holding her by the shoulder as he had held the gratified small-part actor who played Rosencrantz in New York. Dikon heard him draw in his breath as he always did when he collected himself to rehearse. In the silence of that warm evening amidst the reek of sulphur and against the nebulous thermal background, the beautiful voice spoke quietly:—

"'*O God, I could be bounded in a nutshell and count myself a king of infinite space, were it not that I had bad dreams.*'"

Dikon was irritated and disturbed by Barbara's rapturous silence, and infuriated by the whispered, "Thank you" with which she finally ended it. "She's making a perfect little ass of herself," he thought, but he knew that Gaunt would not find her attitude excessive. He had an infinite capacity for absorbing adulation.

"Can you go on?" Gaunt was saying. "*Which dreams—*"

"'*Which dreams indeed are ambition, for the very substance of the ambitious is merely the shadow of a dream.*'"

"'*A dream itself is but a shadow!*' Do you hear this, Dikon?" cried Gaunt. "She knows the lines." He moved forward again, Barbara at his side. "You've got a voice, my child," he said. "How have you escaped the accent? Do you know what you've been talking about? You must hear the music, but you must also achieve the meaning. Say it again: thinking—'*Which dreams indeed are ambition.*'" But Barbara fumbled the second time, and they spoke the line backwards and forwards to each other as they crossed the pumice to the house. Gaunt was treating her to an almost indecent helping of charm, Dikon considered.

The lights were up in the house and Mrs. Claire was hurriedly doing the blackout. She had left the door open and a square of warmth reached across the verandah to the pumice. Before they came to its margin Gaunt checked Barbara again.

"We say good night here," he said. "The dusk becomes you well. Good night, Miss Claire."

He turned on his heel and walked towards his rooms.

"Good night," said Dikon.

She had moved into the light. The look she turned upon him was radiant. "You're terribly lucky, aren't you?" said Barbara.

"Lucky?"

"Your job. To be with him."

"Oh," said Dikon, "that. Yes, of course."

"Good night," said Barbara, and ran indoors.

He looked after her, absently polishing his glasses with his handkerchief.

v

Barbara lay in bed with her eyes wide-open to the dark. Until this moment she had denied the waves of bliss that lapped at the edge of her thoughts. Now she opened her heart to them.

She passed the sequence of those few minutes in the dusk through and through her mind, examining each moment, feeling again its lustre, wondering at her happiness. It is easy to smile at such fervours, but in her unreasoned ecstacy she reached a point of pure enchantment to which she would perhaps never again ascend. The experience may appear more touching but its reality is not impugned if it is recorded that Gaunt, at the same time, was preening himself a little.

"Do you know, Dikon," he said, "that strange little devil quivered like a puppy out there in the dusk." Dikon did not answer and after a moment Gaunt added: "After all it's pleasant to know that one's work can reach so far. The Bard and sulphuric phenomena! An amusing juxtaposition, isn't it? One lights a little flame, you know. One carries the torch."

CHAPTER V

MR. QUESTING GOES DOWN
FOR THE SECOND TIME

The more blatant eccentricities of the first evening were not
repeated during the following days, and the household at
Wai-ata-tapu settled down to something like a normal
routine. The Colonel fatigued himself to exhaustion with
Home Guard exercises. His wife and daughter, overtaxed by
the new standard they had set themselves, laboured
incessantly in the house. Gaunt, following Dr. Ackrington's
instructions, sat at stated hours in the Springs, took short
walks, and began to work steadily on his book. Dikon filed
old letters and programmes which had to be winnowed for
use in the autobiography. Gaunt dictated for two hours every
morning and evening, and expected Dikon's shorthand notes
to be translated into typescript before they began work on the
following day. Dr. Ackrington dealt austerely in his own
room with the problems of comparative anatomy. On
Wednesday he announced that he was going away for a week,
and, when Mrs. Claire said gently that she hoped there was
nothing the matter, replied that they would all be better if
they were dead, and drove away. Colly, who had been a
signaller in the 1914 war, recovered from the surprise of
Simon's first advance, and spent a good deal of time in the
cabin helping him with his Morse. Simon's attitude to Gaunt
was one of morose suspicion. As far as possible he avoided
encounters, but on the rare occasions when they met, his
behaviour was remarkable. He was not content to remain
altogether silent, but would suddenly roar out strange
inquiries and statements. He asked Gaunt whether he
reckoned the theatre did any good in the world, and, when
Gaunt replied with some heat that he did, inquired the price
of seats. On receiving this information he said instantly that a
poor family could live for a week on the price of a stall and

that there ought to be a flat charge all over the house. Gaunt's book had gone badly that morning and his leg was painful. He became irritable and a ridiculous argument took place.

"It's selfishness that's at the bottom of it," Simon shouted. "The actors ought to have smaller wages, see? What I reckon, the thing ought to be run for the good of everybody. Smaller wages all round."

"Including the stage staff? The workmen?" asked Gaunt.

"They all ought to get the same."

"Then I couldn't afford to keep your friend Colly."

"I reckon he's wasting his time anyway," said Simon, and Gaunt walked away in a rage.

Evidently Simon confided this conversation to Colly, who considered it necessary to apologize for his new friend.

"You don't want to pay too much attention to him, sir," Colly said, as he massaged his employer's leg that evening. "He's a nice young chap. Just a touch on the red side. He's a bit funny. It's Mr. Questing that's upset his apple-cart, reely."

"He's an idiotic cub," said Gaunt. "What's Questing got to do with the price of stalls?"

"He's been talking big business, sir. Young Simon thinks he's lent a good bit to the Colonel on this show. He thinks the Colonel can't pay up and Mr. Questing's going to shut down on them and run the place on his pat. Young Simon's that disgusted he's taken a scunner on anything that looks like smart business."

"Yes, but—"

"He's funny. I had it out with him. He told me what he'd been saying to you, and I said he'd acted very silly. 'I've been with my gentleman for ten years,' I told him, 'and there's not much we don't know about the show business. I seen him when he was a small-part actor playing a couple-of-coughs-and-a-spit in stock,' I said, 'and believe you me he's worked for it. He may be a star now,' I said, 'and he may be getting the big money, but how long'll it last?'"

"What the hell did you mean by that?"

"We're not as young as we was, sir, are we? 'You don't want to talk silly,' I said. 'Questing's one thing and my gentleman's another.' But no. 'You're no better than a flunkey,' he says. 'You're demeaning youself.' I straightened him up about that. 'There's none of the blooming valley

about me,' I says, 'I'm a dresser and make-up, and what I do
on the side is done by me own choice. I'm in the game with my
gentleman.' 'It's greed for money,' he howls, 'that's ruining
the world. Big business started this war,' he says, 'and when
we've won it us chaps that did the fighting are going to have a
say in the way things are run. The Questings'll be wiped right
off the slate.' That's the way he talks, you see, sir. Mind, I feel
sorry for him. He's got the idea that his dad and ma are going
to just about conk out over this business and to his way of
thinking Questing's as good as a murderer. He says Smith
knows something about Questing and that's why he had to
jump for it when the train came. You've had fifteen minutes
on them muscles and that'll do you."

"You've damned nearly flayed me alive."

"Yes," said Colly, flinging a blanket over his victim and
going into the next room to wash his hands. "He's morbid, is
young Sim. And of course Mr. Questing's little attempts at
the funny business with Miss Barbara kind of put the pot on
it."

Dikon, who had been clattering his typewriter, paused.

"What's that?" said Gaunt, suddenly alert.

"Had you missed the funny business, sir?" said Colly from
the next room. "Oh, yes. Quite a bit of trouble she has with
him, I understand."

"What did I tell you, Dikon?"

"The way I look at it," Colly went on, appearing in the
doorway with a towel, "she's capable. No getting away from
it, and you can't get domestic labour in this country without
you pay the earth, so Questing thinks he'll do better to keep
her when the old people go."

"But damn it," Dikon said angrily, "this is insufferable.
It's revolting."

"That's right, Mr. Bell. That's what young Sim thinks.
He's worked it out. Questing'll try putting in the fine work,
making out he'll look after the old people if she sees it in the
right light. Coo! It's a touch of the old blood-and-thunder
dope isn't it, sir? Mortgage and all. The villain still pursued
her. Only the juvenile to cast, and there, as we say in *The
Dream,* sir, is a play fitted. I used to enjoy them old pieces."

"You talk too much, Colly," said Gaunt mildly.

"That's right, sir. Beg pardon, I'm sure. Associating with

young Mr. Claire must have brought out the latent democracy in me soul. I tell him there's no call to worry about his sister. 'It's easy seen she hates his guts,' I said, if you'll excuse me."

"I'll excuse you altogether. I'm going to work."

"Thank you, sir," said Colly neatly, and closed the door.

He would perhaps have been gratified if he had known how accurately his speculations about Barbara were to be realized. It was on that same evening, a Thursday, nine days before the Maori concert, that Questing decided to carry forward his hitherto tentative approach to Barbara. He chose the time when, wearing a shabby bathing dress and a raincoat, she went for her four-o'clock swim in the warm lake. Her attitude towards public bathing had been settled for her by her mother. Mrs. Claire was nearly forty when Barbara was born, and her habit of mind was Victorian. She herself had grown up in an age when one ducked furtively in the ocean, surrounded by the heavy bell of one's braided serge. She felt apprehensive whenever she saw her daughter drop her raincoat and plunge hastily into the lake clad in the longest and most conservative garment obtainable at the Harpoon Cooperative Stores. Only once did Barbara attempt to make a change in this procedure. Stimulated by some pre-war magazine photographs of fashionable nudities on the Lido, she thought of sun-bathing, of strolling in a leisurely, even a seductive manner down to the lake, not covered by her raincoat. She showed the magazines to her mother. Mrs. Claire looked at the welter of oiled limbs, glistening lips and greased eyelids. "I know, dear," she said turning pink. "So very common. Of course newspaper photographers would never persuade the really, really *quite* to be taken, so I suppose they are obliged to fall back on these people."

"But, Mummy, they're not 'these people'! Look, there's . . ."

"Barbara darling," said Mrs. Claire in her special voice, 'some day you will understand that there are folk who move in rather *loud* vulgar *sets,* and who may seem to be very *exciting,* and who I expect are all very *rich.* But, my dear," Mrs. Claire had added, gently, exhibiting a photograph of an enormously obese peer in bathing shorts, supported on the one hand by a famous *coryphee* and on the other by a

fashionable prizefighter—"my dear, they are not Our Sort."
And she had given Barbara a bright smile and a kiss, and
Barbara had stuck to her raincoat.

On the occasion of his proposal, Mr. Questing, who did
not care for sitting on the ground, took a campstool to the far
end of the lake, placed it behind some manuka scrub near the
diving board, and, fortified by a cigar, sat there until he spied
Barbara leaving the house. He then discarded the cigar,
waited until she was within a few feet of his hiding place, and
stepped out to meet her.

"Well, well, well," said Mr. Questing. "Look who's here!
How's the young lady?"

Barbara clawed the raincoat about her and said she was
very well.

"That's fine," said Mr. Questing. "Feeling good, eh?
That's the great little lass." He laughed boisterously and
manoeuvred in an agile manner in order to place himself
between Barbara and the diving board. "What's your hurry?"
he asked merrily. "Plenty of time for the bathing-beauty
stuff. What say we have a wee chin-wag, You, Me, & Co.,
uh?"

Barbara eyed him with dismay. What new and odious
development was this? Since the extraordinary scene on the
evening of Smith's accident, she had not encountered
Questing alone and was almost unaware of the angry
undercurrents which ran strongly through the normal course
of life at Wai-ata-tapu. For Barbara was carried along the
headier stream of infatuation. She was bemused with calf-
love, an infant disease which, caught late, is doubly virulent.
Since that first meeting in the dusk, she had not seen much of
Gaunt. She was so grateful for her brief rapture and, upon
consideration, so doubtful of its endurance, that she made no
attempt to bring about a second encounter. It was enough to
see him at long intervals, and receive his greeting. Of
Questing she had thought hardly at all, and his appearance at
the lake surprised as much as it dismayed her.

"What do you want to see me about, Mr. Questing?"

"Well now, I seem to have the idea there's quite a lot I'd
like to talk to Miss Babs about. All sorts of things," said Mr.
Questing, dropping his voice to a fruity croon. "All sorts of
things."

"But—would you mind—you see I'm going to..."

"What's the big hurry?" urged Mr. Questing, in his best synthetic American. "Wait a bit, wait a bit. The lake won't get cold. You ought to do some sun-bathing. You'd look good if you bronzed, Babs. Snappy."

"I'm afraid I really can't . . ."

"Look," said Mr. Questing with emphasis. "I said I wanted to talk to you and what I meant was I wanted to talk to you. You've no call to act as if I'd made certain suggestions. What's the idea of all this shrinking stuff? Mind, I like it in moderation. It's old-world. Up to a point it pleases a man, but after that it's irritating and right now's the place where you want to forget it. We all know you're the pure-minded type by this time, girlie. Let it go at that."

Barbara gaped at him. "There's a camp-stool behind that bush," he continued. "Come and sit on it. I'll say this better if I keep on my feet. Be sensible, now. You're going to enjoy this, I hope. It's a great little proposition when viewed in the correct light."

Barbara looked back at the house. Her mother appeared hurrying along the verandah. She did not glance up, but at any moment she might do so and the picture of her daughter, *tete-a-tete* with Mr. Questing instead of swimming in the lake, would certainly disturb her. Yet Mr. Questing stood between Barbara and the lake and, if she tried to dodge him, might attempt to restrain her. Better get the extraordinary interview over as inconspicuously as possible. She walked round the manuka bush and sat on the stool; Mr. Questing followed. He stood over her smelling of soap, cigars and scented *cachous*.

"That's fine and dandy," he said. "Have a cigarette. No? O.K. Now, listen, honey, I'm a practical man and I like to come straight to the point, never mind whether it's business or pleasure and you might call this a bit of both. I got a proposition to put up which I think is going to interest you a whole lot, but first of all we'll clear the air of misunderstandings. Now I don't just know how far you're wise to the position between me and your dad."

He paused, and Barbara, full of apprehension, hurriedly collected her thoughts. "Nothing!" she murmured. "I know nothing. Father doesn't discuss business with us."

"Doesn't he, now? Is that the case? Very Old-World in his

notions, isn't he? Well, now, we don't expect the ladies to take a great deal of interest in business so I won't trouble you with a lot of detail. Just the broad outline," said Mr. Questing making an appropriate gesture, "so's you'll get the idea. Now, you might put it this way, you might say that your dad's under an obligation to me."

You might indeed, Barbara thought, as Mr. Questing's only too lucid explanation rolled on. It seemed that five years ago when he first came to Wai-ata-tapu to ease himself of lumbago, he had lent Colonel Claire a thousand pounds, at a low rate of interest, taking the hostel and springs as security. Colonel Claire was behind with the interest and the principal was now due. Mr. Questing clothed the bare bones of his narrative in a vestment of playful hints and nudges. He wasn't, he said, a hard man. He didn't want to make it too solid for the old Colonel, not he. "But just the same—" *cliche* followed *cliche*, business continued to be business, and more and more dubious grew the development of his theme until at last even poor Barbara began to understand him.

"No!" she cried out at last. "Oh, no! I couldn't. Please don't!"

"Wait a bit, now. Don't act as if I'm not making a straight offer. Don't get me all wrong. I'm asking you to marry me, Babs."

"Yes, I know, but I can't possibly. Please!"

"Don't run away with the idea it's just a business deal. It's not." Mr. Questing's voice actually faltered and if Barbara had been less frantically distracted she might have noticed that he had changed colour. "To tell you the truth I've fallen for you, kid," he continued appallingly. "I don't know why, I'm sure. I like 'em snappy and kind of wise as a general rule and if you'll pardon my candour you're sloppy in your dress and, boy, are you simple! Maybe that's exactly why I've fallen. Now don't interrupt me. I'm not dizzy yet and I know you're not that way about me. I don't say I'd have asked you if I hadn't got a big idea you'd run this joint damn well when I showed you how. I don't say I haven't put you on the spot where it's going to be hard to say no. I have. I knew where I could get in the fine work, seeing how your old folks are placed, and I got it in. I'll use it all right. But listen, little girl"—Mr. Questing on a sudden note of fervour breathed out his final *cliche*—"I want you," he said hoarsely.

To Barbara the whole speech had sounded nightmarish.
She quite failed to realize that Mr. Questing thought on these
standardized lines and spoke his commonplaces from a full
heart. It was the first experience of its kind that she had
endured, and he seemed to her a terrible figure, half-
threatening, half-amorous. When she forced herself to look
up and saw him in his smooth pale suit, himself pale, slightly
obese and glistening, and found his eyes fixed rather greedily
upon hers, her panic mounted to its climax, and she thought:
"I shan't like to refuse. I must get away." She noticed that his
expensive watch-chain was heaving up and down in an
agitated rhythm about two feet away from her nose. She
sprang to her feet and, as if she had released a spring in Mr.
Questing, he flung his arms about her. During the following
moments the thing she was most conscious of was his
stertorous breathing. She brought her elbows together and
shoved with her forearms against his waistcoat. At the same
time she dodged the face which thrust forward repeatedly at
hers. She thought: "This is frightful. This is the worst thing
that has ever happened to me. I'm hating this." Mr. Questing
muttered excitedly: "Now, now, now," and they tramped to
and fro. Barbara tripped over the camp stool and rapped her
shin. She gave a little yelp of pain.

And upon this scene came Simon and Dikon.

ii

Gaunt had announced that he would do no work after all
and Dikon, released from duty, decided to go for a walk in
the direction of the Peak. He had an idea that he would like to
see for himself the level crossing and the bridge where Smith
had his escape from the train. He found Simon and asked
him to point out the short cut to the Peak road. Simon, most
unexpectedly, offered to go with him. They set out together

along the path that ran past the springs and lake. They had
not gone far before they heard a confused trampling and a
sharp cry. Without a word but on a single impulse, they ran
forward together and Barbara was discovered in Mr.
Questing's arms.

Dikon was an over-civilized young man. He belonged to a
generation whose attitude of mind was industriously ironic.
He could accept scenes that arose out of crises of the nerves,
they were a commonplace of the circle into which his
association with Gaunt had introduced him. It was
inconceivable that any young woman of those circles would
be unable to cope with the advances of a Mr. Questing or, for
a matter of that, fail to lunch and dine off such an attempt
when she had dealt with it. Dikon's normal reaction to
Barbara's terror would perhaps have been a feeling of
incredulous embarrassment. After all they were within a few
hundred yards of the house in broad daylight. It was up to her
to cope. He could never have predicted the impulse of pure
anger that flooded through him, and he had time actually to
feel astonished at himself. It was not until afterwards that he
recognized the complementary emotion which arose when
Barbara ran to her brother. Dikon realized then that he
himself was a lay figure and felt a twinge of regret that it was
so.

Simon behaved with more dignity than might have been
expected of him. He put his arm across his sister's shoulders
and in his appalling voice said: "What's up, Barbie?" When
she did not answer he went on: "I'll look after this. You cut
along out of it."

"Hey!" said Mr. Questing. "What's the big idea?"

"It's nothing, Sim. Sim, it's all right, really."

Simon looked over her shoulder at Dikon. "Fix her up,
will you?" he said, and Dikon answered: "Yes, of course,"
and wondered what was expected of him. Simon shoved her,
not ungently, towards him.

"Great hopping fleas," Mr. Questing expostulated,
"what's biting you now! There's not a damn thing a man can
do in this place without you all come milling round like
magpies. You're crazy. I try to get a little private yarn with
Babs and you start howling as if it was the Rape of the What-
have-you Women."

"Go and boil your head," said Simon. "And Barbie, you buzz off."

"I really think you'd better," Dikon said, realizing that his function was to remove her. She murmured something hurriedly to Simon and turned away. "All right, all right," said Simon, "don't you worry." They left Simon and Questing glaring at each other in ominous silence.

Dikon followed her along the path. She started off at a great rate, with her head high, clutching her raincoat about her. They had gone some little way before he saw that her shoulders were quivering. He felt certain that all she wanted of him was to leave her to herself, but he could not make up his mind to do this. As they drew nearer to the house they saw Colonel and Mrs. Claire come out on the verandah and begin to set up their deck-chairs. Barbara stopped short and turned. Her face was stained with tears.

"I can't let them see," she said.

"Come round by the other path."

It was a track that skirted the Springs and came out near the cabins. A brushwood fence screened it from the verandah. Half-way along, Barbara faltered, sat on the bank, buried her face in her arms and cried most bitterly.

"Oh God, I'm so sorry," said Dikon confusedly. "Have my handkerchief. I'll turn my back, shall I? Or shall I?"

She took the handkerchief with a woebegone attempt at a smile. He sat beside her and put his arm round her.

"Never mind," he said. "He's quite preposterous. A ridiculous episode."

"It was *beastly.*"

"Well, confound the fellow, anyway, for upsetting you."

"It's not only that. He—he—" Barbara hesitated and then with a most dejected attempt at her trick of over-emphasis sobbed out: "He's got a *hold* on us."

"So Colly was right," Dikon thought. "It *is* the old dope."

"If only Daddy had never met him! And what Sim's doing now, I can't imagine. If Sim loses his temper he's frightful. Oh dear," said Barbara blowing her nose very loudly on Dikon's handkerchief, "what have we all done that everything should go so hideously wrong with us? Really, it's exactly as if we dotted scenes about the place like booby-traps for Mr. Gaunt and you. And he was so heavenly about the other time, pretending he didn't mind."

"It wasn't pretence. He told the truth when he said he adored scenes. He does. He even uses them in his work. Do you remember in the *Jane Eyre,* when Rochester, without realizing what he did, slowly wrung the necks of Jane's bridal flowers?"

"Of course I do," said Barbara eagerly. "It was terrible but sort of noble."

"He got it from a drunken dresser who flew into a rage with the star she looked after. She wrenched the heads off one of the bouquets. He never forgets things like that."

"Oh."

"You're feeling a bit better now?"

"A bit. You're very kind, aren't you?" said Barbara rather as if she saw Dikon for the first time. "I mean, to take trouble over our frightfulness."

"You must stop being apologetic," Dikon said. "So far I've taken no trouble at all."

"You listen nicely," Barbara said.

"I'm almost ghoulishly discreet, if that's any recommendation."

"I do so wonder what Sim's doing. Can you hear anything?"

"We've come rather far away from them to hear anything. Unless, of course, they begin to scream in each other's faces. What would you expect to hear? Dull thuds?"

"I don't know. *Listen!*"

"Well," said Dikon after a pause, "that *was* a dull thud. Do you suppose that Mr. Questing has been felled to the ground for the second time in a fortnight?"

"I'm afraid Sim's hit him."

"I'm afraid so too," Dikon agreed. "Look."

From where they sat they could see the patch of manuka scrub. Mr. Questing appeared, nursing his face in his handkerchief. He came slowly along the main path and as he drew nearer they saw that his handkerchief was dappled red. "A dong on the nose, by gum," said Dikon. When he arrived at the intersection, Mr. Questing paused.

"I'm going—He'll see me. I can't—" Barbara began, but she was too late. Mr. Questing had already seen them. He advanced a short way down the side path and, still holding his handkerchief to his nose, addressed them from some considerable distance.

"Look at this," he shouted. "Is it a swell set-up, or is it? I like to do things in a refined way and here's what I get for it. What's the matter with the crowd around here? Ask a lady to marry you and somebody hauls off and half kills you. I'm going to clean this dump right up. Pardon me, Mr. Bell, for intruding personal affairs."

"Not at all, Mr. Questing," said Dikon politely.

Mr. Questing unguardedly removed his handkerchief and three large red blobs fell on his shirt front. "Blast!" he said violently and stanched his nose again. "Listen, Babs," he continued through the handkerchief. "If you feel like changing your mind, I won't say the offer's closed, but if you want to do anything you'll need to make it snappy. I'm going to pack them up, the whole crowd of them. I'll give the Colonel till the end of the month and then *out*. And, by God, if I'd got a witness I'd charge your tough young brother with assault. By God, I would. I'm fed up. I'm in pain and I'm fed up." He goggled at Dikon over the handkerchief. "Apologizing once again, old man," said Mr. Questing, "and assuring you that you'll very shortly see a big change for the better in the management of this bloody dump. So long, for now."

iii

Long after the events recorded in this tale were ended, Dikon, looking back at the first fortnight at Wai-ata-tapu, would reflect that they had suffered collectively from intermittent emotional hiccoughs. For long intervals the daily routine would be uninterrupted and then, when he wondered if they had settled down, they would be convulsed and embarrassed by yet another common spasm. Not that he ever believed, after Mr. Questing's outburst, that there was much hope of the Claires settling back into their old way of life. It seemed to Dikon that Mr. Questing had been out for blood. A marked increase in Colonel Claire's vagueness, together with an air of bewildered misery, suggested that he had been faced with an ultimatum. Dikon had come upon Mrs. Claire on her knees before an old trunk, shaking her head over Edwardian photographs and aimlessly arranging them in heaps. When she saw him she murmured something about clinging to one's household goods wherever one went. Barbara, who had taken to confiding in Dikon, told him that she had sworn Simon to secrecy over the incident by the lake, but that Questing had been closeted with her father for half an hour, still wearing his blood-stained shirt, and had no doubt given the Colonel his own version of the affray. Dikon had described the scene by the lake to Gaunt, and half-way through the recital, wished he had left it alone. Gaunt was surprisingly interested. "It really is most *intriguing*," he said, rubbing his delicate hands together "I was right about the girl, you see. She *has* got something. I'm never mistaken. She's incredibly *gauche,* she talks like a madwoman, and she grimaces like a monkey. That's simply because she's raw, uncertain of herself. It's the bone one should look at. Show me good bone, and a pair of eyes, give me a free hand, and I'll create beauty. She's roused the unspeakable Questing, you see."

"But Questing has his eye on the place."

"Nobody, my dear Dikon, for the sake of seven squalid mud puddles is going to marry a woman who doesn't attract him. No, no, the girl's got something. I've been talking to her. Studying her. I tell you I'm never mistaken. You remember that understudy child at the Unicorn? I saw there was something in her. I told the management. She's never looked back. It's a flair one has. I could . . ." Gaunt paused, and took his chin between his thumb and forefinger. "It would be rather fun to try," he said.

With a sensation of panic, Dikon said: "To try what, sir?"

"Dikon, shall I make Barbara Claire a present? What was the name of the dress shop we noticed in Auckland? Near the hotel? Quite good? You must remember. A ridiculous name."

"I don't remember."

"Sarah Snappe! Of course. Barbara shall have a new dress for this Maori concert on Saturday. Black, of course. It must be terribly simple. You can write at once. No, perhaps you should go to Harpoon and telephone, and they must put it on to-morrow's train. There was a dress in the window, woolen with a dusting of steel stars. Really quite good. It would fit her. And ask them to be kind and find shoes and gloves for us. If possible, stockings. You can get the size somehow. And underclothes, for God's sake. One can imagine what hers are like. I shall indulge myself in this, Dikon. And we must take her to a hairdresser and stand over him. I shall make her up. If Sarah Snappe doesn't believe you're my secretary you can ring up the hotel and do it through them." Gaunt beamed at his secretary. "What a child I am, after all, Dikon, aren't I? I mean this is going to give me such *real* pleasure."

Dikon said in a voice of ice: "But it's quite impossible, sir."

"What the devil do you mean!"

"There's no parity between Barbara Claire and an understudy at the Unicorn."

"I should damn well say there wasn't. The other little person had quite a lot to start with. She was merely incredibly vulgar."

"Which Barbara Claire is not," said Dikon. He looked at his employer, noted his air of peevish complacency and went on steadily. "Honestly, sir, the Claires would never understand. You know what they're like. A comparative stranger to offer their daughter clothes!"

"Why the hell not?"

"It just isn't done in their world."

"You've become maddeningly class-conscious all of a sudden, my good Dikon. What is their world, pray?"

"Shall we say proudly poor, sir?"

"The suspicious-genteel, you mean. The incredibly, the insultingly stupid *bourgeoisie* who read offence in a kindly impulse. You wish me to understand that these people would try to snub me, don't you?"

"I think they would be very polite," Dikon said, and tried not to sound priggish, "but it would, in effect, be a snub. I'm sure they would understand that your impulse was a kind one."

Gaunt's face had bleached. Dikon, who knew the danger signals, wondered in a panic if he was about to lose his job. Gaunt walked to the door and looked out. With his back still turned to his secretary he said: "You will go into Harpoon and give the order over the telephone. The bill is to be sent to me, and the parcel to be addressed to Miss Claire. Wait a moment." He went to his desk and wrote on a slip of paper. "Ask them to write out this message and put it in the parcel. No signature, of course. You will go at once, if you please."

"Very well, sir," said Dikon.

Filled with the liveliest misgivings he went out to the car. Simon was in the garage. Gaunt had been granted a traveller's petrol license and Simon had offered to keep the magnificent car in order. Gloating secretly, he would spend hours over slight adjustments; cleaning, listening, peering.

"I still reckon we might advance the spark a bit," he said without looking at Dikon.

"I'm going into Harpoon," said Dikon. "Would you care to come?"

"I don't mind."

Dikon had learnt to recognize this form of acceptance. "Jump in then," he said. "You can drive."

"I won't come at that."

"Why not?"

"She's not my bus. Not my place to drive her."

"Don't be an ass. I've got a free hand and I'm asking you. You can check up the engine better if you're driving, can't you?"

He saw desire and defensiveness struggling together in Simon. "Get on with it," he said and sat firmly in the passenger's place.

They drove round the house and up the abominable drive. Dikon glanced at Simon and was touched by his look of inward happiness. He drove delicately and with assurance.

"Running well, isn't she?" asked Dikon.

"She's a trimmer," said Simon. As the car gathered speed on the main road he lost his customary air of mulishness and gained a kind of authority. Bent on dismissing the scene with Gaunt from his thoughts, Dikon lured Simon into talking about his own affairs, his impatience to get into uniform, his struggles with Morse, his passionate absorption with the war in the air. Dikon thought how young Simon would have seemed among English youth of his own age and how vulnerable. "I'm coming on with the old dah-dah-dit, though," Simon said. "I've made my own practice transmitter. It's got a corker fulcrum, too. I'm not so hot at receiving yet, but I can get quite a bit of the stuff on the short wave. Nearly all code, of course, but some of it's straight English. Gosh, I wish they'd pull me in. It's a blooming nark the way they keep you hanging about."

"They'll miss you on the place."

"We won't be on the place much longer, don't *you* worry. Questing'll look after that. By cripey, I sometimes wonder if it's a fair pop, me going away when that bloke's hanging round." They drove on in silence for a time and then, without warning, Simon burst into a spate of bewildered protest and fury. It was difficult to follow the progress of his ideas: Questing's infamy, the Colonel's unworldliness, Barbara's virtue, the indignation of the Maori people, and the infamy of big business and vested interests were inextricably mixed together in his discourse. Presently, however, a new theme appeared. "Uncle James," said Simon, "reckons the curio business is all a blind. He reckons Questing's an enemy agent."

Dikon made a faint incredulous noise. "Well he might be," said Simon combatively. "Why not? You don't kid yourself they haven't got agents in New Zealand, do you?"

"Somehow he doesn't strike me as the type—"

"They don't knock round wearing masks and looking tough," Simon pointed out with an unexpected touch of his uncle's acerbity.

"I know, I know. It's only that one hears such a lot of palpable nonsense about spies that the whole idea is suspect. Like arrow poison in a detective story. Why does Dr. Ackrington think—"

"I don't get the strength of it myself. He wouldn't say much. Only dropped hints that we needn't be so sure Questing'd kick Dad off the place. Were you in this country when the *Hippolyte* was torpedoed?"

"No. We heard about it, of course. It was a submarine, wasn't it?"

"That's right. The *Hippolyte* put out from Harpoon at night. She went down in sight of land. Uncle James reckoned at the time that the raider got the tip from someone on shore."

"Questing?" said Dikon, and tried very hard to keep the note of scepticism from his voice.

"Yeah, Questing. Uncle James dopes it out that it's been Questing's idea to get this place on his own ever since he lent Dad the money. He reckons he's been acting as an agent for years and that he'll use the Springs as his headquarters with bogus patients and as likely as not a secret transmitting station."

"Oh, Lord!"

"Well, anyway he's acted pretty crook, hasn't he? I don't think it's so funny. And if the old dead-beats at Home hadn't been too tired to take notice, perhaps we wouldn't have been looking so silly now," Simon added vindictively. "Chaps like Questing ought to be cleaned right up, I reckon. Out of it altogether. What'd they do with them in Russia? Look here," Simon continued, "I'll tell you something. The night before the *Hippolyte* went down there was a light flashing on the Peak. Some of the chaps over at the Kainga, Eru and Rewi Te Kahu and that gang, had gone out in a boat from Harpoon and they said they saw it. Uncle James has seen it since. Everybody knows there's a reinforcement sailing any time now. What's Questing doing, where does he go half the time? He's messing round on the Peak, isn't he? Why did he try to put Bert Smith under the train?" Dikon attempted to speak and was firmly talked down. "Accident my foot," said Simon. "He ought to be charged with attempted murder. The police round here seem to think they amount to something, I reckon they don't know they're born."

"Well," Dikon said mildly, "what action do you propose to take?"

"There's no need to be sarcastic," Simon roared out. "If you want to know what I'm going to do I'll tell you. I'm going to stay up at nights. If Questing goes out I'll slip after him and I'll watch the Peak. My Morse'll be good enough for what he does. It'll be in code, of course, but if it's Morse he's using I'll spot it. You bet I will, and by gum I'll go to the station at Harpoon and if they won't pull him in on that I'll charge him with attempted murder."

"And if they don't care for that either?"

"I'll do *something*," said Simon. "I'll do *something*."

CHAPTER VI

ARRIVAL OF SEPTIMUS FALLS

Friday, the day before the concert, marked the beginning of a crescendo in the affairs of Wai-ata-tapu. It began at breakfast. The London news bulletin was more than usually ominous and the pall of depression that was in the background of all New Zealanders' minds at that time seemed to drag a little nearer. Colonel Claire, looking miserable, ate his breakfast in silence. Questing and Simon were both late for this meal, and one glance at Simon's face convinced Dikon that something had happened to disturb him. He had black marks under his eyes and an air of angry satisfaction. Mr. Questing, too, looked as if he had not slept well. He spared them his customary sallies of matutinal playfulness. Since their drive to Harpoon two days ago, Dikon had tried to adjust his idea of Mr. Questing to that of a paid enemy agent. He had even kept awake for an hour or two beyond his usual time watching the face of Rangi's Peak. But, although Mr. Questing announced his intention each night of dining at the hotel in Harpoon and had not returned when the rest of the party went to bed, the Peak changed from wine to purple and from purple to black outside Dikon's window and no points of light had pricked its velvet surface. At last he lost patience with watching and fell asleep. On both mornings he woke with a dim recollection of hearing a car come round the house to the garage. Simon, he knew, had watched each night and he felt sure that the second vigil had been fruitful. Dikon fancied that Questing had delivered a final notice to the Claires, as at Friday's breakfast they bore an elderly resemblance to the Babes in the Wood. They ate nothing and he caught them looking at each other with an air of bewilderment and despair.

Smith, who seemed to be really shaken by the jump from

the bridge, breakfasted early, a habit that kept up the tradition that he worked for his keep.

The general atmosphere of discomfort and suspense was aggravated by the behaviour of Huia, who after placing a plate of porridge before Dr. Ackrington, burst into tears and ran howling from the room.

"What the devil's the matter with the girl?" he demanded. "I've said nothing."

"It's Eru Saul," said Barbara. "He's been waiting for her again when she goes home, Mummy."

"Yes, dear. Ssh!" Mrs. Claire leant towards her husband and said in her special voice: "I think, dear, that you should speak to young Saul. He's *not* a desirable type."

"Oh, damn!" muttered the Colonel.

Mr. Questing pushed his chair back and walked quickly from the room.

"That's the joker you ought to speak to, Dad," said Simon, jerking his head at the door. "You've only got to look at the way he carries on with—"

"Please, dear!" said Mrs. Claire, and the party relapsed into silence.

Gaunt breakfasted in his room. On the previous evening he had been restless and irritable, unable to work or read. He had left Dikon to his typewriter and, on an unaccountable impulse, elected to drive himself along the appalling coastal road to the north. He was in a state of excitement which Dikon found ridiculous and disturbing. During six years of employment Dikon had found their association pleasant and amusing. His early hero-worship of Gaunt had long ago been replaced by a tolerant and somewhat detached affection, but ten days at Wai-ata-tapu had wrought an alarming change in this attitude. It was as if the Claires, muddle-headed, gentle, and perhaps a little foolish, had proved to be a sort of touchstone to which Gaunt had been brought and found wanting. And yet Dikon, distressed by this change, could not altogether agree with his own judgment. It was the business of the dress for Barbara, he recognized, that had irritated him most. He had accused Gaunt of a gross error in taste and yet he himself had learnt to mistrust and deride the very attitude of mind that the Claires upheld. Was it not, in fact, an ungenerous attitude that forbade the acceptance of a generous gift, an attitude of self-righteous snobbism?

And exploring unhappily the backwaters of his own impulses he asked himself finally if perhaps he resented the gift because he was not the author of it.

The rural mail-car passed along the main highway at about eleven o'clock in the morning, and any letters for the Springs were left in a tin post-box on the top gate. Parcels too big for the box were merely dumped beneath it. The morning was overcast and Gaunt was in a fever lest the Claires should delay the trip to the gate and the parcel from Sarah Snappe be rained upon. Dikon gathered that the gift was to remain anonymous but doubted Gaunt's ability to deny himself the pleasure of enacting the part of fairy godfather. "He will drop some arch hint and betray himself," Dikon thought angrily. "And even if she refuses the blasted dress she'll be more besotted on him than ever."

After breakfast Mrs. Claire and Barbara, assisted in a leisurely manner by Huia, bucketed into their household duties with their customary air of laying back their ears and rushing their fences. Simon, who usually fetched the mail, disappeared and presently it began to rain.

"The oaf!" Gaunt fulminated. "He will lurch up the hill an hour late and bring down a mass of repellent pulp."

"I can go up if you like, sir. The man always sounds his horn if he has anything for us. I can go as soon as I hear it."

"They would guess that we expected something. Even Colly No, they must fetch their own detestable mail. She must receive her parcel at their hands. I want to see it, though. I can stroll out for my own letters. Good God, a second deluge is descending upon us. Perhaps, after all, Dikon, *you* had better go for a stroll and casually pick up the mail."

Dikon looked at the rods of water that now descended with such force that they spurted off the pumice in fans, and asked his employer if he did not think it would seem a little eccentric to stroll in such weather. "Besides, sir," he pointed out, "the mail-car cannot possibly arrive for two hours and my stroll would be ridiculously protracted."

"You have been against me from the outset," Gaunt muttered. "Very well, I shall dictate for an hour."

Dikon followed him indoors, sat down, and produced his

shorthand pad. He was dying to ask Simon if he had succeeded in his vigil.

Gaunt walked up and down and began to dictate. *"The actor,"* he said, *"is a modest warm-hearted fellow. Being, perhaps, more highly sensitized than his fellow man he is more sensitive..."*

Dikon hesitated. "Well, what's wrong with that?" Gaunt demanded.

"Sensitized, sensitive!"

"Death and damnation!... *he is more responsive,* then, *to the more subtle..."*

"More, sir, and *more."*

"Then delete the second *more.* How often am I to implore you to make these paltry amendments without disturbing me?... *to the subtle nuances, the delicate half-tones of emotion. I had always been conscious of this gift, if it is one, in myself."*

"Do you mind repeating that, sir? The rain makes such a din on the iron roof I can scarcely hear you. I got the *subtle nuances."*

"Am I, then, to compose at the full pitch of my lungs?"

"I could trot after you with my little pad in my hand."

"A preposterous suggestion."

"It's leaving off, now."

The rain stopped with the abruptness of subtropical downpours, and the ground and roofs of Wai-ata-tapu began to steam. Gaunt became less restive and the dictation proceeded along lines that Dikon, in his new mood of open-eyed criticism, considered all too typical of almost any theatrical autobiography. But perhaps Gaunt would rescue his book by taking a line of defiant egoism. He seemed to be drifting that way. There was a growing flavour of: "This is the life story of a damn' good actor who isn't going to spoil it with gestures of false modesty"; a fashionable attitude, and no doubt Gaunt had decided to adopt it.

At ten o'clock Gaunt went down to the Springs with Colly in attendance, and Dikon hurried away in search of Simon. He found him in his cabin, a scrupulously tidy room where wireless magazines and text-books were set out on a working bench. He was in consultation with Smith, who broke off in the middle of some mumbled recital and with a grudging acknowledgment of Dikon's greeting sloped away.

In contrast to Smith, Simon appeared to be almost
cordial. Dikon was not quite sure how he stood with this
curious young man, but he had a notion that his passive
acceptance of the role cast for him in the lake incident as the
remover of Barbara, and his suggestion that Simon should
drive the car, had given him a kind of status. He thought that
Simon disapproved of him on general principles as a parasite
and a freak, but didn't altogether dislike him.

"Here!" said Simon. "Can you beat it? Questing's been
telling Bert Smith he won't put him off *after* all, when he
cleans us up. He's going to keep him on and give him good
money. What d'you make of that?"

"Sudden change, isn't it?"

"You bet it's sudden. D'you get the big idea, though?"

"Does he want to keep him quiet?" Dikon suggested
cautiously.

"I'll say! Too right he wants to keep him quiet. He's
windy. He's had one pop at rubbing Bert out and he's made a
mess of it. He daren't come at that game again so he's trying
the other stuff. 'Keep your mouth shut and it's O.K. by me.'"

"But honestly—"

"Look, Mr. Bell, don't start telling me it's 'incredible.'
You've been getting round with theatrical sissies for so long
you don't know a real man when you see one."

"My dear Claire," said Dikon with some heat, "may I
suggest that speaking in the back of your throat and going
out of your way to insult everybody that doesn't is not the
sole evidence of virility. And if real men spend their time
trying to kill and bribe each other, I infinitely prefer my
theatrical sissies." Dikon removed his spectacles and
polished them with his handkerchief. "And if," he added,
"you mean what I imagine you to mean by 'sissies,' allow me
to tell you you're a liar. And furthermore, don't call me Mr.
Bell. I'm afraid you're an inverted snob."

Simon stared at him. "Aw, dickon!" he said at last, and
then turned purple. "I'm not calling you by your Christian
name," he explained hurriedly. "That's a kind of expression.
Like you'd say, 'Come off it.'"

"Oh."

"And a sissy is just a chap who's kind of weak. You know.
Too tired to take the trouble. English!"

"Like Winston Churchill?"

"Aw, to hell!" roared Simon, and then grinned. "All right, all right!" he said. "You win. I apologize."

Dikon blinked. "Well," he said sedately, "I call that very handsome of you. I also apologize. And now, do tell me the latest news of Questing. I swear I shan't boggle at sabotage, homicide, espionage, or incendiarism. What, if anything, have you discovered?"

Simon rose and shut the door. He then shoved a packet of cigarettes at Dikon, leant back with his elbows on his desk and, with his own cigarette jutting out of the corner of his mouth, embarked on his story.

"Wednesday night," he said, "was a wash-out. He went into Harpoon and had tea at the pub. You call it 'dinnah.' The pub keeper's a cobber of his. Bert Smith was in town and he says Questing was there all right. He gave Bert a lift home. Bert was half-shickered or he'd have been too windy to take it. He's on the booze again after that show at the crossing. It was then Questing put it up to him he could stay on after we'd got the boot. Yes, Wednesday night's out of it. But last night's different. I suppose he got his tea in town, all right, but he went over to the Peak. About seven o'clock I biked down to the level crossing—and, by the way, that light's working O.K. I hid up in the scrub. Three hours later, along comes Mr. Questing in his bus. Where he gets the juice is just nobody's business. He steams off up the Peak road. I lit off to a possie I'd taped out beforehand. It's a bit of a bluff that sticks out on the other side of the inlet. Opposite the Peak, sort of. At the end of a rocky spit. I had to wade the last bit. The Peak's at the end of a long neck, you know. The seaward side's all cliff, but you can climb up a fence line. But the near face is *easy* going. There's still a trace of a track the Maori people used when they buried their dead in the old crater. About half-way up it twists and you could strike out from there to the seaward face. There's a bit of a shelf above the cliff. You can't see it from most places, but you can from where I was. I picked that was where he'd go. From my possie you look across the harbour to it, see? It was a pretty solid bike ride, but I reckoned I'd make it quicker than Questing'd climb the Peak track. He's flabby. I had to crawl up the rock to get where I wanted. Wet to the middle, I was. Did I get cold! I'll say. And soon after I'd got there she blew up wet from the sea. It was lovely."

"You don't mean to say you bicycled to that headland beyond Harpoon? It must be seven miles."

"Yeh, that's right. I beat Questing hands down, too. I sat on that ruddy bluff till I just about froze to the rock, and I'll bet you anything you like I never took me eyes off the Peak. I looked right across the harbour. There's a big ship in and she was loading in the blackout. Gee, I'd like to know what she was loading. I bet Bert Smith knows. He's cobbers with some of the wharfies, him and Eru Saul. Eru and Bert get shickered with the wharfies. They were shickered last night, Bert says. I don't think it's so hot going round with—"

"The Peak and Mr. Questing," Dikon reminded him.

"O.K. Well, just when I thought I'd been had for a mug, it started. A little point of light right where I told you on the seaward face. Popping in and out."

"Could you read it?"

"Neow!" said Simon angrily in his broadest twang. "If it was Morse it was some code. Just a lot of *t*'s and *i*'s and *s*'s. He *wouldn't* use plain language. You bet he wouldn't. There'd be a system of signals. A long flash repeated three times at intervals of a minute. 'Come in. I'm talking to you.' Then the message. Say five short flashes: 'Ship in port.' That'd be repeated three times. Then the day she sails. One long flash: 'To-night.' Two short flashes: 'To-morrow.' Three short flashes. 'To-morrow night.' Repeat. Then a long interval, and the whole show all over again. What I reckon," Simon concluded, and inhaled a prodigious draught of smoke.

"But did you, in fact, see the sequence you've described?"

With maddening deliberation Simon ground out his cigarette, made several small backward movements of his head which invested him with an extraordinary air of complacency, and said: "Six times at fifteen-minute intervals. The end signal was three flashes each time."

"Was it, by George!" Dikon murmured.

"'Course I haven't got the reading O.K. May be something quite different."

"Of course." They stared at each other, a sense of

companionship weaving between them.

"But I'd like to know what that ship's loading," Simon said.

"Was there any answering flash out at sea? I couldn't know less about such things."

"I didn't pick it. But I don't reckon she'd do anything. If it's a raider I reckon she'd come in close on the north side of the Peak, so's to keep it between herself and Harpoon, and wait to see. There's nothing but bays and rough stuff up the coast north of the Peak."

"How long did you stay?"

"Till there was no more signalling. The tide was in by then. By heck, I didn't much enjoy wading back. He beat me to it coming home. Me blinking tyre had gone flat on me and I had to pump up three times. His bus was in the garage. By cripey he's a beaut. Wait till I get him. That'll be the day."

"What will you do about it?"

"Bike into town and go to the police station."

"I'll ask for the car."

"Heck, no, I'll bike. Here, you'd better not say anything to him."

"Who?"

Simon jerked his head.

"Gaunt? I can't promise not to do that. You see we've discussed Questing so much, and Colly talks to Gaunt and you've talked to Colly. And anyway," said Dikon, "I can't suddenly begin keeping him in the dark about things. You've got a fantastic idea of Gaunt. He's—dear me, how embarrassing the word still is—he's a patriot. He gave the entire profit of the last three weeks' Shakespearean season in Melbourne to the war effort."

"Huh," Simon grunted. "Money."

"It's what's wanted. And I'd like to talk to him about last night for another reason. He took the car out after dinner. Once in a blue moon he gets a sudden idea he wants to drive. He may have noticed a light out to sea. He said he'd go up the coast road to the north."

"And what he's done to the car is nobody's business. It's a terrible road. Have you looked at her? Covered in mud and scratched all over the wings. It's not his fault he didn't bust up the back axle in a pot-hole. He's a shocking driver."

Dikon decided to ignore this. "What about Dr. Ackring-ton?" he said. "After all he was the first to suspect something. Oughtn't you to take his advice before you make a move?"

"Uncle James doesn't see things my way," said Simon aggressively, "and I don't see things his way. He thinks I'm crude and I think he's a nark and a dugout."

"Nevertheless I think I should tell him."

"I dunno where he's got to."

"He's returning to-morrow, isn't he? Wait till he comes before you do anything."

A motor horn sounded on the main road.

"Is that the mail?" cried Dikon.

"That's right. What about it?"

Dikon looked out of the window. "It's beginning to rain again."

"What of it?"

"Nothing, nothing," said Dikon in a hurry.

ii

It was Barbara, after all, who went first to get the mail. Dikon saw her run out of the house with her mackintosh over her shoulders, and heard Mrs. Claire call out something about the rain spoiling the bread. Of course. It was the day for the bread, thought Dikon, who had reached the second-ary stage of occupation when the routine of a household is becoming familiar. With an extraordinary sensation of approaching disaster he watched Barbara go haring up the hill in the rain. "But it's ridiculous," he told himself, "to treat a mere incident as if it was an epic. What the devil has come upon me that I can do nothing but fidget like an old woman over this damn' girl's clothes. Either she refuses or she accepts them. Either she guesses who sent for them or she doesn't. The affair will merely become an anecdote, amusing or dull. To hell with it."

The little figure ran over the brow of the hill and disappeared.

Dikon, obeying orders, went to tell his employer that the mail was in.

Barbara was happy as she ran up the hill. The rain was soft on her face; thin like mist, and warm. The scent of wet earth was more pungent than the reek of sulphur, and a light breeze brought a sensation of the ocean across the hills. Her spirit rose to meet it, and all the impending disasters of Wai-ata-tapu could not check her humour. It was impossible for Barbara to be unhappy that morning. She had received in small doses during the past week an antidote to unhappiness. With each little sign of friendliness and interest from Gaunt, and he had given her many such signs, her spirit danced. Barbara had not been protected against green-sickness by inoculations of calf-love. Unable to compete with the few neighboring families whom her parents considered "suit-able," and prevented by a hundred reservations and prej-udices from forming friendships with the "unsuitable," she had ended by forming no friendships at all. Occasionally she would be asked to some local festivity, but her clothes were all wrong, her face unpainted, and her manner nervous and uneven. She alarmed the young men with her gusts of frightened laughter and her too eager attentiveness. If her shyness had taken any other form she might have found someone to befriend her, but as it was she hovered on the outside of every group, making her hostess uneasy or irritable, refusing to recognize the rising misery of her own loneliness. She was happier when she was no longer invited and settled down to her course of emotional starvation, hardly aware, until Gaunt came, of her sickness. How, then, could the financial crisis, still only half-realized by Barbara, cast more than a faint shadow over her new exhilaration? Geoffrey Gaunt smiled at her, quiet prim Mr. Bell sought her out to talk to her. And, though she would never have admitted it, Mr. Questing's behaviour, odious and terrifying as it had been at the time, was not altogether ungratifying in retrospect. As for his matrimonial alternative to financial disaster, she contrived to hide the memory of it under a layer of less disturbing recollections.

The parcel from Sarah Snappe lay under the mailbox,

half obscured by tussock and loaves of bread. At first she thought it had been left there by mistake, then that it was for Gaunt or Dikon Bell; then she read her own name. Her brain skipped about among improbabilities. Unknown Auntie Wynne had sent another lot of alien and faintly squalid cast-offs. This was the first of her conjectures. Only when she was fumbling with the wet string did she notice the smart modern lettering on the label and the New Zealand stamps and postmark.

It lay under folds of tissue-paper, immaculately folded. She might have knelt there in the wet grass for much longer if a gentle drift of rain had not dimmed the three steel stars. With a nervous movement of her hands she thrust down the lid of the box and pulled the wrapping paper over it. Still she knelt before it, haloed in mist, bewildered, her hands pressed upon the parcel. Simon came upon her there. She turned and looked at him with a glance half-radiant, half-incredulous.

"It's not meant for me," she said.

He asked what was in the parcel. By this time she had taken off her mackintosh and wrapped the box in it. "A black dress," she said, "with three stars on it. Other things, underneath. Another box. I didn't look past the dress. It's not meant for me."

"Auntie Wynne."

"It's not one of Auntie Wynne's dresses. It's new. It came from Auckland. There must be another Barbara Claire."

"You're nuts," said Simon. "I suppose she's sent the money or something. Why the heck have you taken your mac off? You'll get wet."

Barbara rose to her feet clutching the enormous package. "It's got my name on it. Barbara Claire, Wai-ata-tapu Spa, via Harpoon. There's an envelope inside, too, with my name on it.

"What was in it?"

"I didn't look."

"You're dopey."

"It can't be for me."

"Gee whiz, you're mad. Here, what about the bread and the rest of the mail?"

"I didn't look."

"Aw, hell, you're mad as a meat-axe." Simon opened the letter-box. "There's a postcard from Uncle James. He's coming back to-night. A telegram for Mum from Auckland. That's funny. And a whole swag for the boarders. Yes, and look at the bread kicking round in the dirt. No trouble to you. Wait on."

But Barbara, clutching the parcel, was running down the hill in the rain.

Gaunt waited on the verandah in his dressing gown; "very dark and magnificent," thought Dikon maliciously. Whatever the fate of the dress, whatever Barbara's subsequent reaction, Gaunt had his reward, Dikon thought, when she ran across the pumice and laid the parcel on the verandah table, calling her mother.

"Hullo," said Gaunt. "Had a birthday?"

"No. It's something that's happened. I can't understand it." She was unwrapping the mackintosh from the parcel. Her hands, stained with housework but not yet thickened, shook a little. She unfolded the wrapping paper.

"Is it china that you handle it so gingerly?"

"No. It's—My hands!" She ran down the verandah to the bathroom. Simon came slowly across the pumice with the bread and walked through the house.

"Did you tell them what to write?" Gaunt asked Dikon. "Yes."

Barbara returned, shouting for her mother. Mrs. Claire and the Colonel appeared looking as if they anticipated some new catastrophe.

"Barbie, not *quite* so noisy, my dear," said her mother. She glanced at her celebrated visitor and smiled uncertainly. Her husband and her brother did not stroll about the verandah in exotic dressing gowns, but she had begun to formulate a sort of spare code of manners for Gaunt, who, as Dikon had not failed to notice, spoke to her nicely and repeatedly of his mother.

Barbara lifted the lid from her box. Her parents, making uncertain noises, stared at the dress. She took up the envelope. "How can it be for me?" she said, and Dikon saw that she was afraid to open the envelope.

"Good Lord!" her father ejaculated. "What on earth have you been buying?"

"I haven't, Daddy. It's—"

"From Auntie Wynne. How kind," said Mrs. Claire.

"That's not Wynne's writing," said the Colonel suddenly.

"No." Barbara opened the envelope and a large card fell on the black surface of the dress. The inscription in green ink had been written across it somewhat flamboyantly and in an extremely feminine script. Barbara read it aloud.

"If you accept it, then its worth is great."

"That's all," said Barbara, and her parents began to look baffled and mulish. Simon appeared and repeated his suggestion that the Aunt had sent a cheque to the shop in Auckland.

"But she's never been to Auckland," said the Colonel crossly. "How can a woman living in Poona write cheques to shops she's never heard of in New Zealand? The thing's absurd."

"I must say," said Mrs. Claire, "that although it's very kind of dear Wynne, I think it's always nice not to make mysteries. You must write and thank her just the same, Barbie, of course."

"But I repeat, Agnes, that it's not from Wynne."

"How can we tell, dear, when she doesn't write her name? That's what I mean when I say we would rather she put in a little note as usual."

"It's not her writing. Green ink and loud flourishes! Ridiculous."

"I suppose she wanted to puzzle us."

Colonel Claire suddenly walked away, looking miserable.

"Mayn't we see the dress?" asked Gaunt.

Barbara drew it from the box and sheets of tissue-paper fell from it as she held it up. The three stars shone again in the folds of the skirt. It was a beautifully simple dress.

"But it's charming," Gaunt said. "It couldn't be better. Do you like it?"

"Like it?" Barbara looked at him and her eyes filled with tears. "It's so beautiful," she said, "that I can't believe it's true."

"There are more things in the box, aren't there? Shall I hold the dress?"

He took it from her and she knelt on the chair, exploring feverishly. Dikon, whose orders had been to give Sarah

Snappe *carte-blanche,* saw that she had taken him at his word. The shell-coloured satin was dull and heavy and the lace delicately rich. There seemed to be a complete set of garments. Barbara folded them back, lifted an extraordinarily pert and scanty object, turned crimson in the face and hurriedly replaced it. Her mother stepped between her and Gaunt. "Wouldn't it be best if you took your parcel indoors, dear?" she said with poise. Barbara blundered through the door with the box and, to her mother's evident dismay, Gaunt followed, holding the dress. A curious scene was enacted in the dining-room. Barbara hesitated between rapture and embarrassment, as Gaunt actually began to inspect the contents of the box while Mrs. Claire attempted to catch his attention with a distracted resume of the distant Wynne's dual office of aunt and godmother, Dikon looked on, and Simon read the morning paper. The smaller boxes were found to contain shoes and stockings. "Bless my soul," said Gaunt lightly. "It's a trousseau."

Colonel Claire appeared briefly in the doorway. "It must be James," he said, and walked away again, quickly.

"Uncle James!" cried Barbara. "Mother, could it be Uncle James?"

"Perhaps Wynne wrote to James," began her mother, and Simon said from behind his paper: "She doesn't know him."

"She knows *of* him," said Mrs. Claire gravely.

"You've got that telegram in your hand, Mum," said Simon. "Why don't you read it? It might have something to do with Barbie's clothes."

They all stared at her while she read the telegram. Her expression suggested astonishment, followed by the liveliest consternation. "Oh, *no,*" she cried out at last. "We *can't* have another. Oh dear!"

"What's up?" asked Simon.

"It's from a Mr. Septimus Falls. He says he's got lumbago and is coming for a fortnight. What *am* I to do?"

"Put him off."

"I can't. There's no address. It just says 'Kindly reserve single room Friday and arrange treatment lumbago staying fortnight Septimus Falls.' Friday. *Friday!*" wailed Mrs. Claire. "What *are* we to do? That's to-day."

iii

Mr. Septimus Falls arrived by train and taxi at 4:30,
within a few minutes of Dr. Ackrington, who picked up his
own car in Harpoon. By some Herculean effort the Claires
had made ready for Mr. Falls. Simon moved into his cabin,
Barbara moved into Simon's room, Barbara's room was
made ready for Mr. Falls. He turned out to be a middle-aged
Englishman, tall but bent forward at a wooden angle and
leaning heavily on his stick. He was good-looking, well-
mannered, and inclined to be bookishly facetious.

"I'm so sorry not to give you longer warning," said Mr.
Falls, grunting slightly as he came up the steps. "But this
wretched incubus of a disease came upon me quite suddenly
yesterday evening. I happened to see your advertisement in
the paper and the doctor I consulted agreed that I should try
thermal treatment."

"But we have no advertisement in the papers," said Mrs.
Claire.

"I assure you I saw one. Unless, by any frightful chance,
I'm coming to the wrong Wai-ata-tapu Hot Springs. Your
name *is* Questing, I hope?"

Mrs. Claire turned pink and replied gently: "My name is
Claire, but you have made no other mistake. May I help you
to your room?"

He apologized and thanked her, but added that he could
still totter under his own steam. He seemed to be delighted
with the dubious amenities of Barbara's room. "I can't tell
you," he said in a friendly manner, "how deeply I have grown
to detest suites. I have been living in hotels for six months and
have become so moulded to the *en suite* tradition that I
assure you I have quite a struggle before I can bring myself to
wear a spotted tie with a striped suit. It makes everything very
difficult. Now this—" he looked at Barbara's pieces of
furniture, which, under the brief influence of a domestic
magazine, she had painted severally in the primary colours—
"this will restore me to normal in no time."

The taxi driver brought his luggage, which was of two
sorts. Three extremely new suitcases consorted with a
solitary small one which was much worn and covered with

labels. Mrs. Claire had never seen so many labels. In addition to partially removed records of English and continental hotels, New Zealand place names jostled each other over the lid. He followed her glance and said: "You are thinking that I am 'Monsieur Traveller, one who would disable all the benefits of his own country,' and so forth. The fact is the evil brute got lost and has followed some other Falls all over the country. Would you care for the evening paper? The news, alas, is as usual."

She thanked him confusedly, and retired with the paper to the verandah where she found her brother in angry consultation with Barbara. Dikon stood diffidently in the background.

"Well, old boy," said Mrs. Claire, and kissed him warmly. "Lovely to have you with us again."

"No need to cry over me. I haven't been to the South Pole," said Dr. Ackrington, but he returned her kiss, and in the next second attacked his niece. "Will you stop making faces at me? Am I in the habit of lying? Why should I bestow raiment upon you, you silly girl?"

"But truly, Uncle James? Word of honour?"

"I believe he knows something about it!" Mrs. Claire exclaimed very archly. "Weren't we silly-billies? We thought of a fairy god*mother,* but we never guessed it might be a fairy god*father* at work, did we? Dear James," and she kissed him again. "But you *shouldn't.*"

"Merciful Creator," apostrophized Dr. Ackrington, "do I look like a fairy! Is it likely that I, who for the past decade have urged upon this insane household the virtues of economy and investment—is it likely that I should madly lavish large sums of money upon feminine garments? And pray, Agnes, why are you gaping at that paper? Surely you didn't expect the war news to be anything but disastrous?"

Mrs. Claire gave him the paper and pointed silently to a paragraph in the advertisement columns. Barbara read over his shoulder:—

THE SPA

Wai-ata-tapu Hot Springs

Visit the miraculous health-giving thermal fairyland of the
North. Astounding cures wrought by unique chemical
properties of amazing pools. Delightful surroundings.
Homelike residential private hotel. Every comfort and
attention. Medical supervision. Under new management.

M. QUESTING

The paper shook in Dr. Ackrington's hand, but he said
nothing. His sister pointed to the personal column.

"Mr. Geoffrey Gaunt, the famous English actor, is at
present a guest at Wai-ata-tapu Spa. He is accompanied by
Mr. Dikon Bell, his private secretary."

"James!" Mrs. Claire cried out. "Remember your
dyspepsia, dear. It's so bad for you!"

Her brother, white to the lips and trembling, presented the
formidable spectacle of a man transported by rage. "After
all," Mrs. Claire added timidly, "It *is* going to be true, dear,
we're afraid. He *will* be manager very soon. Of course it's
inconsiderate not to wait. Poor Edward—"

"To hell with poor Edward!" whispered Dr. Ackrington.
"Have you eyes! Can you read! Will you forget for one
moment the inevitable consequences of poor Edward's
imbecility, and tell me how I am to interpret THAT?" His
quivering finger pointed to the penultimate phrase of the
advertisement. "Medical supervision. *Medical supervision!*
My God, the fellow means ME!" Dr. Ackrington's voice
broke into a surprising falsetto. He glared at Barbara, who
immediately burst into a hoot of terrified laughter. He
uttered a loud oath, crushed the newspaper into a ball, and
flung it at her feet. "Certifiable lunatics, the lot of you!" he
raged, and turned blindly along the verandah towards his
own room.

Before he could reach it, however, Mr. Septimus Falls,
doubled over his stick, came out of his own room. The two
limping gentlemen hurried towards each other. A collision
seemed imminent and Dikon cried out involuntarily: "Dr.
Ackrington! Look out, sir."

They halted, facing each other. Mr. Falls said mellifluously: "*Doctor Ackrington?* How do you do, sir? I was about to
make inquiries. Allow me to introduce myself. My name is

Septimus Falls. You, I take it, are the medical superintendent."

Mrs. Claire, Dikon, and Barbara drew in their breaths
sharply as Dr. Ackrington clenched his fists and began to
stutter. Mr. Falls, with the experimental wariness of those
suffering from lumbago, straightened himself slightly and
looked mildly into Dr. Ackrington's face. "I hope to benefit
greatly by your treatment," he said. "Can it possibly be Dr.
James Ackrington? If so I am indeed fortunate. I *had* heard
that New Zealand was so happy as to—But I am sure I
recognise you. The photograph in *Some Aspects of the Study
of Comparative Anatomy,* you know. Well, well, this is the
greatest pleasure."

"Did you say your name was Septimus Falls?"

"Yes."

"Good God."

"I can hardly hope that my small activities have come to
your notice."

"Here!" said Dr. Ackrington abruptly. Come to my
room."

CHAPTER VII

TORPEDO

"It appears," said Dikon later that evening, "that Mr. Falls is a sort of amateur of anatomy and that Ackrington is his god. I am convinced that the revelation came only just in time to avert bloodshed. As it is the doctor seems prepared to suffer the adulation of his rather affected disciple."

"When is Falls going to appear?" asked Gaunt. "Why didn't he dine?"

"I understand he took old Ackrington's advice, had a prolonged stew in the most powerful of the mud baths, and retired sweating to bed. Ackrington suspects a wrong diagnosis and is going to prod his lumbar region."

"A terrifying experience. He tried it on my leg. Dikon, have you ever seen anything like the transformation in that child? She was almost beautiful with the dress in her hands. She will be quite beautiful when she wears it. How can we engineer a visit to the hairdresser before to-morrow evening? With any normal girl it would be automatic, but with Barbara Claire! I'm determined she shall dazzle the native audience. Isn't it a fantastic notion? Metamorphosis at a Maori concert!"

"Yes," said Dikon.

"Of course, if you're going to be contankerous."

"I am not, I assure you, sir," said Dikon, and forced himself to add: "You have given her an enormous amount of pleasure."

"And she suspects nothing." Gaunt looked sharply at his secretary, seemed to hesitate, and then took him by the arm. "Do you know what I'm going to do? A little experiment in psychology. I'm going to wait until she has worn her new things and everybody has told her how nice she looks, until she has been stroked and stimulated and enriched by good

117

clothes, and then, swearing her to secrecy first, I shall tell her where they came from. What do you think she will do?"

"Break her heart and give them up?"

"Not she. My dear chap, I shall be much too charming and tactful. It is a little test I have set myself. You wait, my boy, you wait." Dikon was silent. "Well, don't you think it'll work?" Gaunt demanded.

"Yes, sir. On consideration, I'm afraid I do."

"What d'you mean, *afraid?* We're not going to have this absurd argument all over again, I hope. Damn it, Dikon, you're no better than a croaking old woman. Why the devil I put up with you I don't know."

"Perhaps because I try to give an honest answer to an awkward question, sir."

"I don't propose to make a pass at the girl, if that's what's worrying you. You've allowed yourself to become melodrama-minded, my friend. All this chat of spies and mortgages and sacrificial marriage has blunted your aesthetic judgment. You insist upon regarding a charming episode as a seduction scene on a robust scale. I repeat I have no evil designs upon Barbara Claire. I am not a second Questing."

"You'd be less of a potential danger if you were," Dikon blurted out. "The little fool's not besotted on Questing. Don't you see, sir, that if you go on like this the resemblance to King Cophetua will become so marked that she won't know the difference and will half expect the sequel. She's gone haywire over you as it is."

"Nonsense," said Gaunt. But he stroked the back of his head and small complacent dints appeared at the corners of his mouth. "She can't possibly imagine that my attentions are anything but avuncular."

"She won't know what to imagine," said Dikon. "She's in a foreign country."

"Where the alpine ranges appear to be entirely composed of mole-hills."

"Where, at any rate, she is altogether too much i' the sun. She's dazzled."

"I'm afraid," said Gaunt, "that you are dressing up a very old emotion in a series of classy, and, if I may say so, rather priggish phrases. My good ass, you've fallen for the girl yourself." Dikon was silent, and in a moment Gaunt came behind him and shook him boisterously by the shoulders. "You'll recover," he said. "Think it over and you'll find I'm right. In the meantime I promise you need have no qualms. I shall treat her like porcelain. But I refuse to be deprived of my mission. She shall awake and sing."

With this unconvincing reassurance Dikon had to be content. They said good night and he went to bed.

ii

At twenty minutes past twelve on that same night a ship was torpedoed in the Tasman Sea six miles northwest of Harpoon Inlet. She was the same ship that Simon, from his eyrie of Friday night, had watched loading in the harbour. Later, they were to learn that she was the *Hokianga,* outward bound from New Zealand with a cargo of bullion for the United States of America. It was a very still night, warm, with a light breeze off the sea, and many Harpoon people said afterwards that they heard the explosion. The news was brought to Wai-ata-tapu the following morning by Huia, who rushed in with her eyes rolling and poured it out. Most of the crew was saved, she said, and had been landed at Harpoon. The *Hokianga* had not yet gone to the bottom, and from the Peak it was possible, through field-glasses, to see her bows pointed despairingly at the skies.

Simon plunged into Dikon's room, full of angry triumph, and doubly convinced of Questing's guilt. He was all for leaping on his bicycle and pedalling furiously into Harpoon. In his own words he proposed to stir up the dead-beats at the police station, and the local army headquarters. "If I'd gone yesterday like I wanted to, it wouldn't have happened. By cripey, I've let him get away with it. That was your big idea, Bell, and I hope you're tickled to death the way it's worked out." Dikon tried to point out that even if the authorities at

Harpoon were less somnolent than Simon represented them to be, they would scarcely have been able in twelve hours to prevent the activities of an enemy submarine.

"They might have stopped the ship," cried Simon.

"On your story that you saw lights on the Peak? Yes, I know there was a definite sequence and that it was repeated. I myself believe you're onto something, but you won't move authority as easily as that."

"To hell with authority!" poor Simon roared out. "I'll go and knock Questing's bloody block off for him."

"Not again," said Dikon sedately. "You really can't continue in your battery of Questing. You know I still think you should speak to Dr. Ackrington, who, you say yourself, already suspects him."

In the end Simon, who seemed, in spite of his aggressiveness, to place some kind of reliance on Dikon's advice, agreed to keep away from Questing, and to tell his story to his uncle. When, however, he went to find Dr. Ackrington, it was only to discover he had already driven away in his car saying that he would probably return before lunch.

"Isn't it a fair nark!" Simon grumbled. "What's he think he's doing? Precious time being wasted. To hell with him anyway, I'll think something up for myself. Don't you go talking, now. We don't want everyone to know."

"I'll keep it under my hat," said Dikon. "Gaunt knows, of course. I told you—"

"Oh, hell!" said Simon disgustedly.

Gaunt came out and told Dikon he wanted to be driven to the Peak. He offered a seat in the car to anyone who would like it. "I've asked your sister," he said to Simon. "Why don't you come too?" Simon consented ungraciously. They borrowed the Colonel's field-glasses, and set out.

It was the first time Dikon had been to Rangi's Peak. After crossing the railway line, the road ran out to the coast and thence along a narrow neck of land, at the end of which rose the great truncated cone. So symmetrical was its form that even at close quarters the mountain seemed to be the expression of some grossly simple impulse—the impulse, one would have said, of a primordial cubist. The road ended abruptly at a gate in a barbed-wire fence. A notice, headed

Native Reserve, set out a number of prohibitions. Dikon saw that it was forbidden to remove any objects found on the Peak.

They were not the first arrivals. Several cars were parked outside the fence.

"You have to walk from here," said Simon, and glanced disparagingly at Gaunt's shoes.

"Oh, God! Is it far?"

"*You* might think so."

Barbara cut in quickly. "Not very. It's a good path and we can turn back if you don't think it's worth it."

"So we can. Come on," said Gaunt with an air of boyish hardihood, and Simon led the way following the outside of the barbed-wire fence. They were moving round the flank of the Peak. The turf was springy under their feet, the air fresh with a tang in it. Some way behind them the song of a lark, a detached pinprick of sound, tinkled above the peninsula. Soon his voice faded into thin air and was lost in the mewing of a flight of gulls who came flapping in from seawards. "I never hear those creatures," said Gaunt, "without thinking of a B.B.C. serial." He looked up the sloping flank of the mountain, to where its crater stood black against the brilliant sky. "And that's where they buried their dead?"

Barbara pointed to the natural planes of ascent in the structure of the mountain. "It looks as if they had made a road up to the top," she said, "but I don't think they did. It's as though the hill had been shaped for the purpose, isn't it? They believe it was, you know. Of course they haven't used it for ages and ages. At least, that's what we're told. There *are* stories of a secret burial up there after the *pakehas* came."

"Do they never come here, nowadays?"

"Hardly at all. It's tapu. Some of the younger ones who don't mind so much wander about the lower slopes, but they don't go into the bush and I'm sure they never climb to the top. Do they, Sim?"

"Too much like hard work," Simon grunted.

"No, it's not that, really. It's because of the sort of place it is."

Simon gave Dikon a gloomily significant glance.

"Yeh," he said. "Do what you like up there and nobody's going to ask questions."

"You refer to the infamous Questing," said Gaunt lightly. Simon glared at him and Dikon said hurriedly: "I told you I had spoken to Mr. Gaunt of our little theory."

"That's right," Simon said angrily. "So now we've got to gas about it in front of everybody."

"If you mean me," said Barbara, whom even the mention of Questing could not embarrass that morning, "I know all about what he's supposed to do on the Peak."

Simon stopped short. "You!" he said. "*What* do you know?" Barbara didn't answer immediately, and he said roughly: "Come on. What do you know?"

"Well, only what they're saying about Maori curios."

"Oh," said Simon. "That." Dikon spared a moment to hope that if Simon did well in the Air Force they would not make the mistake of entrusting him with secret instructions.

"And I know Uncle James thinks it's something worse, and . . ." She broke off and looked from one to another of the three men. Dikon blinked, Gaunt whistled, and Simon looked inescapably portentous. "Sim!" cried Barbara. "You're not thinking . . . about *this* . . . the ship? Oh, but it couldn't possibly . . ."

"Here, you keep out of this, Barbie," said Simon in a great hurry. "Uncle James talks a lot of hooey. You want to forget it. Come on."

The track, curving always to the right, now mounted the crest of a low hill. The seaward horizon marched up to meet them. In three strides their whole range of vision was filled with blue. Harpoon Inlet lay behind on their left; on their right Rangi's Peak rose from the sea in a sharp cliff. The fence followed the top of this cliff, leaving a narrow path between itself and the actual verge.

"If you want to see anything," said Simon, "you'll have to get up there. Do you mind heights?"

"Speaking for myself," said Gaunt, "they inspire me with vertigo, nausea, and a strongly marked impulse towards *felo-de-se*. However, having come so far I refuse to turn back. That fence looks tolerably strong. I shall cling to it." He smiled at Barbara. "If you should happen to notice the mad glint of suicide in my eye," he said, "I wish you'd fling your arms round me and thus restore me to my nobler self."

"But what about your leg, sir?" said Dikon. "How's it holding out?"

"Never mind about my leg. You go ahead with Claire. We'll take it in our own time."

Dikon, having gathered from sundry pieces of distressingly obvious pantomime on Simon's part that this suggestion met with his approval, followed him at a gruelling pace up the track. The ocean spread out blandly before them as they mounted. Dikon, unused to such exercise, very rapidly acquired a pain in his chest, a stitch, and a thudding heart. Sweat gathered behind his spectacles. The smooth soles of his shoes slipped on the dry grass, and Simon's hobnailed boots threw dust into his face.

"If we kick it in," said Simon presently, "we can get up to the place where I reckon I saw the signalling on Thursday night."

"Oh."

"The others won't come any farther than this."

They had climbed to a place where the track widened and ran out to a short headland. Here they found a group of some ten or twelve men who squatted on the dry turf, chewed ends of grass and stared out to sea. Two youths greeted Simon. Dikon recognized one of them as Eru Saul.

"What d'you know?" Simon asked.

"She's out there," said Eru. "Going down quick, now. You can pick her up through the glasses."

They had left the Colonel's glasses with Gaunt, but Eru lent them his. Dikon had some difficulty in focussing them but eventually the hazy blue field clarified and in a moment or two he found a tiny black triangle. It looked appallingly insignificant.

"They've been out to see if they could salvage anything," said Eru, "but not a chance. She's packed up all right. Tough!"

"I'll say," said Simon. "Come on, Bell."

Dikon returned the field-glasses, thanked Eru Saul and with feelings of the liveliest distaste meekly followed Simon up the fence line which now rose precipitously before flattening out to encompass a higher shoulder of the Peak. At last they reached a very small platform, no more than a shelf in the seaward face of the mountain. Dikon was profoundly relieved to see Simon, who was well ahead, come to a halt and squat on his heels.

"What I reckon," said Simon as Dikon crawled up beside him, "he must have worked it from here."

Dry-mouthed and still very short-winded, Dikon prepared to fling himself down on the ledge.

"Here!" said Simon. "Better cut that out. Stay where you are. We don't want it mucked up. Pity it rained yesterday."

"And what do you expect to find, may I ask?" asked Dikon acidly. Physical discomfort did not increase his tolerance for Simon's high-handedness. "Are you by any chance building on footprints? My poor fellow, let me tell you that footprints exist only on sandy beaches and in the minds of detective fiction-mongers. All that twittering about bent blades of grass and imprints slightly defaced by rain! In my opinion they do *not* occur."

"Don't they?" returned Simon combatively. "Somebody's been up this track ahead of us. Didn't you pick that?"

"How could I 'pick' anything when you did nothing but kick dust in my glasses? Show me a footprint and I'll believe in it. Not before."

"Good-oh, then. There. What's that?"

"You've just made it with your own flat foot," said Dikon crossly.

"What if I have? It's a print, isn't it? Goes to show."

"Possibly." Dikon wiped his glasses and peered round. "What are *those* things?" he said. "Over by the bank. Dents in the ground?"

He pointed and Simon gave a raucous cry of triumph. "What did I tell you. Prints!" He removed his boots and crossed to the bank. "You better take a look," he said. Dikon removed his shoes. He had a blister on each heel and was glad to do so. He joined Simon.

"Yes," he said. "The footprints after all, and I can tell you exactly how they would be described by the know-alls. 'Several confused impressions of the Booted Foot, two being more clearly defined and making an angle of approximately thirty degrees the one with the other. Distance between inside margins of heel, half an inch. Distance between position of outside margin of big toes, approximately ten inches. This

latter pair of impressions was found in damp clay but had
been protected from recent rain by a bank which overhung
them at a height of approximately three feet.' There's great
virtue in the word 'approximately.'"

"Good-ow!" said Simon on a more enthusiastic inflection
than he usually gave to this odious expression. "Nice work.
Go on."

"Nails in the soles and heels. Toes more deeply indented
than heels. Right foot, four nails in heel; six in sole. Left foot,
three in heel, six in sole. *Ergo,* he lost a nail."

"How much, he lost a nail?"

"*Ergo.* I'm being affected."

"Huh! Yeh, well, what sort of chap is he? Does he act like
Questing? Stands with his heels close together and his toes
apart. Puts more weight on his toes than his heels. Say what
you like, you can deduce quite a bit if you use your nut."

"As, for instance, he must be a dwarf."

"Eye?"

"The bank overhangs the prints at a height of three feet.
How could he stand?"

"Aw heck!"

"Would squatting fill the bill? The other prints show
where he scuffled round trying to settle."

"That's right. O.K., he squatted. For a good long time."

"With his weight forward on his toes," Dikon suggested.
He had begun to feel mildly stimulated. "The day was damp
at the time. Yesterday's rain was easterly and hasn't got in
under the bank. On Thursday night there was a light rain
from the sea."

"Don't I know it? I was away out there, don't forget."

Dikon looked out to his left. The shoulder of the hill hid
Harpoon and the harbour, but Simon's rock was just visible,
a shapeless spot down in the blue. "If you stand on the edge
you can just see the other boulders leading out to it," said
Simon.

"Thanks, I'll take your word for them."

"Gee, can't you see the sand spit under the water clearly
from up here? That's what it'll be like from the air. Coastal
patrol work. Cripey, I wish they'd get on with it and pull me
in."

Simon stood on the lip of the shelf and Dikon looked at

him. His chin was up. A light breeze whipped his hair back from his forehead. His shoulders were squared. Human beings gain prestige when they are seen at a great height against a simple background of sea and sky. Simon lost his uncouthness and became a significant figure. Dikon took off his glasses and wiped them. The young Simon was blurred.

"I envy you," said Dikon.

"Me? What for?"

"You have the right of entry to danger. You'll move out towards it. I'm one of the sort that sit pretty and wait. Blind as a bat, you know."

"Tough luck. Still, they reckon this is everyone's war, don't they?"

"They do."

"Lend a hand to catch this joker Questing. There's a job for you."

"Quite so," said Dikon, who already regretted his digression. "What have we decided? That Questing climbed up here on Thursday night, wearing hobnailed boots. That he signalled to a U-boat information about a ship loading at Harpoon and sailing the following night? By the way, can you visualize Questing in hobnailed boots?"

"He's been mucking about on the Peak for the last three months. He must have learnt sense."

"Perhaps they are hobnailed shoes. Was there moonlight on Thursday night?"

"Not after the rain came up, but he was here by then. There was, before that."

"They'll have to look at all his shoes. Should we perhaps try to make a sort of record of these prints? Glare at them until they leave an indelible impression on our minds and we can take oaths about them hereafter? Or shall I try to make a sketch of them?"

"That's an idea. If they knew their business they'd take casts. I've read about that."

"Who precisely are *they?*" asked Dikon, taking out his notebook and beginning to sketch. "The police? The army? Have we got anything approaching a secret service in New Zealand? What's the matter!" he added angrily. Simon had uttered a loud exclamation and Dikon's pencil skidded across his sketch.

"There's some bloke out here from Scotland Yard. A big pot. There was something about him in the papers a week or two back. They reckoned he'd come here to investigate fifth-columnists, and Uncle James said they ought to be put in jail for giving away official secrets. By cripey, he's the joker we ought to get hold of. Go to the top if you want to get things done."

"What's his name?"

"That's the catch," said Simon. "I've forgotten."

iii

Barbara and Gaunt did not go up the hill after all. They watched Simon and Dikon clinging to the fence and slipping on the sort grass and friable soil.

"I have decided that my leg jibes at the prospect," said Gaunt. "Don't you think it would be much pleasanter to go a little way towards the sea and smoke a cigarette? This morbid desire to look at sinking ships! Isn't it kinder to let her go down alone? I feel that it would be rather like watching the public execution of a good friend. And we know the crew is safe. Don't you agree?"

Barbara agreed, thinking that he was talking to her as if she herself were a good friend. It was the first time they had been alone together.

They found a place near to the sea. Gaunt flung himself down with an air of boyish enthusiasm which would have intensely annoyed his secretary. Barbara knelt, sitting back on her heels, the light wind blowing full in her face.

"Do you mind if I tell you you should always do your hair like that?" said Gaunt.

"Like this?" She raised her hand to her head. The wind flattened her cotton dress. It might have been drenched in rain, so closely did it cling to her. She turned her head quickly, and Gaunt, as quickly, looked again at her hair. "Yes. Straight off your face and brushed fiercely back. No frizz or nonsense. Terribly simple."

"Orders?" said Barbara. It was so miraculously easy to talk to him.

"Please."

"I'm afraid I'll look very bony."

"But that's how you should look when you have good bones. Do you know that soon after we met I told Dikon I thought you had—But I'm making you self-conscious, and that's bad manners, isn't it? I'm afraid," said Gaunt with a sort of aftermath of the Rochester manner, "that I'm accustomed to say pretty much what I think. Do you mind?"

"No," said Barbara, suddenly at a loss.

It was years, Gaunt thought, since he had met a young woman who was simply shy. Nervous, or deliberately coy young women, yes; but not a girl who blushed with pleasure and was too well-mannered to turn away her head. If only she would always behave like this she would be charming. He was taking exactly the right line with her. He began to talk to her about himself.

Barbara was enchanted. He spoke so intimately, as if she were somebody with a special gift of understanding. He told her all sorts of things. How, as a boy in school, he had been set to read the "Eve of Crispian" speech from *Henry V,* and had started in the accepted wooden style which he now imitated comically for her amusement. Then, so he told her, something had happened to him. The heady phrases began to ring through his voice. To the astonishment of his English master (here followed a neat mimicry of the English master) and, strange to say, the enthralment of his classmates, he gave the speech something of its due. "There were mistakes, of course. I had no technique beyond an instinctive knowledge of certain values. But—" he tapped the breast pocket of his coat—"it was *there.* I knew then that I must become a Shakespearean actor. I heard the lines as if someone else spoke them:—

> *"And Crispin Crispian shall ne're go by,*
> *From this day to the ending of the world,*
> *But we in it shall be remembered."*

Gulls mewed overhead and the sea thudded and dragged at the coast, a thrilling accompaniment, Barbara thought, to the lovely words.

"Isn't there any more?" she asked greedily.

"Little ignoramus! There's a lot more." He took her hand. "You are my Cousin Westmoreland. Listen, my fair cousin." And he gave her the whole speech. It was impossible for him to be anything but touched and delighted by her eagerness, by the tears of excitement that stood in her eyes when he ended. He still held her hand. Dikon, limping over the brow of the hill ahead of Simon, was just in time to see him lightly kiss it.

Dikon drove back with Simon, completely mum, beside him in the front seat. Gaunt and Barbara, after a few desultory questions about the wreck, were also silent, a circumstance that Dikon mistrusted, and with some reason, for Barbara was lost in enchantment. One glance at her face had been all too enlightening. "Besotted," Dikon muttered to himself. "What has he been up to? Telling her the story of his life, I don't doubt, with all the trimmings. Acting his socks off. Kissing her hand. By heaven, if the place had a second floor, before we knew where we were he'd be treating her to the balcony scene. Romeo with fibrositis! The truth is, he's reached the age when a girl's ignorance and adulation can make a fool of a man. It's revolting." But although he allowed himself to fume inwardly, he would have resented and denied such imputations against Gaunt from any outsider, for not the least of his troubles lay in his sense of divided allegiance. He reflected that, Barbara apart, he liked his employer too much to enjoy the spectacle of him making a fool of himself.

When they returned to the house they found Mr. Septimus Falls and Mr. Questing sitting in deck-chairs side by side on the verandah, a singular association. Dikon had implored Simon to show no signs of particular animosity when he encountered Questing, but was nevertheless very much relieved when Simon grunted a word of thanks to Gaunt and walked off in the direction of his cabin. Barbara, with a radiant face, ran straight past Questing into the house. Gaunt, before leaving the car, leant forward and said: "I haven't been so delightfully entertained for years. She's a darling and she shall certainly be told who sent the dress."

Dikon drove the car round to the garage.

When he returned he found that Questing, having introduced Septimus Falls to Gaunt, had adopted the manner of a sort of referee or ring-master. "I've been telling this gentleman all the morning, Mr. Gaunt, that you and he must get together. 'Here's our celebrated guest,' I said, 'with nobody to provide him with the correct cultural stimulus until you came along.' It seems this gentleman is a great student of the drama, Mr. Gaunt."

"Really?" said Gaunt, and contrived to suggest a distaste of Questing without positively insulting Falls.

Falls made a deprecating and slightly precious gesture. "Mr. Questing is too generous," he said. "The merest tyro, I assure you, sir. Calliope rather than Thalia commands me."

"Oh, yes?"

"There you are!" cried Mr. Questing admiringly. "And I don't even know what you're talking about. Mr. Falls has been telling me that he's a great fan of yours, Mr. Gaunt."

His victims laughed unhappily and Falls, with an air of making the best of a bad business, said: "That, at least, is true. I don't believe I've missed a London production of yours for ten years or more."

"Splendid," said Gaunt more cordially. "You've met my secretary, haven't you? Let's sit down for pity's sake." They sat down. Mr. Falls hitched his chair a little nearer to Gaunt's.

"I've often thought I should like to ask you to confirm or refute a pet theory of mine," he said. "It concerns Horatio's very palpable lie in reference to the liquidation of Rosencrantz and Guildenstern. It seems to me that in view of your brilliant reading of Hamlet's account of the affair—"

"Yes, yes. I know what you're at. *'He never gave commandment for their death.'* Pure whitewash. What else?"

"I have always thought the line refers to Claudius. Your Horatio—"

"No, no. To Hamlet. Obviously to Hamlet."

"Of course the comparison is absurd, but I was going to ask you if you had ever seen Gustave Grundgen's treatment—"

"Grundgen's? But that's Hitler's tame actor, isn't it?"

"Yes, yes." Mr. Falls made a little movement, gave a little yelp, and clapped his hand to the small of his back. "This odious complaint!" he lamented. "Yes, that is the fellow. A ridiculous performer. You never saw anything like the Hamlet. Madder and madder and madder does he grow, and they think he's marvellous. I witnessed it. Before the war, of course. Naturally."

"Naturally!" said Questing with a loud laugh.

"But we were speaking of the play. I have always considered—" And Mr. Falls was off on an extremely knowledgeable discussion of the minor puzzles of the play. Six years' association with Shakespearean productions had not killed Dikon's passion for Hamlet and he listened with interest. Falls was a good talker if an affected one. He had all sorts of mannerisms, nervous movements of his hands that accorded ill with his face, which was tranquil and remarkably comely. He had taken out a pipe, but, instead of lighting it, emphasized the points in his argument by knocking it out against the leg of his deck-chair. "To make *three* acts where in the text there are *five!*" he said excitedly, and the dottle from his pipe flew about Mrs. Claire's clean verandah as he illustrated his theme with appropriate and angry raps on the chair leg: "Three, mind you, three, three! In God's name, why not leave the play as he wrote it?"

"But we do play it in its entirety, sometimes."

"My dear sir, I know you do. I am enormously grateful as all Shakespeareans must be. Do forgive me. I am riding my hobby-horse to death, and before you of all people. Arrogant presumption!"

"Not a bit of it," said Gaunt cheerfully. "I've been off my native diet long enough to have developed an inordinate appetite for it. But I must say I fail to see your point about the acts. Since we must abridge..."

Barbara looked out of the dining-room door, saw Questing still there, and hesitated. Without pausing in his argument, Gaunt put out his hand, inviting her to join them. She sat beside Dikon on the step. "This will be good for you, my child," said Gaunt in parenthesis, and she glowed ardently. "What on earth has happened to her?" Dikon wondered. "That's the same dress, better than the others because it's simpler, but the same. She's brushed her hair back since we came in, and that's an improvement, of course, but what's happened to *her?* I haven't heard a hoot from the

girl for days, and she's stopped pulling faces." Gaunt had
begun to talk about the more difficult plays, of *Troilus and
Cressida*, of *Henry VI*, and finally of *Measure for Measure*.
Falls, still beating his irritating tattoo, followed him eagerly.

"Of course he was an agnostic," he cried—"the most
famous of the soliloquies proves it. If further proof is needed
this play provides it."

"You mean Claudio? I played him once as a very young
actor. Yes, that speech! It's death without flattery, isn't it? It
strikes cold.

> *"Ay, but to die, and go we know not where;*
> *To lie in cold obstruction, and to rot . . ."*

Gaunt's voice flattened out to a horrid monotone and his
audience stirred uneasily. Mrs. Claire came to one of the
windows and listened with a doubtful smile. Fall's pipe
dropped from his hand and he leant forward. The door of Dr.
Ackrington's room opened and he stood there, attentive.
"Do go on," said Mr. Falls. The icy sentences went forward.

> *"To be imprison'd in the viewless winds . . ."*

Mr. Questing, always polite, tiptoed across the verandah,
and retrieved the pipe. Falls seemed not to hear him.
Questing stood with his pipe in his hand, his head on one
side, and an expression of proprietary admiration on his face.

> *". . . to be worse than worst*
> *Of those that lawless and incertain thought*
> *Imagine howling."*

A shadow fell across the pumice. Smith, unshaven and
looking very much the worse for wear, appeared from the
direction of the cabin, followed by Simon. They stopped
dead. Smith passed a shaky hand across his face and pulled
at his underlip. Simon, after a disgusted stare at Gaunt,
watched Questing.

Gaunt drew to the close of the short and terrifying speech.
Dikon reflected that perhaps he was the only living actor who

could get away with Shakespeare at high noon on the verandah of a thermal spa. That he had not embarrassed his listeners but had made some of them coldly uneasy was very apparent. He had forced them to think of death.

Questing, after clearing his throat, broke into loud applause, tapping Mr. Falls's pipe enthusiastically against the verandah post. "Well, well, well," cried Mr. Questing. "If that wasn't an intellectual treat! Quite a treat, Mr. Falls, wasn't it?"

"My pipe, I believe," said Mr. Falls, politely, and took it. "Thank you." He turned to Gaunt. "Of course you may lay the agnosticism of those lines at the door of character and set against them a hundred others that are orthodox enough, but my own opinion—"

"*As You Like It* has always been *my* favourite," said Mrs. Claire from the window. "Such a pretty play. All those lovely woodland scenes. Dear Rosalind!"

Dr. Ackrington advanced from his doorway. "With all this modern taste for psychopathological balderdash," he said, "I wonder you get anyone to listen to the plays."

"On the contrary," said Gaunt stuffily, "there is a renaissance."

Huia came out—clanging her inevitable bell. The Colonel appeared from his study looking vaguely miserable.

"Is that lunch?" he asked. "What have you been talking about? Sounded as if someone was making a stump speech or somethin'."

Barbara whispered hurriedly in her father's ear.

"Eh? I can't hear you," he complained. "What?" He stared at Gaunt. "Out of a play, was it? Good Lord." He seemed to be faintly disgusted, but presently an expression of complacency stole over his face. "We used to do quite a bit of theatrical poodle-fakin' when I was a subaltern in India," he said. "They put me into one of their plays once. Damn' good thing. D'you know it? It's called *Charley's Aunt*."

iv

Throughout lunch it was obvious to Dikon that Simon was big with some new theory. Indeed, so eloquent were his glances that neither Questing nor anybody else, Dikon thought, could possibly mistake their meaning. Dikon himself was in a state of mind so confused that he seemed to be living in the middle of a rather bad dream. Anxiety about Barbara, based on an emotion which he refused to define, a disturbing change in his own attitude towards his employer, and an ever-increasing weight of apprehension which the war bred in all New Zealanders at that time—all these elements mingled in a vague cloud of uneasiness and alarm. And then there was Questing. In spite of Simon's discoveries, in spite, even, of the witness of the torpedoed ship, Dikon still found it difficult to cast Questing for the role of spy. Indeed, he was still enough of a New Zealander to doubt the existence of enemy agents in his country at all, still inclined to think that they existed only as bugaboos in the minds of tiresome old ladies and clubmen. And yet . . . mentally he ticked off the points against Questing. Had he tried to bring about Smith's destruction, and if so, why? Why did he pretend that he had been to Pohutukawa Bay, when, as Dr. Ackrington had proved by his pitfall, he hadn't been near the place? If he visited the Peak only to hunt for curios, why should he have six times flashed his signal of three, five, and three, from a place where obviously no curios could be buried? He couldn't help looking at Questing, at his smooth, rather naive face, his businessman's clothes, his not altogether convincing air of commercial acumen. Were these the outward casings of a potential murderer, who was quietly betraying his country? Irrelevantly, Dikon thought: "This war is changing the values of my generation. There are all sorts of things that we have thought funny that we shall never think funny again." For perhaps the first time he contemplated coldly and deliberately a possible invasion of New Zealand. As he thought, the picture clarified. An emotion long dormant, rooted in the very soil of his native country, roused in him, and he recognized it as anger. He realized, finally, that he could no longer go on as he was. Somehow, no matter how uselessly, he, like Simon, must go forward to danger.

It was with this new determination in his mind that he visited Simon in his cabin after lunch. "Did you guess I wanted to see you?" asked Simon. "I didn't like to drop the hint over there. He might have spotted it."

"My dear old thing, the air was electric with your hints. What's occurred?"

"We've got him," said Simon. "Didn't you pick it? Before lunch? Him and his pipe?"

Dikon gaped at him.

"Missed it, did you?" said Simon complacently. "And there you were sitting where you might have touched him. What beats me is why he did it. D'you reckon he's got it so much on his mind he's acting kind of automatically?"

"If I had the faintest idea what you were talking about, I might attempt to answer you."

"Aren't you conscious yet? I was sitting in here trying to dope things out when I heard it. I snooped round to the corner. All through the hooey Gaunt and Falls were spilling about Shakespeare or someone. It was the same in every detail."

"For pity's sake, what was the same in every detail?"

"The tapping. A long one repeated three times. Dah, dah, dah. Then five short dits. Then three shorts. Then the whole works repeated. The flashes from the cliff all over again. So what have you?"

They stared at each other. "It just doesn't make sense," said Dikon. "Why? Why? Why?"

"Search me."

"Coincidence?"

"The odds against coincidence are long enough to make you dizzy. No, I reckon I'm right. It's habit. He's had to memorize it and he's gone over and over it in his mind before he shot the works on Thursday night . . ."

"Hold on. Hold on. Whose habit?"

"Aw hell," said Simon disgustedly. "You're dopey. Who the heck are we talking about?"

"We're talking about two different people," said Dikon excitedly. "Questing had picked up that pipe just before you came on the scene. It wasn't Questing who tapped out your blasted signal. It was Mr. Septimus Falls."

CHAPTER VIII

CONCERT

The telephone at Wai-ata-tapu was on a party line. The Claires' tradesmen used it, and occasional week-end trippers who rang up to give notice of their arrival. Otherwise, until Gaunt and Dikon came, it was seldom heard. The result of housing a celebrity, however, had begun to work out very much as Mr. Questing had predicted. During the first weekend, quite a spate of visitors had arrived, ostensibly for thermal *divertissements*, actually, so it very soon transpired, with the object of getting a close-up view of Geoffrey Gaunt. These visitors, with an air of studied nonchalance, walked up and down the verandah, delayed over their tea, and attempted to pump Huia as to the whereabouts of the celebrity. The hardier among them came provided with autograph books which passed, by way of Barbara, from Huia to Dikon and thence to Gaunt, who, to the astonishment of Mrs. Claire, cheerfully signed every one of them. He kept to his room, however, until the last of the visitors, trying not to look baffled, had lost patience and gone home. Once, but only once, Mr. Questing had succeeded in luring him onto the verandah, and on Gaunt's discovering what he was up to had been treated to such a blast of temperament as sent him back into the house nervously biting his fingers.

On this particular Saturday afternoon, though there were no trippers, the telephone rang almost incessantly. Was it true that there was to be a concert that evening? Was Mr. Geoffrey Gaunt going to perform at it? Could one obtain tickets and, if so, were the receipts to go to the patriotic funds? So insistent did these demands become that at last Huia was dispatched over the hill for definite instructions from old Rua. She returned, laughing excitedly, with the message that everybody would be welcome.

The Maori people are a kindly and easy-going race. In temperament they are so vivid a mixture of Scottish Highlander and Irishman that to many observers the resemblance seems more than fortuitous. Except in the matter of family and tribal feuds, which they keep up with the liveliest enthusiasm, they are extremely hospitable. Rua and his people were not disturbed by the last-minute transformation into a large public gathering of what was to have been a private party between themselves and the Springs. Huia, who returned with Eru Saul and an escort of grinning youths, reported that extra benches were being hurriedly knocked up, and might they borrow some armchairs for the guests of honour?

"Py korry!" said one of the youths. "Big crowd coming, Mrs. Keeah. Very good party. Te Mayor coming too, all the time more people."

"Now, Maui," said Mrs. Claire gently, "why don't you speak nicely as you did when you used to come to Sunday school?"

Huia and the youths laughed uproariously. Eru sniggered.

"Tell Rua we shall be pleased to lend the chairs. Did you say the Mayor was coming?"

"That's right, Mrs. Keeah. We'll be having a good party, all right."

"No drink, I hope," said Mrs. Claire severely, and was answered by further roars of laughter. "We don't want Mr. Gaunt to go away thinking our boys don't know how to behave, do we?"

"No fear," said Maui obligingly. Eru gave an offensive laugh and Mrs. Claire looked coldly at him.

"Plenty tea for everybody," said Maui.

"That will be very nice. Well now you may come in and get the chairs."

"Grandfather's compliments," said Huia suddenly, "and he sent you this, please."

It was a letter from old Rua, written in a style so urbane that Lord Chesterfield might have envied its felicity. It suggested that though the Maori people themselves did not venture to hope that Gaunt would come in any other capacity than that of honoured guest, yet they had been made aware of certain rumours from a *pakeha* source. If, in Mrs. Claire's opinion, there was any foundation of truth in these rumours, Rua would be grateful if she advised him of it, as certain preparations should be made for so distinguished a guest.

Mrs. Claire in some perturbation handed the letter over to Dikon, who took it to his employer.

"Translated," said Dikon, "it means that they're burning their guts out for you to perform. I'm sure, sir, you'd like me to decline in the same grand style."

"Who said I was going to decline?" Gaunt demanded. "My compliments to this old gentleman, and I should be delighted to appear. I must decide what to give them."

"You could fell me with a feather," said Dikon to Barbara after early dinner. "I can't imagine what's come over the man. As a general rule platform performances are anathema to him. And at a little show like this!"

"Everything that's happening's so marvellous," said Barbara, "that I for one can't believe it's true."

Dikon rubbed his nose and stared at her.

"Why are you looking at me like that?" Barbara demanded.

"I didn't know I was," said Dikon hastily.

"You're thinking I shouldn't be happy," she said with a sudden return to her owlish manner, "because of Mr. *Questing* and *ruin* staring us in the *face*."

"No, no. I assure you that I'm delighted. It's only . . ."

"Yes?"

"It's only that I hope it's going to last."

"Oh." She considered him for a moment and then turned white. "I'm not thinking about that. I don't believe I mind so very much. You see, I'm not building on anything. I'm just happy."

He read in her eyes the knowledge that she had betrayed herself. To forestall, if he could, the hurt that her pride would suffer when it recovered from the opiate Gaunt had administered, Dikon said: "But you can build on looking very nice to-night. Are you going to wear the new dress?"

Barbara nodded. "Yes. I didn't change before dinner because of the washing-up. Huia wants to get off. But that's not what I mean about being happy . . ."

He cut in quickly. She must not be allowed to tell him the

true reason for her bliss. "Haven't you an idea who sent it to you?"

"None. Honestly. You see," said Barbara conclusively, "we don't know anyone in New Zealand well enough. You'd have to be a great friend, almost family, wouldn't you, to give a present like that? That's what's so puzzling."

Mr. Questing appeared from the dining-room in all the glory of a dinner jacket, a white waistcoat and his post-prandial cigar. As far as anybody at the Springs knew, he had not been invited to the concert, but evidently he meant to take advantage of its new and public character.

"What's all this I hear about a new dress?" he asked genially.

"I shall be late," said Barbara, and hurried into the house. Dikon reflected that surely nobody in the world but Mr. Questing would have had the gall, after what had happened by the lake, to attempt another three-cornered conversation with Barbara and himself. In some confusion, and because he could think of nothing else to say, Dikon murmured something about the arrival of an anonymous present. Mr. Questing took it very quietly. For a little while he made no comment, and then, with a foxy look at Dikon, he said: "Well, well, well, is that so? And the little lady just hasn't got a notion where it came from? Fancy that, now."

"I believe," said Dikon, already regretting his indiscretion, "that there is an aunt in India."

"And the pretty things come from Auckland, eh?"

"I don't think I said so."

"That's quite all right, Mr. Bell. Maybe you didn't," Mr. Questing conceded. "Between you and me, Mr. Bell, I know all about it."

"What!" cried Dikon, flabbergasted. "You do! But how the devil...?"

"Just a little chat with Dorothy Lamour."

"With...?"

"My pet name for the Dusky Maiden," Mr. Questing explained.

"Oh," said Dikon, greatly relieved. "Huia."

"Where do you reckon it came from, yourself?" asked Mr. Questing with an atrocious wink.

"The aunt, undoubtedly," said Dikon firmly, and on the

wings of a rapid flight of fancy he added: "She's in the habit of sending things to Miss Claire who writes to her most regularly. A very likely explanation is that at some time or another Miss Claire has mentioned this shop."

"Oh yeah?" said Mr. Questing. "Accidentally-done-on-purpose, sort of?"

"O.K., O.K., Mr. Bell. Quite so. You mustn't mind my little joke. India," he added thoughtfully. "That's quite a little way off, isn't it?" He walked away, whistling softly and waving a cigar. Dikon uttered a few very raw words under his breath. "He's guessed!" he thought. "Blast him, if he gets a chance he'll tell her." He polished his glasses on his handkerchief and stared dimly after the retreating figure of Mr. Questing. "Or will he?" he added dubiously.

ii

Although it had been built with European tools, the meetinghouse at the native settlement followed the traditional design of all Maori buildings. It was a single room surmounted by a ridged roof which projected beyond the gable. The barge-boards and supporting pillars were intricately covered in the formidable mode of Polynesian art. Growing out of the ridge-pole stood a wooden god with outthrust tongue and eyes of shell, squat, menacing, the symbol of the tribe's fecundity and its will to do battle. The traditional tree-fern poles and thatching had been replaced by timber and galvanized iron, but, nevertheless, the meeting-house contrived to distil a quintessence of savagery and of primordial culture.

The floor space, normally left clear, was now filled with a heterogeneous collection of seats. The Claires' armchairs, looking mildly astonished at their own transplantation, were grouped together in the front row. They faced a temporarily erected stage which was decked out with tree-fern, exquisitely woven cloaks, Union Jacks and quantities of fly-blown paper streamers. On the back were hung coloured prints of three Kings of England, two photographs of former premiers, and an enlargement of Rua as an M.P. On the platform stood a hard-bitten piano, three chairs and a table bearing the insignia of all British gatherings, a carafe of untempting water and a tumbler.

The Maori members of the audience had been present more or less all day. They squatted on the floor, on the edge of the stage, on the permanent benches along the sides and all over the verandah and front steps.

Among them was Eru Saul. Groups of youths collected round Eru. He talked to them in an undertone. There was a great deal of furtive giggling and sudden guffaws. At intervals Eru and his following would slouch off together and when they returned the boys were always noisier and more excited. At seven o'clock Simon, Colly and Smith arrived with three more chairs from Wai-ata-tapu. Colly and Simon stood about looking self-conscious, but Smith was at once absorbed into Eru Saul's faction.

"Hey, Eru!" said Smith, who had a pair of pumps in his pocket. "Do we wind up with a dance?"

"No chance!"

"No fear you don't wind up with a dance," said a woman's voice. "Last time you wind up with a dance you got tight. If you can't behave yourselves you don't have dances."

"Too bad," said Smith.

The owner of the voice was seated on the floor with her back against the stage. She was Mrs. Te Papa, an old lady with an incredibly aristocratic head tied up in a cerise handkerchief. Over her European dress she wore, in honour of the occasion, a magnificent flax skirt. She was the leading great-grandmother of the *hapu* and, though she did not bother much about her title, a princess of the Te Rarawas. Being one of the last of the old regime she had a tattooed chin. From her point of vantage she was able to call full-throated greetings and orders to members of her clan as they drifted in and out or put finishing touches to the decorations. She spoke always in Maori. If one of the younger fry answered her in English she reached forward and caught the offender a good-natured buffet. One of the oddities of contemporary Maori life may be seen in the fact that, though some of the people in outlying districts use a fragmentary and native-sounding form of English, yet they have only a rudimentary knowledge of their own tongue.

At half-past seven visitors from Harpoon and the surrounding districts began to appear. Old Rua Te Kahu came in wearing a feather cloak over his best suit and, with great urbanity, moved among his guests. Mrs. Te Papa rose magnificently and walked with the correct swinging gait of her youth to her appointed place.

At a quarter to eight a party of five white gentlemen, unhappily dressed in dinner suits and carrying music, were ushered into a special row of seats near the platform. These were members of the Harpoon Savage Club, famous throughout the district for their rendering in close harmony of Irish ballads. The last of them, an anxious small man, carried a large black bag, for he was also a ventriloquist. They were followed by a little girl with permanently waved hair who was dressed in frills, by her fierce mother, and by a firmly cheerful lady who carried a copy of *One Day When We Were Young*. It was to be a mixed entertainment.

An observer might have noticed that while the ladies of the district exchanged many nods and smiles, occasionally pointing at each other, with an air of playful astonishment, their men merely acknowledged one another by raising their eyebrows, winking, or very slightly inclining their heads to one side. This procedure changed when the member for the district came in as he shook hands heartily with almost everybody. At five minutes to eight the Mayor arrived with the Mayoress and shook hands with literally anyone who confronted him. They were shown into armchairs. By this time all the seats except those reserved for the official party were full and there were Maoris standing in solid groups at the far end of the hall, or settling themselves in parties on the floor. With the arrival of their guests they became circumspect and quiet. Those beautiful voices, that can turn English into a language composed almost entirely of deep-throated vowels, fell into silence, and the meeting-house buzzed with the noise made by white New Zealanders in the mass. It became very hot and the Maori people thought indulgently that it smelt of *pakeha*, while the *pakehas* thought a little less indulgently that it smelt of Maori.

At eight o'clock a premature wave of interest was caused by the arrival of Colonel Claire, Mr. Questing and Mr. Falls. They had walked over from the Springs, crossing the native thermal reserve by the short cut. Mrs. Claire, Barbara, Dr. Ackrington and Gaunt were to be driven by Dikon and would arrive by the main road. The three older men were ushered up to the official chairs, but Simon at once showed the whites of his eyes and backed away into a group of young Maoris where he was presently joined by Smith, who was still very puffy and pink-eyed, and by Colly.

Mrs. Te Papa was heard to issue an order. A party of girls in native dress came through the audience and mounted the stage. They carried in each hand cords from which hung balls made from dry leaves. Rua took up his station outside the door of the meeting-house. He was an impressive figure, standing erect in the half-light, his feather cloak hanging rigidly from his shoulders. So had his great-grandfather stood to welcome visitors from afar. Near to him were leading men among the clan and, in the offing, Mrs. Te Papa and other elderly ladies. Most of the Maori members of the audience turned to face the back of the meeting-house and as many as could do so leant out of the windows.

Out on the road a chiming motor horn sounded, and at least twenty people said importantly that they recognized it as Gaunt's. The conglomerate hum of voices rose and died out. In the hush that followed, Rua's attenuated chant of welcome pierced the night air.

"Haere mai. E te ururangi! Na wai taua?"

Each syllable was intoned and prolonged. It might have been the voice of the night wind from the sea, a primal voice, strange and disturbing to white listeners. Out in the dark Mrs. Te Papa and her supporters leant forward and stretched out their arms. Their hands fluttered rhythmically in the correct half-dance of greeting. Rua was honouring Gaunt with the almost forgotten welcome of tradition. The mutations of a century of white men's ways were pulled like cobwebs from the face of a savage culture, and the Europeans in the meeting-house become strangers.

As they moved forward from the car Gaunt said: "But we should reply. We should know what he is saying, and reply!"

"I'm not certain," said Dikon, "but I've heard at some time what it is. I fancy he's saying we've got a common ancestor, in the first parents. I think he asks us to say who we are."

"It's not really very *sensible*," Mrs. Claire murmured. "They *know* who we are. Some of their customs are not at all nice, I'm afraid, but they really mean this to be quite a compliment, poor dears."

"As of course it is," said Gaunt quickly. "I wish we could answer."

On a soft ripple of greetings from the Maori party he moved forward and shook hands with Rua. "He's at his best," Dikon thought. "He does this sort of thing admirably."

With Mrs. Claire and Gaunt leading, they made a formal entrance and for the first time Dikon saw Barbara in her new dress.

iii

She had been late and the rest of the party were already in the car when she ran out, huddled in a wrap of obviously Anglo-Indian origin. Apologizing nervously she scrambled into the back seat and Dikon had time only to see that her head shone sleekly. Gaunt had funked the hairdressing and make-up part of his plan, and when Dikon caught a glimpse of Barbara's face he was glad of this. She had paid a little timid attention to it herself. Mrs. Claire sat beside Dikon, Barbara between Gaunt and her uncle in the back seat. When they had started, Dikon thought, unaccountably, of the many many times that he had driven Gaunt out to parties, of the things that were always said by the women who went with them, of how they so anxiously took the temperature of their own pleasure; of restaurants and night-clubs reflecting each other's images like mirrors in a tailor's fitting-room; of the end of such parties and of Gaunt's fretful displeasure if the sequel was not a success; of money pouring out as if from the nerveless hands of an imbecile. Finally he thought of how, very gradually, his own reaction to this routine had changed. From being excited and stimulated he had become acquiescent and at last an addict. He was roused from this unaccountable retrospect, by Mrs. Claire who, twisting her plump little torso, peered back at her daughter. "Dear," she said, "isn't your hair rather odd? Couldn't you fluff it forward a little, softly?" And Gaunt had said quickly: "But I have been thinking how charming it looked." Dr. Ackrington, who up till now had not uttered a word, cleared his throat and said he supposed they were to suffer exquisite discomfort at the concert. "No air, wooden benches, smells and caterwauling. Hope you expect nothing better, Gaunt. The natives of this country have been ruined by their own inertia and the criminal imbecility of the white population. We- sent missionaries to stop them eating each other and bribed them with bad whisky to give us their land. We cured them of their own perfectly good communistic system, and taught them how to loaf on government support. We took away their chiefs and gave them trade-union secretaries. And for mating customs that agreed very well with them, we substituted, with a sanctimonious grimace, disease and holy matrimony."

"James!"

"A fine people ruined. Look at the young men! Spend their time in . . ."

"James!"

Gaunt, with the colour of laughter in his voice, asked if the Maori Battalion didn't prove that the warrior spirit lived again.

"Because in the army they've come under a system that agrees with them. Certainly," said Dr. Ackrington triumphantly.

For the remainder of the short drive they had been silent.

It was too dark outside the meeting-house for Dikon to see Barbara at all clearly. He knew, however, that she had left the cloak behind her. But when she walked before him through the audience, he saw that Gaunt had wrought a miracle. Dikon's connection with the theatre had taught him to think about clothes in terms of art, and it was with a curious mixture of regret and excitement that he now recognized the effect of Barbara's transformation upon himself. It had made a difference and he was not sure that he did not resent this. He felt as if Gaunt had forestalled him. "In a little while," he said, "even though I had not seen her like this, I should have loved her. *I* ought to have been the one to show her to herself."

She sat between Gaunt and her uncle. There were not enough armchairs to go round, and Dikon slipped into an extremely uncomfortable seat in the second row. "Definitely the self-effacing young secretary," he said to himself. In a state of great mental confusion he prepared to watch the concert, and ended by watching Barbara. The girls on the platform broke rhythmically into the opening dance. They were led by a stout lady who, turning from side to side, cast extraordinarily significant glances about her, and made Dikon feel rather shy.

Of all the Maori clans living in this remote district of the far North, Rua's was the least sophisticated. They sang and postured as their ancestors had done and their audience was spared Maori imitations of popular ballad-mongers and crooners. The words and gestures that they used had grown out of the habit of a primitive people and told of their canoes, their tillage, their mating, and their warfare. Many of the songs, sacred to the rites of death, are not considered suitable for public performance, but there was one they sang that night that was to be remembered with a shudder by everyone who heard it.

Rua, in a little speech, introduced it. It had been composed, he said, by an ancestress of his on the occasion of the death of a maiden who unwittingly committed sacrilege and died in Taupo Tapu. He repeated the horrific legend that, one night on the hill-top, he had related to Smith. The song, he explained, was not a funeral dirge and therefore not particularly tapu. His eyes flashed for a moment as he glanced at Questing. He added blandly that he hoped the story might be of interest.

The song was very short and simple, a minor thread of melody that wavered about through a few plain phrases, but the hymn-like over-sweetness of some of the other songs was absent in this one. Dikon wondered how much its icy under-current of horror depended upon a knowledge of its theme.

In the penultimate line a single girl's voice rang out in a piercing scream, the cry of the maiden as she went to her death in the seething mud cauldron. It left an uncomfortable and abiding impression, which was not dispelled by the subsequent activities of the Savage Club quartette, the ventriloquist, the infant prodigy, or the determined soprano.

Gaunt had said that he would appear last on the programme. With what Dikon considered ridiculous solicitude, he had told Barbara to choose for him and she had at once asked for the Crispian Day speech: "The one we had this morning." "Then he *was* spouting the Bard by the sad sea waves," thought Dikon vindictively. "Good God, it's nauseating."

Gaunt said afterwards that he changed his mind about the opening speech because he realized that his audience would demand an encore, and he thought it better to finish up with the *Henry V*. But Dikon always believed that he had been influenced in his choice by the echo of the little song about death. For after opening rather obviously with the Bastard's speech on England, he turned sombrely to Macbeth.

> *"I have almost forgot the taste of fears..."*

and continued to the end

> *"...it is a tale*
> *Told by an idiot, full of sound and fury,*
> *Signifying nothing."*

It is a terrible speech and Gaunt's treatment of it, a deadly calm monotone, struck very cold indeed. When he had ended there was a second's silence, "and then," Dikon said afterwards to Barbara, "they clapped because they wanted to get some warmth back into their hands." Gaunt watched them with a faint smile, collected himself, and then gave them *Henry V* with everything he'd got, bringing the Maori members of his audience to their feet, cheering. In the end he had to do the speech before Agincourt as well.

He came down glowing. He was, to use a phrase that has been done to death by actors, a great artist, but an audience meant only one thing to him: it was a single entity that must

fall in love with him, and, as a corollary, with Shakespeare.
Nobody knew better than Gaunt that to rouse an audience
whose acquaintance with the plays was probably confined to
the first line of Antony's oration was very nice work indeed.
Rua, pacing to and fro in the traditional manner, thanked
him first in Maori and then in English. The concert drew to
an uproarious conclusion. "And now," said Rua, "the King."

But before the audience could get to its feet Mr. Questing
was on his and had walked up on the platform.

It is unnecessary to give Mr. Questing's speech in detail.
Indeed, it is almost enough to say that it was a *tour de force* of
bad taste, and that its author, though by no means drunk,
was, as Colly afterwards put it, ticking-over very sweetly. He
called Gaunt up to the platform and forced him to stand first
on one foot and then on the other for a quarter of an hour.
Mr. Questing was, he said, returning thanks for a real
intellectual treat but it very soon transpired that he was also
using Gaunt as a kind of bait for possible visitors to the
Springs. What was good enough for the famous Geoffrey
Gaunt, he intimated, was good enough for anybody. Upon
this one clear harp he played in divers keys while the party
from Wai-ata-tapu grew clammy with shame. Dikon, filled
with the liveliest apprehension, watched the glow of
complacency die in his employer's face to be succeeded by all
the signs of extreme fury. "My God," Dikon thought, "he's
going to throw a temperament." Simultaneously, Barbara,
with rising terror, observed the same phenomena in her
uncle.

Mr. Questing, with a beaming face, at last drew to his
insufferably fulsome conclusion, and the Mayor, who had
obviously intended to make a speech himself, rose to his feet,
faced the audience, and let out a stentorian bellow.

"*For-or* . . ." sang the Mayor encouragingly.

And the audience, freed from the bondage of Mr.
Questing's oratory, thankfully proclaimed Gaunt as a jolly
good fellow.

But the party was not yet at an end. Steaming trays of tea
were brought in from outside, and formidable quantities of
food.

Dikon hurried to his employer and discovered him to be
in the third degree of temperament, breathing noisily

through his nostrils and conversing with unnatural politeness. The last time Dikon had seen him in this condition had been at a rehearsal of the fight in "Macbeth." The Macduff, a timid man whose skill with the claymore had not equalled that of his adversary, continually backed away from Gaunt's onslaught and so incensed him that in the end, quite beside himself with fury, he dealt the fellow a swinging blow and chipped the point off his collarbone.

Gaunt completely ignored his secretary, accepted a cup of strong and milky tea, and stationed himself beside Barbara. There he was joined by Dr. Ackrington, who, in a voice that trembled with fury, began to apologize, none too quietly, for Questing's infamies. Dikon could not hear everything that Dr. Ackrington said, but the word "horsewhipping" came through very clearly several times. It struck him that he and Barbara, hovering anxiously behind these two angry men, were for all the world like a couple of seconds at a prize-fight.

Upon this ludicrous but alarming pantomime came the cause of it, Mr. Questing himself. With his thumbs in the armholes of his white waistcoat he balanced quizzically from his toes to his heels and looked at Barbara through half-closed eyes.

"Well, well, well," Mr. Questing purred in a noticeably thick voice. "So we've got 'em all on, eh? And very nice too. So she didn't know who sent them to her? Fancy that, now. Not an idea, eh? Must have been Auntie in India, huh? Well, well, well!"

If he wished to cause a sensation, he met with unqualified success. They gaped at him. Barbara said in a small desperate voice: "But if it wasn't . . . ? It couldn't have been . . . ?"

"I'm not saying a thing," cried Mr. Questing in high glee. "Not a thing." He leered possessively upon Barbara, dug Dr. Ackrington in the waistcoat and clapped Gaunt on the back. "Great work, Mr. Gaunt," he said. "Bit highbrow for me, y'know, but they seemed to take it. Mind, I was interested. I used to do a bit of reciting myself at one time. Humorous monologues. Hope you liked the little pat on the back I gave you. It all helps, doesn't it? Even at a one-eyed little show like this," he added in a spirituous whisper, and, laughing easily, turned to find Rua at his elbow. "Why, hullo, Rua," Mr. Questing continued without batting an eyelid. "Great little show. See you some more." And, humming the refrain of the song about death, he moved forward to shake hands heartily with the Mayor. He made a sort of royal progress to the door and finally strolled out.

Later, when it was of enormous importance that he should remember every detail of the next few minutes, Dikon was to find that he retained only a few disconnected impressions. Barbara's look of desolation: Mr. Septimus Falls in pedantic conversation with Mrs. Claire and the Colonel, both of whom seemed to be wildly inattentive; the startling blasphemies that Gaunt whispered as he looked after Questing—these details only was he able to focus in a field of hazy recollections.

It was Rua, he decided afterwards, who saved the situation. With the adroitness of a diplomat at a difficult conference, he talked through Dr. Ackrington's furious expostulations and, without appearing to hurry, somehow succeeded in presenting the Mayoral party to Gaunt. They got through the next few minutes without an actual flare-up.

It must have been Rua, Dikon decided, who asked a member of the glee club to strike up the National Anthem on the meeting-house piano.

As they moved towards the entrance, Gaunt, speaking in a furious whisper, told Dikon to drive the Claires home without him.

"But . . ." Dikon began.

"Will you do as you're told?" said Gaunt. "I'm walking."

He remembered to shake hands with Rua and then slipped up a side aisle and out by the front door. The rest of the party became involved in a series of introductions forced upon them by the Mayor and, escaping from these, fell into the clutches of a very young reporter from the *Harpoon Courier* who, having let Gaunt escape him, seized upon Dikon and Mrs. Claire.

At last Dr. Ackrington said loudly: "I'm walking."

"But James, dear," Mrs. Claire protested gently. "Your leg!"

"I said I was walking, Agnes. You can take Edward. I'll tell Gaunt."

Before Dikon, who was separated from him by one or two people, could do anything to stop him, he had edged between a row of chairs and gone out by the side aisle.

"Then," said Dikon to Mrs. Claire, "perhaps the Colonel would like to come with us?"

"Yes, yes," said Mrs. Claire uneasily. "I am sure . . . Edward! Where is he?"

He was some way ahead. Dikon could see his white crest moving slowly towards the door.

"We'll catch him when we get outside," he said.

"Quite a crush, isn't it?" said Mr. Falls at his elbow. "More like the West End every moment."

Dikon turned to look at him. The remark seemed to be not altogether in character. Mr. Falls raised an eyebrow. A theatrical phrase in common usage came into Dikon's mind. "He's got good appearance," he thought.

"I'm afraid the Colonel has escaped us," said Mr. Falls.

As they moved slowly down the aisle Dikon was conscious of a feeling of extreme urgency, a sense of being obstructed, such as one sometimes experiences in a nightmare. Barbara's distress assumed a disproportionate significance. Dikon was determined that she should not be hoodwinked by Mr. Questing's outrageous hint that he had sent the dress, yet he could not tell her that Gaunt had done so. And where was Gaunt? In his present state of mind he was capable of anything. It was highly probable that at this very moment he was hot on Questing's track.

At last they were out in the warm air. The night was clear and the stars shone brightly. The houses of Rua's *hapu* were dimly visible against the blackness of the hills. A tall fence of manuka poles showed dramatically against the night sky, resembling in the half-light the palisade that had stood there in the days when the village was a fort. Most of the visitors had already gone. From out of the dark came the sound of many quiet voices and of one, a man's, that seemed to be raised in anger. "But it is a Maori voice," Dikon said. In a distant hut one or two women broke quietly into the refrain of the little song. So still was the air that in the intervals between these sounds Taupo-tapu and the lesser mud pots could be heard, placidly working in the dark, out on the native reserve: *plop plop-plop,* a monstrously domestic noise.

Dikon was oppressed by the sensation of something

primordial in which he himself had no part. Three small
boys, their brown faces and limbs scarcely discernible in the
shadow of the meeting-house, suddenly darted out in front of
Barbara and Dikon. Striking the ground with their bare feet
and slapping their thighs they sketched the movements of the
war-dance. They thrust out their tongues and rolled their
eyes. *"Eee-e! Eee-e,"* they said, making their voices deep. A
woman spoke out of the dark, scolding them for their
boldness and calling them home. They giggled skittishly and
ran away. "They are too cheeky," the invisible woman's voice
said profoundly.

The Colonel and Mr. Falls had disappeared. Mrs. Claire
was still by the meeting-house, engaged in a long conversation with Mrs. Te Papa.

"Let's bring the car round, shall we?" said Dikon to
Barbara. He was determined to get a word with her alone.
She walked ahead of him quickly and he followed, stumbling
in the dark.

"Jump into the front seat," he said. "I want to talk to you."
But when they were in the car he was silent for a time,
wondering how to begin, and astonished to find himself so
greatly disturbed by her nearness.

"Now listen to me," he said at last. "You've got hold of the
idea that Questing sent you those damned clothes, haven't
you?"

."But of course he did. You heard what he said. You saw
how he looked." And with an air of simplicity that he found
very touching she added: "And I did look nice, didn't I?"

"You little ninny!" Dikon scolded. "You did and you do
and you shall continue to look nice."

"You knew that wasn't true before you said it. Shall I have
to give it back myself, do you imagine? Or do you think my
father might do it for me? I suppose I ought to hate my lovely
dress but I can't quite do that."

"Really," Dikon cried, "you're the most irritating girl in a
quiet way that I have ever encountered. Why should you
jump to the conclusion he did it? The man's slightly tight
anyway. See here, if Questing sent you the things, I'll buy
Wai-ata-tapu myself and run it as a lunatic asylum."

"How can you be so certain?"

"It's a matter of psychology," Dikon blustered.

"If you mean he's not the sort of person to do a thing like that," said Barbara with some spirit, "I think you're quite 'wrong. You've seen how frightful his behaviour can be. He just wouldn't know it isn't done."

Dikon could think of no answer. "I don't know anything about that," he said disagreeably. "I merely think it's idiotic to say he had anything to do with it."

"If you think I'm idiotic," said Barbara loudly, "I wonder you bother to mix yourself up in our affairs at all." And she added childishly in a trembling voice: "Anyway it's quite *obvious* that you think I'm *hopeless*."

"I you want to know what I think about you," Dikon said furiously, "I think you deliberately make the worst of yourself. If you didn't pull faces like a clown and do silly things with your voice you'd be remarkably attractive."

"Good Lord, that's absolutely impertinent!" cried Barbara, stung to anger. "How *dare* you," she added, "how *dare* you speak about me like that!"

"You asked for an honest opinion..."

"I didn't. So you've no business to give it." As this statement was true Dikon made no attempt to counter it. "I'm uncouth and crude and I irritate you," Barbara continued.

"Then stop talking!" Dikon shouted. He did not mean to kiss her, he was telling himself. He had not even thought of doing so. It was by some compulsion that it happened, some chance touch upon an emotional reflex. Having begun, there seemed to be no reason why he should stop, though an onlooker in his brain was saying quite distinctly: "This is a pretty kettle of fish."

"You *beast!*" Barbara muttered. *"Beast. Beast!"*

"Hold your tongue!"

"Barbie!" called Mrs. Claire. *"Where are you?"*

"Here!" shouted Barbara at the top of her voice.

By the time Mrs. Claire came up to them Barbara was out of the car.

"Thank you, dear," said her mother. "You needn't have moved. I'm so sorry I was such a long time. Mr. Falls has been looking for Edward but I'm afraid he's gone." She got in beside Dikon. "I don't think we need to wait. Jump in, dear, we mustn't keep Mr. Bell any longer."

Barbara's hand was on the door and Dikon had reached out towards the self-starter. They were arrested by a cry which, though it endured for no longer than two seconds, filled the night so shockingly that it hung on the air as a sensation after it had ceased to be a sound.

An observer would have seen in the half-light that their faces were all turned in one direction as if their heads had been jerked by a wire. On the silence that followed upon the scream there came again the monstrously domestic noise of a boiling pot.

CHAPTER IX

MR. QUESTING GOES DOWN
FOR THE THIRD TIME

They were not alone for more than two minutes. A subdued hubbub had broken out in the village around them. Doors were opened and slammed. A woman's voice—was it Mrs. Te Papa's?—was raised in a long wail.

"What," asked Mrs. Claire steadily, "was that dreadful noise?"

They began to protect themselves with improbabilities. It was the small boys trying to frighten them. It was someone repeating the death cry of the girl in the song. The last suggestion came from Dikon, and as soon as he had made it he felt its reflection in his hearers.

"Will you wait here by the car?" he said. "I'd better go and see if anyone's in trouble out there." He moved his hand towards the pools. The open space before the meeting-house was filled with shadowy forms. The woman broke out again into a wail. Other voices joined hers: *"Aue! Aue! Taukiri e!"* Rua spoke authoritatively out of the darkness and the wailing stopped.

"Get into the car, Barbara, and wait," said Dikon.

"You mustn't go out there by yourself."

"I've got a torch in the car. In the rack above your head, Mrs. Claire. May I have it?" Mrs. Claire gave it to him.

"Not by yourself," said Barbara. "I'm coming too."

"Please stay here. It's probably nothing at all, but I'd better look."

"Stay here, dear," said Mrs. Claire. "Keep to the white flags, Mr. Bell, won't you?"

Dikon called into the darkness: "Mr. Te Kahu! What's wrong?"

"Who is that?" Rua's voice held a note of surprise. "I know of nothing that is wrong. Someone has cried out. Where are you?"

Mrs. Claire put her head out of the car window. "Here we are, Rua."

Dikon switched on his torch, shouted that he was going to the thermal reserve, and set out.

The village was surrounded by a manuka fence. The only path across the thermal region started at a gap in this fence and Dikon found his way there easily enough. He could hear the pools working. The reek of sulphur grew stronger as he moved towards the gap. He felt and dimly saw wraiths of steam. When he put his hand to his face he found it was damp with condensed vapour. Now he was outside the hedge, his torch-light found the white flags. He followed them. The ground beneath his feet quivered. Alongside the path a mud pot no bigger than a saucepan worked industriously, forming ringed bosses that swelled and broke interminably. But to his left an unseen vent hissed. He caught sight of a steaming pool. The path mounted and then encompassed the mound of an old geyser. A mass of whitish-grey sinter rose up in front of Dikon and his path veered sharply to the right.

He had felt himself to be very much alone and was startled to see the figure of a man, clearly silhouetted against a pale background of sinter. At first Dikon thought this man stood with his back towards him but as he moved forward he discovered that they were face to face. The man's head was bent forward. Some trick of shadow, or perhaps of Dikon's nerves, suggested that the stranger had turned sharply and now stood ready to defend himself. So vivid was this impression that Dikon halted.

"Who's that?" he said loudly.

"I was about to ask you the same question," said Mr. Septimus Falls. "I see now that it is Mr. Bell. I thought you were to drive back to the Springs."

"We heard someone scream."

"Yes?"

"It seemed to be in this direction. Has anything happened?"

"I have seen nothing."

"But you must have heard it."

"One could scarcely escape hearing it."

"What are you doing here?" Dikon asked.

"I came to look for Colonel Claire."

"Where is he?"

"As I have explained, I have seen nobody. I hope he has reached the hill and gone home."

Dikon looked across to where the hill that separated them from the Springs stood black agains the stars.

"You hope?" he said.

"Have you a good nerve?" asked Mr. Falls. "I think you have."

"Why do you ask that, for God's sake!"

"Look here."

Dikon moved towards him and he at once turned about and led the way to the base of a hillock. The eruptive noises were now much louder. Falls waited for Dikon and took him by the elbow. His fingers were like steel. Dikon saw that they stood at a junction of red-and-white-flagged tracks on the native side of the mound above Taupo-tapu. It was on the summit of this mound that Dikon and Gaunt had stood on the evening that they first saw Taupo-tapu.

"When I came to look for Colonel Claire," said Falls, "I stood for a moment in the gap in the fence. As I looked, a man's figure appeared against the sky-line. He carried a torch and I saw him in silhouette. He must have been somewhere near the extinct geyser you passed a moment ago. I was about to hail him when I noticed that he wore an overcoat, and then I knew that it couldn't be the Colonel so I let him go. I'd looked for Colonel Claire all over the village and I now decided that he must have gone home by way of the reserve and by this time would have got too far for it to be worth while calling him back. I stood there idly waiting for the figure of the man in the overcoat to appear again on the sky-line, as it was bound to do when he climbed this hillock. I knew that it would be a little time before you left so I paused long enough to take out my pipe and fill it. I remember thinking how ancient the half-seen landscape felt, and how alien. I don't know if it was long, perhaps it was half a minute, before I realized that the man in the overcoat was taking a long time to reach the hillock. I wondered if he, like myself, stood listening to the working of this hell-brew. Then I heard the scream."

He paused. Dikon thought: "There's no need for him to continue. I know what he's going to say."

"I ran along this track," said Mr. Falls, "until I reached the top of the hillock. There was nobody there. I ran down the far side and called. There was no answer."

He paused again, and Dikon said: "I didn't hear you."

"The hillock was between us ... I turned and looked back and it was then I remembered that the path on the crest of the hillock was broken. I was aware of it all the time, but I had attached no significance to it and had taken the small gap in my stride. I was flashing my torch here and there, you see, and at this moment it happened to catch the raw edge. I returned. As you see, the hillock falls away in a steep bank immediately above the big mud pot. Taupo-tapu, they call it, don't they? The path runs along the edge of this bank. Look."

He flashed his torch-light, a very powerful beam, on the crest of the hillock. Dikon could see clearly where the gap had eaten into the path. The inside of his mouth was dry. "Then ... it had happened?" he said.

"Of course I looked down. I suppose I expected to see something unspeakable. There was nothing, you understand. Nothing at all."

"Yes—but ..."

"Nothing. Nothing at all. The rings and blisters formed and broke. The mud has a kind of lustre at night. I then followed the path right over to the big hill above the Springs. I went almost to the house but there was nobody. I came back here and saw you walking towards me."

Whether by accident or design, Mr. Falls switched on his torch and its strong beam shone full in Dikon's eyes. He moved his head but the light followed him. He said thickly: "I'm going up there. To look."

"I think you had better not do that," said Mr. Falls.

"Why?"

"It should be left undisturbed. We can do nothing."

"But you've already disturbed it."

"Not more than I could help. Very little. Believe me, we can do nothing here."

"It's all a mistake," said Dikon violently. "It means nothing. The path may have fallen in a week ago."

"You forget that we came that way to the concert. It has fallen in since then."

"Since you know all the answers," said Dikon unevenly,

"perhaps you'll tell me what we do next. No, I'm sorry. I expect you're right. Actually, what *do* we do next?"

"Establish the identity of the man in the overcoat, don't you think?"

"You mean—find the members of the party. To see . . . Yes, you're quite right. For God's sake let's go back."

"By all means let us go back," said Mr. Falls. "But you know there was only one member of the party who wore an overcoat, and that was Mr. Questing."

ii

They had agreed to tell Mrs. Claire and Barbara that they had met nobody on the reserve and leave it at that. The short drive home was made ghastly by Mrs. Claire's speculations on the origin of the scream. She was full of comfortable explanations which, Dikon felt, she herself did not altogether believe. The Maori people, she said, were so excitable. Always playing foolish pranks. "I expect," she ended on a note that was almost tranquil, "they just thought they'd give us a good fright."

Barbara, on the other hand, was completely silent. "It was in another age," Dikon thought, "that I kissed her." But he did not believe that it was because of the kiss that she was silent. "She knows something has happened," he thought. It was a relief to hear Mrs. Claire say that after such a late night they must pop straight off to bed.

When they had returned to the Springs, Dikon let his passengers out and drove the car round to the garage. He saw Mrs. Claire and Barbara walk along the verandah towards their rooms. He parked the car and returned to find Mr. Falls waiting for him on the verandah.

They had agreed that Dr. Ackrington should be consulted. It was not until now that Dikon remembered how scattered the various departures from the concert had been. Mr. Questing's enormities, Gaunt's fury, and the Colonel's disappearance seemed now to be profoundly insignificant. But he knew a moment's unreasoning panic as they crossed the verandah to the dining-room. He didn't know what he had expected to find but it was extraordinarily disconcerting to hear Gaunt's voice, angrily scolding.

"I maintain, and anybody who knows me will bear this out, that I am an amazingly even-tempered man. But mark this: when I get angry I get *angry* and by heaven I'll give him hell. 'Do you realise,' I shall say, 'that I—I whom you have publicly insulted—have refused to make a concert-platform appearance before royalty? Do you realize...'"

Dikon and Mr. Falls walked into the dining-room. Gaunt was sitting on one of the tables. His hand was raised and his eyes flashed. Dikon had time to remark that his employer was now coasting on the down-grade of a bout of temperament. When he began to talk the worst was usually over. Beside him on the table stood a bottle of his own whisky to which he had evidently been treating Dr. Ackrington and Colonel Claire. The Colonel sat with a tumbler in his hand. His hair was ruffled and his mouth was not quite closed. Dr. Ackrington appeared to be listening with angry approval to Gaunt's tirade.

"Come and have a drink, Falls," said Gaunt. "I've just been telling them—" He broke off and stared at his secretary. "And may I ask what's the matter with you?"

They were all staring at Dikon. He thought: "I suppose I look sick or something." He sat at one of the tables and, resting his head on his hand, listened to Mr. Falls giving an exact repetition of the story he had already told to Dikon. He was heard in utter silence and it was some time after he had finished that Dr. Ackrington said in a voice that seemed foreign to him: "He may, after all, have returned. How do you know that he hasn't returned? Have you looked?"

"By all means let us look," said Falls. "Bell, perhaps you wouldn't mind?"

Dikon went along the verandah to Mr. Questing's room. The pearl-grey worsted suit was neatly disposed on a chair, ties that had a familiar look hung over the looking-glass, the bed was turned back and a suit of remarkably brilliant pyjamas with a violent puce motif was laid out. The room smelt strongly of the cream Mr. Questing had used on his hair and, indefinably, of him. Dikon shut the door and went on to look, with an unhurried precision that surprised himself, through any other rooms where Questing might conceivably be found. He could hear Simon practising Morse in the cabin and through the open door saw that he and Smith were together there. On his return he saw Colly cross the verandah with a suit of Gaunt's over his arm. Dikon returned to the dining-room and again sat down at the table. Nobody asked him if he had seen Questing.

Colonel Claire said suddenly: "Yes, but I don't understand why it should have happened."

Mr. Falls was very patient. "A probable explanation might be that he walked too near the edge and it gave way."

"The only explanation, surely," said Dr. Ackrington sharply.

"Do you think so?" asked Mr. Falls politely. "Yes, perhaps you are right."

"Would it be possible," asked Dikon suddenly, "to branch off from the path and return to the *pa* by another route?"

"There you are!" cried Colonel Claire with childish optimism. "Why didn't somebody think of that?"

"Utterly impossible, I should say," said Dr. Ackrington crisply. "Where's the boy? And Smith? They ought to know."

"Dikon will find them," said Gaunt. "God, this can't be true! It's monstrous, it's unthinkable. I—I won't have it."

"You'll have to lump it," thought Dikon as he went off to the cabin.

They were still there. Dikon interrupted Simon in the middle of a heated dissertation on fifth columnists in New Zealand. The sinking of the ship, together with all the other crises of the past week, had been forgotten in this new and supreme horror, but now Dikon thought suddenly that if Questing had indeed been an agent, it would have been better for him to have faced discovery and a firing squad than to have met his fate in Taupo-tapu. He told Simon briefly what they believed to have happened, and was inexpressibly shocked by the way he took it.

"Packed up, is he?" said Simon angrily. "Yeah, and now they'll *never* believe me. What a bastard!"

"Cursing and swearing about the poor bastard when he's dead," said Mr. Smith reproachfully. "You ought to be bloody well ashamed of yourself." He stirred uneasily and disseminated a thick spirituous odour. "What a death!" he added thickly. "Give you the willies to think about it, wouldn't it?" He shivered and rubbed the back of his hand across his mouth. "I had one or two over at the *pa* with the boys," he explained needlessly.

Dikon was disgusted with both of them. He said shortly that they were wanted in the dining-room, and walked out, leaving them to follow. Simon caught up with him. "Bert's not so good," he said. "He's had a couple."

"Quite obviously."

Smith lurched between them and took them by the arms. "That's right," he agreed heavily, "I'm not so good."

When Dr. Ackrington questioned them about a possible means of returning to the Maori settlement by any route other than the flagged path, they said emphatically that it could not be done. "Even the Maoris," said Smith, staring avidly at the whisky bottle, "won't come at that."

"You can forget it," said Simon briefly. "He couldn't do it."

Gaunt, with a beautifully expressive gesture, covered his eyes with his hands. "This will haunt me," he said, "for the rest of my life. It's in here." He beat the palms of his hands against his temples. "Indelibly fixed. Hag-ridden by a memory."

"Fiddlesticks," said Dr. Ackrington briskly.

Gaunt laughed acidly. "Perhaps I am exceptional," he said with a kind of tragic airiness.

"Well," said the Colonel most unexpectedly, "if you don't mind, James, I think I'll go to bed. I feel rather sick."

"Good God, Edward, are you demented? Is it possible that you have ever been in a position of authority? When, as we are forced to believe, you were responsible for the conduct of a regiment, did you meet the threat of native uprisings by feeling sick and taking to your bed?"

"Who's talking about native uprisings? The natives of this country don't do that sort of thing. They give concerts and mind their own business."

"You deliberately misconstrue my meaning. The threat of danger—"

"But," objected Colonel Claire, opening his eyes very wide, "we aren't threatened with danger at the moment, James. Either Questing has fallen into a boiling mud cauldron, poor feller, in which case we can do nothing, or else, you know, he hasn't, in which case there is nothing the matter with him."

"Good God, man, we've an extremely grave responsibility."

Colonel Claire said loudly: "What in heaven's name do you mean?"

Dr. Ackrington beat the air with both hands. "If this appalling accident has happened—I say, *if* it has happened, then the police must be informed."

"Very well, James," said the Colonel. "Inform them. I am all for handing over to the proper authorities. Falls would be the one to do that, you know, because he almost saw it happen. Didn't you?" he asked, gazing mournfully at Mr. Falls.

"I was not as close as that, I think," said Mr. Falls. "But you are perfectly right, sir. I should inform the police. In point of fact," he added after a pause, "I have already done so. While Bell was parking the car."

They gaped at him. "I felt," he added modestly, "that the responsibility of taking this step devolved upon myself."

Dikon expected Dr. Ackrington to bristle at this disclosure, but it appeared that his enormous capacity for irritation was exhausted by his brother-in-law, upon whom he now turned his back.

"Is it remotely possible," he asked Mr. Falls, "that the fellow came on here and has made off somewhere or another?" He looked hard at his nephew. "Such a proceeding," he said, "would not be altogether out of character."

"His car's in the garage," said Simon.

"Nevertheless he may have gone."

"I'm afraid it's impossible," said Falls precisely. "If he followed the path I must have seen him."

"And there was the scream," Dikon heard himself say.

"Exactly. But I agree that we should form a search-party. Indeed, the police have suggested that we do so before they take any steps in the matter. I make one stipulation. Let us avoid the path past Taupo-tapu."

"Why?" demanded Simon, instantly truculént.

"Because the police will wish to make an examination."

"You talk as if it was murder," said Gaunt loudly. Smith gave a violent snuffle.

"No, I assure you," said Mr. Falls politely. "I only talk as if there will be an inquest."

"You can't have an inquest without a body," said Simon.

"Can't you? But in any case—"

"Well!" Simon demanded. "What?"

"In any case there may be a body. Later on. Or part of one," Mr. Falls added impassively.

"And now I'm afraid I really am going to be sick," said the Colonel. He hurried out to the verandah and was.

iii

The search-party was formed. The Colonel, having recovered from his nausea, astonished them all by offering to go to the Maori settlement and make inquiries.

"If they've got wind of it, as you seem to suggest, Bell, they'll work themselves up into a state. In my experience, half the trouble with native people is not lettin' them know what you're up to. The poor feller's been killed on their property, you know. That makes it a bit tricky. I think I'd better have a word with old Rua."

"Edward," said his brother-in-law, "you are incomprehensible. By all means go. The Maori people appear to understand you. They are to be congratulated."

"I'll come with you, Dad," said Simon.

"No, thank you, Sim," said the Colonel. "You can help with the search-party. You know the terrain, and may prevent anyone else falling into a geyser or somethin'." He gazed in his startled fashion at Mr. Falls. "I don't catch everything people say," he added, "but if I understand you, he must be dead. I mean, why scream? And you say there was nobody else about. Still, you'd better have a look round, I suppose. I think before I go over to the *pa*, I'd better tell Agnes."

"Need Agnes be told yet?"

"Yes," said the Colonel, and went away.

As Mr. Falls still insisted that the section of the path above Taupo-tapu was not to be used, the only way to the native settlement was by the main road. It was agreed that the Colonel should drive there in Dr. Ackrington's car, satisfy the Maori people, and organize a thorough search of the village. Meanwhile the rest of the party would explore the hills, thermal enclosures, and paths round the Springs. Dikon felt sure that none of them had the smallest expectation of finding Questing. The search seemed futile and horrible but he welcomed it as something that staved off for a time the moment when he would have to think closely about Questing's death. He was busy shoving away from his thoughts the too vivid picture that formed itself about the memory of a falsetto scream.

It was decided that Dr. Ackrington should take the stretch of kitchen garden and rough paddock behind the house, Dikon the hill, Smith and Simon the hot springs, their surrounding path, and the rough country round the warm lake. Mr. Falls proposed to follow the path across the native thermal reserve until he came within a short distance of Taupo-tapu. The Colonel had suggested that Questing might have broken his ankle and fallen. Nobody believed in this theory. Gaunt said hurriedly that there seemed nowhere for him to go. "I am ready to do anything, anything possible, anything in reason," he said, "but I am deeply shaken and if you can manage without me I shall be grateful." They decided to manage without him. Dikon was uncomfortably aware that the other men had dismissed Gaunt as useless and that Simon, at least, had done so with contempt. He watched

Simon speak in an undertone to Smith and was miserably angry when Smith glanced at Gaunt and sniggered. So far from being an understatement, Gaunt's description of himself was, Dikon realized, accurate. Gaunt was profoundly shocked. His hands were unsteady and his face pinched. Lines, normally dormant, netted the corners of his eyes. It was not in Gaunt to conceal emotion but it was an error to suppose that because his distress was unchecked, it was not authentic.

Dikon set out along the path by the Springs to the hill. While they were indoors the moon had risen. Its light brought into strange relief the landscape of Wai-ata-tapu. Plumes of steam stood erect above the pools. Shadows were graved like caverns in the flanks of the hill, but while the higher surfaces, as if drawn in wood by an engraver, were strongly marked in passages of silver and black, the lower planes were wreathed in vapour through which rose manuka bushes, stiffly pallid. These, when Dikon brushed against them, gave off an aromatic scent. As always, in moonlight, there was a feeling of secret expectancy in the air.

Simon caught up with Dikon by the brushwood fence. "Here," he said. "I want you."

Dikon felt unequal to Simon but he waited. "Don't you reckon we're dopey if we let that bloke go off on his pat?" Simon demanded.

"Who are you talking about?" asked Dikon wearily.

"Falls. He seems to think he amounts to something, shooting out orders. Who is he anyway? If I got him right this morning when he did his stuff with the pipe he's the bird that knows the signals. And if he knows the signals he was in with Questing, wasn't he? He's just a bit too anxious about his cobber, in my opinion. We ought to watch him."

"But if Questing's dead what can Falls, if he *is* an agent, do about it?"

"I'm not a mathematician," said Simon obscurely, "but I reckon I can add up the fifth column when the answer's two plus two."

"But he telephoned the police."

"*Did* he? *He* says he did. The telephone's in Dad's office. You can't hear it from the dining-room. How do we know he used it?"

"Well, stop him if you like."

"He's lit off. Streaked away before we got started. Where's his lumbago?"

"How the hell do I know! He's shed it in your marvellous free sulphuric-acid baths," said Dikon, but he began to feel uneasy.

"O.K., call me a fool. But you're doing the hill. If I were you I'd keep a look-out across the reserve while you're at it. See what Mr. Falls's big idea is when he goes along the path. Why does he want to keep everyone off it except himself? How do we know he won't go over the ground above the mud pot? Know what I reckon? I reckon he's dead scared Questing dropped something when he took the toss. He's going to look for it."

"Pure conjecture," Dikon muttered. "However, I'll watch."

Smith, like some unattractive genie, materialized out of a drift of steam. "Know what I reckon?" he began and Dikon sighed at the repetition of this persistent phrase. "I reckon it's blind justice. After what he tried on me. I'd rather a train killed me than Taupo-tapu, by God. Give you the willies, wouldn't it? What's the good of looking for the poor bastard when he's been an hour in the stock pot?"

Dikon swore at Smith with a violence that surprised himself. "It's no good howling at me," said Smith, "you can't get away from the facts. C'mon, Sim."

He moved on towards the lake.

"He reeks of alcohol," said Dikon. "Is it wise to let him loose?"

"He'll be O.K.," said Simon. "I'll keep the tags on *him*. You look after Falls."

Dikon stood for a moment watching them fade into wraiths as they turned into the Springs' enclosure. He lit a cigarette and was about to strike out for the hill when he heard his name called softly.

"Dikon!"

It was Barbara in her red flannel dressing gown and felt slippers, running across the pumice in the moonlight. He went to meet her. "You called me by my first name," he said, "so perhaps you've forgiven me. I'm sorry, Barbara."

"Oh, that!" said Barbara. "I expect I behaved stupidly.

You see, it hasn't happened to me ever before." And with an owlish imitation of somebody else's wisdom she quoted: "It's always the woman's fault."

"You little goat," said Dikon unsteadily.

"I didn't come out to talk about that. I wanted to ask you what's happened."

"Hasn't your father—?"

"He's talking to Mummy. I know by his voice that it's something frightful. They won't tell me, they never do. I must know. What are you all doing? Why are you out here? Uncle James has brought his car round and I saw Sim and Mr. Smith go out together. And when I met *him* on the verandah he looked so terrible. He didn't answer when I spoke to him—just walked away to his room and slammed the door. It's something to do with what we heard, isn't it? Please tell me. Please do."

"We think there may have been an accident."

"To whom?"

"Questing. We don't know yet. He may have just wandered off somewhere. Or sprained his ankle."

"You don't believe that." Barbara's arm in its red flannel sleeve got out as she pointed to the hill. "You think something's happened, out there. Don't you? Don't you?"

Dikon took her by the shoulders. "I'm not going to conjure up horrors," he said, "before there are any to conjure. If you take my tip you'll follow suit. Think what a frightful waste of the jim-jams if we find him cursing over a fat ankle, or if he merely went home to supper with the Mayor. I'm sure he adores mayors."

"And so, who screamed?"

"Sea-gulls," said Dikon shaking her gently. "Banshees. Maori maidens. Go home and do your stuff. Make cups of tea. Go to bed. Men must search and women must sleep and if you don't like me kissing you don't look at me like that."

He turned her about and shoved her away from him. "Flaunting about in your nightgown," he said. "Get along with you."

He watched her go and then, with a sigh, set out for the hill.

He thought he would climb high enough to get a comprehensive view of the native thermal reserve and the

land surrounding it. If anything stirred down there he should
stand a good chance of seeing it in the bright moonlight. He
found the track that Rua used on his evening walks and felt
better for the stiff climb. Someone had suggested half-
heartedly that they should at intervals call out to Questing
but Dikon could not bring himself to do this. A vivid
imagination stimulated by the conviction that Questing was
most horridly dead made the idea of shouting his name quite
appallingly stupid. However, he had promised to search so he
climbed steadily until he reached a place where the reserve
was spread out before him in theatrical relief. It had the
curious and startling unreality of an infra-red photograph.
"If it wasn't so infernally alive," he thought, "it would be like
a lunar landscape." He could see that the reserve was more
extensive than he had imagined it to be. It was pocked all
over with mud pots and steaming pools. Far out towards its
eastern border he caught a glimpse of a delicate jet that
spurted from its geyser and was gone. "It's a lost world,"
Dikon thought. He reflected that a man lying in one of the
inky shadows would be quite invisible and decided that he
had had his climb for nothing. He looked at the slopes of the
hill immediately beneath him. The short tufts of grass and
brush were motionless. He wandered about a little and was
going to turn back when he sensed, rather than saw, that
beneath him and out to his left, something had moved.

His heart and his nerves were jolted before his eyes had
time to tell him that it was only Mr. Septimus Falls, moving
quietly along the white-flagged path across the reserve. As far
as he could make out, Mr. Falls was bent forward. Dikon
remembered Simon's theory and wondered if, after all, it was
so preposterous. But Mr. Falls was still well within the
bounds that he himself had set though he walked fairly
rapidly towards the forbidden territory. Dikon realized with
a sudden pang of interest that he was moving in a very
singular manner, running when he was in the moonlight and
dawdling in the shadows. The mound above Taupo-tapu was
easily distinguishable; Mr. Falls had almost reached the limit
of his allotted patrol. "Now," Dikon said, "he must turn."

At that moment a cloud passed before the face of the
moon and Dikon was alone in the dark. The reserve, the
path, and Mr. Falls had all been blotted out.

Clouds must have come up from the south while Dikon climbed the hill, for the sky was now filled with them, sweeping majestically to the north-east. A vague sighing told him that a night wind had arisen and presently his hair lifted from his forehead. He had brought his torch but he was unwilling to disclose himself. He had told nobody of his intention to climb high up the hill. He saw that in a minute or two the moon would reappear and he waited, peering into the darkness, for the moment when Mr. Falls would be revealed.

It was not long, perhaps no more than a minute, before the return of the moonlight. After its brief eclipse the strange landscape seemed to be more sharply defined; mounds, craters, pools and mud pots, all showed clearly He could even see the white flags along the path. But Mr. Falls had completely disappeared.

iv

"Really," Dikon thought, "if I go all jitter-bug after the problematical death of a man who was almost certainly an enemy agent, I'm not likely to be a howling success in the blitz. No doubt Mr. Falls is pottering about in the shadows. In a moment he will reappear."

He waited and watched. He could hear his watch tick. Away to the east a night bird cried out twice. He saw a light moving about in the native village and wondered if it was Colonel Claire's. Two or three more sprang up. They were searching about the village. Once, far below on the other side of the hill, he heard Simon and Smith call to each other. An interval in the vast procession of clouds left the face of the moon quite clear. But still Mr. Falls remained invisible.

"I can't stand this any longer," Dikon thought. He had taken three strides downhill when a brilliant point of light flashed on the mound above Taupo-tapu and was gone, but

not before the image of a stooping man had darted up in
Dikon's brain. The flash was not repeated but in a little while
the faintest possible glow of reflected light appeared behind
the mound. "Why, damn and blast the fellow," thought
Dikon, "he's messing about on forbidden territory!"

His only emotion was that of fury; his impulse, to plunge
downhill, cross the path and catch Falls red-handed. He had
actually set out to do this when a shattering fall taught him
that he could not run downhill and at the same time keep his
eye on a distant spot on the landscape. When he had picked
himself up and recovered his torch, which had rolled
downhill, he heard a thin sweet whistle threading its way
through an air that transported Dikon with astounding
vividness into the wings of a London theatre.

> *Come away, come away, Death,*
> *I am slain by a fair cruel maid.*

Mr. Septimus Falls was walking briskly back along the
path, whistling his way home.

He had reached the foot of the hill and turned its flank
before Dikon, cursing freely, was half-way down. The thin
whistle changed into a throaty baritone and the last Dikon
heard of the singer was a doleful rendering of the song which
begins: "*Fear no more the heat of the sun.*"

The jolts and stumbles of his journey downhill took the
fine edge off his temper and by the time he had reached the
bottom he was telling himself that he must go warily with
Falls. He paused, lit a cigarette and made some attempt to
sort out the jumble of events, suspicions and conjectures that
had collected about the person and activities of Maurice
Questing.

Questing had visited Rangi's Peak and the Maori people
believed he had gone there to collect forbidden curios. When
Smith attempted to spy on Questing he had narrowly escaped
death under a train and at the time had believed Questing had
done his best to bring about the accident. Had Smith, then,
been on the verge of stumbling across evidence which would
incriminate Questing? Subsequently Questing had offered to
keep Smith on at the Springs and pay him a generous wage.
This sounded like bribery on Questing's part. Simon and Dr.

Ackrington were convinced that Questing's main object in visiting the Peak was to flash signals out to sea. This theory was strongly borne out by Simon's investigations on the night before the ship went down. Questing had manoeuvred to get possession of Wai-ata-tapu, and, when he was about to take over, Septimus Falls had arrived, making certain that he would not be refused a room. Mr. Falls had made himself pleasant. He had talked comparative anatomy with Dr. Ackrington, and Shakespeare with Gaunt. He had also tapped out something that Simon declared was a repetition of the signal flashed from the Peak. Had this been an intimation to Questing that Falls himself was another agent? Why had Falls been at such pains to ensure that nobody inspected the path above Taupo-tapu? Was it because he was afraid that Questing might have left some incriminating piece of evidence behind him? If so, what? Papers? Some object that might be recovered from the cauldron? For the first time Dikon forced himself to consider the possibility of anything being recovered from the cauldron, and was sickened by a procession of unspeakable conjectures.

He decided that as soon as he returned he would tell Dr. Ackrington what he had seen. "I shan't tell Simon," he decided. "His present theory will lead him to behave like the recording angel's off-sider whenever he sets eyes on Falls."

And Gaunt? His first impulse was not to tell Gaunt. It was an impulse based on some instinctive warning which he did not care to recognize. He told himself that knowledge of this new development would only add to Gaunt's nervous distress and that no good purpose would be served by speaking to him.

As he walked briskly along the path towards the Springs, he was conscious of a feeling of extreme dissatisfaction and uneasiness. There was at the back of his mind some apprehension which he had not yet acknowledged. He felt that a further revelation was to come and that within himself, unadmitted to his thoughts, was the knowledge of what it would be. The air of the little Maori song came back to him and with it, like a chain jerked out of dark waters, sprang the sequence of ideas he was so loath to examine.

It was with a sense of extreme depression that he finally reached the house.

The dining-room was in darkness but a light shone faintly round the edge of the study window. The Colonel's blackout arrangements were not entirely successful. Dikon could hear the drone of voices—the Colonel's, he thought, and Dr. Ackrington's—and he tapped at the door and the Colonel called out in a high voice: "Yes, yes, yes? Come in."

They sat together, portentously, after the manner of elderly gentlemen in conclave. They seemed to be distressed. With a trace, or so Dikon thought, of his old regimental manner, the Colonel said: "Come to report, Bell? That's right. That's right."

Feeling rather like a blushing subaltern, Dikon stood by the desk and gave his account. The Colonel, as usual, stared at him with his eyes wide-open and his mouth not quite closed. Dr. Ackrington looked increasingly perturbed and uncomfortable. When Dikon had finished there was a long silence and this surprised him, for he had anticipated that from Dr. Ackrington, at least, there would be a display of wrath in the grand manner. Dikon waited for a minute and then said: "So I thought I'd better come straight back and report."

"Exactly so," said the Colonel. "Perfectly correct. Thank you, Bell." And he actually gave a little nod of dismissal.

"This," thought Dikon, "is not good enough," and he said: "The whole affair seemed so very suspicious."

"No doubt, no doubt," said Dr. Ackrington very quickly. "I'm afraid, Bell, you've merely been afforded a momentary glimpse into a mare's nest."

"Yes, but look here, sir . . ."

Dr. Ackrington raised his hand. "Mr. Falls," he said, "has already informed us of this incident. We're satisfied that he acted advisedly."

"Quite. Quite!" said the Colonel, and touched his moustache. Again with that air of dismissal, he added: "Thank you, Bell."

"This is *not* the army," Dikon thought furiously, and stood his ground.

Dr. Ackrington said: "I think, Edward, that perhaps Bell is entitled to an explanation. Won't you sit down, Bell?"

With a sense of bewilderment Dikon sat down and waited. These two amazing old gentlemen appeared to have effected a swap of their respective personalities. As far as his native mildness would permit, the Colonel had now assumed an air of austerity: Dr. Ackrington's manner, on the contrary, was almost propitiatory. He glanced sharply at Dikon, looked away again, cleared his throat, and began.

"Falls," he said loudly, "had no intention of infringing the bounds that he himself had set upon the extent of his investigation. You will remember that the area between the two points where the red-flagged path deviated from the white-flagged one was to be regarded as out of bounds. He had arrived at the first red flag on this side of Taupo-tapu and was about to turn back when he was arrested by a suspicious noise."

Dr. Ackrington paused for so long that Dikon felt obliged to prompt him.

"What sort of noise, Sir?" he asked.

"Somebody moving about," said Dr. Ackrington, "on the other side of the mound. He waited for a moment, listening. Then a light flashed out. Under the circumstances Falls decided—rightly, in my opinion—that he'd go forward and establish the identity of this person. As quietly as possible and very slowly, he crept up the mound and looked over it."

With a sudden dart that made Dikon jump, Colonel Claire thrust a box of cigarettes at him, muttering the preposterous phrase: "No need for formality." Dikon refused a cigarette and asked what Mr. Falls had discovered.

"Nothing!" said the Colonel opening his eyes very wide. "Nothing at all. Damned annoyin'. What!"

"The fellow either heard Falls coming," said Dr. Ackrington, "or else he'd finished whatever game he was up to and bolted while Falls was climbing the mound; in my opinion the more likely explanation. He'd a good start and although Falls went some way down the other side and flashed his torch, there wasn't a sign of anybody. Fellow had got clean away."

"I see, sir," he said. "Obviously, I've been barking up the wrong tree. But Simon and I had some further cause for believing Mr. Falls to be a rather mysterious person."

He paused, wishing he had held his tongue.

"Well," said Dr. Ackrington sharply, "what was it, what was it?"

"I thought perhaps Simon had told you."

"Simon hasn't honoured me with his theories which, I have no doubt, constitute a plethora of wild-cat speculations."

"Not quite that, I think," Dikon rejoined and he related the story of Mr. Falls and his pipe. To this recital they listened with ill-concealed impatience; indeed it had the effect of restoring Dr. Ackrington to his customary form. "Damn and blast that cub of yours, Edward," he shouted. "What the devil does he mean by concocting these fables and broadcasting them in every quarter but the right one? He knew perfectly well that I regarded Questing's visit to the Peak with the gravest suspicion, he goes haring off by himself, picks up what may prove to be vital information, and tells me nothing whatever about it. In the meantime a ship goes down and an agent from whom we should have got valuable information goes and get lost in a mud pot. Of all the blasted, self-sufficient young popinjays..." He broke off and glared at Dikon. "As a partner in this conspiracy of silence, perhaps you will be good enough to offer an explanation."

Dikon was in a quandary. Though he had refused to be bound to secrecy by Simon he felt that he had betrayed a trust. To tell Dr. Ackrington that he had urged a consultation and that Simon had refused it would be to present himself as an insufferable prig. He said he understood that Simon had every intention of going to the police with his story. Far from pacifying Dr. Ackrington this statement had the effect of still further inflaming him, and Dikon's assurances that so far as he knew Simon had not yet consulted an authority did little to calm him.

The Colonel bit his moustache and apologized to his brother-in-law for Simon's behaviour. Dikon attempted to lead the conversation back to Mr. Falls and was instantly snubbed for his pains.

"Sheer twaddle and moonshine," Dr. Ackrington fumed. "The young ass had his head full of his precious signal and no doubt heard it in everything. What was it?" he demanded. Fortunately Dikon remembered the signal and repeated it.

"Makes no sense in Morse," said the Colonel unhappily. "Four *t*'s, four *5*'s, a *t*, and *i*, and an *s*. Ridiculous, you know, that sort of thing."

"My good Edward, I don't for an instant doubt the

significance of this signal as flashed from the Peak. Do you imagine that Questing would communicate in intelligent Morse code to an enemy raider: 'Ship sails tomorrow night kindly sink and oblige yours Questing'?" He gave an unpleasant bark of laughter. "It's this tarradiddle about Falls and his pipe that I totally discredit. The man's full of nervous mannerisms. I've observed him. He's forever fiddling with his pipe. And will you be good enough to tell me, Mr. Bell, how one distinguishes between a long and a short tap? Pah!"

Dikon thought this over. "By the intervals between the taps?" he suggested timidly.

"Indeed? Would Simon be able, without warning, so to distinguish?"

"The *t*'s would sound very like a collection of *o*'s and *m*'s," said the Colonel.

"I never heard such high-falutin' piffle in my life," added Dr. Ackrington.

"I don't profess to read Morse," said Dikon huffily.

"And you never will if you take lessons from Falls and his pipe. He's a reputable person and not altogether a fool on the subject of comparative anatomy. I may add that we have discovered friends in common. Men of some standing and authority."

"Really, sir?" said Dikon demurely. "That, of course, completely exonerates him."

Dr. Ackrington darted a needle-sharp glance at Dikon and evidently decided that he had not intended an impertinence. "I consider," he said, "that Falls has behaved with admirable propriety. I shall speak to Simon to-night. It's essential that he should not go shouting about this preposterous theory to anyone else."

"Quite," said the Colonel. "We'll speak to him."

"As for the interloper at Taupo-tapu, it was doubtless one of your Maori acquaintances, Edward, disobeying orders as usual. By the way, you must have been there at the time. Did you notice any suspicious behaviour?"

The Colonel rubbed up his hair and looked miserable. "Not to say suspicious, James. Odd. They see things differently, you know. I don't pretend to understand them. Never have. I like them, you know. They keep their word and so on. But of course they're a superstitious lot. Interestin'."

"If you found their behaviour this evening so absorbing," said Ackrington acidly, "perhaps you will favour us with a somewhat closer description of it."

"Well, it's difficult, you know. I expected to find they'd all gone to bed, but not a bit of it. They were hangin' about the *marae* in groups and a good many of them seemed to be in the hall; not tidyin' up or anything—just talkin'. Old Mrs. Te Papa seemed to be in a great taking-on. She was in the middle of a long speech. Very excited. Some of them were at that beastly wailin' noise. Rua was on the verandah with a lot of the older men. Funny thing," said the Colonel and stared absently at Dikon without completing his sentence.

"What, my dear Edward, was a funny thing?"

"Eh? Oh! I was going to say, funny thing he didn't seem surprised to see me." The Colonel gave a rather mad little laugh and pointed at his brother-in-law. "And funnier still," he said, "when I told them what we thought had happened to Questing, they didn't seem surprised about that, either."

CHAPTER X

ENTRANCE OF SERGEANT
WEBLEY

Dikon was despatched with orders to find Simon and send him to his father in ten minutes' time. He had Simon rather heavily on his conscience. Thinking longingly of his bed he went once more to the cabin. The sky was overcast and a light drizzle was falling. Dikon was assailed by a feeling of profound depression. He found Simon still up and still closeted with Smith, in whom the effects of alcohol had faded to a condition of stale despair.

"My luck all over," Smith said lugubriously as soon as he saw Dikon. "I land a permanent job with good money and the boss fades out on me. Is it tough or is it tough?"

"You'll be O.K., Bert," said Simon. "Dad'll keep you on. I told you."

"Yeah, but what a prospect. I'm not saying anything against your dad, Sim, but he's onto a good thing with me and he knows it. If I liked to squeal on him your dad'd be compelled by law to give me hotel wages. I'm not complaining, mind, but that's the strength of it. I'd have done good with Questing."

Dikon said: "I find it difficult to reconcile your disappointment with your former statement that Questing tried to run a train over you."

Smith stared owlishly at him. "He satisfied me about that," he said. "It wasn't like he said at the time. The signal was working O.K. but his car's got one of them green talc sunscreens. He was looking through it and never noticed the light turn red. He took me along and showed me. I went crook at the time. Him and me hadn't hit it off too well and I taped it out he'd tried to fix me up for keeps but I had to hand it to him when he showed me. He was upset, you know. But I said I'd overlook it."

"With certain stipulations, I fancy," said Dikon drily.

"Why not!" cried Smith indignantly. "He owed it to me, didn't he? I was suffering from shock and abrasions. You ask the Doc. My behind's like one of them monkeys', yet. I'd got a lot to complain about, hadn't I, Sim?" he added with an air of injury.

"I'll say."

"Yeah, and what's Mr. Bell's great idea talking as if it was me that acted crook?"

"Not a bit of it, Mr. Smith," said Dikon soothingly. "I only admire your talents as an opportunist."

"Call a bloke names," said Smith darkly, "and never offer him a drink even though he *is* supposed to be a blasted guest." He brooded, Dikon understood, on Gaunt's bottle of whisky.

"All the same, Bert," said Simon abruptly. "I reckon you were pretty simple to believe Questing. He was only trying to keep you quiet. You wouldn't have seen your good money, don't you worry."

"I got it in writing," shouted Smith belligerently. "I'm not childish yet. I got it in writing while he was still worried I'd turn nasty over the train. Far-sighted. That's me."

Dikon burst out laughing.

"Aw, turn it up and get to hell," roared Smith. "I'm a disappointed man. I'm going to bed." He gave an indignant belch and left them.

"He'd be all right," said Simon apologetically, "if he kept off the booze."

"Have you told him about your own views on Questing?"

"Not more than I could help. You can't be sure he won't talk when he's got one or two in. He still reckons Questing went up to the Peak for curios. I didn't say anything. You want to keep quiet about the signals."

"Yes," agreed Dikon and rubbed his nose. "On that score I'm afraid you're not going to be very pleased with me." And he explained that he had told the whole story to the Colonel and Dr. Ackrington. Simon took this surprisingly well, reserving his indignation for Mr. Falls's behaviour at Taupo-tapu which Dikon now revealed to him. In Simon's opinion Falls had no right, however suspicious the circumstances, to exceed the limit that he himself had set. "I don't like that joker," he said. "He's a darned sight too plausible."

"He's no fool."

"I reckon he's a crook. You can't get away from those signals."

Rather apprehensively Dikon advanced Dr. Ackrington's views on the signals. "And I must confess," he added, "that to me it seems a likely explanation. After all, why on earth should Falls take such an elaborate and senseless means of introducing himself to Questing. All he had to do was to take Questing on one side and present his credentials. Why run the danger of someone spotting the signal? It doesn't make sense."

Unable to answer this objection, Simon angrily reiterated his own views. "And if you think I'm dopey," he stormed, "there are others that don't. You may be interested to hear I went to the police station this afternoon." He observed Dikon's astonishment with an air of satisfaction. "Yes," he said, "after you told me it was Falls tapped out the signal, I hopped on my bike and got going. I know the old sergeant and I got onto him. He started off by acting as if I was a kid but I convinced him. Well, anyway," Simon amended, "I stuck to it until he let me in to see the Super."

"Well done," Dikon murmured.

"Yes," Simon continued, stroking the back of his head, "I was an hour in the office. Talking all the time, too. And they were interested. They didn't say much, you know, but they took a lot of it down in writing and I could see they were impressed. They're going to make inquiries about this Falls. If Uncle James and Dad reckon they know better than the authorities why should I worry? Wait till the police pull in their net. That'll be the day. They're not as dumb as I thought they were. I'm satisfied."

"Splendid," said Dikon. "I congratulate you. By the way, I was to ask you to go and see your father and I may as well warn you that you're going to be bound over to secrecy about your theory of Falls's signals with the pipe. And now I think I shall go to bed."

He had reached the door when Simon stopped him. "I forgot to tell you," said Simon. "I asked them the name of this big pot out from Home. They looked a bit funny on it and I thought they weren't going to tell me but they came across with it in the end. It's Alleyn. Chief Detective-Inspector Alleyn."

ii

Dikon's notions as to the legal proceedings arising out of the circumstances of Questing's disappearance were exceedingly vague. Half-forgotten phrases about presumption of death after a lapse of time occurred to him. He had speculated briefly about Questing's nationality and next-of-kin. He had never anticipated that on the following morning he would wake to find several large men standing about the Claires' verandah, staring at their boots, mumbling to each other, and exuding the unmistakable aroma of plain-clothes policemen.

This, however, was what he did find. The drone of voices awakened him; the light was excluded from his room by a massive back which actually bulged through the open window. Dikon put on his dressing gown and went to see his employer. He had looked in on Gaunt before going to bed and had discovered him to be in a state of nervous prostration, undergoing massage from Colly. Dikon, having been told for God's sake to let him alone, had left the room followed by Colly. "Oh, my aunt!" Colly had whispered, jerking his thumb at the door. "High strikes with bells on. A fit of the flutters with musical honours. We're in for a nice helping of ter-hemperament, sir, and no beg pardons. Watch out for skids, and count your collars. We'll be out on tour again to-morrow." He turned down his thumbs. "Colly!" Gaunt had yelled at this juncture. "Colly! Damnation! *Colly!*" And Colly had darted back into the bedroom.

Remembering this episode, Dikon approached his employer with some misgivings. He listened at the door, caught a whiff of Turkish tobacco, heard Gaunt's cigarette cough, tapped and walked in. Gaunt, wearing a purple dressing gown, was propped up in bed, smoking. When Dikon asked how he had slept he laughed bitterly and said nothing. Dikon attempted one or two other little opening gambits all of which were received in silence. He was about to make an uncomfortable exit when Gaunt said: "Ring up that hotel in Auckland and book rooms for to-night."

With a feeling of the most utter desolation Dikon said: "Then we are leaving, sir?"

"I should have thought," said Gaunt, "that it followed as the night the day. I do not book rooms out of sheer elfin whimsy. Please settle with the Claires. We leave as soon as possible."

"But, sir, your cure?"

Gaunt shook a finger at him. "Are you so grossly lacking in sensibility," he asked "that you can blandly suggest that I, with the loathsome picture of last night starting up before my eyes whenever I close them, should steep my body, *mine*, in seething mud?"

"I hadn't thought of it like that," said Dikon lamely. "I'm sorry. I'll tell the Claires."

"Pray do," said Gaunt and turned his shoulder on him.

Dikon went to find Mrs. Claire and encountered Colly on the way. Colly turned his eyes up and affected to dash a tear from them. The phrase, "He's too cheeky," formed itself in Dikon's thoughts and instantly reminded him of the small brown boys who had grimaced in the moonlight. He continued on his way without an answering gesture. He ran the Colonel to earth in his study where he was closeted with a large dark man with a high colour, wearing an uneventful suit and a pair of repellent boots. This person turned upon Dikon a hard speculative stare.

"Sergeant Webley," said the Colonel. Sergeant Webley rose slowly.

"How do you do, sir?" he said in a muffled voice. "Mr....?"

"Bell," said the Colonel.

"Ah, yes. Mr. Bell," repeated Sergeant Webley. He half-opened his hand, which was broad, flat and flabby with lateral creases. He seemed to peer into its palm. Dikon realized with a stab of alarm that he was consulting a small note-book. "That's right," repeated Sergeant Webley heavily. "Mr. Dikon Bell. Would that be a kind of nickname, sir?"

"Not at all," said Dikon. "It was given me in my baptism."

"Is that so, sir? Very unusual. Old English perhaps."

"Perhaps," said Dikon coldly. Webley cleared his throat and waited.

"Sergeant Webley," said the Colonel uncomfortably, "is making some inquiries..."

"Yes, of course," said Dikon hurriedly. "I'm sorry I interrupted, sir, I'll go."

"No need for that, Mr. Bell," said Webley with a sort of fumbling cordiality. "Very glad you looked in. Quite an unfortunate affair. Yes. Take a seat, Mr. Bell, take a seat."

With a claustrophobic sensation of something closing in upon him, Dikon sat down and waited.

"I understand," said Webley, "that your movements last night were as follows." He flattened his note-book on his knees and began to read from it. "But I've heard all this before," Dikon thought. "I've read it a hundred times in airliners, on the decks of steamers, in hotel bedrooms." And he saw yellow dust-jackets picturing lethal weapons, clutching hands, handcuffs, and men like Mr. Webley squinting along the barrels of revolvers. More in answer to his thoughts than to Webley's questions he cried aloud: "But it was only an accident!"

"In a case of this sort, Mr. Bell, disappearance of the party concerned under circumstances pointing to demise, we make inquiries. Now, you were saying?"

His heavy interrogation began to take on a kind of lifeless rhythm: question, answer, pause, while Sergeant Webley wrote and Dikon fidgeted, and again, question. It was a colourless measure reiterated drearily with variations. Under its burden Dikon walked again down a narrow track, through a gap in a hedge, and across a barren place where white flags showed clearly. Beyond the drone of Webley's voice a single scream rose and fell like a jet from a geyser.

Webley was very insistent about the scream. Was Dikon positive that it had come from the direction of the mud cauldron? Sounds were deceptive, Webley said. Might it not have come from the village? Dikon was quite positive that it had not and, on consideration, said he would swear that it had arisen close at hand in the thermal region. Where precisely had he been when he first saw Mr. Falls? Here Webley unfolded a large-scale and extremely detailed map of the district. Dikon was able to find his place on the map and, a punctual wraith, Mr. Falls walked again towards him in the starlight. "Then you'd say he was about half-way between you and the mud pot?" The sense of impending horror which had haunted Dikon ever since he woke was now intensified and translated physically into a dryness of the throat. "About that," he said.

Webley looked up from the map, his pale finger still flattened on the point where Dikon had stood. "Now, Mr. Bell, how long would you say it was from the time you left Mrs. and Miss Claire until the moment you first saw Mr. Falls?"

"No longer than it takes to walk fairly briskly from the car to the point under your finger. Perhaps a couple of minutes. No more."

"A couple of minutes," Webley repeated, and stooped over his note-book. With his head bent, so that his voice sounded more muffled than ever, he said much too casually: "You're in young Mr. Claire's confidence, aren't you, Mr. Bell?"

"In what sense?"

"Didn't he tell you about his ideas on Mr. Questing?"

"He talked to me about them. Yes."

"And did you agree with him?" asked Webley, raising his florid face for a moment to look at Dikon.

"At first I considered them fantastic."

"But you got round to thinking there might be something in it? Did you?"

"I suppose so," said Dikon and then, ashamed of answering so guardedly, he said firmly: "Yes, I did. It seems to me to be inescapable."

"Is that so?" said Webley. "Thank you very very much, Mr. Bell. We won't trouble you any more just now."

Dikon thought: "I seem to be forever getting my *conge.*" He said to the Colonel: "I really came to tell you, sir, that Mr. Gaunt has been very much upset by this appalling business and thinks he would like to get away, for a time at least. He's most anxious that you should know how much he appreciates all the kindness and consideration that he has been shown and ... and," Dikon stammered, "and I hope that after a little while we may return. I'm so sorry to bother you now but if I might settle up ...?"

"Yes, yes, of course," said the Colonel with obvious relief. "Quite understandable. Sorry it's happened like this."

"So are we," said Dikon. "Enormously. I'll come back a little later, shall I? We'll be leaving at about eleven." He backed away to the door.

"Just a minute, Mr. Bell."

Webley had been stolidly conning over his notes, and Dikon, in his embarrassment, had almost forgotten him. He now rose to his feet, a swarthy official in an ugly suit. "You were thinking of leaving this morning were you, Mr. Bell?"

"Yes," said Dikon. "This morning."

"You and Mr. Geoffrey Gaunt and Mr. Gaunt's personal vally?" He wetted his thumb and turned a page of his notebook. "That'd be Mr. Alfred Colly, won't it?"

"Yes."

"Yes. Well, now, we'll be very sorry to upset your arrangements, Mr. Bell, but I'm just afraid we'll have to ask you to stay on a bit longer. Until we've cleared up this little mystery, shall we say?"

With a sense of plunging downwards in a lift that was out of control, Dikon said: "But I've told you everything I know, and Mr. Gaunt had nothing whatever to do with the affair. I mean he was nowhere near. I mean . . ."

"Nowhere near, eh?" Webley repeated. "Is that so? Yes. He didn't drive home in his car, did he? Which way did Mr. Gaunt go home, Mr. Bell?"

And now Dikon was back in the meeting-house, and Gaunt, shaking with rage, was pushing his way out along the side aisles as if propelled by an intolerable urge. He was engulfed in a crowd of people who stared curiously at him. He showed for a moment in the doorway and was gone.

Dikon was recalled by Webley's voice. "I was asking which way Mr. Gaunt went home from the concert, Mr. Bell."

"I don't know," said Dikon. "If you like I'll go and ask him."

"I won't trouble you to do that, Mr. Bell. I'll ask Mr. Gaunt myself."

iii

We are slow to recognize disaster, quick to erect screens between ourselves and a full realization of jeopardy. Perhaps the idea of something more ominous than accident had lain dormant at the back of Dikon's thoughts. As there are some diseases that we are loath to name, so there are crimes with which we refuse consciously to associate ourselves. Though Dikon was oppressed by the sense of an approaching threat, his conscious reaction was to wonder how in the world under these new restrictions he was to cope with Gaunt. Thus, by a process of mental juggling, the minor was substituted for the major horror.

He said: "If you're going to see Mr. Gaunt perhaps I may come with you. I don't know if he's up yet."

Webley looked thoughtfully at him and then with an air of heartiness which Dikon found most disconcerting he said: "That'll do very very nicely, Mr. Bell. We like to do things in a friendly way. If you don't mind introducing me to Mr. Gaunt, I'll just explain the position to him. I'm quite sure he'll understand."

"Are you, by God!" thought Dikon, and led the way along the verandah.

As they approached Gaunt's rooms, Colly came out staggering under the weight of a wardrobe trunk. Webley gave him that hard stare with which Dikon was to become so familiar. "You'd better take that thing away, Colly," said Dikon.

"Take it away?" asked Colly indignantly. "I've only just brought it out. What am I supposed to be, sir? Atmosphere in the big railway-station scene or what?" He glanced shrewdly at Webley. "Pardon me, Chief-Inspector," he said. "There's no corpse in this trunk. Take a look if you don't believe me, and don't muck up our underwear. We're fussy about details."

"That'll be quite all right, Colly," said Webley. "Stay handy, will you? I'd like to have a yarn with you."

"Rapture as expressed in six easy poses," said Colly. "Yours to command." He winked at Dikon. "If you're looking for His Royal Serenity, sir," he said, "he's in his barf."

"We'll wait," said Dikon. "In here, will you, Mr. Webley?" They waited in Gaunt's sitting-room. Colly, whistling limpidly, staggered away under the trunk.

"That kind of joker's out of our line in New Zillund," said Webley. "He's different from what you'd have thought. A bit too fresh, isn't he? Not my idea of a vally."

"Colly's a dresser," said Dikon, "not a valet. He's been a long time with Mr. Gaunt, and I'm afraid he's got into the way of thinking he's a licensed buffoon. I'm sorry, Sergeant. I'll just go and tell Mr. Gaunt you're here."

He had hoped to get one word in private with Gaunt, but Webley thanked him and followed him out on the verandah. "Going in for the treatment, is he?" he asked easily. "Just across the way, isn't it? I've never taken a look at these Springs. Been here ten years and never taken a look at them. Fancy that!"

He followed Dikon across the pumice.

It was Gaunt's custom before breakfast to soak for fifteen minutes in the largest of the pools, that which was enclosed by a rough shed. Evidently, Dikon thought, his new abhorrence of thermal activities did not extend to this particular bath.

Closely followed by Webley, Dikon went up to the bathhouse and tapped at the door.

"Who the hell's out there!" Gaunt demanded.

"Sergeant Webley to see you, sir."

"Sergeant *who?*"

"Webley."

"Who's he?"

"Harpoon police force, sir," said Mr. Webley. "Very sorry to trouble you."

There was no reply to this. Webley made no move. Dikon waited uncertainly. He heard a splash as Gaunt shifted in the pool. He had the idea that Gaunt was sitting up, listening. At last, in a cautious undertone, the voice beyond the door called him. Dikon?"

"I'm here, sir."

"Come in."

Dikon went in quickly, closing the door behind him. There was his employer as he had expected to find him, naked, vulnerable, and a little ridiculous, jutting out of the vivid water.

"What *is* all this?"

Dikon gestured. "Is he there?" Gaunt muttered.

Dikon nodded violently and with an attempt at cheerfulness that he felt rang very false, said aloud: "The Sergeant would like to have a word with you, sir."

He groped in his pocket, found an envelope and a pencil and wrote quickly: "It's about Questing. They won't let us go." He went on talking as he showed it to Gaunt: "Shall I send Colly in, sir?"

Gaunt was staring at the paper. Water trickled off his shoulders. His face was pinched and looked old, the skin on his hands was waterlogged and wrinkled. He began to swear under his breath.

On the other side of the door Webley cleared his throat. Gaunt, his lips still moving, looked at the door. He grasped the rail at the edge of the bath and stood upright, a not very handsome figure. "He ought to say something," Dikon thought. "It looks bad to say nothing." Gaunt beckoned and Dikon stooped towards him but he seemed to change his mind and said loudly, "Ask him to wait. I'm coming out."

The morning was warm and humid and the pool Gaunt had left was a hot one, but even when he was wrapped in his heavy bathrobe he seemed to be cold. He asked Dikon for a cigarette. Conscious always of Webley on the other side of the thin wooden wall Dikon forced himself to talk. "I'm afraid this appalling business is going to hold us up a bit, sir. I should have thought of it before." Gaunt suddenly joined in. "Yes, a damned nuisance, of course, but it can't be helped." It all sounded horribly false.

They came out of the bath-house and there was Webley. "Hanging about," thought Dikon, "like Frankenstein's monster." He walked up with them to the house and stayed outside Gaunt's window while he dressed. Dikon sat on the edge of the verandah and smoked. The clouds that had blown up in the night were gone and the wind had dropped. Rangi's Peak was a clear blue. The trees on its flanks looked as if they had been blobbed down by a water-colourist with a full and generous brush. The hill by the springs basked in the sun and high above it the voices of larks reached that pinnacle of shrillness that floats on the outer margin of human perception. The air seemed to hold a rumour of notes rather than an actual song. Three men came round the path by the lake. One of them carried a sack which he held away from him, the others, rakes and long manuka poles. They walked in Indian file, slowly. When they came nearer, Dikon saw that a heavy globule hung from the corner of the sack. It swung to and fro, thickened and dropped with a splat of sound on the pumice. It was mud. The rake and the ends of the poles were also muddy.

He sat still, his cigarette burning down to his fingers, and watched the men. They came over the pumice to the verandah and Webley moved across to meet them. The man with the sack opened it furtively and the others moved between him and Dikon. Webley pushed his black felt hat to the back of his head and squatted, peering. They mumbled together. A phrase of Septimus Falls's came into Dikon's mind and nauseated him. Inside the house Barbara called to her mother. At once the group broke up. The three men disappeared round the far end of the house, carrying their muddy trophies, and Webley returned to his post by Gaunt's window.

Dikon heard the creak of a door behind him. His nerves were on edge and he turned quickly; but it was only Mr. Septimus Falls standing on the threshold of his room.

"Good morning, Bell," he said. "A lovely day, isn't it? Quite unsullied and in strong contrast to the events associated with it. 'Only man is vile.' It is not often that one goes to Hymns A. and M. for profundity of observation but I remember the same phrase occurred to me on the night that war broke out."

"Where were you then, Mr. Falls?"

"'Going to and fro in the earth,'" said Mr. Falls lightly. "Like the devil, you know. In London, to be precise. I didn't see you after your return last night but hear that your vigil on the hill was an uneventful one."

"So they *haven't* told him I was watching him," thought Dikon. "And how did you get on?" he asked.

"I? I was obliged to trespass, and all to no avail. I thought you must have seen me." He smiled at Dikon. "I heard you falling about on your hill. No injuries, I trust? But you are young and can triumph over such mishaps. I, on the contrary, have played the very devil with my lumbar region."

"I thought last night that you seemed remarkably lively."

"Zeal," said Mr. Falls. "All zeal. Wonderful what it will do, but one pays for it afterwards, unhappily." He placed his hand in the small of his back and hobbled towards Webley. "Well, Sergeant," he said, "any new developments?"

Webley looked cautiously at him. "Well, yes, sir, I think we might say there are," he said. "I don't see any harm in telling you we're pretty well satisfied that this gentleman came by his death in the manner previously suspected. My chaps have been over there and they've found something. In the mud pot."

"Not—?" said Dikon.

"No, Mr. Bell, not the remains. We could hardly hope for them under the circumstances, though of course we'll have to try. But my chaps have been there on the look-out ever since it got light. About half an hour ago they spotted something white working about in the pot. Sometimes, they said, you'd see it and sometimes you wouldn't. One of them who's a family man passed the remark that it reminded him of the week's wash."

"And . . . was it?" asked Falls.

"In a manner of speaking, sir, it was. We raked it out and are holding it. It's a gentleman's dress waistcoat. One of those backless ones."

iv

Dikon, at his employer's request, was present at the interview between Gaunt and Webley. Gaunt was at his worst, alternately too persuasive and too intolerant. Webley remained perfectly civil, muffled, and immovable.

"I'm afraid I'll have to ask you to stay, sir. Very sorry to inconvenience you but there it is."

"But I've told you a dozen times I've no information to

give you. None. I'm unwell and I came here for a rest. A rest! My God! You may have my address and if I should be wanted you'll know where to find me. But I know nothing that can be of the smallest help to you."

"Well, now, Mr. Gaunt, we'll just see if that's so. I haven't got round yet to asking you anything, have I? Now, perhaps you wouldn't mind telling me just how you got home last night."

Gaunt beat the arms of his chair and with an excruciating air of enforced control said in a whisper: "How I got home? Very well. Very well. I walked home."

"Across the reserve, sir?"

"No. I loathe and abominate the reserve. I walked home by the road."

"That's quite a long way round, Mr. Gaunt. I understand you had your car at the concert."

"Yes, Sergeant, I had my car. That did not prevent me from wishing to walk. I walked. I wanted fresh air and I walked."

"Who drove the car, sir?"

"I did," said Dikon.

"Then I suppose, Mr. Bell, that you overtook Mr. Gaunt?"

"No. It was some time before we left."

"Longer than fifteen minutes after the concert was over, would you say?"

"I don't know. I haven't thought."

"Mr. Falls puts it at about fifteen minutes. It's a mile and a quarter by the main road, sir," said Webley, shifting his position in order to face Gaunt. "You must be a smart walker."

"The car can't do more than crawl along that road, you know. But I walked fast on this occasion, certainly."

"Yes. Would that be because you were at all excited, Mr. Gaunt? I've noticed that when people are kind of stimulated or excited they're inclined to step out."

Gaunt laughed and adopted, mistakenly, Dikon thought, an air of raillery. "I believe you're a pressman in disguise, Sergeant. You want me to tell you about my temperament."

"No, sir," said Webley stolidly. "I just wondered why you walked so fast."

"You have guessed why. I was stimulated. For the first time in months I had spoken Shakespearean lines to an audience."

"Yes?" Webley opened his note-book. "I understand you left before the other members of your party. With the exception of Mr. Questing, that is. Mr. Questing left before you, didn't he?"

"Did he? I believe he did." Gaunt put his delicate hand to his eyes and then shook his head violently as though he dismissed some unwelcome vision. Next he smiled sadly at Mr. Webley, extended his arms and let them flop. It was a bit of business that he used in "Hamlet" during the penultimate duologue with Horatio. Mr. Webley watched it glumly. "You must forgive me, Sergeant," said Gaunt. "This thing has upset me rather badly."

"It's a terrible affair, sir, isn't it? Was the deceased a friend of yours, may I ask?"

"No, no. It's not that. For it to happen to anyone!"

"Quite so. You must have seen him, I suppose, after you left the hall."

Gaunt took out his cigarette case and offered it to Webley, who said he didn't smoke. Dikon saw a tremor in Gaunt's hand and lit his cigarette for him. Gaunt made rather a business of this and, as they were at it, said something not so much in a whisper as with an almost soundless articulation of his tongue and teeth. Dikon thought it was: "I've got to get out of it."

"I was saying—" said Webley heavily, and repeated his question.

Gaunt said that as far as he could remember he had caught a glimpse of Questing outside the hall. He wasn't positive. Webley kept him to this point and he grew restive. At last he broke off and drew his chair closer to Webley.

"Look here," he said. "I've honestly told you all I know about this poor fellow. I want you to understand something. I'm an actor and an immensely well-known one. Things that happen to me are news, quite big news, at Home and in the States. Bell, as my secretary, will tell you how tremendously careful I have to be. The sort of things that are said about me in print matter enormously. It may sound far-fetched, but I assure you it is not, when I tell you that a few sentences in the hot-news columns, linking my name up with this accident, would be exactly the wrong kind of publicity. We don't know much about this unfortunate man but I've heard rumours that he wasn't an altogether savoury character. That may come out, mayn't it? We'll get hints about it. 'Mystery man dies horribly after hearing Geoffrey Gaunt recite at one-eyed burg in New Zealand.' That's how the hot-columnists will treat it."

"We don't get much of that sort of thing in this country, Mr. Gaunt."

"Good Lord, man, I'm not talking about this country. As far as I'm concerned this country doesn't exist. I'm talking of New York."

"Oh," said Mr. Webley impassively.

"See here," said Gaunt, "I know you've got your job to do. If there's anything more you want to ask, why ask it. Ask it now. But for God's sake don't keep me hanging on here. I can't invite you to come out and have a drink with me but—" Dikon, appalled, saw Gaunt's hand go to the inside pocket of his coat. He got behind Webley and shook his head violently, but Gaunt's note-case was now in his hand and Webley on his feet.

"Now Mr. Gaunt," Webley said with no change whatever in his uninflected and thick voice, "you should know better than to think of that. If you're as careful of your reputation as you've been telling me, you ought to realize that anything of this nature looks very bad indeed if it gets known. Put that case away, sir. We'll let you go as soon as possible but until this black business is cleared up nobody's leaving Wai-ata-tapu. Nobody."

Gaunt drew back his head with a certain characteristic movement which Dikon always associated with an adder.

"I think you're making a mistake, Sergeant," he said with elaborate indifference. "However, we'll leave it as it is for the moment. I'll telephone to Sir Stephen Johnston and ask him to advise me what steps to take. He's a personal friend of mine. Isn't he your Chief Justice or something?"

"That'll be quite in order, Mr. Gaunt," said Webley tranquilly. "His Honour may make some special arrangement. In the meantime I'll ask you to stay here."

"Great God Almighty!" Gaunt screamed out. "If you say

that again I'll lose all control of my temper. How dare you take this attitude with me! The man has been killed by a loathsome accident. You behave, my God, as if he'd been murdered."

"But," said a voice in the doorway, "isn't it almost certain that he has?"

It was Mr. Septimus Falls, standing diffidently on the threshold.

v

"*Do* forgive me," said Mr. Falls in his rather spinster-like fashion. "I *did* tap on the door, I promise you, but you didn't notice. I came to tell Sergeant Webley that he is wanted on the telephone."

"Thank you, sir," said Webley, and went out.

"May I come in?" asked Falls, and came in. "As that large efficient man has tramped away, it seems a propitious moment to review our position."

"Why did you say—*that*—about Questing?" said Gaunt. "Why, in heaven's name?"

"That he has been murdered? Because of several observations I have made. Let me enumerate them. *A*, the attitude of the police seems to me to be more consistent with a homicide investigation than with an inquiry into an accident. *B*, the circumstances surrounding the affair appear to be suspicious; as, for instance, the bite out of the path. Have you ever tried to dislodge a piece of that solidified mud? My dear sir, you couldn't do it unless you positively danced on the spot. *C*, I observed by the light of my torch that the displaced clod had fallen to the foot of the bank. It held the impression of a nailed boot or shoe. Questing was the only man in evening dress, at the concert. *D*, (and, dear me, how departmental I sound), the clod had contained a white flag which lay beside it, the only white flag on that side of the mound. As far as I could see the grooves on the edge of the gap and down the sides of the clod must have been the hold made by the flag standard. I am certain Webley and his satellites have discovered these not inconsiderable phenomena. Which would account for their somewhat implacable attitude towards ourselves, don't you feel? I too have been forbidden to leave Wai-ata-tapu. A tiresome restriction."

"I fail utterly," said Gaunt breathlessly, "to see why these ludicrous details should suggest that there has been foul play."

"Do you? And yet when Hamlet felt the point unbated did he not smell villainy?"

"I haven't the slightest idea what you mean. I still think it monstrous that I, who after all am a guest in this country, should be subjected to this imbecile entanglement in red tape. If the position continues," said Gaunt, speaking very rapidly and looking down his nose at Mr. Falls, "I shall appeal directly to the Governor-General whom I have the honour to know personally."

"This if frightful," thought Dikon. "First a Chief Justice and now a Governor-General. We shall be cabling to the Royal Family if Webley remains unshaken."

At this point Dr. Ackrington appeared in the doorway.

"May I come in?" he asked.

Gaunt waved his hand.

"I don't know whether you realize it," said Dr. Ackrington, taking them all in with a comprehensive glare, "but we are under suspicion of homicide, every man jack of us." He gave an angrily triumphant laugh.

"I refuse to believe it!" Gaunt shouted. "I refuse to be entangled. It was an accident. He was drunk and he stumbled. Nobody is to blame, I least of all. I refuse to be implicated."

"You can refuse till you're black in the face, my good sir," said Dr. Ackrington. "Much good will it do you. You liked him no better than the rest of us, a fact that even this purple monument to inefficiency must stumble across sooner or later."

"Do you mean Sergeant Webley?" asked Falls.

"I do. I'm sorry to say I regard the man as a moron."

"That, if you will forgive me, Dr. Ackrington, is a

mistake. I feel sure that we should be extremely ill-advised to dismiss Webley as a person of no intelligence. And in any case, if, as I am persuaded, Questing has been deliberately sent to an unspeakable death, do we not wish his murderer to be discovered?"

With a faint smile Mr. Falls looked from one face to another. After an uncomfortable interval, Gaunt, Dr. Ackrington, and Dikon all spoke together. "Yes, of course," they said impatiently. "Of course," Dr. Ackrington added. "But I must tell you at the outset, Falls, that if you concur with the official view of this case, I utterly disagree with you. However I merely wish to warn you of the possible, the almost inevitable blunders that will be perpetrated by this person. If he is to be in charge of this case I consider that none of us is safe."

"And what are you going to do about it?" asked Gaunt offensively.

"I intend to call a meeting."

"Good God, how perfectly footling!"

"And why, may I ask? Why?"

"Does somebody propose somebody else as a murderer? Or what?"

"You are facetious, sir," said Dr. Ackrington furiously. "I confess that I did not expect to find you so confident of your own immunity."

"I should like to know precisely what you mean by that, Ackrington."

"Come," said Falls. "Nothing is gained by losing our tempers."

"Nor by the merciless introduction of *cliches*," Gaunt retorted, darting his head at him.

"Are you in there, James?" asked Colonel Claire. His face, slightly distorted, was pressed against the window-pane.

"I'm coming." Dr. Ackrington surveyed his audience of three. "It is my duty," he said grandly, "to inform you that Webley has apparently been recalled to Harpoon. His men have returned to the reserve. At the moment we are not under direct supervision and I suggest that we lose no time in discussing our position. We are meeting in the dining-room in ten minutes. After this conversation I cannot, I imagine, expect to see you there."

"On the contrary," said Falls, "I shall certainly attend."

"And I," said Dikon.

"Obviously," said Gaunt, "I had better be there, if only to protect myself."

"I am delighted that you recognize the necessity," said Dr. Ackrington. "Coming, Edward." He joined his brother-in-law on the verandah.

Mr. Falls did not follow him. To Dikon's embarrassment he stayed and listened with an air of a connoisseur to Gaunt's renewed display of temper. Gaunt had never been averse to an audience at these moments but on this occasion he seemed to be unaware of anyone but Dikon, who received the full blast of his displeasure. He was told that he had bungled the whole affair, that he should never have allowed Webley an interview, that he was totally indifferent to Gaunt's agony of mind. Never before had Dikon found his employer so unreasonably abusive. His own feeling of apprehension mounted with each intemperate phrase. He was ashamed of Gaunt.

This uncomfortable display was brought to an end by a sudden and unnerving clangour outside the window. Huia was performing with vigour upon the dinner bell. Gaunt, abominably startled, uttered a loud oath.

"Is that lunch?" exclaimed Dikon, who had himself been shaken. "Now I come to think of it," he added, "I forgot to have breakfast."

"I fancy it is a summons to the conference," said Falls placidly. "Shall we go in?"

vi

Three of the small dining-tables had been shoved together and at the head of them sat Dr. Ackrington with the Colonel, looking miserable, on his right hand. Simon and Smith sat together at the far end. Simon looked mulish and Smith foggily disgusted. Dr. Ackrington pointed portentously to the chairs on his left. Dikon and Falls sat together; Gaunt, like a sulky schoolboy, took the chair farthest removed from everyone else. The Colonel, evidently feeling that the silence was oppressive, suddenly ejaculated: "Rum go, what?" and seemed alarmed at the sound of his own voice.

"Very rum," agreed Mr. Falls sedately.

Mrs. Claire and Barbara came in. They wore their best dresses, together with hats and gloves, and they carried prayer-books. They contrived to disseminate an atmosphere of English Sunday morning. There was a great scraping of chairs as the men got up. Smith and Simon seemed to grudge this small courtesy, and looked foolish.

"I'm sorry if we are late, dear," said Mrs. Claire. "Everything was a little disorganized this morning." She began to peel the worn gloves from her plump little hands and looked about her with an air of brisk expectancy. Dikon remembered with a start that she conducted a Sunday school in the native village. "We had to come and go by the long way," she explained.

Barbara went off with the prayer-books and returned, without her hat, looking scared.

"Well, sit down, Agnes, sit down," Dr. Ackrington commanded. "Now that you *have* come. Though why the devil you elected to traipse off ... However! I imagine that you had no pupils."

"Not a *very* good attendance," said Mrs. Claire gently, "and I'm afraid they *were* rather inattentive, poor dears."

Dikon was amazed to see that she was quite unruffled. She sat beside her husband and looked brightly at her brother. "Well, dear?" she asked.

Dr. Ackrington grasped the edge of the table with both hands and leant back in his chair.

"It seems to me," he began, "it is essential that we, as a group of people in extraordinary circumstances, should understand one another. I, and I have no doubt all of you, have been subjected to a cross-examination from a person who, I am persuaded, is grossly unfit for his work. I am afraid my opinion of the local police force has never been a high one and Sergeant Webley has said and done nothing to alter it. I may state that I have formed my own view of this case. A brief inspection of the scene of the alleged tragedy would possibly confirm this view but Sergeant Webley, in his wisdom, sees fit to deny me access to the place. Ha!"

He paused, and Mrs. Claire, evidently feeling that he expected an answer, said: "Fancy, dear! What a pity, yes."

Dr. Ackrington looked pityingly at his sister. "I said 'the *alleged* tragedy,'" he pronounced. "The *alleged* tragedy." He glared at them.

"We heard you, James," said Colonel Claire mildly, "the first time."

"Then why don't you say something?"

"Perhaps, dear," said his sister, "it's because you speak so loudly and look so cross. I mean," she went on with an apologetic cough, "one thinks to oneself: 'How cross he is and how loudly he speaks,' and then, you know, one forgets to listen. It's confusing."

"I was not aware," Dr. Ackrington shouted, and checked himself. "Very well, Agnes," he said, dropping his voice to an ominous monotone. "You desire a continuation of the mealy-mouthed procedure of your Sunday school. You shall have it. With a charge of homicide hanging over all our heads, I shall smirk and whisper my way through this meeting and perhaps you will manage to listen to me."

"'*I will roar you,*'" thought Dikon, "'*as 'twere any nightingale.*'"

"You said *alleged*," Mr. Falls reminded Dr. Ackrington pacifically.

"I did. Advisedly."

"It will be interesting to learn why. Undoubtedly," said Mr. Falls mellifluously, "the whole affair is not to be described out of hand as murder. I don't pretend to understand the, shall I call it, technical position of a case like this. I mean, the absence of a body . . ."

"*Habeas corpus?*" suggested Colonel Claire dimly.

"I fancy, sir, that *habeas corpus* refers rather to the body of the accused than to that of the victim. Any one of us, I imagine," Mr. Falls continued, looking amiably round the table, "may be a potential *corpus* within the meaning of the writ. Or am I mistaken?"

"Who's going to be a corpse?" Smith roared out in a panic. "Speak for yourself."

"Cut it out, Bert," Simon muttered.

"Yeah, well I want to know what it's all about. If anyone's going to call me names I got a right to stick up for myself, haven't I?"

"Perhaps I may be allowed to continue," said Dr. Ackrington coldly.

"For God's sake get on with it," said Gaunt disgustedly. Dikon saw Barbara look wonderingly at him.

"As I came along the verandah just now," said Dr. Ackrington, "I heard you, Falls, giving a tolerably clear account of the locale. You, as the only member of our party who had had the opportunity of seeing the track, are at an advantage. If, however, your description is accurate, it seems to me there is only one conclusion to be drawn. You say Questing carried a torch and was using it. How, therefore, could he miss the place where the path has fallen in? You yourself saw it a few moments later."

Mr. Falls looked steadily at Dr. Ackrington. Dikon found it impossible to interpret his expression. He had a singularly impassive face. "The point is quite well taken," he said at last.

"The chap was half-shot," said Simon. "They all say he smelt of booze. I reckon it was an accident. He went too near the edge and it caved in with him."

"But," said Dikon, "Mr. Falls says the clod that carried away has got an impression of a nailed boot or shoe on it. Questing wore pumps. What's the matter?" he ejaculated. Simon, with an incoherent exclamation, had half risen. He stared at Dikon with his mouth open.

"What the devil's got hold of *you?*" his uncle demanded.

"Sim, dear!"

"All right, all right. Nothing," said Simon and relapsed into his chair.

"The footprint which you say you noticed, my dear Falls," said Dr. Ackrington, "*might* have been there for some time. It may be of no significance whatever. On the other hand, and this is my contention, it may have been put there deliberately, to create a false impression."

"Why by?" asked the Colonel. "I don't follow all this. What did Falls see? I don't catch what people say."

"Falls," said Dr. Ackrington, "is it too much to ask you to put forward your theory once more?"

"It is rather the theory which I believe the police will

advance," said Falls. With perfect urbanity he repeated his own observations and the conclusions which he thought the police had drawn from the circumstances surrounding Questing's disappearance. Colonel Claire listened blankly. When Falls had ended he merely said: "Oh that!" and looked faintly disgusted.

Gaunt said: "What's the good of all this? It seems to me you're running round in circles. Questing's gone. He's died in a nightmarish, an unspeakable manner and I for one believe that, like many a drunken man before him, he stumbled and fell. I won't listen to any other theory. And this drivelling about footprints! The track must be covered in footprints. My God, it's too much. What sort of country is this that I've landed in? A purple-faced policeman to speak to me like that! I can promise you there's going to be a full-dress thumping row when I get away from here." His voice broke. He struck his hands on the table. "It was an accident. I won't have anything else. An accident. An accident. He's dead. Let him lie."

"That is especially where I differ from you," said Dr. Ackrington crisply. "In my opinion Questing is very far from being dead."

CHAPTER XI

THE THEORY OF THE
PUT-UP JOB

The sensation he had created seemed to mollify Dr. Ackrington. After a moment's utter silence his hearers all started together to exclaim or expostulate. Dikon was visited by one of those chance notions that startle us by their vividness and their irrelevancy. He actually thought for a moment that Ackrington, of all people, had suggested some return from death. A horrific picture of a resurrection from the seething mud rose in his mind and was violently dismissed. From this fantasy he was aroused by Gaunt, who cried out with extraordinary vehemence: "You're demented! What idiocy is this!" and by Falls who, with an air of concentration, raised his hand and succeeded, unexpectedly, in quelling the rumpus.

"I assure you," he said, "if he was uninjured and moving, I must have seen him. But perhaps, Dr. Ackrington, you think that he was uninjured and still."

"I see you take my point," said Ackrington, who, as usual, seemed ready to tolerate Falls. "In my opinion the whole thing was an elaborately staged disappearance."

"Do you mean he's still hangin' about?" cried the Colonel, looking acutely uncomfortable.

"Of course," Mrs. Claire said, "we should all be only too thankful if we could believe..."

"Gosh!" said Simon under his breath. "I wish to God you were right."

"Same here," agreed Smith fervently. "Suit me all right, never mind what happened before." His hand moved to the breast pocket of his coat. He opened the coat and looked inside. An unpleasant thought seemed to strike him. "Here!" he said angrily. "Do you mean he's hopped it altogether?"

"I mean that taking into consideration the profound

incompetence of the authorities, he has every chance of doing so," said Ackrington.

"Aw, hell!" said Smith plaintively. "What do you know about that!" He laughed bitterly. "If he's hooked it," he said, "that's the finish. I'm not interested." The corners of his mouth drooped dolorously. He looked like an alcoholic and disappointed clown. "I'm disgusted," he said.

"Perhaps we should let Dr. Ackrington expound," Falls suggested.

"Thank you. I have become accustomed to a continuous stream of interruptions whenever I open my mouth in this household. However."

"Do explain, dear," said his sister. "Nobody's going to interrupt you, old boy."

"For some time," Dr. Ackrington began, pitching his voice on a determined note, "I have suspected Questing of certain activities; in a word, I believe him to be an enemy agent. Some of you have been aware of my views. My nephew, apparently, has shared them. He has not seen fit to consult me and has conducted independent investigations of the nature of which I was informed, for the first time, last night." He paused. Simon kicked his legs about and said nothing. "It appears," Dr. Ackrington continued, "that my nephew has had other confidants. It would be strange under these circumstances if Questing, undoubtedly an astute blackguard, failed to discover that he was in some danger. How many of you, for instance, knew of his real activities on the Peak?"

"I know what he was up to," said Smith instantly. "I told Rua, weeks ago. I warned him."

"Of what did you warn him, pray?"

"I told him Questing was after his grandfather's club. You know, Rewi's adze. I was sorry later on that I'd spoken. I got Questing wrong. It was different, afterwards. He was going to treat me all right." Again, his hand moved to the inside pocket of his coat.

"I too had spoken to Rua. I had received no satisfaction from the police or from the military authorities, and, wrongly perhaps, I conceived it my duty to warn Rua of the true significance of Questing's visit to the Peak. Don't interrupt me," Dr. Ackrington commanded, as Smith began a querulous outcry. "I told Rua the curio story was a blind. I gather that unknown to myself, at least three other persons"—he looked from Simon to Dikon and Gaunt—"were aware of my suspicions. Simon has actually visited the police. As for you, Edward, I tried repeatedly to convince you . . ."

"Yes, but you're always goin' on about somethin' or other, James."

"My God!" said Dr. Ackrington quietly.

"Please, dear!" begged Mrs. Claire.

"Is it too much," asked Gaunt on a high note, "to ask that this conversation should grow to a point?"

"May I interrupt?" murmured Falls. "Dr. Ackrington suggests that Questing, feeling that the place was getting too hot for him, has staged his own disappearance in order to make good his escape. We have got so far, haven't we?"

"Certainly. Further, I suggest that he was lying in the shadows when you hunted along the path last night after the scream, and that as soon as you had gone he completed a change of garments. Doubtless he had hidden his new clothes in some suitable cache. He threw the ones he was wearing into Taupo-tapu and made off under cover of the dark. In support of this theory I draw your attention to a development of which Falls has acquainted me. They have salvaged Questing's white waistcoat from Taupo-tapu. How could a waistcoat detach itself from a body?"

"It was a backless waistcoat," Dikon muttered. "The straps might have gone. And anyway, sir, the chemicals in the thing . . ."

But Dr. Ackrington swept on with his discourse. "It is even possible that the person you, Falls, heard moving about when you returned was Questing himself. Remember that he could only get away by returning through the village or by coming on round the hill. No doubt he waited for everything to settle down. He acted, of course, under orders." Dr. Ackrington coughed slightly and looked complacently at Falls. "My theory," he said with a most unconvincing air of modesty, "for what it is worth."

"If you don't mind my saying so, Uncle James," said Simon instantly, "in my opinion it's not so much a theory as a joke."

"Indeed! Perhaps you'll be kind enough..."

"You're trying to tell us that Questing wanted to make a clean get-away. What was his big idea letting out a screech you could hear for miles around?"

"I had scarcely dared to hope that I would be asked that question," said Dr. Ackrington complacently. "What better method could he employ if he wished to protect himself from interruption from the Maori people? Do you imagine that after hearing that scream, there was a Maori on the place who would venture near Taupo-tapu?"

"What about us?"

"It was sheer chance that kept Bell and your mother and sister and Mr. Falls behind. And, most important, please remember that it had been arranged that we should *all* pack into Gaunt's car for the return journey. All, that is, except Questing himself, Simon and Smith. It was an unexpected turn of events when Gaunt, Edward, Falls and I all decided, separately, to walk. He had expected to be practically free from disturbance. The audience was leaving when Questing himself went out."

"And what about this print?" Simon continued exactly as if his uncle had not spoken. "I thought the idea was that somebody had deliberately kicked the clod away. Bell's pointed out that Questing wore pansy pumps."

"Ah!" cried Dr. Ackrington triumphantly. "Aha!" Simon looked coldly at him. "Questing," his uncle went on, "wished to create the impression that he fell in. If my theory is correct he will have made as great a change as possible in his appearance. Rough clothes. Workmen's boots. He waits until he has changed his evening shoes for these boots and then stamps away the edge of the path." Dr. Ackrington slapped the table and flung himself back in his chair. "I invite comment," he said grandly.

For a moment nobody spoke, and then, to Dikon's profound astonishment, one after another, Gaunt, Smith, the Colonel, and Simon, the last somewhat grudgingly, said that they had no comments to offer. It seemed to Dikon that the listeners round the table had relaxed. There was a feeling of expansion. Gaunt touched his forehead with his handkerchief and took out his cigarette case.

Obviously gratified, Ackrington turned to Falls. "You say nothing," he said.

"But I am filled with admiration nevertheless," said Falls. "A most ingenious theory and lucidly presented. I congratulate you."

"What *is* it about the man?" Dikon wondered. "He looks all right, rather particularly so. His voice is pleasant. One keeps thinking he's going to be an honest-to-God sort of fellow and then he prims up his mouth and talks like an affected pedagogue." Out of patience with Falls, he turned to look at Barbara. He had tried not to look at her ever since she came in. Her pallor, her air of bewilderment, and the painful attentiveness with which she listened to everybody and said nothing seemed to Dikon almost unbearably touching. She was watching him now, anxiously, asking him something. She answered his smile with a shadowy one of her own. There was an empty chair beside hers.

"Dikon!"

Gaunt had shouted at him. He jumped and looked round guiltily. "I'm sorry, sir. Did you say something to me?"

"Dr. Ackrington has been waiting for your answer for some considerable time. He wants your opinion on his solution."

"I'm terribly sorry. My opinion?" Dikon thrust his hands into his pockets and clenched them. They were all watching him. "Well, sir, I'm afraid I've been completely addled by the whole affair. I can't pretend to have any constructive theory to offer."

"Then I take it you are prepared to accept mine?" said Ackrington impatiently.

Why had he got the feeling that they were bending their wills upon him, that they sat there boring into his mind with theirs, trying to compel him to something?

"What the devil's the matter with you?" Gaunt demanded.

"Come, come, Bell, if you've nothing to say we must conclude you've no objection."

"But I have," said Dikon, rousing himself. "I've every objection. I don't believe in it at all."

ii

He knew that his explanations sounded hopelessly inadequate. He heard himself stumbling from one feeble objection to another. "I can't disprove it, of course, sir. It might be true. I mean, it's all sort of logical but I mean it's not based on anything."

"On the contrary," said Dr. Ackrington and his very mildness seemed to Dikon to be most disquieting, "it is based on the man's character, on the circumstances surrounding him, and upon the undisputed fact that no body has been found."

"It sounds so sort of bogus, though." Dikon floundered about through a series of slangy phrases which he was quite unaccustomed to use. "I mean it's the kind of thing that they do in thrillers. I mean he wouldn't know there was going to be all that chat at the concert about the girl who fell in Taupo-tapu. Would he? And if he didn't know that then he wouldn't know about the scream keeping the Maoris away."

"My good fool," said Gaunt, "can't you understand that the scream was introduced *because* of the legend? An extra bit of atmosphere. If he hadn't heard the legend and the song he wouldn't have screamed."

"Precisely," said Ackrington.

"Well, Mr. Bell?" asked Falls.

"Yes, that fits in, of course, but I'm afraid it all sort of fits too neatly for me. As if it were concocted, don't you know? Like china packed too closely. No lee-way for jolts. I'm afraid my objections are maddeningly vague but I simply cannot *see* him hiding a disguise in an extinct geyser and tossing his boiled shirt into a mud pot. And then going off—where?"

"It is highly probable that a car was waiting for him somewhere along the road," said Ackrington.

"There's a goods train that goes through at midnight," suggested Smith. "He might of hopped onto that. Geeze, I hope you're right, Doc. It'd give you the willies to think he was stewing over there, wouldn't it?"

Mrs. Claire uttered a cry of protest and Ackrington instantly blasted Smith.

"Cut it out, Bert!" advised Simon. "You don't put things nicely."

"Hell, I said I hoped he *wasn't*, didn't I? What's wrong with that?"

"If you are not satisfied with Dr. Ackrington's theory, Mr. Bell," said Falls, "can you suggest any other explanation?"

"I'm afraid I can't. I haven't seen the print on the clod of mud, of course, but it seems to me it can't be an old one if it suggests that somebody kicked the clod loose. If that's so, it looks as if there has been foul play. And yet I'm afraid I don't think Questing was drunk enough to fall in or even that it's at all likely, if he did put his foot in the gap, that he would go right over. And it seems to be a very chancy sort of trap for a murderer to set, doesn't it? I mean Simon might have gone over, or anybody else who happened to walk that way. How could a murder reckon on Questing being the first to leave the concert?"

"You don't think it was an accident. You can't advance any tenable theory of homicide. You find my theory logical and yet cannot accept it. I think, Mr. Bell," Dr. Ackrington summed up, "you may be excused from any further attempts to explain yourself."

"Thank you very much, sir," said Dikon sincerely. "I think I may."

He walked round the table and sat down by Barbara.

From that moment the other men treated Dikon as an onlooker. It was impossible, they agreed, that in a homicide investigation the police could regard him as a suspect. He was with Mrs. Claire and Barbara when Questing screamed, he drove to the hall and had no opportunity to enter the thermal reserve either before, after, or during the concert. The fact that the path had been intact when the other men walked over to the village excluded him from any suspicion of complicity as far as the displaced clod was concerned. "Even the egregious Webley," said Dr. Ackrington, "could scarcely blunder where Bell is concerned." Dikon realized with amusement that in a way he lost caste by his immunity.

"As for the rest of us," said Dr. Ackrington importantly, "I have no doubt that Webley, in the best tradition of the worst type of fiction, will suspect each of us in turn. For this reason I have thought it well that we should consult together. We do not know along what fantastic corridors his fancy may lead him but it is quite evident from certain questions that he has already put to *me* that he has crystallized upon the footprint. Now, did any of us wear boots or shoes with nails in them?"

Only Simon and Smith, it appeared, had done so. "I got them on now," Smith roared out. "In my position you don't wear pansy shoes. I wear working boots and I wear them all the time." He hitched up his knee and planked a most unlovely boot firmly against the edge of the table. "Anybody's welcome to inspect my feet," he said.

"Thank you so much," Gaunt murmured. "No. Definitely no."

"That goes for me," said Simon. "I've got three pairs. They can look at the lot for mine."

"Very well," said Dr. Ackrington. "Next, they require to know our movements. Perhaps each of us has already been asked to account for himself. You, Agnes, and you, Barbara, are naturally not personally involved. Nevertheless you may be questioned about us. You should be prepared."

"Yes, dear. But if we are asked any questions we tell the truth, don't we? It's so simple," said Mrs. Claire, opening her eyes very wide, "just to tell the truth, isn't it?"

"Possibly. It's the interpretation this incubus may put upon the truth that should concern us. When I tell you that he has three times taken me through a recital of my own movements and has not made so much as a single note upon my theory of disappearance, you may understand my anxiety."

"Won't he listen to the idea?" asked Gaunt anxiously and then added at once: "No. No. He questioned me in the same way. He suspects one of us." And looking from one to another he repeated: "He suspects one of us. We're in danger."

"I think you underrate Webley," said Falls. "I must confess that I cannot see why you are so anxious. He is following police procedure, which, of necessity, may be a little cumbersome. After all Questing *has* gone and the manner of his going must be investigated."

"Quite right," said the Colonel. "Very sensible. Matter of routine. What I told you, James."

"And in the absence of motive," Mr. Falls continued, and was interrupted by Dr. Ackrington.

"Motive!" he shouted. "Absence of motive! My dear man, he will find the path to Taupo-tapu littered with alleged motives. Even I—*I* am suspect if it comes to motive."

"Good Lord," said the Colonel, "I suppose you are, James! You've been calling the chap a spy and saying shootin' was too good for him for the last three months or more!"

"And what about you, my good Edward? I imagine your position is fairly well-known by this time."

"James! Please!" cried Mrs. Claire.

"Nonsense, Agnes. Don't be an ostrich. We all know Questing had Edward under his thumb. It's common gossip."

Gaunt shook a finger at Simon. "And what about you?" he said. "You come into the picture, don't you?" He glanced at Barbara, and Dikon wished most profoundly that he had never confided in him.

Simon said quickly: "I've never tried to make out I liked him. He was a traitor. If he's cleared out I hope they get him. The police know what I thought about Questing. I've told them. And if I'm in the picture so are you, Mr. Gaunt. You looked as if you'd like to scrag him yourself after he'd finished his little speech last night."

"That's fantastically absurd, I'm afraid. I wouldn't wish my worst enemy to—God, I can't even bear to think of it."

"The police won't worry about how you think, Mr. Gaunt. It's the way you acted that'll interest them."

"Too right," said Smith rather smugly. Gaunt instantly turned on him.

"What about you and your outcry?" said Gaunt. "Three weeks ago you were howling attempted murder and breathing revenge."

"I've explained all that," shouted Smith in a great hurry. "Sim knows all about that. It was a misunderstanding. Him and me were cobbers. Here, don't you go dragging that up and telling the police I threatened him. That'd be a nasty way to behave. They might go thinking anything, mightn't they, Sim?"

"I'll say."

"Naturally, they'll have their eye on you," said Gaunt with some enjoyment. "I should say they'll be handing you the usual warning in less than no time."

Smith's eyes filled with tears. He thrust a shaking hand into the breast pocket of his coat and pulled out a sheet of paper which he flung onto the table. "Look at it!" he cried. "Look at it. Him and me were cobbers. Gawd spare me days, we buried the bloody hatchet, Morry Questing and me. That's what he was going to do for me. Look at it. Written out by his own hand in pansy green ink. Pass it round. Go on."

They passed it round. It was a signed statement written in green ink. The Colonel at once recognized the small businesslike script as Questing's. It undertook, in the event of Questing becoming the proprietor of Wai-ata-tapu, that the bearer, Herbert Smith, would be given permanent employment as outside porter at a wage of five pounds a week and keep.

"You must have made yourself very unpleasant to extract this," said Gaunt.

"You bet your boots I did!" said Mr. Smith heartily. "I got him while my bruises were still bad. They were bad, too, weren't they, Doc?"

Dr. Ackrington grunted. "Bad enough," he said.

"Yeh, that's right. 'You owe it to me, Questing,' I said and then he drove me over the the level crossing and showed me how it happened, him looking through the coloured sunscreen at the light. 'That may be a reason but it's no excuse,' I said. 'I could make things nasty for you and you know it.' So then he asks me what I want and after a bit he comes across with this contract. After that we got on well. And now, what's it worth? Dead or bolted it makes no odds, me contract's a wash-out."

"I should keep it, nevertheless," said Dr. Ackrington.

"Too right, I'll keep it. If Stan Webley starts in on me—"

"I had an idea," said Mr. Falls gently, "that we were going to discuss alibis."

"You're perfectly right, Falls. It's utterly beyond the power of man, in this extraordinary household, to persuade any single person to keep to the point for two seconds together. However. Now, we left this infernal concert severally. Questing went out first. You followed him, Gaunt, after an interval of perhaps three minutes. Not more."

"What of it?" Gaunt demanded, at once on the offensive.

He added immediately, "I'm sorry, Ackrington. I'm behaving
badly, I know." He looked at Mrs. Claire and Barbara. "Will
you forgive me?" he said. "I don't deserve to be forgiven, I
know, but this business had jangled my nerves to such an
extent I hardly know what I'm saying. I'm a bit run-down, I
suppose, and—well, it's hit me rather hard, for some stupid
reason."

Mrs. Claire made soft consolatory noises. For the life of
him Dikon could not stop himself looking at Barbara. Until
now, Gaunt had completely disregarded her but the famous
charm had suddenly reappeared and he was smiling at her
anxiously, pleading with her to understand him. Barbara met
this advance with a puzzled frown and turned away. Then, as
if ashamed of this refusal, she raised her head and, finding
that he was still watching her, blushed. "I'm so sorry," said
Gaunt and Dikon thought he made this last apology
indecently personal. Barbara answered it with an unexpected
gesture. She gave an awkward little bow. "She's got good
manners," thought Dikon. "She's a darling." He saw that her
hands were working together under the edge of the table and
wished he could tranquillize them with his own. When he
listened again to the conversation he found that Gaunt was
giving an account of his movements after the concert.

"I don't pretend I wasn't angry," he said. "I was furious.
He'd behaved abominably, using my name as a blurb for his
own squalid business. I thought the best thing I could do was
to go out and apply fresh air to the famous temperament.
That's what I did. There was nobody about. I lit a cigarette
and walked home by the road. I don't think I can prove to the
strange Mr. Webley that I did precisely that, but it happens to
be the truth. I regained my temper in the process. When I
arrived here I went to my room. Then I heard voices in the
dining-room and thought that a drink might be rather
pleasant. I came to the dining-room bringing a bottle of
whisky with me. I found Colonel Claire and Dr. Ackrington.
That's all."

"Quite so," said Ackrington. "Thank you. Now, Gaunt,
your best move, obviously, is to find some witness to your
movements. You say there is none."

"I'm positive. I've told you."

"But it's more than possible some of the Maori people

hanging round the doorway saw you walk away. The same observers might already have seen Questing go off in the opposite direction. I myself followed close after you but you had already disappeared. However, I heard distant voices that seemed to me to come from the far side of the village, the side nearest the main road. Possibly the owners of these voices saw you. It was with the object of collecting such data that I suggested we should call this meeting."

"I saw nobody," said Gaunt, "and I heard no voices."

"Did you hear the scream?" asked Simon.

"No, I heard nothing," said Gaunt easily and smiled again at Barbara.

"Then," said Dr. Ackrington importantly, "I may proceed with my own statement."

"No, wait a bit, James."

Colonel Claire drove his fingers through his hair and gazed unhappily at his brother-in-law. "I'm afraid we can't let things go like this. I mean, since you've insisted on us thrashing the thing out between us one mustn't keep back anything, must one? Gaunt's statement may be quite all right. I don't know. But at the same time . . ."

Dikon saw Gaunt turn white while his lips still held their smile. Gaunt did not look at the Colonel, his eyes still rested on Barbara, but they stared blankly, now. He did not speak and after glancing uncomfortably at him the Colonel went on.

"You remember," he said, "I went back to the *pa* last night."

"Well?" said Ackrington sharply as he paused.

"Well, I think I told you that they were all excited. They said a lot of things that at the time I felt I'd better keep to myself. I used to take that line in India, pretty much, when there was trouble with the natives. Wait a bit before handin' on anything they tell you or you may land yourself in a mess. It's the best way in my opinion. But when we agree to give full reports on our movements and there's evidence that a report may *not* be full, well then it's one's duty to speak. That's my view."

"Your ethics, my dear Edward, may be admirable. No doubt they are. But having decided to reveal that which you formerly held locked in your bosom, will you be kind enough to come to the point and, in fact, reveal it."

"All right, James. Don't start rattlin' me, there's a good chap. It's only this. One of the boys over there said that during Questing's speech he went up to a *whare* near the road. I'm afraid they'd got a keg of beer there stowed away for the evening. Young Eru Saul, it was. He said that some minutes later he heard a couple of *pakehas* having a fearful row. At least, one of them was abusin' the other like a pickpocket and the other seemed to be half-laughin' and half-jeerin'. 'Made him get very angry,' was the way Saul put it. He didn't understand what it was all about but he listened to it until he heard one of them call the other a bloody liar (please forgive me, Agnes, I have been against your attendin' this meetin' from the beginnin') and threaten to do something or another that Saul couldn't catch. Then there was a long pause. He got tired of it and went back to the beer. He heard someone walk past the *whare* and went out to see who it was. Of course it was dark but he left the door open. They're very careless about the blackout over there, my dear. I think we ought—"

"*Will you get on, Edward?*"

"Very well, James. The light from the door showed up this person and Saul said it was Gaunt. He said he'd recognized the angry voice as Gaunt's as soon as he heard it and he's quite certain the other man was Questing."

iii

During the next five minutes Dikon underwent as many changes of temperament as Gaunt himself at his worst. Incredulity, panic, sympathy, shame and irritation in turn possessed him as Gaunt first denied, then admitted and finally explained away his interview with Questing. He began by suggesting that the Colonel's informant had either made up his story of a quarrel or else mistaken the principals. The Colonel remained unshaken.

"I'm sorry," he said gently. "I don't think there was any mistake, you know."

"The youth was probably tight. Isn't he the fellow you've had to get rid of, Mrs. Claire?"

"Eru Saul? Yes. Yes. I'm afraid he really *is* an unsatisfactory boy. No home influence, alas. One of those *unfortunate* cases," said Mrs. Claire meaningly. "We've tried to give him a good start but he's drifted back. Such a pity, yes."

Gaunt shook a finger at the Colonel: "You say yourself he'd been at the beer."

"Yes, I know I do, but he wasn't a bit tight and I'm sure he believed he was speaking the truth."

"All right, Colonel." Gaunt raised his hands and let them fall on the table. "I give up. I met the man and told him precisely what I thought of him. I'm sorry it's had to come out. Another bit of most undesirable publicity. If my agent was here he'd give me absolute hell, wouldn't he, Dikon? My one desire was to keep out of this extremely distasteful affair. I'm perfectly certain that Dr. Ackrington is right and that the whole thing's a put-up job. Frankly, I'm tremendously anxious that my name should not appear and that is precisely why I hoped to avoid any mention of this encounter. I've been foolish. I realize that. I apologize."

"It's just too bad about you," said Simon. "You're in it with the rest of us. Why the heck should *you* get away with a pack of lies!"

"You're perfectly right, of course," said Gaunt. "Why should I?"

"If people start talking about murder—" began Smith confusedly, and Gaunt at once interrupted him.

"If there's talk of murder," he said, "I fancy this story gives *me* a complete alibi. Young Saul says that he saw me walking up to the main road. As a matter of fact I remember passing the lighted hut. I distinctly noticed a smell of beer. The thermal region's in the opposite direction. I suppose I should be grateful to the dubious Mr. Saul."

"You should be thankful you haven't landed yourself in a

damned equivocal position," said Dr. Ackrington, staring at
Gaunt. "I pass over the more serious view, which we should
be perfectly justified in taking, of your attempt to keep us in
the dark. I merely advise you to make quite sure of this alibi
you have just thought of."

"It is quite genuine, I promise you," said Gaunt easily.
"Might we get on with someone else's movements?"

"Well, of all the bloody nerve—" began Simon.

"Simon!" said his parents together and the Colonel
added, "You'll apologize to your mother and sister,
immediately, Simon. And to Mr. Gaunt."

Dikon, in his distress, had time to reflect that the Claires
were a little too good to be true. Simon muttered his apology.

"Suppose," Mr. Falls suggested, "we get on with the other
narratives. Yours, for instance, Ackrington."

"By all means. I shall begin by stating flatly that if I could
have got at Questing last night I should certainly have given
him fits. I left the hall with every intention of giving him fits. I
couldn't find him. I heard voices in the distance; in the light of
Gaunt's amended statement, I presume they were his and
Questing's voices but I did not recognize them. I had it in my
head that Questing would be half-way across the thermal
reserve and I hurried along with the idea of catching him up. I
did not find him. I carried on and came home."

"May one know why you wanted to tackle him?" asked
Falls.

"Certainly. His behaviour at the concert. It was the final
straw. Any questions?" asked Dr. Ackrington loudly.

"Too right, Doc, there's a question," said Smith with an
air of the deepest acumen. "Can you prove it?"

"No."

"Oh."

"Any other questions?"

"I should like to know," said Falls, "if you noticed the gap
in the path."

"I am glad, Falls, that you at least have had the
intelligence to ask the only question that can possibly have
any useful bearing on our problem. I did not. I must confess I
don't actually remember seeing the flag, which I admit is
curious. But I'm perfectly certain there was no gap in the
path."

"Might you have missed it, Uncle?" asked Barbara

suddenly and Dikon noticed how the men all looked at her as if a domestic pet had given utterance.

"Conceivably," said Dr. Ackrington. "I don't think so. However. Now you, Edward."

"It's unfortunate," said Gaunt airily, "that nobody saw the doctor whizzing past the geysers."

"I am aware of that. I realize my position. The purple policeman has doubtless put some fantastic interpretation upon the circumstance. I agree that I am unfortunate in that I was unobserved."

"But you *were* observed, James," said the Colonel, opening his eyes very widely. "I observed you, you know."

iv

The Colonel seemed to be mildly gratified by his brother-in-law's reception of this news. He smiled gently and nodded his head at Dr. Ackrington, who gaped at him, opened and shut his mouth once or twice, and finally swore swiftly under his breath.

"I was behind you, you know," Colonel Claire added. "Walkin'."

"I didn't suppose, Edward, that you cycled through the thermal region. May I ask why you have not mentioned this before?"

Colonel Claire returned the classic answer: "Nobody asked me," he said.

"Were you hard on his heels the whole way, Colonel?"

"Eh? No, Falls. No, you see he went so fast. I caught sight of him when I got to that gap in the hedge round the village and then the bumps in the ground hid him. Then I saw him again when I got to the top of the mound. He was nearly over at the hill by then."

"I must say it's not my idea of a cast-iron alibi," said

Gaunt, who seemed to welcome any chance of scoring off Dr.
Ackrington. "Two little peeps in the dark with craters and
mounds between you."

"Oh, he had a torch," said the Colonel. "Hadn't you,
James? And, by the way, the scream was *much* later. I was
nearly home when I heard the scream. I thought it was a
bird," added the Colonel.

"What sort of bird, for God's sake?"

"A mutton-bird, James. They make beastly noises at
night."

"There are no mutton-birds round here, Edward."

"Does it matter?" asked Dikon wearily.

"Not two hoots, I should have thought," said Gaunt
bitterly. "I've always detested nature study."

"He *is* sure of himself all of a sudden," thought Dikon.

They ploughed on with the Colonel's story. When asked if
he had noticed the gap in the path he became distressingly
vague and changed his mind with each question as it was put
to him. Falls took a hand. "You say you had a pocket torch,
Colonel. Now my recollection of the gap is that it showed
rather sharp and dark in the torchlight, like a shadow or even
a stain across the outer edge of the path."

"Yes!" the Colonel exclaimed. "That's a jolly good way of
describin' it. Like a black stain."

"Then you did see it?"

"I only said it was a good way of *describin'* it. Vivid."

"Didn't you notice that the white flag at the top was
missing?"

"Ah! Now, did I? You'd notice a thing like that, wouldn't
you?"

Dr. Ackrington groaned and executed a rapid tattoo with
his fingers on the table.

"But then again," the Colonel said, "one saw the *red* flags
going off at the *foot* of the mound, so naturally one wouldn't
follow *them*. And the path is quite sharply defined at that.
One would just follow it up the mound, wouldn't one,
Agnes?"

"What, dear?" said Mrs. Claire, startled by this sudden
demand upon her attention. "Yes, of course. Naturally."

"The hole!" Dr. Ackrington shouted. "The gap! For pity's
sake pull yourself together, Edward. Throw your mind, a

courtesy title for your cerebral arrangements, I fear, back to
your walk up the path. Visualize it. Think. Concentrate."

Colonel Claire obediently screwed up his face and shut his
eyes tightly.

"Now," said Dr. Ackrington, "you are climbing the path,
using your torch. Do you see the white flag on the top of the
mound?"

Colonel Claire, without opening his eyes, shook his head.

"Then, as you reach the top, what *do* you see?"

"Nothing. How can I? I'm flat on my face."

"What!"

"I fell down, you know. Flat."

"What the devil did you do that for?"

"I don't know," said Colonel Claire, opening his eyes very
wide. "Not on purpose, of course. I caught sight of you some
way ahead and I thought to myself, 'Hullo, there goes James,'
and there, at that moment, went I. It gave me quite a fright
because after all one is close to the edge up there. However, I
picked myself up and carried on."

"Did you fall into the hole, dear?" asked Mrs. Claire,
solicitously.

"What hole, Agnes?"

"James seems to think there was a hole," she muttered.

"Did you look to see why you'd fallen? Did you examine
the path with your torch?"

"How could I, James, when the torch had gone out? I fell
on it and it wouldn't go again. But I could see the flags dimly
so I was all right."

"I'm so glad you weren't hurt, dear," said his wife.

"And so there, in effect," said the Colonel quite cosily, "we
are."

"Precisely nowhere," said Dr. Ackrington. "I take it you
can't produce a witness to your movements, Edward?"

"Not unless Questing saw me. And even if he's alive, as we
all seem to have agreed, he's vanished into thin air, so that's
no good, is it?"

Dr. Ackrington pointed at his nephew. "You," he said.

"Bert and Colly and I were together," said Simon. "A chap
from Harpoon gave us a lift back. Ernie Priest, it was. Some
of the boys over there wanted us to stay for a drink but I don't
think it's so hot getting dragged in on those parties. It was
Eru Saul's gang and I draw the line there. Ernie had a bottle

of beer in the car. We had one with him and he dropped us up at the front gate. That's right, isn't it, Bert?"

"I'll say," said Smith moodily.

"Did any of you leave the hall during the performance?" asked Falls.

"You did, didn't you, Bert?"

"What if I did!" cried Smith, instantly on the defensive. "Sure, I did. I went out with two of the boys for a quick one. There's some people when they've got a drink on the place has the decency to offer you one." He looked accusingly at Gaunt. "*Some* people, I said," he added. "Not everyone."

"Who were the two youths?" Dr. Ackrington demanded.

"Eru Saul and Maui Matai."

"Did you separate at all, Mr. Smith?" asked Falls.

"That's right, pick on me. We did *not.* We stuck together and we got back in time to hear his nibs screeching his socks off."

"Are you talking about me?" asked Gaunt, bristling.

"That's right."

"I should be glad to know at what point in my performance I could be said, even by a drunken Philistine, to screech."

"'*Once more into the blasted breeches, pals,*'" said Smith in a shrill falsetto. "'*Once more.*' We could hear you all the way down the path. Does it hurt you much?"

"Cut it out, for Pete's sake, Bert," whispered Simon and stifled a laugh.

"I resent this," said Gaunt breathing noisily.

"My dear Gaunt, surely not?" soothed Mr. Falls. "A piquant incident! You will dine off it when the undesirable publicity has subsided. I should like to ask Mr. Smith and Mr. Claire," he went on, "if they and Mr. Gaunt's man remained in the hall until the general exodus."

"Yes," said Simon, glaring at him.

"Did you see Questing go out?" asked Dr. Ackrington.

"Too right we did," said Smith—"he was talking to us. Well, to me. Very pleased with his bit of a speech and skiting about it. It was while we were with some of the Maori gang, wasn't it, Sim? Outside the hall."

"That's right. And d'you know what I reckon he was doing?"

"You're asking me!" said Smith. "He was passing over the

doings. Had a bottle in his overcoat pocket. One of those flatties."

"Brandy," said Simon.

"Yeh. I saw him slip it to young Maui Matai. It's like what I told Rua. He was keeping in with the young lot. That's why Maui asked us to have one. I could of done with it, too," confessed Smith.

"Well, and then Ernie Priest came along," Simon explained, "and the four of us sloped off up to his car."

"Leaving Questing with those Maori youths?" asked Falls.

"That's right," said Smith.

"Interesting!" Falls murmured. "And your Maori friends said nothing to you of this, Colonel?"

"They wouldn't. They know what we think about the whole business of giving spirits to the natives."

"I suppose so. Yes, yes," said Gaunt in an exhausted voice.

"Ah, yes," said Mr. Falls blandly. "Quite so. Afterwards. I take it," he went on with his air of precision, "that this meeting doesn't wish for a repetition of my own extremely inconclusive statement? I understand that you have all become acquainted with it."

"That's right," said Simon before anyone else could answer. "We know you were just about on the spot when he yelled. We know you took pretty good care to keep us off the path while you went back there yourself. We know you wouldn't have had to say anything if Bell hadn't come along and found you. You're the only one of the lot of us except Uncle James that's seen this gap in the path. You seem to have got hold of the idea that everything you say goes for gospel. Well, by cripey, it doesn't for mine. By my idea you've had a free run of the hot air round here for a bit too long. There's one other thing we know about you. What about the stuff with your pipe?"

"Simon!" said his father and uncle together.

"What about it? Come on. What about it?"

"Simon, will you..."

"No, no, please!" begged Falls. "Do let us hear about this. I'm completely baffled, I assure you. Did you say my *pipe?*"

"I'm not saying another thing, Uncle. Keep your shirt on."

Colonel Claire looked coldly at his son and said: "You'll

come and speak to me afterwards, Simon. In the meantime you will be good enough to say nothing. I am ashamed of you."

"Damned young cub," Dr. Ackrington began, and his sister at once said: "No, James, please. It's for his father to speak to him, dear, if he's done wrong."

"*I'm* sorry," Simon muttered ungraciously. "I didn't mean to..."

"That will do," said his father.

"Well," said Falls, "since this seems to be another little mystery that is to remain unsolved, perhaps, Ackrington, you would sum up for us."

"Certainly. I'm afraid," said Dr. Ackrington, clearing his throat, "that beyond establishing a species of alibi in three cases, and also clarifying the situation generally, we do not appear at first glance to have attained very much."

"Hear, hear," said Gaunt.

"Nevertheless," continued Dr. Ackrington, quelling him with an acid stare, "there are certain valuable points to be noted. The gap in the path was not there before the concert. I didn't see it on my return and as Claire was close behind me it seems most unlikely, indeed impossible, that it could have appeared before he got there or that even he could have missed it. We are agreed that the clod of mud could only have been dislodged by considerable force and we know that it bears the deep impress of a nailed boot. The only two members of our party wearing nailed shoes or boots appear to have alibis. Questing must have entered the thermal reserve after Claire and I had crossed it and after his scene with Gaunt. What was he doing in the interim?"

"Having one with the boys?" Smith suggested.

"Possibly. That can be checked. Now, we have discovered nothing to contradict my theory of a put-up job. On the other hand we've narrowed down the margin for murder. If the clod was dislodged with the idea of Questing putting his foot into the gap and falling over, this fictitious murderer must have dodged out after you, Edward, had gone by. He must have danced and stamped about, revealing himself on the sky-line if you'd happened to glance back, and, having completed his work, come on here or returned to the *pa*. During this period Gaunt had quarrelled with Questing, and gone up to the main road; Simon and Smith were drinking in somebody's car after consorting for a time with certain Maoris; while Bell, Agnes, and Barbara had gone to Gaunt's car." Dr. Ackrington looked triumphantly round the table. "We are completely covered for the crucial time. What's the matter, Agnes?"

Mrs. Claire was weaving her small plump hands. "Nothing really, dear," she said gently. "It's only—I know nothing about such things, of course, nothing. But I do read some of Edward's thrillers, and it always seems to me that in the stories they make everything rather more elaborate than it would be in real life."

"This is not a discussion on the dubious realism of detective fiction, Agnes."

"No, dear. But I was wondering if perhaps we were not a little inclined to be too elaborate ourselves? I mean, it's very clever of you to think of all the other things, and I don't pretend I can follow them; but mightn't it be simpler if somebody had just hit poor Mr. Questing?"

Dikon broke a dead silence by saying. "Mrs. Claire, you make me want to stand up and cheer."

CHAPTER XII

SKULL

Dikon's was the only voice lifted in praise of Mrs. Claire's unexpected theory. Her brother, after looking at her in blank astonishment, told her roundly that she was talking nonsense. He explained, as if to a child, that a blow from a hidden assailant would not account for the displaced clod of mud and that even in a struggle, which could scarcely have taken place without Falls hearing it, the path was altogether too firm for any portion of it to give way. The Colonel supported him, saying that when the iron standards for the flags were driven in the Maoris had used a sledge-hammer. Mrs. Claire said that of course they were right, and they looked uneasily at her.

Barbara said: "Even if the police *do* think someone attacked him, haven't we proved that none of us could have been there at the time?"

"Bravo!" cried Gaunt. "Of course we have."

"As far as that goes," said Simon, "there is one of us who could have knocked him over." He looked at Falls.

"I?" said Falls. "Dear me, yes. So I could. So I could."

"After all," said Simon, "they'll only have your word for it that you didn't know what happened. Bell heard Questing scream and went out there. And what did he find? You. Alone."

"I was not wearing hobnail boots, however."

"Lucky for you, I reckon. And talking about these boots, there's something else I've got to tell you. Questing owned a pair of boots with sprigs. I can prove it."

Dikon had seen enough of Simon by this time to know that a piece of portentous information burnt holes in the pockets of his reticence. He frowned at Simon. He even tried to stave him off by an effort of the will but it was no good.

Out came the story of their climb up Rangi's Peak, out came
a description of the hobnailed footprints.

"And if the police show me this clod of mud I reckon I can
tell if it's the same print. Anyway they can go up the Peak and
look for themselves. With any luck the prints'll still be there."

With this recital he bounded into popular favour. Dr.
Ackrington, after a comparatively mild blast on the danger
of withholding information, declared that Simon, by his vigil
on the rock, had gone far towards proving that Questing was
the signaller. If Questing was the signaller it was almost
certain, said Dr. Ackrington, that the prints on the ledge were
his prints. If these corresponded with the impression on the
detached clod then they might well prove to be a determining
factor.

"You may depend upon it," cried Dr. Ackrington, "the
damned blackguard's a hundred miles away if he hasn't got
clean out to sea, and wherever he is, he's wearing those
blasted boots."

Steps sounded outside, followed by a muffled grumble of
voices. Dikon turned to look. Through the wide windows of
the dining-room the men at the table watched Webley's three
assistants cross the pumice and come towards the verandah.
Dikon was visited by a sensation of unreality, a feeling that
the mental and physical experiences of this interminable
morning were repeating themselves exactly. For the men
walked in the same order that they had adopted when he last
saw them. They carried again their muddy rakes and poles,
and one of them held away from him a heavy sack from
which a globule of mud formed and dropped. And just as,
before, his heart had jolted against his ribs, so it jolted again.
As the men drew near the verandah they saw the party in the
dining-room. They paused and the two groups looked at each
other through the open windows. A car came down the drive.
Webley and an elderly man got out. The men with the sack
moved towards them and again there was a huddled
inspection.

Mrs. Claire and Barbara, who sat with their backs to the
windows, followed the direction of their companions' gaze,
and half turned.

"Wait a moment, Agnes," said Dr. Ackrington loudly.
"Will you attend to me? Never mind the windows now. Mind
what I say. Barbara, will you listen!"

"Yes, James."

"Yes, Uncle James."

They turned dutifully. Dikon, sharing Dr. Ackrington's desire that Barbara should not see the men outside, got to his feet and moved behind her chair. Dr. Ackrington spoke loudly and rapidly. Colonel Claire and his wife and daughter looked at him. The others made no pretense of doing so, and Dikon tried to read in their faces the progress of the men beyond the window.

". . . I repeat," Dr. Ackrington was saying, "that it's as clear as daylight. Questing, having changed into workmen's clothes and heavy boots, stamped away the clod from the path, threw his evening clothes into the cauldron and bolted. We were meant to presume accidental death."

"I still think it was incredibly stupid of him to forget that he would leave prints," said Dikon. He saw Simon's eyes widen as he watched the men beyond the windows.

"He thought the clod would fall into the cauldron, Bell. It must be by the merest fluke that it did not do so."

Simon's hands were clenched. Falls raised an eyebrow. Dr. Ackrington himself, looking, as they did, beyond the windows, paused and then added rapidly: "If Questing is found before he gets clean away, he will be wearing hobnail boots. I'll stake my oath on it."

Simon was on his feet pointing. "Look!"

Now they all turned.

The group of men outside the window parted. Webley had taken something from the sack. He held it up. It was a heavy boot and it dripped mud.

ii

They were all shown the boot. Webley brought it into the dining-room and displayed it, standing on a sheet of newspaper in the middle of the table, and exuding a strong smell of sulphur. He wiped away most of the mud. The surface of the leather was pulpy and greatly disfigured, some of the metal eyelets had fallen out and the upper had become detached in places from the sole. There were, however, still two hobnails in the heel, though the others had fallen out.

Webley wiped his large flat hands on a piece of rag and looked woodenly at his trophy.

"I'd be obliged," he said, "if any of you ladies or gentlemen could put an owner on this. We've got its mate outside."

Nobody spoke.

"We fished them out with a hay-fork," Webley said. "Don't any of you gentlemen recognize it?"

Dr. Ackrington made a brusque movement. "Yes, Doctor?" Webley said at once. "You were going to say something?"

"I believe—I think that quite possibly they were Questing's."

"His? But you told me he wore evening shoes, Doctor."

"Yes. There's a new development, however. My nephew— Perhaps we should explain."

Simon cleared his throat. "I told them about it down at your show, Sergeant. It was during my investigation on the Peak."

Dikon wondered if for a fraction of a second Webley had looked resigned, if his singularly inexpressive face had been blurred momentarily with the glaze of boredom. He passed his flat fingers over his jowl, stared at Simon and said: "Oh, yes?" Simon embarked with a great air of consequence upon an account of their visit to the Peak. He forgot to include Dikon in his recital. "The night before when I was out on the rock, I picked that Questing was signalling from this ledge on the Peak. That's why I went straight up there yesterday morning. Soon as I got there I looked for footprints and did I find them! Two beauties. Squatting on his heels, he'd been, under the lee of the bank. Here! You let me have a look at the soles of the boots and I reckon I'll tell you if they made these prints on the Peak. That's a fair pop, isn't it?"

Webley went out and returned with the second boot. It was further advanced in disintegration than its mate. He laid them on the sides with their soles towards Simon.

"Some of the sprigs are gone," he said. "You can see where they've been, though. How about it?"

Simon leant forward portentously and stared at the boots. He counted under his breath and his face grew redder and redder.

"How about it?" repeated Webley.

"Give us a chance," said Simon. He laughed uncomfortably. "I've just got to think. You know. You have to concentrate on a thing like this."

"That's right," said Webley impassively.

Simon concentrated.

Gaunt lit a cigarette. "The young investigator seems to be going into a trance," he said. "I don't think I shall wait for the revelation. May I be excused?"

"Don't you start being funny," said Simon angrily. "This is important. You stay where you are." Dikon took out his notebook and Simon pounced on it. "Here! Why didn't you give me that before?" He ruffled the pages. "This is what I wanted all the time, Mr. Webley. I saw the significance of these prints right away and I got Bell to make a sketch of them. Wait till I find it."

"Was Mr. Bell up there with you?"

"That's right. Yes, I took him along as a witness. Here," cried Simon in triumph, "here it is. Look at that."

Dikon, having made the sketch, had a pretty clear recollection of the prints. He decided that they might have been made by the boots on the table. Such hobnails as remained, as well as the scars left by those that had fallen out, corresponded, he thought, with the impressions he had copied. Webley, breathing placidly through his mouth, shielded the sketch with his hand and compared it with his muddy exhibits. He looked at Dikon.

"Would you have any objection, Mr. Bell, to my taking possession of this page?"

"None."

"That'll be quite O.K., Mr. Webley," said Simon magnificently.

"Much obliged, Mr. Bell," said Webley and neatly detached the page.

Gaunt said: "And in what condition is our fugitive Questing now, Dr. Ackrington? Is he galloping away to some hide-out, dressed in dungarees and patent-leather pumps, or is he capering about in the rude nude?"

Dr. Ackrington darted a glance of loathing at Gaunt and said nothing.

Webley said: "You've been telling them about your theory, have you, Doctor? Disappearance, eh? You'll find it difficult to fit in these boots, won't you?"

"The difficulty," said Dr. Ackrington, "is not insuperable. Isn't it at least possible that Questing realized he had left recognizable footprints and threw the boots he had intended to wear into the cauldron?"

"You are as nimble in the concoction of unlikelihoods," said Gaunt, "as a Baconian nosing in the plays of Shakespeare."

"An utter irrelevancy, Gaunt. A little while ago you supported my contention. I find your change of attitude incomprehensible."

"I'm afraid that on consideration I find all your theories equally irrelevant *and* incomprehensible. I'm afraid that for me, however selfishly, the point of interest lies in the fact that whether Questing slipped, was pushed, or escaped, I cannot, in the wildest realms of conjecture, be purported to have had anything to do with the event. If I'm wanted, Sergeant Webley, I shall be in my room."

"That'll be quite O.K., thank you, Mr. Gaunt," said Webley and watched him go.

iii

When Gaunt had gone, the meeting dissolved into a series of mumbled duologues. Dikon heard Webley say that he wanted to look through their rooms. Mrs. Claire said that he would find them dreadfully untidy. It appeared that Huia, stimulated to the point of hysteria by the events of the last twelve hours, was incapable of performing her duties. She slept over at the native village which, Mrs. Claire explained, she reported to be seething with terrified speculations.

"They get such strange ideas, you know," said Mrs. Claire to Webley. "One tries to tell them that all their old superstitions are wrong but still they are there—underneath."

Dikon thought that Webley pricked up his ears at this. However the Sergeant merely said in his sluggish way that he would rather the rooms were not touched and that he hoped nobody would object to his looking through them. He added the ominous request that they should all remain on the premises as he would like to see them again. He went off with the Colonel in the direction of the study. Mr. Falls looked after them meditatively.

Dikon went to see his employer and found him on the sofa with his eyes closed.

"Well?" said Gaunt, without opening his eyes.

"Well, sir, the meeting's dissolved."

"I've been thinking. The Maori youth must be found. The youth who saw me go up to the main road."

"Eru Saul?"

"Yes. They must get a statement from him. It will establish my alibi." He opened his eyes. "You'd better tell the empurpled Sergeant."

"He's not to be approached at the moment, I fancy," said Dikon, who did not care at all for this suggestion.

"Well, don't leave it too long. After all it's of some slight importance since it protects me from a charge of homicide," said Gaunt bitterly.

"Is there anything else I can do?"

"No. I'm utterly prostrated. I want to be left alone."

Hoping that this mood would persist, Dikon went outside. There was no one about. He crossed the pumice sweep and wandered up and down the path by the warm lake. Wai-ata-tapu was unusually silent. The familiar morning sounds of housework were not to be heard or the voices of Mrs. Claire and Barbara screeching companionably to each other from different rooms. He could see Huia moving about in the dining-room. Presently Smith and Simon walked round the house, Simon discoursing magnificently. Webley came out of the study, unlocked the door of Questing's room and went in. Dikon was over-stimulated and so restless that he was unable to think closely about Questing's disappearance or indeed about anything. He was conscious that he had been frustrated at the moment of departure upon an emotional journey; he was both dissatisfied and apprehensive.

Presently Barbara came out of the house. She looked about her in a desultory fashion and, after a moment, caught sight of him. He waved vigorously. She hesitated and then, with a backward glance, came to meet him.

"What have you been doing all this time?" he asked.

"I don't know. Nothing. I ought to be seeing about lunch but I can't settle down."

"Nor I. Couldn't we sit down for a moment? I've been pounding to and fro like a sentry until I feel quite worn-out."

"I feel I ought to be doing something or another," said Barbara. "Not just sitting."

"Well, perhaps we could march up and down together."

"Oh, Dikon," Barbara said, "what is it that's waiting for us? Where are we going?"

He had no answer to this and after a moment she said: "You don't think he's alive, do you?"

"No."

"Do you think somebody killed him?" She looked into his face. "Yes, that is what you think," she said.

"Not for any logical reason. I can't work it out. I'm like your mother, I can't go all elaborate over it. I certainly can't believe in Dr. Ackrington's theory. He's so hell-bent on making everything fit into the mould of his own idea. Intellectually he's as obstinate as a mule, it seems to me."

"Uncle James turns everything into a kind of argument. Even terribly serious things. He can't help it. The most ordinary conversation with Uncle James can turn in the twinkling of an eye into a violent argument. But, though you mightn't think it, he *is* open to conviction. In the end. Only by that time you're so exhausted you've forgotten what it's all about."

"I know. The verdict goes by default."

"Would that be the way the scientific mind works?"

"How should I know, my dear?"

"I should like to ask you something," said Barbara after a silence. "It's nothing much but it's been worrying me. Suppose this does turn out to be—" She hesitated.

"Murder? One feels rather shy about uttering that word, doesn't one? Do you prefer the more classy 'homicide'?"

"No, thank you. Suppose it is murder, then. The police will want to know every tiny little thing about last night, won't they?"

"I suppose so. It's what one imagines. A prolonged and dreary winnowing."

"Yes. Well now, please don't fly into another rage with me because I really couldn't bear it, but ought I to tell them about my new dress?"

Dikon gaped at her. "Why on earth?"

"I mean, about him coming up to me and talking as if he'd given it to me."

Appalled by the possible implication of this project Dikon said roughly: "Good Lord, what tomfoolery is this!"

"There!" said Barbara.. "You're livid again. I can't think why you lose your temper every time I mention the dress. I still think he did it. He's the only person we knew who wouldn't see that it was an impossible sort of thing to do."

Dikon took a deep breath. "Listen," he said. "I told Questing the blasted clothes were almost certainly a present from your Auntie Whatnot in India. He remarked that India was a long way away and I've no doubt he thought he'd take a gamble and pretend he was the little fairy godfather. He was simply trying to make capital. And anyway," Dikon added, hearing his voice turn flat, "you must see that all this can have no possible bearing on the case. You don't want to go trotting to the police with tatty little bits of gossip about your clothes. Answer any questions that are put to you, you silly child, and don't muddle the poor gentlemen. Barbara, will you promise?"

"I'll think about it," said Barbara gravely. "It's only that I've got a notion in my head that somehow or another my dress does fit into the picture."

Dikon was in a quandary. If Gaunt was forced to acknowledge the authorship of the present to Barbara, his fury against Questing would be brought out in stronger relief, an unpleasant development. Dikon scolded, ridiculed, and pleaded. Barbara listened quietly and at last promised that she would say nothing of the dress without first telling him of her intention. "Though I must say," she added, "that I can't see why you're getting into such a tig over it. If, as you say, it's completely irrelevant, it wouldn't matter much if I did tell them."

"You might put some damn-fool idea into their thick heads. The mere fact of you lugging the wretched affair into the conversation would make them think there was something behind it. Let it alone, for pity's sake. What they don't know won't hurt them."

He kept her with him a little longer. He had an idea that she'd substitute this nonsense about the dress for a more important discussion which, at the last moment, she had funked. He saw her look unhappily at the door into Gaunt's rooms. At last, twisting her hands together, she said very solemnly: "I suppose you've had a lot of *experience*, haven't you?"

"I must say you do astonish me," cried Dikon. "What sort of experience? Do you imagine I'm dyed deep in strange sins?"

"Of course not," said Barbara turning pink. "I meant you must have had a good deal of experience of the Artistic Temperament."

"Oh, that. Well, yes; we come at it rather strong in our line of business, you know. What about it?"

Barbara said rapidly: "People who are very sensitive—" she corrected herself—"I mean, highly sensitized, are terribly vulnerable, aren't they? Emotionally they're a skin short. Sort of. Aren't they? Things hurt them more than they hurt us." She glanced doubtfully at Dikon. "This," he thought, "is pure Gaunt; a paraphrase, I shouldn't wonder, of the stuff he sold her while I was sweating up that mountain."

"I mean," Barbara continued, "that it would be wrong to expect them to behave like less delicately adjusted people when something emotionally disintegrating happens to them."

"Emotionally . . . ?"

"Disintegrating," said Barbara hurriedly. "I mean you can't treat porcelain like kitchen china, can you?"

"That," said Dikon, "is the generally accepted line of chat."

"Don't you agree with it?"

"For the last six years," said Dikon cautiously, "part of

my job has been to act as a shock-absorber for tempera-
ments. You can't expect me to go all dewy-eyed over them at
my time of life. But you may be right."

"I hope I am," said Barbara.

"The thing about actors, for instance, that makes them
different from ordinary people is that they are technicians of
emotion. They are trained not to suppress but to flourish
their feelings. If an actor is angry, he says to himself and to
everyone else, 'My God, I am angry. This is what I'm like
when I'm angry. This is how I do it.' It doesn't mean he's
angrier or less angry than you or I, who bite our lips and feel
sick and six hours later think up all the things we might have
said. He says them. If he likes someone, he lets them know it
with soft music and purring chest notes. If he's upset he puts
tears in his voice. Underneath he's as nice a fellow as the next
man. He just does things more thoroughly."

"You do sound cold-blooded."

"Bless me soul, I take pinches of salt whenever I enter a
stage-door. Just as a precautionary measure."

Barbara's eyes had filled with tears. Dikon took her hand
in his. "Do you know why I've said all this?" he asked. "If I
was a noble-minded young man with gentlemanly instincts, I
should go white to the lips and in a strangulated voice agree
with everything you say. Since I can't pretend we're not
talking about Gaunt I should add that it is our privilege to
sacrifice ourselves to a Great Artist. Because I'm Gaunt's
secretary I should say that my lips were sealed and stand on
one side like a noble-minded dumb-bell while you made
yourself miserable over him. I don't behave like this because
I'm not such a fool, and also because I'm falling very deeply
in love with you myself. There are Webley and your father
going into a huddle on the verandah so we can't pursue this
conversation. Go back into the house. I love you. Put that on
your needles and knit it."

iv

Somewhat shaken by his own boldness, Dikon watched Barbara run into the house. She had given him one bewildered and astonished glance before she turned tail and fled. "So I've done it," he thought, "and how badly! No more pleasant talks with Barbara. No more arguments and confidences. After this she'll fly before me like the wind. Or will she think it her duty to hand me a lemon on a silver salver and tell me nicely that she hopes we'll still be friends?" The more he thought about it the more deeply convinced did he become that he had behaved like a fool. "But it's all one," he thought. "She's never even looked at me. All I've done is to make her rather more miserable about Gaunt than she need have been."

Webley and the Colonel were still huddled together on the verandah. They moved and Dikon saw that between them they held a curious-looking object. Seen from a distance, it resembled a gigantic wishbone adorned with a hairy crest. It was by this crest that they held it, standing well away from the two shafts, one of which was wooden while the other glinted dully in the sunlight. It was a Maori adze.

Webley looked up and saw Dikon, who instantly felt as though he had been caught spying on them. To dispel this uncomfortable illusion, he walked over and joined them.

"Hullo, Bell," said the Colonel. "Here's a rum go." He looked at Webley. "Shall we tell him?" he asked.

"Just a minute, Colonel," said Webley, "just a minute. I'd like to ask Mr. Bell if he's ever seen this object before."

"Never," said Dikon. "To my knowledge, never."

"You were in Questing's room last night, weren't you, Mr. Bell?"

"I glanced in to see if he was there. Yes."

"You didn't look in any of his boxes?"

"Why should I?" cried Dikon. "This isn't a corpse-in-a-trunk mystery. Why on earth should I? Anyway," he added lamely after a glance at Webley's impassive face, "I didn't."

Webley, still holding the adze by its hairy crest, laid it carefully on the verandah table. The haft, intricately carved, was crowned by a grimacing manikin. The stone blade, which had been worked down to a double edge with a rounded point, projected, almost at right angles to the haft, from beneath the rump of the maniken.

"They used to dong one another with those things," said Dickon. "Did you find it in Questing's room?"

The Colonel glanced uncomfortably at Webley, who merely said: "I think we'll let old Rua take a look at this, Colonel. Could you get a message over to him? My chaps are busy out there. I'd rather nobody touched this axe affair and anyway it'd be as well to get Rua away from the rest of his gang."

"I'll go," Dikon offered.

Webley looked him over thoughtfully. "Well now, that's very kind of you, Mr. Bell," he said.

"Trophies of the chase, Sergeant?" asked Mr. Falls, suddenly thrusting his head out of his bedroom window which was above the verandah table. "Do forgive me. I couldn't help overhearing you. You've found a magnificent expression of a savage art, haven't you? And you wish for an expert opinion? May I suggest that Bell and I go hand-in-hand to the native village? We can, as it were, keep an eye on each other. A variant of the adage that one should set a thief to catch a thief. Do you follow me?"

"Well, sir," said Webley, watching him carefully, "there's no call to put it like that. At the same time, if you two gentlemen care to stroll over to the *pa*, I'm sure I'd be much obliged."

"Splendid!" cried Mr. Falls gaily. "May we go by the short route? It will be much quicker and since, as I imagine, the cauldron is all set about with your myrmidons, neither of us will have an opportunity to add articles of evening dress to the seething mud. You could give us a chit to your men, no doubt."

Greatly to Dikon's astonishment, and somewhat to his dismay, Webley raised no objection to this project. Dikon and Mr. Falls set out, by the all too familiar path, for the native reserve. Mr. Falls led the way, limping a little it is true, but not, it seemed, greatly inconvenienced this morning by his lumbago.

"I must congratulate you," he said pleasantly, "on the attitude you adopted at our rather abortive conference. You felt that our anatomist's flights into the realms of conjecture were becoming fantastic. So, I must confess, did I."

"You did!" Dikon ejaculated. "Then, I must say..." He stopped short.

"You were about to say that I didn't contradict him. My dear sir, you saved me the trouble. You propounded my views to a nicety."

"I'm afraid I find that difficult to believe," said Dikon dryly.

"You do? Ah, yes, of course. You regard me as the prime suspect. Very naturally. Do you realize, Mr. Bell, that if I'm tried for murder, you will be the chief witness for the prosecution? Why, bless my soul, you almost caught me red-handed. Always presuming that my hands were red."

Mr. Falls's face was habitually inscrutable and naturally the back of his head was entirely so. Dikon walked behind him and felt himself to be at a loss. He tried to keep his voice as colourless as Mr. Falls's own. "Quite so," he said. "But I tell myself that as guilty person you might have shown more enthusiasm for Dr. Ackrington's theory. No murder, no murderer."

"Unbounded enthusiasm would hint at a lack of artistry, don't you feel?"

"The others exhibited it," said Dikon. Mr. Falls gave a little chuckle. "Yes," he agreed, "their relief was almost tangible, wasn't it? Now you, as the only one of the men with a really formidable alibi, were also the only man to exhibit scepticism."

"Mr. Falls," said Dikon loudly, "what's your idea? Do you think he's dead?"

"Yes."

"Murdered?"

"Oh, yes. Rather. Don't you?"

By this time they had reached the borders of the thermal region. Remembering the lunar landscape of last night Dikon thought that by day it looked only less strange. There, in the distance, the geyser's jet was, for a flash of time, erected like a plume in the air. Here, the path threaded its way between quaking ulcers; there, the white flags drooped from their iron standards. There, too, on the crest of the mound above Taupo-tapu, were Mr. Webley's men, black figures against a sombre background, figures that stooped, thrust downwards, and then laboriously lifted.

"One can't believe in things like this," said Dikon under his breath.

Mr. Falls had very sharp ears. "Horrible, isn't it?" he said. And again it was impossible to find in his voice the colour of his thought. He waved his stick. "The whole place," he said, "is impossibly Doré-esque, don't you feel?"

"I find it so difficult to believe that it's entirely impersonal."

"The Maori people make no attempt to do so, I understand."

Now they had drawn close to the mound. Dikon said to himself: "It is nothing. Falls will hand over Webley's authority and we shall walk quickly over the mound. I shall look at the path between Falls's feet and my feet and in a moment it will begin to lead downhill. And then I shall know that my back is turned to Taupo-tapu. It is nothing."

But as they climbed the mound the distance between them widened and Dikon didn't hear what Falls said to the men. Why were they waiting? Why this long mumbled colloquy? He looked up. The path was steep on that side of the mound and his eyes were on a level with the men's knees.

"Can't we get on with it?" he heard himself say angrily.

One of the men pushed past him and stumbled down the path.

Falls said: "Wait a moment, Bell." The man who had blundered down the path began to make retching noises.

The men on the top of the mound—there were two of them now besides Falls—squatted close to each other as if they held a corroboree. One of them let go a pitchfork he held and it rattled down the path. Falls stood up. His back was towards the light but Dikon saw that his face was bleached. He said: "Come on, Bell." Although Dikon desired most passionately to turn and escape by the path along which they had come, his muscles sent him forward.

It would have been much worse, of course, if they hadn't covered it, but, though the sack was thick, it was wet. It followed the shape beneath it in a hard eloquent curve. Dikon's imagination found sockets in the shadows beneath the curve. One of the men must have pushed him forward.

Falls waited for him on the far side at the foot of the mound, but as soon as Dikon reached him he turned and led the way onwards to the gap in the manuka hedge. Here a man stood on guard.

Even when they were beyond the fence he could still hear the sound of Taupo-tapu, the grotesquely enlarged domestic sound of a boiling pot.

CHAPTER XIII

LETTER FROM
MR. QUESTING

Strangely enough the sensation that was uppermost in Dikon's mind was one of embarrassment. He would have to speak to Falls about what they had seen, and like a man who hesitates before making a speech of condolence he did not know how to form his phrases. Should he say: "I suppose that was Questing's head under the sack"? Or, "That settles it"? Or, "That disposes of Ackrington's theory, doesn't it?" It was impossible to find the right phrase. He was so occupied with his preposterous difficulty and, at the same time, suffered such a violent feeling of nausea that he didn't notice Eru Saul and was startled when Falls spoke to him.

"Hello," said Mr. Falls. "Can you direct me to Mr. Rua Te Kahu's house?"

Dikon thought that Eru must have been standing in a recess in the hedge, perhaps peering through the twigs, and that he had turned quickly as they came up to him. He was coatless, and wore his puce-coloured shirt. Bits of dry manuka stuck to it and to the front of his waistcoat.

Mr. Falls pointed the ferrule of his stick at the recess. "Can you see the working party from here?" He squinted through an opening in the manuka. "Ah, yes. Quite clearly." He picked a twig off the front of Eru's waistcoat. "Terrible affair, isn't it?" he said. "And now, as we have a message for Mr. Te Kahu from the police, would you mind directing us?"

Eru said: "Have they found him?"

"'A part of him.' Forgive the inadvertent quotation. His skull to be exact."

243

"'Struth!" Eru whispered and showed his teeth. He turned and walked quickly up the path to the *marae* and they followed him. Old Mrs. Te Papa sat on the verandah floor with her back against the meeting-house wall. When she saw them she shouted something in Maori and Eru replied briefly. Her response was formidable. She flung up her hands and pulled her shawl over her face.

"*Aue! Aue! Aue! Te mamae i au!*" wailed Mrs. Te Papa.

"Good God!" cried Mr. Falls nervously. "What's she doing?"

"I've told her," said Eru sulkily. "She's going to *tangi*."

"To wail," Dikon translated. "To lament the dead. Think of an Irish wake."

"Really. Extraordinarily interesting."

Mrs. Te Papa continued to wail like a banshee while Eru led them to the largest of the cottages that stood round the *marae*. Like its fellows it was shabby. Its galvanized iron roof was corroded by sulphur.

"That's it," said Eru, and made off.

Attracted by Mrs. Te Papa's cries, other women came out of the houses and, calling to each other, trooped towards the meeting-house. Eru was joined by three youths. They stood with their hands in their pockets, watching Mr. Falls and Dikon. Dikon still felt very sick, and hoped ardently that he would not disgrace himself before the youths.

Mr. Falls was about to tap on the door when it opened and old Rua stood upon the threshold. Mrs. Te Papa shouted agitatedly. He answered her in Maori and waited courteously for his visitors to announce their errand. Falls delivered Sergeant Webley's message and Rua at once said that he would come with them. He shouted, and a small girl ran out of the house, bringing the grey blanket he wore on his shoulders. "It is as well," he said tranquilly, but with a faint glint in his eyes, "to give instant obedience when it is a policeman who asks. Let us go." He turned off as if to follow the track that led to the main road.

"We've got the Sergeant's permission to cross the reserve," said Mr. Falls.

"It will be better by the road," said Rua.

"It's very much further," Falls pointed out.

"Then we should take Mrs. Te Papa's car." Again Rua

shouted and Mrs. Te Papa broke off in the middle of a desolate wail to say prosaically: "All right, you take him but he won't go."

"We shall take him," said Rua, "and perhaps he will go."

"Eru can make him go," Mrs. Te Papa remarked and she hurled an order across the *marae*. Eru detached himself from the group of young men and slouched off behind the houses.

"Thank you so much, Mrs. Te Papa," said Falls, taking off his hat.

"You are very welcome," she replied, and composed herself for a further lamentation.

Mrs. Te Papa's car was not so much a car as a mass of wreckage. It stood in a back yard in a little pool of oil, sketchily protected by the remains of its own fabric hood. One of its peeling doors hung disconsolately from a single hinge. It was markedly bandy and had that look of battered gentility that belongs to very old-fashioned vehicles.

Rua opened the only door that was shut and said: "Do you prefer front or back?"

"I shall sit in back with you, if I may," said Falls.

Dikon climbed into the front. Eru wrenched at the starting handle, and, as though he had dug a thumb in her ribs, the old car gave a galvanic start and set up a terrific commotion. "Ah!" Rua shouted cheerfully. "She goes, you see." Having been left in gear, she almost ran over her driver. However, Eru flung himself in as she passed, and in a moment they were jolting up the hill. The noise was appalling.

"I see no reason," Mr. Falls began in a stentorian voice. "why you should not be told the object of Sergeant Webley's message."

Dikon slewed round in his seat to gaze in consternation at Mr. Falls. He met the unwinking stare of old Rua, huddled comfortably in his blanket.

"Webley wants your opinion on a native weapon," Falls continued. "A beautiful piece, it seems to me, a collector's piece." Rua said nothing. "I should call it an adze but perhaps that is incorrect. Let me describe it."

He described it with extraordinary accuracy and in such detail that Dikon was first amazed at his faculty of observation and then extremely suspicious of it. Could Mr.

Falls possibly have seen all these things through his window during the brief time that the adze was on the verandah table?

"One thing struck me very forcibly," Mr. Falls was saying. "The figure at the head of the haft has got, not one protruding tongue, but two. Two long protruding tongues, side by side. The little god, if indeed he is a god, holds one in each of his three-fingered hands. Between the fingers there are small pieces of shell and beneath them the tongues are encircled by a narrow band."

"You are driving too fast, Eru," said old Rua, to Dikon's profound relief. Mrs. Te Papa's car, bucketing down a steep incline, had developed a curious flaunting movement which, he felt certain, its back axle could sustain no longer. Eru checked her with a jerk.

"The band itself," Mr. Falls continued mellifluously in the comparative silence, "is most delicately carved. One marvels at the skill of your ancient craftsmen, Mr. Te Kapu. When one considered that their tools were those of a stone age—What did you say?"

Rua had made some ejaculation in his native tongue.

"Nothing," he said. "Drive carefully, Eru. You are too impetuous."

"But it seems to me that across this band some other hand has graved three vertical furrows. The design is repeated all over the weapon, but in no other place do these three lines occur. Now how do you explain that?"

Rua did not answer at once. Eru trod violently on the accelerator, and Dikon repressed a cry of dismay as Mrs. Te Papa's car responded with a shattering leap. Rua's words were lost in the din of progress. "Wait . . . impossible . . . until I see . . ."

He roared at Eru and at the same time Dikon turned to protest against this new turn of speed. He saw, with astonishment, that the half-caste's lips were trembling, that his face was livid. "He must be feeling like I feel," thought Dikon. "He must have seen everything through the hole in the manuka hedge."

Mr. Falls leant forward and tapped Eru on the shoulder. He started violently.

"I hear you missed the star turn at the concert last night," said Mr. Falls.

"We heard some of it," said Eru. "It was all right, too!"

"Mr. Smith tells me you missed the earlier speeches. I do hope you returned in time for the magnificent Saint Crispin's Eve."

"Was that when he said something about the old dugouts being asleep while him and the boys was waiting for the balloon to go up?"

"'And gentlemen in England now a-bed'?"

"Yeh, that's right. We heard that one. It was good, too."

"Marvellous," said Mr. Falls, and sat back in his seat. "Marvellous, wasn't it?"

They arrived intact at Wai-ata-tapu. The adze had been removed, evidently to the Colonel's study, as Rua was at once taken there, Falls, rather unnecessarily, ushering him in. Dikon was left alone with Eru Saul in Mrs. Te Papa's palpitating car. "Hadn't you better turn off your engine?" he suggested. Eru jumped and switched back the key. "Have a cigarette?" said Dikon.

"*Ta.*" He helped himself with trembling fingers.

"This is a bad business, isn't it?"

"It's terrible all right," said Eru, staring at the study window.

Dikon got out and lit his own cigarette. He was feeling better. "Where did they find it?" Eru demanded.

"What? Oh, the axe. I don't know."

"Did they find it in *his* stuff?"

"Whose?" said Dikon woodenly. He was determined to know nothing. Eru electrified him by jerking his head, not at Questing's room but at Gaunt's.

ii

"That's where he hangs out, isn't it?" said Eru. "Your boss?"

"What the hell do you think you're talking about?" said Dikon violently.

"Nothing, nothing!" said Eru, showing the whites of his eyes. "I was only kidding. You don't want to go crook over a joke."

"I can't see anything amusing in your extraordinary suggestion that a Maori axe should be discovered in Mr. Gaunt's room."

"O.K., O.K. I only wondered if he was one of these collectors. They'll come at anything, if they're mad on it. You know. Lose their respect for other people's property."

"Let me assure you that Mr. Gaunt is not a collector."

"Good oh. He's not. Let it go."

Dikon turned on his heel and walked toward his own room. It was in his mind to go straight to Gaunt. His idea of Gaunt, by no means an unrealistic one, had been defaced by the events of the day. He felt a strange necessity to see Gaunt for himself, alone, to try if it was possible to re-establish their old relationship. He had not gone more than six paces when he was arrested by a terrific rumpus which seemed to come from the Colonel's study. It was old Rua. His voice was raised in a roar as formidable as any with which his ancestors had led their clans to battle. The words at first were indistinguishable. Dikon thought that he made out ejaculations in Maori and occasional words of English. A babble of consolatory phrases broke out. The Colonel, Sergeant Webley and Mr. Falls seemed to be making an attempt to placate him. He roared them down. "It is the Toki-poutan-gata-o-Tane. It is the weapon of my grandfather, Rewi. It is a matter of offence against a most sacred and tapu possession. It must be returned immediately. *Immediately!*"

"Wait on, wait on," Dikon heard Webley mumble. "You'll get it back all right."

"I shall have it back immediately. I shall appeal to the native land courts. I shall go to the Minister for Native Affairs," Rua stormed and Dikon was reminded vividly of his employer. The rumpus broke out with renewed enthusiasm. Mrs. Claire came out from the dining-room.

"Oh, Mr. Bell," she whispered, "*what* now?" She laid a plump hand on his arm, a hand which he thought the more touching for its calluses and stains. "It's Rua, isn't it?" she said.

"Something about his grandfather's axe," Dikon muttered. "He's very cross with Webley for holding onto it."

"Oh, dear! One of those *silly* superstitions. Sometimes one almost loses hope. And yet, you know, he's a regular communicant."

The regular communicant, at this moment, came charging out of the study roaring like a bull and flourishing the ancestral adze. Webley and the Colonel were hot on his heels. Mr. Falls followed in a more leisurely manner.

"He's ruining the prints," Webley shouted in great agitation. "It's most irregular."

Rua plunged blindly along the verandah. Mrs. Claire moved forward to meet him. He fetched up short. He was breathless, and his eyes flashed. He stamped twice with his heavy boot and shook the adze. "It is an outrage!" he panted.

"Now, Rua," said Mrs. Claire placidly. "It's not at all good for you to work yourself up like this and it's not a nice way to behave in somebody else's house. I'm ashamed of you."

Webley approached cautiously and Rua backed away from him.

"I obey the gods," said Rua. "He robbed the grave of my ancestor. The fury of Tane has fallen upon him. My grandfather Rewi is avenged." It occurred to Dikon that all this grandiloquence would have sounded more impressive in the native tongue. Mrs. Claire seemed to be of this opinion. She administered a crisp scolding, her hands folded at her waist, while Rua, still clutching his preposterous trophy, rolled his eyes and seemed to be in two minds whether to go for Webley or beat a retreat.

Upon this scene, half-comic, half-ominous as all scenes at Wai-ata-tapu seemed fated to appear, came Huia, nervously twisting her hands. She edged her way round the dining-room door and along the back of the verandah. Her gaze was fixed upon her great-grandfather. At the same time Simon appeared round the corner of the house and Barbara, carrying a tray, drifted through the dining-room and paused at the windows. Dr. Ackrington loomed up behind her, peered through the window and, seeing what was afoot, limped out to the verandah. A moment later Dikon heard a movement in Gaunt's rooms. It was as though the characters in a loosely constructed drama had begun to converge upon a focal point.

Huia's face had lost its warmth of colour. She and the old man stared at each other, seeming to communicate. He raised the adze slowly. The crest of hair quivered. *"Haere mai,"* said Rua. "Come here to me."

She crept a little nearer. He began to speak to her in their own tongue but soon checked himself. "You do not understand me. You know little of the speech of the children of Tane. Very well. Let your shame be made known in the tongue of the *pakeha.*" He looked about him, commanding the attention of his hearers. "Many months ago, feeling myself draw near to the path that goes down to the final abode, I spoke with my eldest grandson who now fights with our battalions in a strange country. To him I confided the secret of the hiding place of this weapon, a secret which has been known only to the *ariki*, the first-born, of each generation of my family. Beyond the manuka bushes where we spoke, unknown to me, this girl lay dreaming. I discovered her when my grandson had left me. I questioned her and she told me that since I had spoken in our own tongue she had not understood me. Look at her now and judge if she deceived me." He moved towards her. She pressed herself against the wall and watched him. "To whom did you betray the resting place of Rewi's *toki?* Answer me. To whom?"

She made a timid abortive gesture, half-raising her hand. Then, as if Rua had menaced her, she shot out her arm and pointed at Eru Saul.

iii

Throughout the scenes that followed Dikon had the feeling that he was peering into some room which at first seemed to be quite dark. But, he thought, out of the shadow nearer objects presently appeared so that first the figure of Huia and then that of Eru were distinguishable, while behind these, in deeper shadow, more significant forms awaited the slow adjustment of his vision.

Eru faced old Rua with an air strangely compounded of terror and effrontery. Dikon fancied that a struggle was at work in the half-caste, between his European and his native impulses. If this was so the Maori, under Rua's dominance, was the more potent agent. A shabby attempt at defiance soon broke down. Eru began with protestations and ended with a confession.

"I never touched it. I never took it. I never seen it before."

"You knew where it rested. Huia, answer me. You told him where it was hidden?"

Huia nodded and burst into tears. Eru threw a venomous glance at her.

"So you, Eru, stole it and took money for it from this man Questing?"

"I never! I never knew he'd got it. I hadn't got any time for him."

"Huia, did you tell Questing?"

"No! *No!* Never. I never tell anyone but Eru. It was long time ago. I told Eru for fun when we go together. Nobody else. Eru told him."

"If I'd thought it was for that bastard," said Eru, "I'd never of told nobody." And with extraordinary venom he added: "You and your fancy *pakeha*. I might've picked Questing was at the back of it. Why the hell didn't he say it was for Questing?"

"To whom *did* you speak of this matter? Answer me."

"Come on, Eru," said Webley. "You won't do yourself any good by holding out on it. There's a serious charge mixed up in this business, don't forget. You want to put yourself right, don't you?"

"I told Bert Smith," Eru muttered and Dikon thought he saw a little farther into the darkness of that shrouded room: not to the end, he thought, but a little farther. Webley moved forward and said to Simon, "Find Bert, will you?"

"O.K.," said Simon.

When he appeared Smith was querulous and uneasy.

"Can't a bloke have *any* time to himself?" he demanded and then saw the adze in Rua's hand. "By cripey!" he said. "By cripey, it's Rewi's axe." He looked at Rua and drew a deep breath. "So he stuck to it, *after* all," he said.

"Who stuck to what?" asked Webley. "Take a look at that axe, Bert. Have you ever seen it before? Come on."

Smith cautiously approached Rua, who drew back. "You'll have to let him see it, Rua," said Webley. "Come on, now."

"It's all right," said Smith. "I've never seen it but I know what it is all right. I'd heard all about it."

"You stole it—" Rua began and Smith, in a great hurry, interrupted him. "Not on your life, I didn't! You haven't got anything on me. I might of known where it was and I might of told him but I never went curio hunting on the Peak. No bloody fear, I didn't."

"You told Questing where it was?" Dr. Ackrington demanded. "Why?"

"Just a minute, Doctor, if *you* please," Webley intercepted. "Now then, Bert. What was the idea, telling Questing?"

"He asked me." And now it was Questing's large face that showed in the dark.

"Asked you to find out? *And* paid you for your trouble, eh?" said Webley.

"All right. Put it that way. Nothing criminal in passing on a bit of information, is there? He asked me to find out and I found out. Eru told me. Come on, Eru. You told me, you know you did."

"You said it was for the other bloke," Eru said breathlessly.

"What other bloke?" Webley demanded. Eru once again jerked his head at Gaunt's rooms. "Him," he said. And Dikon now saw into the farthest corner of his imaginary room.

In the silence that followed, Mr. Falls said: "There seems to be a multiplicity of blokes all passing on information like a hot potato. Are we to understand, Sergeant Webley, that the deceased, on behalf of Mr. Gaunt, bribed Mr Smith to bribe Mr. Saul, is it? Thank you—Mr. Saul, to obtain information as to the *locale* of this exquisite weapon?"

"It looks as if that's about the strength of it, sir."

"You damn' well choose your words!" said Smith

indignantly. "Who's talking about bribes? It was between friends. Him and me were cobbers, weren't we, Sim?"

"I thought he tried to put you under the train, Bert," said Webley."

"Oh, my Gawd, do I have to go into that again!" apostrophized Mr. Smith with evident fatigue. "We got it all ironed out. Here. Take a look." He lugged out his written agreement with Questing and thrust it at Webley.

"Let it go," said Webley. "You showed me that before. We won't trouble you any more just now, Bert."

"So *you* say," Smith grumbled and, carefully folding his precious document, wandered morosely into the dining-room.

Webley turned to Rua. "Look, Rua. You can see by what's been said that we've got to keep hold of your grand-dad's axe. We'll give you a receipt for it. You'll get it back all right."

"It should not be touched. You do not understand. I myself, holding it, am now tapu."

"Rua, Rua!" chided Mrs. Claire softly.

"Sergeant Webley," said Falls, "Please correct me if I am wrong, but suppose Mr. Te Kahu gave you his undertaking that when the adze is needed by the police he will allow them to have it? Could it not in the meantime be entrusted to the Colonel? The Colonel is your friend, Mr. Te Kahu, isn't he? Suppose you went with him to his bank and left it there for safe-keeping? How would that be? Colonel, what do you say?"

"Eh?" said the Colonel. "Oh, certainly, if Webley agrees."

"Sergeant?"

"I'll be satisfied, sir."

"Well, then?" Falls turned to Rua.

The old man looked at the weapon in his hands. "You will think it strange," he said, "that I, who have in my time led my people towards the culture of the *pakeha,* should now grow quarrelsome over a silly savage notion. Perhaps in our old age we return to the paths of our forbears. The reason may put on new garments but the heart and the blood are constant. From the haft of the weapon there flows into my blood an influence darker and more potent than all the *pakeha* wisdom I have stored in my foolish old head. But, as you say, Colonel Claire is the friend of my people. To him I submit."

Falls went into his room and came out with that heavily belabelled case which Mrs. Claire had noticed on his arrival. He placed it, open, upon the table, and Rua laid the adze in it.

"If it remains in Colonel Claire's hands," he said, "I am satisfied." He turned to Eru. "You are not of the Maori people. In the days when this *toki* was fashioned your breed was unknown. Yet the punishment of Tane shall reach you. It were better that you had died in Taupo-tapu. I forbid you to return to our people." After this final burst of magnificence Rua added placidly, "I myself can drive Mrs. Te Papa's car."

And drive it he did, sitting upright at the wheel, his blanket about his shoulders, bouncing slightly as he negotiated the inequalities of the pumice track.

Huia, sobbing noisily, ran into the house followed by the gently clucking Mrs. Claire. Eru moistened his lips and, without another word, set off up the track.

"That's a very embarrassing old gentleman."

Gaunt had strolled along the verandah, smoking a cigarette. He had dressed that morning in a travelling suit and looked an extraordinarily incongruous figure. His clothes, his hands, and his hair were as little in harmony with Wai-ata-tapu as would have been those of Sergeant Webley in the Ritz. Webley at once fastened on him.

"Now, Mr. Gaunt."

"Well, Sergeant?"

"You must have heard what's been said. Is it correct that you wanted to get hold of this weapon?"

"I should have liked to buy it, certainly. I have a taste for barbaric ornament."

"Did you offer to buy it?"

"I told Questing I should like to see it first. Not unnaturally. My secretary had related the story of Rewi's axe. When Questing came to me a few nights ago and littered the place up with obscure hints that he could if he would and so on, I confess my curiosity was stimulated. But I assure you that I did not commit myself in any way."

"Do you realize that the removal of property from a native reserve is a criminal offence?" Dr. Ackrington demanded.

"No. Is it really? Questing told me the old gentleman was prepared to sell but that he didn't want the rest of his tribe to know. He said we should have to be very hush-hush."

"Did you know anything about this, Mr. Bell?" asked Webley, turning his dark face towards Dikon.

"Oh, no," said Gaunt easily. "I didn't mention it to anybody. Questing was rather particular about that."

"I'll be bound he was," said Webley with a nearer approach to bitterness than Dikon had thought him capable of expressing.

"It was really too bad of him to involve me in a dubious transaction, you know. I resent it," said Gaunt. "And I must say, Sergeant, you seem to me to be working yourself into a tig over an abortive attempt at theft while an enemy agent bustles into obscurity. Why not deny yourself your passion for curios and catch Mr. Questing?"

Dikon opened his mouth and shut it again. He was looking at Mr. Falls, upon whose lips were painted the faintest trace of a smile.

"But we have found Mr. Questing," said Webley dully. Gaunt's hands contracted and he gave a sharp exclamation. Dikon saw again the hard curve of an orb under wet sacking.

"Found him?" said Gaunt softly. "Where?"

"Where he was lost, Mr. Gaunt. In Taupo-tapu."

"My God!"

Gaunt looked at his fingers, seemed to hesitate, and then turned on his heel and walked back along the verandah. As he reached his own rooms he said loudly with a sort of sneer: "That takes the icing off old Ackrington's gingerbread, doesn't it! I beg your pardon, Doctor. Do forgive me. I'd forgotten you were here."

He went into his room and they heard him shout for Colly.

Mr. Falls broke an awkward silence by saying: "What a very gay taste in shirts Mr. Eru Saul displays, doesn't he?"

Eru, a desolate figure, had plodded up the drive as far as the last turn that was visible from the house. His puce-coloured sleeves were vivid in the sunlight.

Barbara leant out of the open window and said nervously: "He always wears that shirt. One wonders if it's ever washed."

Dikon, expecting Dr. Ackrington's outburst to come at

any moment, said hurriedly: "I know. He wore it on the day of Smith's accident."

"So he did."

"No, he didn't," said the Colonel unexpectedly.

They stared at him. "But, Daddy, he *did*," said Barbara. "Don't you remember he came into the dining-room to sort of confirm Mr. Smith's account and he was wearing the pink shirt? Wasn't he, Sim?"

"What the heck's it matter?" Simon asked. "He was, as a matter of fact."

"He couldn't have been," said the Colonel.

Dr. Ackrington began in a high voice, "In the name of all that's futile, Edward, will you—" and stopped short. "The shirt was pink," he said loudly.

"No."

"It was pink, Edward."

"It couldn't have been, James."

Webley said heavily: "If you'll excuse me I'll get on with it," and casting a disgusted look at the Colonel he returned to Questing's room.

"I know it wasn't pink," the Colonel went on.

"Did you *see* the fellow's shirt?"

"I suppose I must have, James. I don't remember that, but I have it in my head that it was blue. People talked about the feller's blue shirt."

"Well, it wasn't blue, Dad," said Simon. "It was that same godalmighty affair he's got on now."

"I don't catch what people say, but I did catch that. Blue."

"This is extremely interesting," said Mr. Falls. "Here are three people swearing pink and one blue. What about you, Bell?"

"I'm on both sides," said Dikon. "It was puce but I agree with the Colonel that Questing said it was blue."

"It is extraordinary to me," said Dr. Ackrington, "that you can all moon about, arguing like magpies over a perfectly footling affair, when the discovery of Questing's body puts us all in a damned equivocal position."

"I am interested in the man in the ambiguous shirt. Could we not have Mr. Smith's opinion?" suggested Mr. Falls. "Where is he?"

Without moving, Simon yelled: "Hey, Bert!" and in due course Smith reappeared.

Mr. Falls said: "I wonder if you can settle an argument. Do you remember that on the evening of your escape from the train, Mr. Questing said that he left you to the attentions of a man in a blue shirt?"

"Uh?"

Mr. Falls repeated his question.

"That'd be Eru Saul. He brought me home. What of it?"

"Wearing a blue shirt?"

"Yeh, that's right."

"It was pink," said Dr. Ackrington and Simon together.

"If Questing said it was blue it must've been blue," said Smith crossly. "I was that knocked about I wouldn't notice whether the man was wearing a pansy shirt or a pair of rompers. Yeh, I remember. It was blue."

"You're colour-blind," said Simon. "It was pink."

He and Smith argued hotly. Smith walked away muttering and Simon shouted after him. "You're making out it was blue because he said it was blue. You'll be telling us next he went to Pohutukawa Bay that afternoon, like he said he did."

Smith stopped short. "So he did go to the Bay," he yelled.

"Yeh? And when Uncle James said wasn't it a pity the pootacows weren't in bloom he said yes, too bad. And they were blazing there all the time."

"He did go to the Bay. He took Huia. You ask Huia. Eru told me. So get to hell," added Smith and disappeared.

"What do you know about that!" Simon demanded. "Here, do you reckon Eru changed his shirt in our kitchen? Or was it another man on the hill that Questing saw?"

"He did *not* go to Pohutukawa Bay," said his uncle. "I bowled him over. I completely bowled him over. *Huia!*"

After a short delay Huia, still weeping, appeared in the doorway.

"What you want?" she sobbed.

"Did you go in Mr. Questing's car to Pohutukawa Bay on the day when Smith was nearly run over?"

"I never do anything bad with him," roared poor Huia, relapsing into pidgin English. "Only go for drive to te Bay and come back. Never stop te engine, all time."

"Did you see the pootacows?" asked Simon.

"How can we go to Pohutukawa Bay and not see *pohutukawas*? Of course we see *pohutukawas* like blazes all over te shop."

"Did Eru Saul change his shirt in the kitchen that night?"

"What te devil you ask me nex'! Let me catch him change his shirt in my kitchen."

"Oh, gee!" said Simon disgustedly and Huia plunged back into the house.

"It must be nearly lunch time," the Colonel remarked vaguely. He followed Huia indoors and shouted for his wife.

"This is a madhouse," said Dr. Ackrington.

Webley came out of Questing's room. "Mr. Bell," he said, "may I trouble you, please?"

iv

"I couldn't feel more uncomfortable," Dikon thought as he walked along the verandah, "if I'd killed poor old Questing myself. It's extraordinary."

Webley stood on one side at the door, followed Dikon inside and shut it. The blind was pulled down and the light was on so that Dikon was vividly reminded of his visit of the previous night. The pearl-grey worsted suit was still neatly disposed upon a chair. The ties and the puce-coloured pyjamas were in their former position. Webley went to the dressing-table and took up an envelope. Dikon saw with astonishment that it was addressed to himself in the neat commercial script of Smith's talisman.

"Before you open this, Mr. Bell, I'd like to have a witness." He put his head round the door and mumbled inaudibly. Mr. Falls was cautiously admitted.

"A witness before or after the fact, Sergeant?" he asked archly.

"A witness to the fact, shall we say, sir?"

"But why in heaven's name did he write to me?" Dikon murmured.

"That's what we'll find out, Mr. Bell. Will you open it?"

It was written in green ink on a sheet of business paper on which printed titles were set out, representing Mr. Questing as an indent agent and representative of several firms. It bore the date of the previous day and was headed: "Private and Confidential."

Dear Mr. Bell [Dikon read],

You will be somewhat surprised to receive this communication. An unexpected cable necessitates my visiting Australia and I am leaving for Auckland first thing tomorrow morning to see about a passage by air. I shall not be returning for some little while.

Now, Mr. Bell, I should commence by telling you that I appreciate the very very happy little relationship that has obtained since I first had the pleasure of contacting you. The personal antagonism that I have encountered in other quarters has never entered into our acquaintance and I take this opportunity of thanking you for your courtesy. You will note that I have endorsed this letter p. and c. It is rather particularly so and I am sure I can rely upon you to keep the spirit of the endorsement. If you are not prepared to do so I will ask you to destroy this letter unread.

"I can't go on with this," said Dikon.

"If you don't, sir, we will. He's dead, remember."

"Oh, hell!"   •

"You can read it to yourself if you like, Mr. Bell," said Webley, keeping his eyes on Mr. Falls, "and then hand it over."

Dikon read on a little way, made an ejaculation and finally said: "No, by George, you shall hear it." And he read the letter aloud.

Now, Mr. Bell, I am going to be very frank with you. You may have understood from remarks that have been passed that I have become interested in certain possibilities regarding a particular district not ten miles distant from where you are located.

Mr. Falls murmured: "Enchanting circumlocution."
"That'll be the Peak," said Webley, still watching him.
"Quite."

I have in the course of my visits made certain discoveries.
To put it bluntly, on Friday last, the evening before the S.S.
Hokianga was torpedoed off this certain place, I was on the
latter and I observed certain suspicious occurrences. They
were as follows. Being on the face overlooking the sea, my
attention was arrested by a light which flashed several times
from a spot some way farther up the slope. For personal
reasons I was undesirous of contacting other persons. I
therefore remained where I was, some nine feet off the track,
lying behind some scrub. From here I observed a certain
person, who passed by and was recognized by myself but
who did not notice me. This morning, Saturday, I learnt of
the sinking of the *Hokianga* and at once connected it with the
above incident. I sought out the person in question and
accused him straight out of being an enemy agent. He denied
it and added that if I went any further in the matter he would
turn the tables on myself. Now, Mr. Bell, this puts me in a
very awkward spot. My activities in this particular place have
leaked out and there are some who have not hesitated, as I am
well aware, to put a very very nasty interpretation on them. I
am not in a position to right myself against any accusations
this person might bring and in *his* position he is more likely to
be believed than I am. I was forced to give an undertaking
that I would not say that I had seen him. He adopted a very
threatening attitude. I do not think he trusts me. I don't mind
admitting I'm uneasy. He seemed to think I had inside
information about his code of signals, which is not the case.
Now, Mr. Bell, I am a man of my word but I am also a
patriot. I venerate the British Commonwealth of Nations and
the idea of a spy in God's Own Little Country gets my goat
good and proper. Hence this letter.
So it seems to me, Mr. Bell, that the best thing I can do is
to fix up this little matter of business across the Tasman right
away. I shall tell Mrs. C. I am going in the morning.
So I drop you this line which I shall post before taking the
air for Aussie. You will note that I have kept my undertaking
to this person and have not mentioned his name. I trust you,

Mr. Bell, not to communicate the matter of this letter to anyone else, but to take what action you think best in all other respects.

Again expressing my appreciation for our very pleasant association.

> With kind regards,
> Yours faithfully,
> Maurice Questing

Dikon folded the letter and gave it to Webley.

"*'I do not think he trusts me,'*" quoted Mr. Falls. "How right he was!"

"Yes," Dikon agreed and added. "He was right about another thing too. He was an appalling scamp, but I always rather liked him."

Huia rang the luncheon bell.

CHAPTER XIV

SOLO BY SEPTIMUS FALLS

Before they left the room Webley showed Dikon how Questing had already packed most of his clothes. Webley had forced open a heavy leather suitcase and found it full of pieces of greenstone, implements, and weapons; the fruits, he supposed, of many night's digging on the Peak. Rewi's adze, Webley said, had been locked apart in another case. Dikon guessed that Questing had planned to show it to Gaunt when they returned from the concert and had kept it apart for that purpose.

"Do you suppose he meant to try and sell the other stuff in Australia?" he asked.

"That might be the case, Mr. Bell, but he would never have got it past the Customs examination. The export of such things is strictly prohibited."

"Or perhaps," Mr. Falls suggested, "he was merely a passionate collector. There are men, you know, who without any real appreciation for such things, become obsessed with a most imperative desire to acquire them. Scrupulous in other things they are entirely unscrupulous in that."

"He was a pretty keen man of business," Dikon said.

"I'll say he was," said Webley. "We've found blue-prints for a new Wai-ata-tapu hotel and ground that'd make Rotorua look like Shanty-town. Wonderful place he'd planned to make of it."

He put Questing's letter in a large envelope, made a note of its contents across the back, and asked Dikon and Falls to sign it. They went out and he locked the door after them.

"Well," said Dikon as they walked along the verandah. "I never quite believed he was a spy."

"It seems to leave the field wide-open again, doesn't it?" Mr. Falls murmured.

"For an enemy agent who is also a murderer?"

"It is a strong presumption. Have you any objection, Webley, to our making this new development known to the rest of our party?"

Webley was close behind them. Mr. Falls stopped and turned to await his answer. It was a long time coming.

"Well, no," said Webley at last. "There's no objection to that. I can't exactly stop you, can I, Mr. Falls?"

"I mean, with an enemy in our midst, isn't it a wise policy to put everyone on the alert as it were? Will you go in, Bell?"

"After you," said Dikon.

"Mr. Falls and I," said Webley, "are going to wash our hands. Don't wait for us, Mr. Bell."

Upon this sufficiently broad hint, Dikon went in to lunch.

The rest of the party was already seated. Dikon joined his employer. Dr. Ackrington and the Claires, with the exception of Simon, were at the large family table. Simon sat apart with his friend Mr. Smith. Mr. Falls, when at last he and Webley came in, went to his own table close by.

"Do you mind if I join you, sir?" said Webley and did so.

"But I am honoured, Sergeant. As my guest, I hope?"

"No, no, sir, thanking you, all the same," said Webley. "I see there's a place laid, that's all."

He had made a mistake, it seemed. There was no second place laid at Mr. Falls's table but Huia, still very woebegone, rectified this, and he sat down.

"Nice of you to join me, Dikon," said Gaunt loudly. "I appear to be in disgrace."

Barbara turned her head swiftly and as swiftly looked away again.

"I forgot to say," Gaunt added, "that Questing asked fifty guineas for the adze. I shall always wonder if the price was excessive. I must ask the embarrassing old gentleman."

Nobody answered his sally. Gaunt thrust out his chin and gave Dikon one of his hard bright glances.

Luncheon went forward in a silence that was only broken by Sergeant Webley's conscientious attention to his food. At an early stage of this uncomfortable meal Dikon, who faced the windows, saw two of Webley's men come round the shoulder of the hill carrying a covered stretcher between them. They disappeared behind the manuka hedge, taking the roundabout path to the cabins. This unmistakable incident killed what little appetite he had. In a minute or two the men, without their burden, appeared on the verandah. Here they were joined by a young man in grey flannel trousers and a sports coat whom Dikon had no difficulty in recognizing as a representative of the press. This new arrival, with an air of innocent detachment, stared in at the windows. Webley looked at him with lack-lustre eyes and shook his head. The two plain-clothes men hung about near the door. The pressman sat on the verandah step and lit his pipe. The party in the dining-room, though aware of these proceedings, paid no attention to them. "The resemblance to the monkey-house at feeding time grows more pronounced every second," thought Dikon. Huia collected the plates and, when Mrs. Claire was not watching her, tipped uneaten pieces of cold meat onto one dish. As if by agreement, Mrs. Claire and Barbara went out together. Smith sucked his teeth savagely, muttered "Excuse me" and slouched out to the verandah. The pressman looked up hopefully and spoke to him but evidently got an uncompromising answer. He let Smith move off, looking wistfully after him.

In heavy silence the remaining seven men finished their meal.

"One can hardly hear oneself speak for the buzz of gay inconsequent chatter," said Gaunt. "I think I shall relax for half an hour."

He pushed back his chair.

"There is, after all, sufficient reason for our silence," said Mr. Falls."

Something in his attitude, though he had not risen, and some new quality in the tone of his voice, which was a deep one, brought a sudden stillness upon his hearers.

"When one is in danger of arrest," said Mr. Falls, "one does not feel disposed for chatter. May I, however, claim the attention of the company for a moment? Sergeant Webley, will you indulge me?"

Webley, who had made a brusque movement when Gaunt's chair scraped on the floor, leant the palms of his hands on the table and, looking attentively at Falls, said: "Go ahead, sir."

"I don't know," said Mr. Falls, "whether you are all

devotees of detective fiction. I must confess that I am. It is argued, in respect of these tales, that they bear little or no relation to fact. Police investigation, we protest, is not a matter of equally balanced motives, tortuous elaborations, and a final revelation in the course of which the investigator's threat hangs like an *ignis fatuus* over first one and then another of the artificially assembled suspects. It is rather the slow amassment of facts sufficient to justify the arrest of someone who has been more or less suspect from the moment the crime was discovered. Sergeant Webley," said Mr. Falls, "will correct me if I am wrong."

Sergeant Webley cleared his throat sluggishly. One of the men outside the window looked over his shoulder into the room, turned away again, and moved out of sight.

"However that may be," Falls continued, and they listened to him with confused attention as if he had, without warning, thrust an embarrassing ceremony upon them, "however that may be, I detect some resemblance in our present assembly to those arbitrary musters, and with the permission of Sergeant Webley I should like, before we break up, to clear the memory of Mr. Maurice Questing. Mr. Questing was *not* an enemy agent."

Here Dr. Ackrington broke out with some violence and was not silenced until an account of Questing's letter had, by a sort of forcible feeding, been rammed down the gullet of his understanding. He took it rather badly. The recovery of Questing's skull had evidently been broken to him but this final blow to the very corner-stone of all his theories seemed literally to horrify him. He turned quite pale, his protestations ceased, and he waited in silence for Falls to go on.

"Not only was Questing innocent of espionage but, if we are to believe his letter, he actually recognized and accused the real culprit, who adopted a threatening attitude, and, by a species of blackmail, extracted an undertaking from Questing that he would not betray him. Questing suggests that when they parted they were mutually distrustful of one another, and I suggest that fright, rather than business, prompted his sudden decision to go to Australia. He felt himself to be in danger just as we now feel ourselves to be in danger, and, in a figure that he himself might have used, he passed the buck to Mr. Bell. I think he must have written that letter just before we left for the concert. I happened to pass his open door and saw him with his elbows squared on his table. As you know, some three hours later he was killed."

"Will you excuse me," said Gaunt. "I don't want to be difficult but, as I've tried to point out before, I've been extremely upset by this unspeakably horrible affair and I'm afraid I just haven't got the kind of mind that revels in *post mortems*. I'm sorry. I shall leave you to it."

"One moment, Mr. Gaunt," said Falls. "You're upset, I fancy, not so much by the knowledge that Questing died very horridly, as by the fear that you yourself might be implicated."

"I won't have this!" cried Gaunt, and sprang to his feet. "I resent this, bitterly."

"Do sit down. You see,' said Mr. Falls, looking amiably about him, "in spite of ourselves we are becoming the orthodox muster of suspects. Here is Mr. Gaunt who quarrelled with Mr. Questing because Mr. Questing used his name as an advertisement, and because he pretended he was the author of a gift that Mr. Gaunt himself had made."

Barbara started galvanically. Gaunt began to accuse Dikon. "So I've got you to thank—"

"No," said Falls. "My dear Gaunt, who but you could have made this gift? A quotation from Shakespeare on the card? Written by the shop assistant? You see I have heard all about it. And, if that was not enough, your very expressive face betrayed you most completely last night, when Questing spoke of her enchanting dress to Miss Barbara. You looked—please forgive the unhappy phrase—positively murderous. Was it not the memory of this that led you to conceal your subsequent quarrel with Questing? It seems to me you had quite a lot to agitate you when Questing was killed."

"I have explained to the point of hysteria that I was anxious to avoid publicity. Good God, who ever committed murder for such a motive? Sergeant Webley, I beg that you—"

"I quite agree," said Falls. "Who ever did? May I pass on, for the moment, to another of our suspects? Mr. Smith."

"Here, you lay off Bert!" shouted Simon. "He's right out of this. He'd got his agreement."

"His motive," Mr. Falls continued precisely, "appears at

first to be revenge. Revenge for an attempt on his life."

"Revenge, my foot. They buried the hatchet."

"In order to resurrect a much more valuable one in the form of Rewi's adze. Yes, yes, I agree that the revenge motive breaks down but it does well enough for a red herring. Dr. Ackrington: your motive, at first, would seem to be a kind of quintessence of fury. You believed Questing to be a traitor and you could find little support in your effort to bring him to book."

"It's perfectly obvious to me now, Falls, that the man was done to death by someone from the native settlement. No doubt some wretched youth in the pay of the enemy."

"Ah! The Maori theme. Shall we leave that for the moment? Now, in your case, Colonel, the motive is much more credible. Forgive me for introducing a painful theme but your position was, I'm afraid, only too clear. Questing's extraordinary assumption of proprietorship alone would have betrayed it. He was, as Mr. Bell remarked a little while ago, a keen man of business. Have you not benefited greatly by his death..."

"Cut that out!" Simon cried out angrily. "You damn' well lay off my father."

"Be quiet, Simon," said the Colonel.

"...as indeed," Mr. Falls completed his sentence, "have all the members of your family?" He looked at his hands, lightly clasped on the table. "The Maori element," he said, and paused. "Revenge for the violation of a sacred object? Not an inconsiderable motive. To my mind, a perfectly credible motive. But did anybody beside Mr. Gaunt, outside the Old Firm, as I feel tempted to call the Smith-Questing-Saul link-up, know of the disappearance of the adze? And beyond that there seems to be a jealousy theme centering round your maid, Colonel. Questing appears to have supplanted the man with the debatable shirt. Eru. Eru Saul."

"But my dear Falls," said Dr. Ackrington, "you seem to accept Questing's letter. Surely, then, the murderer is the spy?"

"Certainly. It is most probable. The point I am leading up to is this. It seems to me that in this case motive should, for the moment, be disregarded. There are too many motives. Let us look instead at circumstances. At fact."

"Oh, for God's sake," Gaunt said wearily.

"Four apparently inexplicable points have interested me enormously. The railway signal. Eru Saul's shirt. The *pohutukawa* trees. The misplaced flag. It seems to me that if an explanation is found that will apply equally to these four parts, then we shall have gone a long way towards solving the whole. These are factual things."

"How about yourself?" Simon demanded abruptly. "If it comes to facts you look pretty fishy, don't you?"

"I am coming to myself," said Mr. Falls modestly. "I look extremely fishy. I have left myself to the last because what I have to say, or part of it, is in the nature of a confession."

Webley looked up quickly. He moved his chair back a little and shifted the position of his great feet.

"When I left the hall," said Mr. Falls, "I went immediately into the thermal reserve. I have stated that I saw Questing ahead of me and recognized him by his overcoat. I have also stated that I paused and lit my pipe, that I then heard Questing scream, and that a few moments later Bell came along from the direction of the village. I had no alibi. Later, having insisted that none of us should return to the scene of the crime, I myself returned there. You saw me from the hill, did you not, Bell? I was obliged, by the nature of my errand, to use my torch. I heard you plunging down the hillside and realized that you must have seen me. On my return I informed Colonel Claire and Dr. Ackrington of my visit to the forbidden territory. Later, I believe, they told you I had given, as an excuse, a story that I had heard someone moving about on the other side of the mound. This was untrue. There was nobody there. And now," Falls continued, "I come to the last episode in my story." With a swift movement he thrust his hand inside his jacket.

Simon scrambled to his feet with an inarticulate cry.

"Grab him!" he shouted. "Grab him! Quick! Before he takes it! *Poison!*"

ii

But it was not a phial or deadly capsule that Mr. Falls drew from the inner pocket of his coat, but a strip of semi-transparent yellow substance which he held up before Simon, who was already half-way across the floor.

"You alarm me terribly," said Mr. Falls. "What on earth are you up to?"

"Sit down, boy," said Dr. Ackrington, "you're making a fool of yourself."

What the blazes are you gettin' at, Sim?" asked his father. "Plungin' about like that?"

Gaunt laughed hysterically and Simon turned on him.

"All right, laugh! The man stands there and tells you he lied, and you think it's funny. All along, I've said there was something fishy about him." His face was scarlet. He addressed his father and uncle. "I told you. I told you he tapped out the code signal. It's there under your noses and you won't do anything."

"Ah!" said Mr. Falls. "You noticed my experiment on the verandah, did you? I thought as much. You have what used to be called a speaking countenance, Claire."

"You admit it was the code signal? You admit it?"

"Certainly. An experiment to test Questing. I had an unfortunate result. He picked up the pipe. Quite innocently, of course, but it conveyed an unhappy impression, not only to you but to someone much more closely interested. His murderer."

"That's right," said Simon. "You."

"But I see," Mr. Falls continued urbanely, "that you are looking at this piece of yellow celluloid which I hold in my hand. I cut it off Questing's sun-screen on his car. Its colour is important. Colour, indeed, plays a significant part in our story. If you look at a red object through this celluloid it becomes a different shade of red, but it is still red. If you look at a green object through it, a similar phenomenon occurs. A blue-green, such as one may see on a railway signal, merely becomes a slightly warmer yellowish green. If Questing said that he mistook the red signal because he saw it through this celluloid, he lied."

"Yes, but damn it all..." Simon began, and got no further.

"Questing stated that on the occasion of his almost fatal signal to Mr. Smith at the railway bridge, Eru Saul wore a blue shirt, but we know that he wore a pink one. Did he lie again? That same evening he fell into Dr. Ackrington's trap, and agreed that there was no bloom on the trees at Pohutukawa Bay, when, as a matter of fact, the Bay was, and still is scarlet with blossom. Again, did he lie? Dr. Ackrington, most naturally, concluded that he had not been to the Bay, but we know now that he had. Here I should tell you, in parenthesis, that Mr. Questing's pyjamas and ties exhibit a recurrent theme of the peculiar shade of puce which it seems he did not recognize in Eru Saul's shirt. Now we come to the final scene."

Webley got quickly to his feet. One of the men on the verandah opened the door and came in. He, too, moved quietly. Dikon thought that only he and Gaunt had seen him and his manoeuvre. Gaunt looked quickly from this man to Webley.

"Questing," said Mr. Falls, "carried a torch when he crossed the thermal reserve. The moon was not yet up and he flashed his torch-light on the white flags that marked the path he must follow. When he reached the mound above Taupo-tapu, over which the track passes, he would see no white flags ahead of him for the one on the top had been displaced. He would, however, see the faded red flags marking the old path on which Taupo-tapu has now encroached. There are several mounds on both sides of Taupo-tapu and they look much alike by torch-light.

"My contention is that Questing followed the red flags and so came by his death. My contention is that Questing's murderer is the man who knew that he was colour-blind."

iii

A sharp flick to that fascinating toy, the kaleidoscope, will transfer a jumble of fragments into a symmetrical design. To Dikon, it seemed that Mr. Falls had administered just such a flick to the confused scraps of evidence that had collected about the death of Maurice Questing. If the completed pattern was not yet fully visible it was because there was some defect, not in the design, but in Dikon's faculty of observation. The central motif, the pivot of the system, was still hidden from him but it began to emerge as Falls, disregarding the sharp exclamations that broke from his listeners, and the emphatic slap with which Dr. Ackrington brought his palm down on the table, went on steadily with his exposition. The affectations, and the excessive urbanity of manner, were no longer noticeable in his speech. He was grave and relentlessly methodical.

"Now, it is a characteristic of persons afflicted with colour-blindness that they are most reluctant to admit to this defect. The great Hans Gross has noted this curious attitude and says that a colour-blind person, if he is forced to confess to his affliction, will behave as if he was guilty of some crime. Questing, when challenged by Dr. Ackrington with an attempt to cause the death of Mr. Smith, instead of admitting that he could not distinguish the red signal from the green, said that the signal was not working. Mr. Smith told you that, later on, Questing gave him the story of the celluloid sun-screen."

"Yes, but look here . . ." Simon began and stopped short. "On your way," he said.

"Thank you. It is also characteristic of these people that they confuse green with red and they have a predilection for that peculiar shade of pink, kaffir pink or puce as it is sometimes called, which, apparently, seems to them to be blue. A patch of red if seen by green torch-light might appear to these people to be colourless. At any rate, with the white flag removed, Questing, if colour-blind, would have no standard of comparison and would most certainly accept the red flag to be white and accept it as such. Accepting for the moment my theory of Questing's colour-blindness, let us see how it squares up with the evidence of the track. Sergeant

Webley," said Mr. Falls with a slight return to his old
mellifluous style, "will correct me if I am wrong. My own
investigation took place by torch-light, remember."

He smiled apologetically and took the tip of his nose
between his thumb and forefinger. "I saw," he said, "that the
clod of displaced earth, or solidified mud as I believe it to be,
had split away from the iron flag standard. I could see the
groove made by the standard in the broken section of the
bank. The heel marks made by the famous nailed boot were
immediately behind it, as well as on the clod itself. These
suggested a possibility that the heel stabs had been used with
the object of loosening the standard rather than dislodging
the clod. If one kicked at such a standard in the dark one
would make a few dud shots. The standard itself lay a little
distance away from the clod. They had both fallen on a
narrow shelf of firm ground at the edge of the cauldron.

"Both flag and path were intact when we went to the
concert. Of the returning party nobody remembers seeing the
flag but, on the other hand, nobody remembers seeing the
gap in the path. But Colonel Claire, who was the last to go
through before the tragedy, tells us he fell when he reached
the top of the mound."

"Eh?" said the Colonel with one of his galvanic starts.
"Fell? Yes. Yes, I fell."

"Is it possible, Colonel, that you trod on the clod already
loosened by the removal of the flag and that it gave way
beneath you, causing you to stumble forward?"

"Wait a bit," said the Colonel. "Let's think."

He shut his eyes and screwed up his face. His moustache
twitched busily.

"While Edward is lost in contemplation," said Dr.
Ackrington, "I should like to point out to you, Falls, that if
your theory is correct, the flag was removed after we had
entered the hall."

"Yes."

"And it was intended, originally, that we should all crowd
into Gaunt's car for the return journey."

"A point well taken," said Mr. Falls.

"And that the half-caste fellow left the hall during the
performance."

"Returning in time to hear Mr. Gaunt's masterly
presentation of the Saint Crispin's Eve speech."

"The speech before Agincourt, wasn't it?"

"We shall see. Yes, Colonel?"

The Colonel had opened his eyes and relaxed his moustache. "Yes," he said. "That's what it was. Astonishin' I didn't think of it before. The ground gave way. By George, I might have gone over, you know. What?"

"A most fortunate escape," said Mr. Falls gravely. "Well now, gentlemen—I have almost done. It seems to me that only one explanation will agree with all the facts I have mentioned. Questing's murderer was a man with hobnailed boots. He threw the boots into Taupo-tapu. He had visited the Peak, for the boots correspond with Bell's sketch of the prints. He had access to the reserve during the concert. He knew Questing was colour-blind, and was most anxious that we should not discover this fact. He was an enemy agent and Questing knew it. Now what figure in our cast fits all these conditions?"

"Eru, Saul," said Dr. Ackrington.

"No," said Falls. "Herbert Smith."

iv

It was Simon who was making the greatest outcry: Simon protesting that Bert Smith wouldn't hurt a fly, that he couldn't have done it, that he had tried to join up, that he was all right as long as he kept off the liquor. It was Simon who, with a helpless slackening of his voice, repeated that Falls had no right to bring this accusation and, finally, that Falls did it to protect himself. The Colonel and Dr. Ackrington tried to silence him. Webley attempted to get him out of the room, but he held his ground and in the end he talked himself to a standstill. His lips trembled, he made a gesture of relinquishment. Like an exhausted child, he stumbled clumsily to a seat, beat on the table with his fists, and at last was silent.

"Smith!" said Gaunt. "Lord, what an anticlimax! They

must be hard-up for cogs in the fifth-column set-up in this country if they found a job for Smith."

"I'm afraid he is a very small cog," replied Falls.

The Colonel said: "He's been with us for years."

"I am not entirely convinced," said Dr. Ackrington importantly. "How are you so damned positive that Smith knew Questing was colour-blind? He may have *believed* the story of the sun-screen."

"He was never told that story. According to Smith, Questing drove him to the crossing and showed him the light through the screen, which Smith said was green but which, as you see, is yellow. *He's* not colour-blind, you know; he knew Questing wrote with green ink. The sun-screen story was invented after the murder, for our benefit. He had to explain why he had suddenly become friendly with Questing. He had to produce his precious letter. Above all things, we mustn't know of Questing's defective sight. His insistence, this morning, that Questing must have been right about the colour of Eru Saul's shirt is only explicable in that light. Of course Questing gave Smith the real explanation of his failure to see the signal. Questing agreed to keep him quiet, and incidentally used him as a go-between in his curio hunts. All went well until Questing discovered him on the Peak and accused him of espionage. The goose that laid the golden eggs had to be killed."

"Then the Maori theme," said Dikon. "Eru Saul, the stolen adze, and the violation of tapu, were all subsidiary factors?"

"In a way, yes. Eru Saul told me that when he returned to the concert, after going for a drink with Smith, he heard Mr. Gaunt recite a speech about *'old dug-outs being asleep while him and the boys waited for the balloon to go up.'* This seemed to me to be a recognizable paraphrase of *'gentlemen in England now a-bed,'* which is part of the Saint Crispin speech. But Smith told us that as he returned to the hall he heard Mr. Gaunt shout a sentence which he rendered as: *'Once more into the blasted breeches, pals.'* Unmistakably the opening line of the Agincourt speech, the last item in Mr. Gaunt's recital, which he gave only after prolonged and enthusiastic demands for an encore."

"Bert wouldn't know," Simon said. "He wouldn't know. It's all one to Bert."

"There is a time lag of some five or six minutes between the beginning of the Crispin speech and the beginning of the Agincourt speech. Would you put it at that, Gaunt?"

"I think so," said Gaunt automatically.

"Time enough for Smith to re-enter the doorway with his companions and, while all eyes were focussed on you, to slip out again and run to the reserve. Time enough, when he could not wrench it out, for him to kick the standard until it was loosened, and then drop it over the edge. Time enough to think of the evidence left by his boots and throw them overboard. Time enough to run back to the hall and be standing there, close by his friends, when the lights went up." He turned to Simon. "You were with him after the concert?" Simon nodded. "Did you notice his feet?" Simon shook his head.

"Mr. Gaunt's man was with you, wasn't he?"

"Yes."

"Could we speak to him, I wonder?"

Webley nodded to the man at the door. He went out and returned with Colly.

"Colly," said Mr. Falls. "What sort of boots was Mr. Smith wearing when you went home last night?"

"Not boots at all, sir," said Colly instantly. "Soft shoes."

"Did you walk over to the hall with him before the concert?"

"Yessir. We went over early with extra chairs."

"Was he wearing shoes then?" Webley demanded.

Colly jumped and said: "You're that small, Inspector, I never see you. No, he was wearing boots then. 'E took 'is shoes in 'is pocket, 'case we finished up with a dance."

"Did he carry his boots home?" asked Webley.

"I never see them," said Colly, and looked uneasy.

"O.K."

Colly glanced unhappily at Simon and went out.

Webley walked over to the man at the door.

"Where is he?" he asked.

"In his room, Mr. Webley. We're watching it."

"Come on, then," said Webley, and they went out, their boots making a heavy trampling sound that died away in the direction of Smith's room.

CHAPTER XV

THE LAST OF
SEPTIMUS FALLS

"It's no good asking me to work up a grain of sympathy for him," said Dikon. "There's no capital punishment in this country now. He'll spend the rest of his life in gaol, and a damned lucky let-off it is for him. He's a dirty little spy and a still dirtier murderer. It's poor old Questing I can't bear to think about."

"Oh, *don't.*"

"I'm sorry, Barbara darling. No, I won't call you 'Barbara darling.' In our giddy theatrical circles we call people 'darling' when we can't remember their names. I shall call you something calmly Victorian. Barbara, love. Barbara, my dear. Now, don't take umbrage. It doesn't hurt you, and it gives me a certain hollow satisfaction. How far shall we walk?"

"To the sea?"

"My feet will turn into smouldering sponges, but I'm game. Come on."

They walked on in silence under a pontifical sky.

"It seems more like a week ago than two days," said Barbara at last.

"I know. Exit Smith in custody. Exist Mr. Septimus Falls in a trail of glory and soon, alas, exit us."

"How soon?"

"He talks about next week. We've got to stay for the inquest. He's much better, you know. Your anatomical uncle says he doesn't think there will be a recrudescence of the fibrositis, which is, I consider, a magic phrase."

"Where will he go?" asked Barbara in a flat voice.

"To London. He wants to take a company out on tour. The Bard in the blitz. Fit-ups. Play anywhere. It's a grand idea," said Dikon and added, "I'm leaving him."

"*Leaving* him? But why?"

"To have one more shot at enlisting. If they won't like me any better here than they did in Australia I shall return with Gaunt. There must be *something* for a blind bat to do. They say they use everybody at Home. I shall wear battle-dress, and sit in a black little cellar at the end of the longest passage of an obscure building, typewriting memoranda for a Minor Blimp. Will you write to me?"

Barbara didn't answer. "Will you?" he insisted and she nodded.

"Fancy!" Dikon said after a moment. "There are tears in your eyes because he's going and here am I, ready to howl like a banshee at the notion of leaving you. There's no sense in it."

Barbara stopped short and glared at him. "It's not for that," she said. "You're not as sharp as I thought you were. It's because—well, it's partly because I've been living in a *hollow mockery.*" She brought this out in her old style, turning her eyes up and the corners of her mouth down.

"Don't do that to your nice face," said Dikon.

"I'll do what I like with my face," said Barbara with spirit. "If my face irritates you, you needn't look at it. You talk about being fond of me but all you want to do is fiddle about with me until you've made me into a bad imitation of some beastly glamour girl."

"No, honestly. Honestly not. I wouldn't mind if you screamed at me because I sniff when I read and bite my nails. You can made one face after another with the virtuosity of a Saint Vitus and I shall still love you. Why have you been living in your 'hollow mockery'?"

"I've been such a frightful fool. Slopping all over him because I thought he was like Mr. Rochester and all the time he's just vain and selfish and rather common. Pretending his soul was lacerated by what happened and all that time he was just afraid he'd be mixed up in it. I'm so ashamed of myself."

"Oh," said Dikon.

"And for him to give me those things. And look at me as if I was a *cheap plaything*—I didn't make a face. You can't say I made a face."

"You never batted an eyelash. But you're too hard on him. He's kind-hearted, and he gives presents like you'd shell peas. Model dresses are no more than a couple of rosebuds to him."

"And when Daddy told him, very nicely, that I couldn't possibly accept them he behaved *frightfully*. He said: 'She can etc. well turn an etc. nudist if it amuses her.' Sim heard him."

"That," said Dikon, controlling his voice, "is because he'd been dealt rather a stiff smack in the pride. It's a bit galling to have your presents returned with quiet dignity. He felt like two-penn'orth of dirt and that made him angry and bewildered."

"Well, I'm sorry, but he really ought to have known better. And don't let's talk any more about the things because, however much I try, I can't pretend I didn't like them." Barbara looked at Dikon. "Which makes the whole thing rather comic, I suppose."

"Bravo, Miss Claire," said Dikon. He took her arm and to his great astonishment felt her hand slip into his own.

"You will write to me, won't you?" said Dikon. "If the war lasts a long time you will forget what I'm like, but I shall come back."

"Yes," said Barbara. "Come back."

ii

"That," said Mr. Falls, "is about all, I fancy. I'm going down to Wellington as soon as the inquest's over. Hush-hush conversations with the P.M. and the Commissioner and so on. I'm afraid we've only caught a sprat, but at least it will show the seriousness of the position."

"Yes," said the Superintendent. "We'd got into the way of thinking these things don't reach us down here. The boys go away, reinforcement after reinforcement, and then it gets a bit closer and we begin building up our home forces, but we don't somehow think in terms of fifth columnists. Or the general public don't. We've been very fortunate to have you."

"I'll say!" said Mr. Webley. "You know, sir, there was the

old doctor writing in and writing in and yet the thing looked somehow ridiculous. He had hold of the wrong end of the stick, of course, but the idea was right."

"Yes," said the Superintendent heavily, "the idea was right."

Mr. Falls said: "Dr. Ackrington behaved very well. As you know I got him to come and see me in Auckland. That was after I'd had his letter. But I didn't decide to go to Wai-ata-tapu until the next day when you people suggested it. There was no time to warn him and we met face to face on the verandah while I was doing my decrepit dilettante stuff. He didn't turn a hair. He backed me up nobly. We had to take the Colonel into our confidence, of course and that *was* a bit tricky. And while I'm handing out bouquets I should like to say how every grateful I am to Webley. He was extraordinarily good over the whole show."

"There you are, Sergeant!" said the Superintendent.

"He insisted on my doing the summing-up business. We both thought that as the espionage aspect of the thing was an open secret among them, it was best to let them know the truth. Simon Claire, for one, would have raised a hell of a dust if there had been any doubt left in his mind. As it is, they have all undertaken to say nothing. If you can adjourn the inquest and hold things over for a little it will give me a chance to dig a bit deeper before the principals realize quite how much we know."

"You don't want to appear at all, I gather?"

"Mr. Septimus Falls will have to give evidence, I'm afraid, but he will not return to Wai-ata-tapu."

Sergeant Webley passed his hand over his face and gave a low chuckle.

They all stood up and the Superintendent held out his hand. "It's been a real privilege," he said. "I'm sure Webley has felt like that about it."

"I'll say! A great day for me, sir."

"We'll meet again, I hope, with a bigger catch."

They shook hands. "I'll warrant we do," said the Superintendent, "with you on the job. Good-bye, Mr. Alleyn. Good-bye."

THE END